TO MAURA
& GRAHAM -

TO A WONDERFUL

COUPLE

BEST WISHES AND
ALL THE BEST TO
MY NEW SISTER + BROTHER
IN LAW

David's *child*

NICK MARCIANO

a novel

David's *child*

TATE PUBLISHING *& Enterprises*

Published by Tate Publishing & Enterprises, LLC
127 E. Trade Center Terrace | Mustang, Oklahoma 73064 USA
1.888.361.9473 | www.tatepublishing.com

Tate Publishing is committed to excellence in the publishing industry. The company reflects the philosophy established by the founders, based on Psalm 68:11,
"The Lord gave the word and great was the company of those who published it."

Published in the United States of America
ISBN: 978-1-61777-805-6
1. Fiction / Christian / General
2. Fiction / Suspense
11.07.13

Special thanks go to
Murray, Bertha, Dom, and Siobhan
for their grateful contributions. You guys are the best.

CHAPTER ONE

David Turner didn't exercise much, yet had what was considered a healthy physique. He stood at five feet, eleven inches, and tipped the scales at one hundred and seventy-five pounds. Friends were amazed at how he could eat half a pizza the night before and wake up lighter the next day. Born with light green eyes and dirty blond hair, at the age of forty-two he had people guessing his true age, estimating thirty, perhaps thirty-two at the most. If he wasn't the thriving writer that he was born to be, he might have been in competition with Hugh Grant for the leading role in "chick flicks." If he shaved his head, grew a three- to four-day stubble on his face, Hollywood's machine could easily have transformed him into a revenge-seeking action hero. But he was a placid, peaceful man who loved life, adored his family, and who also happened to be a very successful, well-known author, turning out bestsellers as though giving out candy. David Turner was that talented.

This one particular morning began as all mornings did, or so David thought. No one could have foreseen, least of all by him, that today his wonderful life was to change forever. It all began when he was seated in front of his computer, polishing up the last chapter of his current novel, when a state trooper's cruiser slowly pulled into his driveway. The car was impossible to miss; David's desk rested in front of a large French framed window, giving him an excellent view of the outside. He saved the page he had been working on for the past few minutes, pulled back his chair, and stood up, finding it amusing as the plump officer wriggled from side to side, struggling to get out of his car.

The trooper looked comical in appearance, with his thin moustache, thick-rimmed glasses, and a face so round that it could have easily been mistaken for a Halloween mask. He may have looked awkward, but there was nothing amusing about the way he acted, carefully checking his clipboard and glancing back and forth at the property until he located the mailbox. The numbers stamped on the pole matched his. He had the correct address. This was the home of David Turner, devoted church attendee, famed author of inspiring novels, and most respected for his generous charity donations.

David watched the trooper neatly tuck his shirt into his pants and carefully wipe the top of both boots on the back of his pant leg. Months earlier, the local police station had been subjected to unfair criticism from a disgruntled reporter who was charged with drunk driving. Though only fifty miles north of Los Angeles, this small town of Bolton, with a very small population, when compared to its southern neighbour, took itself seriously, especially at how the police presented themselves.

David thought for a moment, wondering whether Diane had paid the parking ticket she received months ago and if this was the reason for this man's untimely visit. Anticipating a knock at any second, he walked to the door, swung the door open, and smiled at the policeman. The sombre expression on the trooper's face was not one reserved for a mere parking ticket. It alarmed him. A specific scene from the film, *Saving Private Ryan* flashed through his mind, the part where an official from Western Union knocks on the door to inform a mother that three of her sons had died while serving their country. He quickly dismissed the thought, as his writer's imagination gone wild.

"Would David Turner reside here?" the trooper softly asked.

"Yes, that would be me."

The trooper pulled out a handkerchief from his pant pocket and wiped the perspiration off his forehead.

"May I come in please?" he asked shoving the damp handkerchief back into his rear pocket.

David didn't want to know the reason for this visit. He didn't want to hear what this funny-looking man had to say. He only wish was that he would go back into his car and drive away so that he could return to his novel.

"Sorry, Mr. Turner. May I come in?" he asked again in a lower tone.

"If this is over a parking ticket I regret wasting your time. I will pay right away," he replied, firmly holding onto the doorknob and blocking the trooper's path.

"No, Mr. Turner. This is not about a parking ticket," he half whispered.

For unknown reasons, David grinned and lowered his head, focusing on his left slipper, the one with the hardened coffee stain. "I just noticed a coffee stain on top of my slipper," he lied. That stain had been on that same slipper for weeks. He didn't know why he brought this up in front of a stranger except to make light of this uncomfortable situation and to persuade himself that this was all a ridiculous misunderstanding. "As soon as my wife returns from shopping, I'll just have to ask her to go back out and buy me a new pair."

The trooper didn't want to look down at David's slippers and didn't. He was not interested in any coffee stain.

"May I come in please?" he asked for the third time.

"Yes, I'm sorry. Please come in," he apologized, finally releasing the knob, taking half a dozen steps backwards and allowing the trooper to enter at his own pace.

Once inside, the trooper reluctantly removed his hat. For years he had been given the responsibility of informing people that their loved ones were never coming home again and blamed the stress that came along with it as the sole reason for his receding hairline.

The few remaining strands of healthy hair on the right side of his head were neatly brushed over to the left, managing to cover a small portion of his bald spot. He fidgeted the hat a few times before placing it horizontally on his chest, approximately four inches above his leather belt.

"Are you married to Diane Turner?"

David felt a commanding shiver take full control of his body. He had felt this way only twice in his life—once the day he almost drowned at the beach, when he lost his breath and needed his older brother to keep his head above water, and the second time when he was a passenger on board a booming 747. The jet was cruising along at thirty-six thousand feet when the engines cut off for a few seconds before restarting. Both incidents had given him a feeling of vulnerability and defencelessness. Those were the times when you asked God why he had abandoned you and immediately afterwards start making deals with him, promising the Almighty anything as long as he intervened.

"Yes, Diane is my wife," he confirmed, clearing his throat.

The trooper cleared his throat louder and then paused long enough before saying, "I'm sorry to report to you that your wife was involved in a fatal car accident this morning."

David took as many steps backwards as he could until his back touched the wall. He looked at the wedding photo of him and Diane on the opposite wall next to the trooper. Next to that wedding picture hung a most recent photo taken only weeks ago of a very pregnant Diane, sitting on the edge of a water fountain, comically pointing to her oversized stomach with her left hand and holding an ice cream cone with her right.

"I will have to ask you to come with me to identify the body, sir."

Turning pale and too shaken to emotionally react to Diane's unexpected death, he asked, "What about the baby … what about my child?"

"I think it's best that you see for yourself, Mr. Turner."

CHAPTER TWO

S even years later …
   David placed the razor blade down and splashed warm
water over his entire face, savouring the warm sensation. It made
him feel like a million dollars even if it only lasted for a brief
second, making him feel optimistic about anything and everything. With a bit of luck, today would be the day he would recapture the discipline required by all true authors, which was to ignore
all distractions, excuses and just write. Over the past few years, he
found writing to become a painful and lonely experience, and if he
wasn't careful, these feelings could in due course create the ideal
situation for writer's block. He wasn't alone. No writer ever wanted
to admit they had become a victim of this enigma. To an author,
writer's block was a filthy word, an admission that they didn't have
any more stories to tell and, in some cases, if not routed, was the
beginning of the end for a career.
   He glanced at the clock radio, noticing he was running behind
schedule. He still had to get Cathy's cereal, check her school
backpack, and then have his fifteen-minute morning chat with
her before the school bus arrived. He valued these one-to-one
chitchats with his daughter. They were irreplaceable, a must to a
family's relationship. They discussed the weather, what was said in
church, the neighbour's dog, placing flowers at Diane's graveside;
it didn't matter to either one. What did matter was that they talked
for at least fifteen minutes each and every morning. It was something they both looked forward to, no matter what the mood; no
matter the situation, the chats made them feel loved and important to each other.

This form of family bonding was introduced to the Turner family back in Scotland by David's late father, and it worked. Though barely four years of age at the time, David still had fond memories of sitting on his father's lap, listening to his stories of the Scottish hero, William Wallace, who was later immortalized by Mel Gibson in the feature film *Braveheart*.

The sink was cleaned. The towels were neatly hung, and the toilet was flushed before David left the washroom. He entered the long corridor, which led to the kitchen area and suddenly came to an abrupt stop. He saw a smiling Cathy already sitting at the table, cereal mixed, backpack zipped, and a proud grin on her face.

"Have you noticed that I am maturing?" she asked, standing up and spreading her arms like a tiny game host model.

"I have," he laughed before entering the kitchen.

"You're two minutes late. We only have thirteen minutes left. No need to worry, though. I already have the subject for the day."

"Which is?"

Cathy sat back down and swallowed a spoonful of cereal, wiping her mouth with a napkin, folding it, and neatly placing it beside the plate. Her manners were impeccable, a clear sign that she was about to ask a favour.

"Another budgie would be nice," she said as though it was a minor issue.

"What do you mean by another budgie?"

"I think we should get another budgie so Mr. Rogers has some-one to talk to."

David looked over to the birdcage noticing the budgie chewing on the iodine salt spool.

"I think our bird friend is perfectly happy living on his own."

Cathy thought for a second or two, analyzing her next move. She lowered the spoon into the cereal, scooping only half a spoon-ful into her mouth this time.

"He looks lonely to me."

"How do you know this?" David smiled, enjoying the cat and mouse game.

"I just know."

"Not good enough. If you really want another budgie then write me a two-page explanation as to why. I'll read it, and depending how well it's written, I'll decide at that time." The phone rang. Both father and daughter cringed. This was their time, bad timing for anyone to be calling, especially if it was *him*. .

"We only have ten minutes left," she reminded her father.

David stood up, walked to the opposite side of the kitchen and looked down at the phone screen. It was *him*—David's publisher, Mr. Steamer. He stared at the hated flashing number, gritting his teeth in anger, refusing to answer it.

"If that's Mr. Steamer you might as well answer it. He'll just keep on calling until you do," reasoned Cathy. Mr. Steamer was not a reasonable man. He was evil and selfish and enjoyed it. It wasn't his physical presence that was intimidating. Some said they were uncomfortable by the way his bushy eyebrows came to a point or the way his neck veins expanded when angered, while others simply melted with fear by the way his eyes appeared to turn a reddish color when things didn't go his way. Past employees who foolishly challenged him and lost would swear they saw the first stage of horns growing from the top of his head. David thought it was all those things and much more, including a Napoleon complex. He tolerated this madman because he paid his bills, generously rewarding him for his novels; however, he made it a point never to socialize with him, the exception—at book signings. Mr. Steamer would stalk him, demanding he stay as long as necessary until each and every fan had his autograph. If David got tired, or if his hand got sore from repeatedly signing his name, Mr. Steamer was there to quickly remind him of his sizeable advance, along with the number of years needed to recoup that money.

"You stay until each and every autograph is signed," he would snarl at David, not caring who overheard him.

"Answer it, Daddy!" Cathy cried out, upset that each additional ring was eating away at valuable seconds.

He reluctantly picked up the phone, and before the receiver even touched his ear, he heard Mr. Steamer's irritating voice lash out at him. "Did you read today's newspaper, *David?*"

David hated many things about his employer, but detested when he ended his sentences with his name, always dragging it out as loud and long as possible for the sole purpose of infuriating him.

"What ever happened to hello?" he asked Mr. Steamer.

"Hellos don't make me money, David," Mr. Steamer barked back. There was an uncomfortable pause between the two men before Mr. Steamer repeated. "Did you read today's paper?"

"Not yet. I was in the middle of talking with my daughter when you called."

"I'd suggest you forgo talking to anyone, get today's newspaper, and check page six of the entertainment section. Unless you have gone blind, you'll see that your latest book is not in the top twenty lists anymore. Neither is your name in block letters. You know what that means, David? It means no one is buying your books as they once did," he continued, raising his voice to a higher pitch.

"That book was never marketed properly, and you know that," he replied, matching Mr. Steamer's tone and waiting like a fool for an answer. He hated these moments of silence. It made him feel like a fool, but, then again, that was Mr Steamer's intention all along.

"If pumping half a million dollars to promote your book is considered improper marketing, then we have a major problem. It only confirms that you are losing touch with reality."

David felt he didn't deserve to be belittled like this, not when six of his last nine novels reached the top of the bestseller list.

"Just tell me what's on your mind," he snapped back, anxious to get back to his daughter.

"That won't be a problem, and I'll be brutally honest. Now tell me, when you wrote that last book, were you suffering from writer's block?"

A nerve had been hit. That was the last thing David wanted to hear.

"You can try to fool whomever you want, David, but not me. I've been in this game long enough to recognize the symptoms."

"I have to go."

"No need to be ashamed. All writers face this impasse. Some snap out of it while others never do. In the meantime there are other topics you could write about, simple ones, which can make me money and where an imagination is secondary."

David tensed. As of late, Mr. Steamer had been hinting that he should write steamy adult books. It was a lucrative market, a quick and easy way to make a healthy profit according to him. From the corner of his eye, he noticed Cathy attempting to get his attention, pointing at the clock and raising seven fingers, each one representing the minutes left before the school bus was due to arrive. He wanted to ripe the phone off the wall in frustration, but what irritated him most was that Mr. Steamer knew Cathy was nearby and could easily have made out the subject of their conversation. Pressing the phone tighter to his ear he calmly said, "I will call you back."

"No need to call me back. I expect you to be in my office Monday morning at ten a.m. I also expect a dozen, one-page drafts for these new books that I can choose from. "

"That's impossible!" he cried out louder than he intended to.

"That's not what I want to hear."

David wanted to tell him what he could do with his money and his threats. He wanted to remind him there were other publishing houses that would eagerly offer him a multi-book deal, but not now. Not with Cathy with-in hearing distance, and though she appeared only interested in their remaining time and not his screaming match with Mr. Steamer, it was a risk he wasn't willing to take.

Cathy lowered one of her fingers, letting him know that six minutes remained, prompting him to hide behind the kitchen wall. With the phone still firmly pressed against his ear. "I will not write adult books!"

"You will do whatever it takes for this publishing house to recoup its money."

"I'm not your slave, Steamer."

"You mean, Mr. Steamer," he replied. "And as far as being my slave, that's another subject for another day. Be in my office Monday morning at ten a.m. If you are not here by one minute past ten, there will be a knock on your door. It will be my lawyer, holding a letter in his hand. At two minutes past ten you will officially be sued. I can afford to turn my lawyers into couriers and make them richer than they already are. By the time this is over, you will be breaking into your daughter's piggy bank for gas money."

"On what grounds?"

"Lawyers invent laws. Mine will come up with something."

"You can threaten me all you want. It's not going to work …" he said.

"It's a shame you don't swear. Cursing is a great way to release tension."

"I won't be there."

"Yes, you will," replied Mr. Steamer before hanging up.

David slammed the receiver down, convinced he got the best of Mr. Steamer, but his shaking hands told him otherwise.

"Are you still on the phone?" he heard Cathy ask.

He hid his trembling hands inside his pockets, took a deep breath, and poked his head around the corner. If she heard any part of that humiliating conversation, she didn't let on, rather she was grinning at him.

"I finished my cereal."

At that instant he wanted to hug her and never let go. She displayed a maturity beyond her years, a gift no seven-year-old child had a right to possess so early in life. He looked beyond her, out of the window, relieved that the school bus had not arrived.

"I'm sorry about this. How can I make it up to you?"

She thought for a moment. "I think we need more bird seed," she shrewdly replied.

He glanced over at the budgie's cage. Strapped to the side was a little lever that stored the seeds. There were two different containers, both half filled, representing another week's worth of food.

"I won't promise anything." He smiled knowing full well she knew what he meant.

She screamed with joy, scooping up her empty cereal bowl, dashing to the sink, and giving it a quick splash.

Again he found himself fascinated by his little princess. More and more, day after day, month after month, she was turning into her mother before his very eyes. The dimples on her cheeks when she smiled, the curls on her long blonde hair, the sound of her laughter, and the way she carried on. He was not a betting man, but he would wager a king's ransom that as Cathy aged, a tiny gap would appear between her two front teeth, identical to Diane's, the same gap that made his late wife more adorable than words could ever describe. Sadly the sound of a muffler was heard, a noise indicating that the school bus was approaching. It had arrived minutes earlier than it had a right to and parked itself in front of the house. Another child would be angry. Another child would be pouting, but not Cathy. She pointed her finger at David and asked, "Are you ready?"

David spread his arms, inviting her to run and throw herself into them as she had done every morning before leaving for school. He caught her in midair, swinging her in circles the traditional three times before stopping, giving her a kiss and gently placing her back down on her feet.

"I love you so much, baby," he told her.

Giving David one final hug, she picked up her backpack and skipped out of the door, followed closely by her father. He took a few steps outside, waved to the bus driver and waited until Cathy climbed safely on board. Minutes later, it drove away, disappearing around the bend, but before he could turn around to go back into the house, something caught his attention. It was the morning newspaper, which lay ten to twelve feet farther down the driveway. He heard the phone ring again betting it was Mr. Steamer, and though he would not answer the call, he could still hear his piercing voice taunting him, daring him to check page six to see for himself that his name was not in block letters and that his latest book was nowhere to be found on the top twenty list.

The phone temporarily stopped ringing only to ring again after a short pause. David felt he had no choice but to see it through. He marched out, picked up the paper, folded it under his arm, and slyly walked back before Mrs. Robinson, the elderly neighbour, had the opportunity to see him. He was in no mood for her.

"Good morning, David," he heard her say through the upstairs, open window.

"Good morning, Mrs. Robinson."

"Cathy looked like a little angel this morning."

"Thank you. I will tell her you said so." He gave her the usual nod and walked back into the house, sitting at the kitchen table and spreading out the newspaper. He ignored all other headlines, selecting the entertainment section and going directly to page six. He had gone to that page many times in his career and in most cases had felt a sense of vanity seeing his name in block letters as the author of a bestseller. His books were always in the top ten, but that was then, and this was now. As of this morning neither his name nor his latest work were anywhere to be found. What made it all the more pathetic was that it scarcely lasted a month in the top ten, only reaching number seven. *Or was it number eight?* he thought. He jumped when the phone rang again, upsetting him to such an extent that he clumsily folded the newspaper, stood up, walked to the window, and stared outside, refusing to accept that his creative skills may have withered.

Mercifully the phone stopped ringing. All he could hope for was that it would not ring again. He walked over to his aged computer, the source of some of his greatest work, and turned it on with every intention of proving to himself that he had not lost his will to write. He sat down. An image of him and Diane lying on a beach somewhere in the Caribbean popped up on the screen. A long time had gone by since that photo was taken, so much so that he didn't even remember the name of that tropical island. Life was so much simpler then, a time when he laughed a lot, a time when he produced some of his greatest work. He remembered thanking God each and every day for giving him the artistic gift of writing, along with an imagination that other authors would be envious of.

David brought up a list of novels he had been working on for the past few years. Some were started and deserted for one reason or another, some were half finished, others barely started, while the rest he just couldn't remember the plots any longer. He searched within himself to find the love of the characters he created and nourished but lacked the interest. It was too much of a chore and more convenient to let these characters languish inside the computer's hard drive. Sitting back, he folded his arms behind his head and thought that today would be a good time to begin a completely new novel. Perhaps a story about a pesky neighbour or a tale of a little girl's love for her budgie or possibly a story of a mean-spirited tycoon who is stripped of his entire fortune and ends up selling shoes in order to survive. All those story lines flashed quickly in and out of his mind, not remaining long enough to be taken seriously.

He eventually forced his fingers onto the keyboard, preparing to write, but at the last second decided to visit his favourite game room, the one which challenged the players to match their wits with the computer. He enjoyed that game immensely and would love to better yesterday's score. His potential new novel would have to wait for the time being.

David entertained himself, playing computer games for what he thought was roughly twenty minutes but in reality was over three hours. When it was over, he realized that he hadn't proven anything other than that Mr. Steamer might be correct after-all. He thought it more honest to get it over with and confess that he simply didn't have the desire to write anymore, to tell Mr. Steamer once and for all that he was seriously considering retiring altogether. Based on his lifestyle and contributions to his charities, he wasn't certain if he had saved enough money; his accountant was the only person who knew the figures. Even if he could continue to donate most of his royalties to the church, what would he do with the rest of his life? Would he seek employment at a college and offer workshops for aspiring writers.

David was in the midst of a serious crisis, and he didn't know what to do about it.

CHAPTER THREE

Nick and his wife of twelve years, Lee, had been up since early dawn preparing for this special occasion. It was now three in the afternoon, and the kitchen table looked absolutely stunning, fit for royalty. The china sparkled, the tablecloth was pressed to the point of being shiny, the knives and forks were spaced out to perfection, and the ice resting inside the bucket kept the champagne chilled. A fresh bouquet of flowers that had been delivered hours earlier stood upright inside a historic vase giving the kitchen a fresh and pleasant aroma, adding to the relaxing atmosphere. The reason for all the lavishness was the anticipated visit from Nick Turner's younger brother, David. In two short hours he, Cathy, and a woman named Jackie would be joining them for dinner.

Normally a very unpretentious man, Nick went all out for this occasion and with good reason. Jackie would be the very first woman David had confessed to an interest in since Diane passed away. Standing at just over six feet and perhaps twenty to twenty-five pounds overweight, Nick was a gentle human being. His face was round, his complexion light, shoulders broad, and his hair a reddish-brown—features inherited from his Scottish background. His enemies could have been counted on one hand, and those were more out of jealously due to his success than an actual hatred of him. Cashing in on profitable stocks a few years back, he was living the American dream by purchasing a pleasant country home spread over six acres. With a small stream running through the property, it was one of the most gorgeous places in the entire county, one of the few places where he felt at ease. The inside was littered with antiques, everything from the rarest Coca Cola billboards to furniture made before the great Civil War. The basement was finished with a fireplace on the east wall and a fifty-six-inch flat screen television on the west wall. On the south side was a long bar resembling a Scottish pub back home, complete with a five-gallon beer keg located at the far end of the counter and a huge Celtic Football Club emblem on the centre of the back wall. Various old photos of Scottish landmarks were scattered throughout, giving Nick the excuse to proudly explain the history behind them when visitors came.

Unfairly labelled a coward by some, Nick would walk away from a conflict rather than face one, doing whatever was necessary to avoid a confrontation. Such was not the case in his younger years while growing up with David in Scotland. In those times he would fight at a drop of a hat if anyone threatened David, receiving his fair share of beatings from older and meaner kids when protecting his younger brother, something he felt compelled to do.

"What did those cost you?" he asked Lee, pointing to the flowers, forever playing the part of the penny-pinching miser, a role he loved to play.

Lee spread the flowers evenly. "They didn't cost me anything … they cost you."

"Was it over fifty dollars?"

Tracie appeared from behind the living room wall, holding the receipt in her tiny hand. "Seventy-five dollars and forty-two cents."

"Between the dentist, the tooth fairy, and those flowers, it would be safe to say I took a financial beating these past few days." He laughed in reference to Tracie's two missing front teeth, a victim of what most seven-year-old kids have to endure before entering their eighth year. He had agreed not to laugh at her dental misfortunes, but it was difficult not to. She simply looked endearing.

"I'm sorry. I didn't mean to laugh," he apologized, holding back another burst.

Tracie didn't seem bothered by her father's ribbing, and when she wiggled her tongue between the gaps and grinned at him, he laughed some more.

This little girl could easily have been mistaken for a doll. She smiled at everything, inheriting her father's good nature and out-look on life. Born the same day as her cousin Cathy, she had an adorable face covered with thirty-seven freckles. She was positive of this figure since both her and Nick made a habit of counting each and every one of them once a week to see if the numbers had changed. Her reddish hair flowed freely down to her shoulders, and, though not as spoiled as Cathy, she did get her way most of the time, especially with Nick, whereas her mother, Lee, was uncompromising. A good example was the thin silver chain wrapped around her tiny neck with her two recently missing teeth fastened on the end. Lee thought it was appalling that she walked around with those disgusting items resting on her chest while Nick had actually drilled miniature holes through them in order that they could be linked through the chain.

Despite their differences and the odd clash, Nick loved his wife dearly and had every reason to feel blessed. He had met her nine years earlier and immediately recognized that he wanted to spend the rest of his life with her. At that time she worked as a librarian and was new to the area, frightened of anything that moved and suffering from agoraphobia—a fear of crowds. Other than going straight to and from work, the only other place she felt secure was inside the comfort of her church, fearing anywhere else would trigger a panic attack.

They saw each other for the first time at Sunday mass, and following a series of conversations she trusted him enough to go out on her very first date with him. Some would say she was very average looking, and they would be correct in their assumption of her. She did little to enhance her appearance. Bright clothing and loud make-up brought attention, something she avoided like the plague. Of average weight for her height of five feet, four inches, her light brown hair was kept long for a reason; she was conscious of the skin around her cheeks. In her teenage years, she had suf-fered from a server case of acne, which left small permanent scars, but to Nick she was the most beautiful woman in the world. They were married a short time later.

David treasured his black Jaguar, loved the aroma of the leather seats, which always smelled new, and the half dozen or so gadgets that he had especially ordered over and above what came with the standard model.

"The tires are good for at least two hundred thousand miles," the salesman had proclaimed at the time of purchase. David doubted they would be, but it didn't matter. That car was one of the few possessions that he splurged on with the money generated from his book sales. Ever since he was a teenager and had seen a billboard promoting this vehicle he was spellbound by the majestic black cat's emblem on the front. True to his nature, he devised a system to offset the guilt for owning this expensive model: whenever he filled it up with gas, he would set aside that same amount and throw it into the collection box when attending church.

He applied the brakes, bringing the Jaguar to a halt approximately one foot behind the white intersection line. This stop, minor as it was, caused an instant build up of hot sticky air inside the car, yet he would not switch on the air conditioning. Every time he was tempted to do so, he was reminded of a documentary he had seen on A&E five years earlier, blaming legionnaire's disease for the death of thirty-nine elderly people in Philadelphia. The virus was traced to an air conditioning unit on the roof of the building. Following the conclusion of that program, he had lost all faith in artificial cool air and didn't want it to blow into his face. Unfortunately, Cathy, who was sitting in the backseat vigorously fanning the air around her with a comic book, did not share his view.

"The light will change soon," he reassured her.

"I'm okay," she replied, quickly lowering the book so as not to concern him.

David's companion, Jackie, sat beside him, not bothered by the high temperature.

"Would you like us to stop and get you a cold drink?" she asked the child.

"No, thank you. I'll be fine."

Too early into their relationship to completely let his guard down, David did feel a sense of comfort with Jackie. Originally, he was hesitant to bring her into his home, uncertain as to how his daughter might react to another woman in his life. So far he hadn't seen any indication of resentment from either side. They were both polite and respectful of each other, and despite their age difference, they seemed to understand that if they didn't try to get along, he'd be placed into an uncomfortable situation.

The light turned green. Slipping out of character for a brief moment, David quickly stepped on the gas pedal, hoping a gust of wind would cool the interior, but all it did was bring in added humidity. He looked up at the rear view mirror. Cathy was fanning herself again.

"We will be on the highway soon," he reassured her, hoping the highway might bring in a more constant flow of air.

Jackie smiled at his pitiful brush with the wild side. She had never met a gentler or kinder human being and found that comical speeding scenario charming.

"Have you ever received a speeding ticket?" she felt the need to ask.

"When I was eighteen, I thought I was a bit of a rebel then, but my father thought otherwise and took my keys away for two weeks. He didn't classify it as punishment but as a learning experience."

"You always talk highly of your father but rarely mention your mother."

Many might have thought that the late Mr. Turner was too hard fisted in his methods, but nothing could have been farther from the truth. He never once laid a hand in anger when it came to his two beloved boys; always fair, yet firm when times called to be firm. It wasn't easy raising David and Nick as a single father. When his wife didn't return from a "*two-week*" trip to India with friends, he realized she would not return at all. Rather than going back to a husband whose sole purpose in life was always to do the right thing, she chose to hide in the jungle looking for tigers, which was far more exciting than a dull marriage. He didn't collapse over the incident; rather he began researching the Turner family tree and discovered he had a relative, his grandfather's brother, living in America. Following several months of communicating with this newfound relative he decided to immigrate to America to begin a new life. He sold all assets in Scotland with the goal of using his finances as a foundation to set up a construction company. It wasn't long before his hard work, combined with sweat and long hours, paid dividends, and his firm grew to become one of the largest and more successful in the area.

"I don't remember much about her to be honest with you, only that she left and didn't want to come back. Thank God my father was strong. He was and continues to be my hero," he explained, sliding his hand over to hers and softly squeezing her three middle fingers. They felt warm, a human contact he had missed over the years. Never in his wildest dreams did he imagine holding another woman's hand, but Jackie made it all so uncomplicated. He accepted her for who she was—a hardworking, trustworthy, kind, and thoughtful person who would share her last dollar with whomever she felt needed it. Always aware of the people around her, she respected their feelings, regardless of how insignificant. It was in sharp contrast to the "female groupies" who had attempted to get close to him in the past due to his celebrity status. The fact that three years ago his picture was on the cover of *People Magazine*, with the heading "America's Most Eligible Bachelor," did not change him. Rather it only embarrassed him and added to his somewhat reclusive behaviour.

Jackie wasn't what people would perceive as stunning, but she had a face that one would find on the front cover of a Sears' catalogue modelling a bright autumn sweater. Her body was average, but average in all the right places; her brown hair was kept in a bob style with a straight bang across her forehead bringing attention to her eyes, which some would say were her best feature. Standing two inches shorter than David, she had been called a Jacqueline Kennedy-Onassis look alike on many occasions, a flattering remark she took to heart.

David met her at a fundraising event, which his priest, Father Mark, had asked him to attend. The elderly priest understood that David's acclaim as a bestselling author would enhance the evening, perhaps even convincing other celebrities to attend. He was correct, for the evening had been a smashing success, raising over fifty thousand dollars. At the end of the night as David stood on the platform, giving thanks to all who attended, he noticed Jackie sitting in the third row, next to Father Mark. She had taken time off her hectic occupation as head of an adoption agency to assist in the fundraiser, and, soon after David's speech, Father Mark introduced the two. The chemistry between them had not gone unnoticed by the holy man, and he was delighted. What had began as small talk slowly carried on into the night, mostly due to one of Father Mark's tales of a spiritual myth in which God trusted a chosen few to raise his children here on earth.

"I can't think of any pair in the world whom God would trust to tutor his children, to school them properly of earthly ethics and morals than the Turner brothers," he told Jackie. All fables came with warnings, and Father Mark's tale was not an exception. He went on to explain that the chosen few would have to prevail against the evil urges of temptation. God would summon his own messengers to test the strength of these individuals, and if for whatever reason they slipped into the dark side, the Almighty would have no choice but to take his children back. A wonderful yarn from a wholesome priest who, at times, tried too hard, thought David.

In a matter of minutes the Jaguar would be passing the graveyard. This was no ordinary graveyard; it was Diane's permanent resting place. She lay rested beneath the largest marble headstone, a place where each and every morning David had fresh flowers brought to it.

Cathy would soon be shouting towards that direction, keeping with tradition ever since she was old enough to understand that her mother was buried there. She grabbed the top window with her right hand and held on as tightly as possible. With her free hand she lifted her body and poked her head out, stretching as far as she could to catch a first glimpse of the many crosses to come. Short on patience and knowing that beyond those crosses was her mother's, she turned her body sideways, tempted to remove the seatbelt.

"Don't you dare!" David cried out.

"But you're driving too fast!"

David whispered to Jackie, "I always drive the same speed, and she always accuses me of the same thing. Soon she'll be telling me to slow down."

"Slow down, Daddy," begged Cathy.

Jackie laughed out loud, immediately turning to face her. "I'm sorry. I didn't mean to laugh," she apologized.

Cathy wasn't paying attention, expecting the memorial park to come into view at any moment. Until then everything else was secondary, including apologies.

"There they are!" shouted Cathy, pointing to the first headstone.

"Do you see Mom's yet?" he asked, foreseeing a burst from her at any moment.

"There it is!" she cried out, pointing her shaky index finger at it. "Do you see it?" she continued as though the sight was new to him. "Hi, Mommy!" she shouted again, not giving David the opportunity to answer her. She then leaned forward, grabbed the head rest in front of her and extended her tiny body forward as far as the seatbelt allowed her to. "Do you think she heard me?"

"I know she did," he grinned.

"We're going to Uncle Nick's!" She shouted back through the open window, taking one last look before the car picked up speed again.

Throughout the whole ordeal and gone unnoticed by David, but not by Cathy, Jackie had whispered her own words at the headstone, telling Diane that David was everything she told her he was. Cathy was thrilled when she heard that. She somehow managed to maneuver her hand between the seat and the car door where Jackie's own hand awaited hers. They squeezed each other's hand for a few seconds before Cathy pulled her hand back.

CHAPTER FOUR

Salt Lake University was similar to other universities in Utah, except for one class that no other campus had nor would ever have. This group of special students consisted of eleven individuals ranging in ages from thirty-three to fifty-five. They all appeared haggard, tired, and showing signs of premature aging, the youngest displaying traces of grayish hair while the oldest possessing a long gray beard. In spite of their abnormal appearance, this unique group of eleven was at all times uplifting and inspiring. Theirs was a class where everyone felt distinctive and comfortable sharing experiences with each other that everyday people on the outside couldn't even begin to fantasize about.

Their weekly schedule rarely changed. From Monday through Thursday, they attended class. Friday and Saturday were days spent as they wished, doing anything from fishing to shopping or just walking in pairs throughout the country side. On Sunday a bus would pick them up at their residence, eight a.m. sharp, and take them to church where they enjoyed a good part of the day. Not only did they participate as a group, but it was understood that they would spend their remaining days together in a huge twenty-room manor owned by a man named Jacob Wright. This wealthy and generous individual, who many teased could be mistaken for Santa Clause due to his own long white beard, rosy cheeks, and a robust frame, paid for all of their food and expenses. He was their savior, mentor, professor, and, to some of the younger ones, a father figure they could easily relate to.

Mr. Wright had individually searched them out, rescuing all eleven at a time when they were at the lowest point of their lives.

In those dark days all eleven were frail and confused, desperately seeking people to believe in their spiritual encounters, and, when society ignored them, deeming the whole lot insane, they all reached a point of contemplating suicide; therefore, it wasn't surprising that when Mr. Wright entered the classroom they clapped as anyone would do for their champion.

"Good morning, class," he greeted then sat down to face his class.

"Good morning, Mr. Wright," they replied simultaneously.

He opened his briefcase. Hidden beneath some documents was a half-eaten chocolate bar. He never outgrew his love for chocolate, starting every morning by nibbling on one end, saving the other half for class. If not for his doctor warning him that a man of his age and size should be very wary of his sugar intake, he would have consumed a dozen or more before the day was through. Looking back at his students, he removed a file of his choice and joked, "Don't we all look perky today?" to the delight of his class and then placed his reading glasses on. "If I'm not mistaken, I believe it is Patrick's turn this morning."

Patrick, a forty-five-year-old student with long hair tied into a ponytail and only one of the few in the group that was clean shaven, stood up. Speaking with a slight lisp he said. "Yes, Mr. Wright. It is my turn."

"Would you be kind enough to come to the front of the class then?"

The room had twelve chairs. Patrick sidestepped the only empty one and eagerly walked to the front of the class, keen on sharing his experiences with the rest. Furthermore, he was grateful that he could disclose extremely sacred incidents with his equivalents and not be classified as a lunatic, something that his closest friends and family had accused him of.

"I was allowed to speak to my deceased wife for over five minutes," he began. "Seconds before we ran out of time, she smiled and said to me, 'Two more years, darling.'"

"Is that when she disappeared into the mist?" asked Mr. Wright, knowing it was.

"Yes. I recall begging for more time but was politely told it was time for her to return and for me to leave."

Mr. Wright heard a soft murmur from the rest of the class. "Can anyone guess what Patrick's wife meant by 'two more years'? Was she attempting to relay a secret message to a husband she had adored when she was alive?" he asked. One of the other students raised his arm. "Yes, Luke."

"I find it highly unlikely," stated Luke. "I don't believe secret messages exist in Heaven for the simple fact that God would know of this."

"Fair assumption," replied Mr. Wright, looking back at Patrick. "What do you think she meant?"

"At that precise moment I thought she was telling me that I had two more years to live before we become a couple again, but I highly doubt she would be in a position to anticipate the future. Only God can do that, and kind as he is, he would not share that information with anyone. Her final three words have haunted me ever since because I simply don't know what she was trying to tell me."

Another student with a possible answer raised his hand.

"Go ahead. Mark."

"I have to believe there was something between Patrick and his wife that would have taken two more years to complete when she was alive," analyzed Mark.

Patrick thought for a moment. "Before she died, we had two years remaining on our mortgage payments. She was so excited about that prospect. It meant we could eventually afford to buy an older house across the street and convert it into a residential home for the aged." He smiled as he remembered. "She would break into this little childish Irish dance at the sheer thought."

The class whispered amongst each other, dissecting his theory and attempting to make sense of it all. Mr. Wright did not interfere; rather he gave them all the time they needed to discuss Patrick's saintly encounter with each other as they themselves would get their opportunity to compare it with their own.

The permanent ugly scar on his right hand, just above his thumb reminded Nick of what could happen if oven mitts were not fitted properly. Two years ago, a protective mitt slipped off his hand. Helplessly holding onto a hot dish, the incident left him with a hideous wound. The pain eventually went away, but the scar remained, making him very self-conscious of it, especially when shaking hands or when signing documents in front of witnesses. It bothered him to such an extent that he had attempted to learn to write with his left hand, abandoning the experiment when it became apparent that he would never master it.

This time he checked and then re-checked that both mitts fitted properly before lowering the oven door and peeking inside. The golden turkey smelled scrumptious and ready to be taken out to cool when the phone at the end of the counter rang. When Lee showed no interest in answering it, Nick held up his mitted hands, showing her that he was not in any position to answer it either. Lee in turn picked up a bowl of fruit, indicating that her hands were also full.

Lee rarely answered the phone unless she absolutely had to. Quite simply, she was frightened, too petrified that it might be a stranger or a marketing call. Nick was well aware of her fears, but there were times like this when he hoped she might make an exception.

"I'll get it," said Tracie running towards the phone.

"If it's your Uncle David, tell him to pick up some ice," Lee shouted at her.

"Hello?" answered Tracie, pausing for a second. "Yes, one moment please," she continued, placing the receiver tight to her stomach so as not to be heard. "It's not Uncle David. It's that man who's always angry."

"I can't take it now," he whispered, suspecting to whom she was referring.

Confused, Tracie looked at Lee for guidance, but her mother was already walking out of the kitchen. She didn't want any part of this phone call, especially from an angry voice. The sound of the oven mitts thrown onto the kitchen counter, followed by mumbling was enough to tell Tracie that her father was not happy to take the call. She passed him the phone and stood aside.

"Where's David?" is all Nick had to hear to know his suspicions were correct. On the other end of the line was Mr. Steamer; one of the few men that he disliked and had no time for.

"Mr. Steamer?" he replied pretending to be surprised.

"Do you know what I hate?" Mr. Steamer began.

Nick bit his lip. He was going to tell him than he most likely disliked life in general but thought better of it. There was no telling the reprisal that awaited his David if he offended this madman.

"I'm sorry. I don't understand."

"I hate phonies. You knew it was me. Why act as if you didn't." Mr. Steamer demanded to know.

"David is not expected here today, and if you'll excuse me, I have to go."

"You Turners make horrible liars." There was a slight pause. "Did you know that even a small turkey can feed up to ten people? I can smell the turkey from here. I can also smell the gravy and know there's not enough ice to chill the champagne as your wife would want it. I count six dishes on the table that are spaced out evenly, and I even know the last time that same china was used. I know everything, so don't tell me that David is not expected. That only insults my intelligence."

Somewhat shaken, Nick wondered how he knew of the turkey. If that was a lucky guess, then how did he know about the china or the champagne? It would be insane to think he possessed super natural powers. Things of that nature only happened in films.

"Talk to me, Nick. Talk to me."

Nick quickly dismissed these thoughts, reminding himself of who he was dealing with. Mr. Steamer was the master intimidator, a man who had been wicked for so long that he could masterfully anticipate other people's thoughts. He recalled, word for word, how David described him: "That man could guess by the tone of a voice as to what a person was doing at any particular time. If drunk, he would know; and if one was in the midst of a weak and desperate moment, he would seize that opportunity and verbally tear into that person's soul."

Nick cleared his throat, "I can give you his cell number. That's the best I can do."

"I pay for his phone and have his cell number!" screamed Mr. Steamer.

"Please don't raise your voice at me. It's not going to get you anywhere. All I can do is repeat what I have told you all along. He is not here, nor is he expected. I am sorry, but I have to go."

"I will remember this conversation, and I will make sure you do as well," he threatened, slamming the phone down.

Tracie stepped in front of Nick, a disturbed frown on her face. Her father had just lied and had to answer for it.

"You lied to that man. You told him that Uncle David was not going to be here."

He had always taught her never to lie. "Lies breed more lies," he would preach every so often just as his father had once preached to him.

"That man I was talking to isn't very nice," he managed to say.

"Does that mean we can lie to bad people?"

Nick had made a fortune in the stock market, knowing when to buy and when to sell. Brokers considered him a genius, forever seeking his advice, respecting his foresight, and knowing he was right more often than not, yet he could not answer the most basic of questions from a seven-year-old.

"One should never lie," he softly confessed.

"Then why did you lie?" she quickly replied, demanding an answer, and when Nick avoided her, she added, "I'm sorry, Daddy, but I need to know."

Nick had to respond or risk appearing like a conman, someone who said one thing and meant a dozen other things. "I was protecting your Uncle David from that man."

"But that doesn't tell me if lying to a bad person is right," she persisted.

Lee called out Nick's name, complaining, of what wasn't of any importance. She couldn't have picked a more opportune time, and he took advantage of it. He picked up the mitts, slid his hands inside and said, "I got a turkey to take out of the oven."

Tracie would ask him again at a later date. That he was certain of.

The Scottish weather was not suited for citric fruit trees, but the constant California sunshine was another matter altogether. That was one of the first things appreciated and taken advantage of when the Turners set foot in their new country. They were pleasantly surprised and felt pampered when all they had to do was stroll behind their home and pull the fruit of their choice off the nearest tree. That was a far cry from having to go to the grocery store, as was the case back home. Hence it wasn't a surprise that Nick surrounded his estate with pear, apple, cherry, and too many peach trees to count. He also took pleasure in growing his own grapes and making his own wine, even though he wasn't much of a drinker. Most of the bottled wine was given to Father Mark who auctioned them off as another form of revenue for the church.

On the right side of the estate stood a huge tree that Nick estimated was well over eighty years old. Four feet above the ground, attached to the trunk of this tree was a constructed play house that he had labored long and hard for weeks to assemble. It had a pitched roof, a door facing the main house, three windows, and was protected all around with waterproof stain. Inside, the walls were smoothly sanded, the floor tiled, and a small desk, complete with two miniature chairs resting in the middle. In the corner was a small chest where Tracie kept crayons, toys, and any other belonging she saw fit. Visitors would often comment on the structure, telling Nick what he never tired of hearing: that it was constructed better than some real homes.

On the property's left side, was a small manmade pond, something that Nick had secretly dreamed of owning all his life and finally had the funds to see it through. Beyond the pond was a hill, and behind it, a hidden dirt road leading to the house. Any car driving towards the property would kick up clouds of dust before becoming visible.

Tracie stood at the edge of the pond, feeding the dozen or so ducks. With wings flapping, they chased every piece of bread thrown at them; the smaller ones protesting when ignored, the dominant ones enjoying things as they were. Normally she was fair, distributing the feed equally, but not today. Today her focus was on that hill, and when she noticed clouds of dust first forming and then swaying horizontally, she knew her cousin Cathy would soon be there. Throwing the rest of the bread into the pond, she ran towards the house, crying out, "They're here!" as though the king and queen of England were about to drop in.

Nick was trimming the remaining pieces of turkey.

"Perfect timing," he mumbled to himself, "Lee, they're here."

Lee used her sleeve to nervously wipe the perspiration off her forehead. "I know, I heard," she replied, inspecting the kitchen table from one end to the other, convinced something was missing. "What did I forget?"

"You always forget the salt and pepper," he said, not looking to see if indeed they were missing.

The instant the Jaguar came to a full stop, Cathy unbuckled the seatbelt, jumped out of the car and ran to meet Tracie. They met halfway, hugged, and waited for David and Jackie to get out of the car.

"Hello, Tracie. This is my new friend, Jackie," said David, placing his arm around Jackie's waist, bringing her close to him.

"I know. Cathy already told me her name was Jackie."

"Nice to meet you, Tracie," grinned Jackie, at the same time staring at the chain dangling around her neck. "Are those teeth?"

"They're my good luck charm," she explained before taking Cathy's hand and pulling her towards the tree house where the cousins immediately entered.

David lead Jackie towards the tree house, close enough for the children to be heard. "Just listen to the way they communicate with each other," said David. "You will find it close to amazing."

Using their thumbs, both girls ran them along each other's foreheads, down their cheeks and ending at the bottom of their chin. Following a slight pause, they began to chant in harmony. It sounded like a song, but it was not a song at all. The syllables weren't recognized as part of the English language, yet the children understood each other.

"What are they saying?" asked Jackie.

"No one knows for sure. They somehow developed their own language while growing up so close together. What we thought was adorable baby talk between them was actually a form of communication that they still use to this day."

"Simply remarkable," said Jackie.

"Hello," welcomed a male voice.

They both looked up at the porch and saw Nick and Lee staring down at them.

"Hello," beamed David. When he realized that neither one of them was looking directly at him, but rather paying attention to Jackie, he quickly removed his arm away from her waist and took two steps to the side, putting distance between them. He seemed lost, not knowing what to do with the arm, and wondered if in the eye of his brother and Lee if he disrespected his late wife in any way. Jackie was only the second serious relationship in his life, and the last thing he wanted to do was offend her, but he felt he did just that by panicking and moving away from her. To Jackie's credit she remained calm, sure of herself, and seemingly understanding of the situation.

" I'm Jackie Ulliman," she announced. "And you must be Nick and Lee."

Nick was relaxed, his gentle demeanor shining as always. "I know. I'm Nick. I'm not sure what her name is, though," he joked, pointing at Lee.

Lee rolled her eyes—a tip off that he had used this gag once too often. "Please come up," she said ignoring Nick altogether.

They both climbed the three stairs needed to reach the top of the porch. As customary, the brothers respectfully shook hands, hugged, and patted each other on the back. In earlier days, David used to greet Lee in a similar fashion, but she made it known through Nick that any contact, including David's, made her uncomfortable. She simply didn't want to be touched.

"Pleasure to meet you," Jackie softly said as she shook Nick's hand. "David has told me many wonderful things about you."

Lee took a small backward step, placed her hands deep inside the apron pockets in order to avoid any potential handshake and mumbled. "It's a pleasure to meet you as well."

An edgy pause followed between the four until Nick broke the silence by saying. "I hope everybody is hungry. I know I am."

The women were the first to enter, and as David was about to follow, Nick held him back.

"Mr. Steamer called here earlier looking for you."

David shook his head. "That man is relentless, calling me a dozen times a day."

"Is he still attempting to alter your writing style?"

David laughed. "Is that your polite way of asking if he's still trying to get me to write adult stories?"

"Is the term *adult stories* your interpretation of porn?" he laughed back.

"I suppose," replied David, the grin on his face quickly diminishing.

"Have you thought about what you're going to do?"

"That's the problem. I don't know what to make of it. There has to be a motive to his madness. He can get any two-bit writer to write that kind of trash for a fraction of the cost."

"Just be careful with that man."

The cousins were still inside the tree house, sitting opposite each other, hands spread on top of the desk, and were in the midst of a deep conversation. This privacy gave them the opportunity to dissect the lie Nick told to Mr. Steamer. This time alone also gave them the freedom to speak in their own language.

"I find it all so very disturbing," said Cathy, fidgeting her hands back and forth on the desk.

"My thought as well, and when I asked if it was proper to lie to 'bad' people, he ignored the subject altogether," Tracie explained using a vocabulary that no seven-year-old would, regardless of what language was spoken.

Deep in thought, Cathy then scratched her chin. "May I suggest a solution?"

"Yes, please, because I am overwhelmed by it all."

"Why not disregard it for the time being? Do not allow it to burden you any further. In days to come, mention it to him once again."

"But we all know that one must never lie," insisted Tracie. "It was horrible to listen to."

"I can imagine," replied Cathy, placing her hand on top of Tracie's to console her. "He did lie to Mr. Steamer and must be held accountable. Perhaps all he needs is a bit soul searching."

"I shall question him again on Wednesday."

"Please let me know me the moment he answers. I am curious as to his reply."

"And what of Mr. Turner?" asked Tracie.

"He indulges in intense conversations with Mr. Steamer, but as of yet, I see the same strength in him as always. Even so, I constantly pray to our Father that he never crosses that line. I love Mr. Turner so much and will miss him terribly if one day he decided to take the wrong path."

"It would be a terrible loss for us all."

"One can only hope," replied Cathy just in time to hear her father shout to them that dinner was on the table.

Dinner was moving along nicely. Everyone did their best to make Jackie feel welcomed, and it was working. Originally a bit reserved, she eventually came around and even debated on some sticky political issues with Nick. That was expected. Nick's political views were centre to right while Jackie's were left to centre. A clash of opinions was inevitable. At one point David was tempted to interfere, concerned that their debating would get out of control, but decided against it. They were sensible adults, both agreeing to disagree. Over all, everyone was having an excellent time. The highlight came when David shared some of his book signing incidents with one particular story standing out from the rest; when autographing his book for a score of fans he overheard an elderly lady brag to another that should Mr. Turner prematurely pass away, her newly autographed book would be more valuable.

"How would you have reacted if she had come back with a violin case?" Nick said, laughing.

"Let's just say that I kept looking over my shoulder," he said, relishing the laughter his story brought out from the rest.

The moment dessert was over, permission was asked and granted to the children to be excused. There seemed to be urgency for them to return back to the tree house.

"I told Nick not to build that tree house. She spends more time in there than here," complained Lee.

"Actually a tree house is the perfect plaything. It represents the first sign of ownership and responsibility," said David.

Lee wouldn't have any of it, grumbling back, "Those two are spoiled rotten."

"Sometimes it is difficult to distinguish whether a child is spoiled or over loved," reasoned Jackie.

"Cathy has been pestering me to buy her a new budgie. Eventually I will get her one but it's not to spoil her but out of love," said David.

"Don't be so naive David. If you buy her that bird, you are paying for her love," stated Lee.

If David had told Lee what he really thought of her absurd statement it would have ruined the dinner. Cathy was his child, and he would raise her how he saw fit. It was of no concern of hers and no secret that bitterness was building up between the two over the years. Sensing a potential disaster, Nick stood up, massaged his full belly, and looked at David. "Why don't we go out and get some fresh air?"

Doctor Musk stood by the doorway, hesitant to walk in unannounced and disturb Mr. Wright's class. All he needed was his attention and got it immediately when Mr. Wright saw him standing there with a sense of urgency. When one of his students turned around to see who Mr. Wright was staring at, so did the others. They all knew Doctor Musk. He was not only Mr. Wright's personal physician, but he was also theirs. Finding it odd that he would appear as he did, the students then looked back at Mr. Wright and soon began whispering amongst each other, much like scared children. Their anxiety alarmed Mr. Wright. He immediately stood up, subconsciously cleared some documents off his desk, and said, "No reason to be concerned, class. Doctor Musk was expected." Most of the class believed him. The others decided it was in their best interest to do so and did. "If you could kindly give me a few minutes, I'll be right back," he continued and readily walked out to meet the doctor.

"I'm sorry for interrupting," the doctor apologized before Mr. Wright had reached him.

"No problem whatsoever," he replied, taking him by the arm and ushering him along the hallway. Once a safe distance from the class, Mr. Wright let go of his arm, smiled, and whispered in jest. "How long are you giving me?"

The doctor attempted to smile back but found he couldn't. He had vowed never to get personal or emotional with his patients, but with a man of Mr. Wright's caliber, it was next to impossible.

"The bowel screening results came back, and they indicate that we should do more tests," he told him as soothingly as he could.

Mr. Wright glanced back at his class, at his eleven students. Tried as they may, they looked lost and vulnerable without him. He would hate to think what would become of them if he were no longer alive. Other than Patrick, and to some extent Luke, there was no one with the strength or experience to replace him.

It was uncertain moments like this that Mr. Wright would focus at the twelfth empty chair and wondered if a clear leader would ever emerge to fill that seat.

David sat on the first step of the porch sipping on a cold glass of ginger ale, and Nick was sitting behind him on the rocking chair drinking warm coffee; both were watching the children playing. The children did their best to entertain their fathers, chasing each other in and out of the tree house and then looking back at them for any sort of reaction.

"Be careful," cried out David, finding it odd that Nick appeared bored by it all. Usually he would be chatting nonstop about the subject he loved best: how one day he was going to expand the pond and then drift into which private school would be best suited for Tracie for the coming year. This time he was unusually quiet, only taking sporadic glances at the children before his attention wandered elsewhere.

The distance between brothers had drifted in different directions over the years, more than either one wanted to admit. Conversations dealing with personal matters had become more difficult to address. Things were kept in with neither brother wanting to be the first to make their problems known. When Diane was still alive it was different. The four of them would go out to dinner, to the theatre, to an amusement park, basically finding any excuse to spend time together. When fans of David stopped him, asking for his autograph, Nick was so proud, constantly boasting to friends about his little brother's literary achievements. But things changed. The Turner family changed. With Lee's paranoia and David never completely recovering from his wife's tragic death, the family structure, although still solid, lost some of its foundation.

Nick stood up, walked around the rocking chair for no reason, and then sat back down. Something was unquestionably bothering him, and if that was his way of letting his brother know, it worked. But David needed small talk beforehand as a prelude. He pointed above the garage at the safety electrical sensor system Nick purchased months back but never got around to having it installed. The main wires were still sticking up in midair, not connected to the principal panel inside the garage. Once connected, a series of invisible sensors were meant to shoot out. If anything or anybody crossed those unseen beams, the system was designed to automatically discharge powerful lights onto the driveway along with every single light in the house. Activated mostly at night, this lighting complex was just another gadget that marketers brainwashed consumers into feeling they couldn't do without.

"You still haven't hired an electrical contractor to install that?" laughed David.

Nick chuckled. "Lee makes a point of harassing me about it every so often."

This bit of humor unconventional as it seemed, worked. Nick was now ready to talk. He leaned his body forward and swung his head from side to side as though a third party might be listening to their conversation.

"Have you heard about a real estate proposal called 'Woodbridge Estates'?" he whispered.

David thought for a moment. "Only what I read in the papers. Something about turning a subsidized area into a high-priced condominium village and giving it the stylish name of Woodbridge Estates."

"That's the one," replied an excited Nick, subconsciously looking behind him again.

David recalled reading about this troubled area known as the "Junction," a district so dangerous that even the police were reluctant to patrol. When they were forced to, they would only enter with a well-armed, well-trained SWAT team as back up. Not only was it unsafe, but it was also one of the highest crime areas, stretching for miles, and one of the few remaining districts that had not been reconstructed following the riots of the early nineties. The people living there had managed to adapt to the conditions and survived as best as they could. In short, they grew so accustomed to being isolated from the outside world that they preferred to be left alone.

"That place is strictly a low-rental subsidized area. I can't see how it could ever be zoned for modern condominiums."

"It will be shortly," replied Nick. Tired of looking over his shoulder, he got up from the rocking chair and sat next to his brother. "I'm thinking of joining a group of investors. Within that group is an individual of influence, a powerful person who has enough political influence to change zoning bylaws," he quietly told him. Eager to explain further, he moved closer to David. "As it stands now, this group can buy that whole area for next to nothing, but once the zoning bylaw changes it will be worth ten times as much."

David gave him time to catch his breath. "I'm surprised. Normally something tragic has to happen before zoning bylaws get changed. Normally for any regulation to change, the person of influence that you speak of needs justification in order to flex his political muscles. I guarantee you that one day you will be reading about that area. It could be anything from a major fire to a mass shooting. Then the liberals will voice their concerns, demanding something be done. That's all the ammunition your friend needs. He'll campaign for the safety of those people, making it easier to have them moved out of their homes.

"Sounds like a conspiracy to me. Perhaps your writer's imagination has gone amok again," laughed Nick.

David didn't laugh back. "I hope you're right. If not, those poor souls will be herded like cattle and taken to who knows where. To be honest with you, the whole scheme sounds an inch from being illegal. I'm surprised you would even want to get involved."

Nick reacted as though his parade was rained on. He pulled away, scratching an imaginary itch on his elbow. "I never really gave their relocation much thought, and as far as being illegal, at least you got a speeding ticket at eighteen. I never did. Maybe, just maybe, I want to do something edgy like this just to see how it feels."

David wasn't sure if his brother was being sarcastic or serious. "I can't tell you what to do. I only wish you the best."

Nick paused for a moment. "It's still a year away. I may change my mind."

Lee was at one end of the kitchen counter. At the opposite, facing her, Jackie wiped the last of the dishes and placed it on top of the others. She checked to see if she had missed anything and discovered a single spoon that somehow was left behind. When picking it up, coincidently Lee grabbed it at the same time. Their hands touched. Lee quickly pulled back, startling Jackie.

"I'm sorry," Jackie apologized.

Embarrassed by the incident, Lee dried the spoon, placed it inside the drawer and said nothing, leaving it up to Jackie to start a conversation, any conversation.

"Thank you for your hospitality," Jackie began.

Lee regretted the "touching" incident but wouldn't apologize for it even though she had taken to Jackie, recalling what her late mother said of first time guests: *"You can tell a woman's upbringing by her conduct immediately after dinner,"* she had told her. *"If that person helps with the dishes, then she was raised properly."* Without a doubt, Jackie had a proper upbringing.

A commotion was heard outside. Both women looked out of the window, noting it was the children chasing each other.

"They seem to get along very well," observed Jackie.

"Better than twins," Lee replied, forcing a smile. "They have so much in common."

"I heard them communicating in their own language. It was remarkable."

"That's only one of the many unique things about those two," Lee said sensing an urge to open up to her so as to offset the awkward incident. "I'm not sure what David has told you about the children, but, I will add this, we are blessed to have them."

"He has told me bits and pieces. I'm sure he'll tell me more when he's ready."

Lee removed her apron, neatly folding and placing it on top of the dinner table. "Has he told you they both officially 'died' only to be brought back to life?"

Others might not have felt comfortable with such a personal topic, but Jackie kept her composure.

"He has told me about losing his wife in a horrific car accident but somehow Cathy was saved."

Lee grimaced, recalling that terrible night. "It was a horrible time for us all. I was nine months pregnant with Tracie and sitting in the hospital waiting room with Nick and David when the doctor walked into the hallway. Next to him was a nurse carrying a clipboard. You can always expect bad news when a nurse walks next to a doctor carrying his clipboard," declared Lee, visibility upset.

"You don't have to tell me any of this."

She did want to tell her and continued with. "The doctor took that clipboard, read the two top lines, and stated that since Diane was dead, they were now concentrating on saving the baby. Maybe it was the shock of seeing David cry that brought on what happened next." Lee's voice began to falter. "I felt an extruding pain inside my stomach. The umbilical cord had wrapped itself around Tracie's neck, choking her, right there in the hospital hallway. I could feel something wasn't right. I could feel Tracie shivering inside me, and, then, nothing. No more movement. I lost consciousness and couldn't remember much after that other than Nick screaming at the doctor to rush me into the nearest delivery room."

Jackie was left speechless. She filled a glass of water and gave it to Lee. Lee drank it without thanking her. Following a lengthy pause, she continued, "I lay in that room, begging God to save my child, while at the same time in the next room, lay Diane mangled beyond recognition.

"I'm so sorry," said Jackie, not certain if Lee even acknowledged the apology.

"I was heavily sedated, not sure of what was happening around me, only hearing voices crying out that Tracie was not breathing. I'll never forget the shock on the doctor's face when she suddenly began to cry. When I lifted my head I saw a nurse wrapping her in a blanket and walking out of the room. Seconds later I also saw another nurse run out of Diane's room carrying another wrapped baby. It was Cathy. They had managed to bring her back to life precisely at the same moment as Tracie."

Lee had said more than she wanted to. Not much more was said between the two women after that.

Cathy and Tracie exchanged a few words. Coming to some sort of agreement, they took each other's hand and skipped to the porch, stopping before their fathers and gazing at them a certain way.

They were about to ask a favour. The two children hesitated, not wanting to be the first to ask. Eventually Cathy took the initiative.

"There's no school tomorrow. Can someone please take us swimming?"

Normally this wouldn't be a problem, but neither man volunteered.

"I have a meeting in the morning," said David, relenting to the fact that he was going to see Mr. Steamer.

"I think your mom wanted to go shopping," was Nick's excuse.

The children said nothing; the expression on their faces said it all. Seconds later Lee and Jackie walked out of the house.

"Why the long faces?" asked Lee.

"They were hoping one of us would take them swimming tomorrow, but it seems we're all busy," explained Nick.

"I can take them if you like. I don't work on Mondays," offered Jackie.

The Turners were presented with an unusual problem. Other than the odd school or church fieldtrip, no one from outside the family had ever taken the children anywhere. They hadn't even had a babysitter in their young lives. While growing up, if David had to honor a commitment, arrangements would be made weeks in advance so that Lee could look after Cathy. The same applied to Nick and Lee, with David always ready to look after Tracie. Though Jackie seemed competent and trustworthy, she was not family.

Lee wasn't ready to break tradition even if it meant insulting David's friend.

"Oh, no," she instantly interrupted. "We would never put you out of your way like that."

"It won't be out of my way at all. In fact, I think it would be fun."

Lee turned her back on everyone and walked into the house—an obvious and poorly disguised act of cowardliness—leaving Nick to solve the problem. He knew better than agree to such a thing.

"Can Miss Jackie take us, Daddy?" asked Tracie.

When Nick didn't answer, the atmosphere intensified, not only for Jackie but also for David. He was willing to trust her and wanted Nick to know that.

"What time do you want Cathy to be ready?" he asked.

"Anytime after nine would be work for me."

"That would be perfect."

"What about me, Daddy? What about me?" cried Tracie.

David felt Lee glaring at him. He was right. She was staring directly at him through the window, stone faced, angry, and fuming.

"What about me?" Tracie continued to plead.

CHAPTER FIVE

No one could have entered this city without knowing that Mr. Steamer was the owner of that magnificent building which served both as his office and his home. That structure was brilliantly constructed deep within the heart of downtown, standing forty stories high and, with its prime location, the envy of all other proprietors. Surrounding the roof's edge, on all four corners, stood six-foot high coppered letters with the words "STEAMER'S PUBLISHING INC." firmly attached to reinforced steel. Below were thousands of windows elegantly fastened to the rest of the building, each with a thin silver trim wrapping, defying any other skyscraper to match its brilliance.

A horde of Mr. Steamer's employees occupied twenty-four floors of this building. Their job was to make money for him, lots of it, and if they could not discover a diamond in the rough, such as another David Turner, they would be replaced before any severance package could take effect. A constant flow of hopeful writers would enthusiastically submit what they considered to be their best work, novels that had taken nearly two years to complete. Ninety-five percent of the time, edgy editors would tell these hopefuls that their writing style or story lines were not suited for STEAMER'S PUBLISHING INC. guidelines.

"You are welcome to come back and try again," they would tell them, unconcerned about the dreams they had just destroyed. The remainder of the building was rented out with extraordinary rental fees attached to it reminding the tenants of the privilege it was to be in the same building as Mr. Steamer.

The penthouse totaled ten thousand square feet. Seven thousand of that was taken up by rows of offices and other private rooms, most notably Lora's and Mr. Steamer's offices. It was extravagant, and there was no other penthouse like it for miles. The doorknobs were sprayed with a thin layer of real gold, and the walls' surrounding trim was all handmade by the most skilled carpenters, chosen specifically for Mr. Steamer by top union leaders. Fourteen-foot ceilings filled with imported spotlight fixtures were one of the many highlights; the massive kitchen being another, with its own specially designed in-house barbeque. There were six washrooms, each with its own double sink units, shower stalls, and Jacuzzi bathtubs. The showers were enclosed with glass sliding doors; inside were chromed shelves particularly constructed to hold every imaginable shampoos and cleaning lotions. The only unusual phase of this penthouse was the bar. Strangely there was no liquor to be found, only bottles of chilled water and fruit juices. The rest of the shelves were displaying photos of Mr. Steamer with an arm wrapped around his "special group of friends" who came from every part of the globe, including the Arctic and Antarctica. Everyone knew of Mr. Steamer's favorite room, a sanctuary where he could relax and be left in peace—his beloved sauna. Custom made to suit his style, it was the one haven that was out of bounds for everyone except Lora.

The penthouse's remaining three thousand square feet was designed as open concept with a reception desk directly in front of the elevator doors and where the receptionist could greet and direct visitors into one of the many waiting areas. There they would wait until Mr. Steamer was ready to receive them; and should they have to wait to see him, a coffee machine was located to the right of the main waiting area. If visitors thought the coffee was complimentary, they were wrong. There were two signs above the coffee machine fastened on the wall—one that instructed everyone to insert four quarters for the brew, fifty cents more for double cream. The other sign reminded everyone that should they require using the company telephone, it would have to be authorized to ensure that the call was not long distance.

Though first-time visitors to Mr. Steamer's office would be impressed, David found it to be cold and unwelcoming. He had been sitting in the waiting area, sinking deeper inside an oversized black leather sofa, wishing he could have been somewhere else. In front of him was a glass-covered table displaying today's newspaper. In the past he would have read most of the editorial segment, a good portion of the world news, and also bits and pieces from the sports section. But he knew if he picked up that paper, he would be enticed to turn to page six to check if his last novel could have miraculously slipped back into the top twenty over night. That was something he'd rather ignore. He only wanted to set things right with Mr. Steamer and to make it absolutely clear that he would not write filth. If Mr. Steamer was in one of his moods and the meeting dragged on, he would simply leave, then make an appointment with his accountant to go over his finances. True, he should have paid more attention in the past to his royalties, but money was never important to him, as it always came easily. If the meeting went in his favour, he could then pass by the pet store, purchase the budgie, and surprise Cathy.

Something else was bothering him. He had accumulated enough experience throughout his career to sense when he was being stared at. He turned towards the receptionist and caught her intently looking at him. She was a young, red-haired beauty, perhaps in her mid-twenties. Taking a quick glance at her nametag, he learned that her name was Lynda Steward.

The blushing receptionist apologized, "I'm sorry, Mr. Turner. I didn't mean to stare."

"No apologies necessary," smiled David.

"I only wanted to tell you that I have read every one of your books."

"I'm sure that news would make Mr. Steamer a very happy man," joked David.

Lynda laughed. "I've been working here for over a week and have yet to see him smile."

David loved her response, something he needed to lift his spirits. "I have known Mr. Steamer for a much longer time, and I have also yet to see him smile," he replied, amusing himself.

Perhaps it was David's casual attitude or possibly Lynda's character was more forward than others, but she had no reservation of asking what any true fan would ask of a celebrity. "Would it be possible to meet for a coffee one day? I can bring one of your books for you to autograph if your schedule permits it."

A personal line had been crossed. David never socialized with any fan, and though Lynda appeared lovely and sweet, she wasn't the first to try and lure him across that line. He had his reasons to be wary recalling one author in particular who had only one bestseller to his credit over a twenty-year span. Over the years David had accidentally ran into this man at celebrity functions. Under his arm he carried with him at all times a rough draft of his potential second bestseller. Curiosity had got the better of David, finding the courage to ask this author how his second novel was coming along. Following a brief conversation, it occurred to David that this man had miraculously lucked out with his very first novel, and there wasn't another one left in him; a true one-hit wonder. Since he had spent all the royalties from his first book, the actual reason he showcased his second book around like he did was to impress the ladies. Eventually sleeping with most of the young female aspiring authors that were in awe of a published author, he never refused a free meal or a place to stay when it was offered to him only to move on to his next fan.

That was not David nor would it ever be.

"There's no need to go for a coffee, but if you bring the book in, I'd love to sign it next time I'm here," he said in a soft and gentle tone. The receptionist responded poorly, her face quickly blushing. It didn't go unnoticed, prompting David to add, "I'm sorry. It's just something I don't do."

Lynda Steward took out a blank pad, loudly slapping it on the desk, and, for no apparent reason other than to let him know she was hurt, began to draw circles. When he saw her childish reaction, he thought it a shame and best to leave her be.

High heels contacting the hard marvel floor were faintly heard, and as they got louder, David recognized them to be Lora's, Mr. Steamer's loyal assistant who was arriving to escort him into Mr. Steamer's office. He checked his watch. It was precisely 10:00 a.m. He switched off his cell phone, got up, and politely said, "It was a pleasure talking to you."

Lynda rudely raised her eyebrows, nodded her head, and returned to drawing circles, only this time applying so much pressure on the pen that the tip cut through three layers of paper.

Lora appeared, immediately smiling at David and doing what she did best—to make him feel welcome.

"Good morning, Mr. Turner. I'm glad you could make it."

David had always respected Lora. There was a sense of class about her, and she always made a point of being thoughtful to whomever she was talking to. Although wary of discussing business when she was near, he admired her for many reasons but mostly for the strength she required to work for an extremist like Mr. Steamer. He always thought that with her articulate vocabulary, combined with her above average intelligence, she might have chose a better career, notably as an anchorwoman in the media field.

"Please follow me," she said, courteously leading the way.

Before leaving, he glanced over one final time at Lynda, but she remained with her head low, pouting, and preferring to ignore him altogether.

The walk along the corridor was a lengthy one; both walls were covered with massive black-and-white photos of the firm's history. Some of them were firmly attached to the wall with permanent chrome clamps while others were purposely slanted, giving them a fresh and modernistic appearance. Every second one was of Mr. Steamer, parading his beaming face, but ironically his oversized glasses hid half of his features. He always appeared larger than life, holding royalty checks with one hand and shaking hands with writers that David had never heard of before. The only colored photo was taken four years ago by *Forbes Magazine*. Mr. Steamer stood on the rooftop of his magnificent building, arms folded, and with the letters "STEAMER'S PUBLISHING INC." behind him; he appeared every bit the media mogul that he was.

David had his share of bestsellers, especially early on in his career, yet there was not one photo of him on either side of the wall. It had bothered him in the past but never enough to ask why. However, there was one question he had always wanted to ask each time he walked through these hallways.

"Do you notice anything different about Mr. Steamer in that picture?" he said, pointing to a photo with the year 1983 clearly printed at the bottom. "And that one." He continued pointing to another on the opposite side of the hall, which indicated the year 2003.

"I can't say that I do."

"Exactly," he replied. "Those pictures are twenty years apart, yet Mr. Steamer doesn't appear to have aged at all. He appears younger and fitter in the most recent photo."

Lora giggled. "It's true; that man never seems to age. I asked him about it once and was told not to be fooled, that at times he feels his true age."

"Which is?"

"No one knows. It's his little secret; although he has admitted to some that it's in the tens of thousands of years." She laughed.

Mr. Steamer leaned over the window edge, giving his full attention to the ailing flower. That plant had been watered and fed as per the florist's instructions, yet it appeared to be dying. He pulled another dead leaf off, mumbling to himself that there were only three left. Undeterred, he used the tip of a gold pen as a mini rake, carefully digging around the stem, hoping to enrich it with fresh air and perchance giving the plant the boost it needed. He then gently wiped the top and bottom of each remaining leaf with a soft tissue, caressing the stem as one would pet a newborn kitten.

Lora opened the door.

"Is David with you?" he snarled without looking back.

"Yes, Mr. Steamer," she replied.

"Do you see a dozen one-page outlines in his hands?"

David shook his head at her, signifying a no answer.

Still stroking the plant's stem, Mr. Steamer said, "Since I'm not getting a reply, I'm assuming the answer is no then?" He then picked up the plant, slowly turned around and completely ignored David, ordering Lora to "Get rid of this plant. It's dying."

"Should I buy a replacement?"

"No need to buy it. If you go inside my safe you will find the purchase receipt of this one. There are still three weeks left on the warranty. Return it to that florist, and bring me another one."

"Yes, Mr. Steamer," she said, taking the plant from him.

"That new receptionist we hired last week. What's her name again?"

"Lynda Steward."

"Yes … the pretty one. On your way out, fire her," he ordered, sitting down at his desk.

"Yes, Mr. Steamer," she replied, giving David a quick smile before departing, not waiting for one in return.

David walked in and sat down, coming face-to-face with his adversary. They resembled two boxers before a heavy weight bout, feeling each other out, searching for a weakness that they could use to their advantage. David looked both woeful and anxious, just the way Mr. Steamer wanted him to be, and in turn Mr. Steamer appeared angry and miserable, just the way David knew he would be.

"You didn't have to fire her," began David.

"Don't you ever get bored of playing a superhero?" He began, "I know I didn't have to fire her, but I did because I can." He leaned forward slightly and then back again, realizing he was moving too quickly for the kill, cheating himself of the chase. "She was getting a grand a week to answer the phone, not to tell you that I don't smile."

David quickly glanced around the room, searching for any hidden listening devices. "How did you know what she said? God, do you have every inch of this place bugged?"

"I don't need any listening devices," he replied back as though he had just been insulted.

"How did you know what she said then?"

"I just did," Mr. Steamer hissed, defying him to ask again.

Frightened of Mr. Steamer's reply, he didn't ask again. If he heard Lynda, then he must have also heard him. It was best to move on. There was nothing he could do for her anyway.

"Stop trying to save the world, David. There are enough parasites making a fortune pretending to do just that. Besides, this planet has become rancid and not worth saving anymore," he said, opening his top drawer, removing a long nail file and beginning to file his thumb nail. "I have discovered something interesting about you, David."

"I'm not interested in what you know and don't know about me, Mr. Steamer. I would prefer we get down to the real reason I'm here."

Mr. Steamer put the nail file down, placed both hands on top of the desk and leaned forward. "You are suffering from writer's block, my dear friend, and it may be permanent." He then pulled back. "The sooner you admit it to yourself, the sooner we can get down to what really matters—making me money."

David didn't expect his insults and accusations so soon, waving them aside. Normally his boss would toy with his opponents, entertaining himself by watching them squirm to a point where they would plead for him to stop. But he considered himself well prepared, almost arrogant. "If that's what you think has happened, then release me from my contract."

Mr. Steamer resumed filing his nail. "That would be so convenient for you, David, but I'm afraid that releasing you from your contract would not be in my best interest. You owe me advance money, which you freely accepted fully aware that your writing days were over and now your problem becomes our problem."

"Over time you will get it all back plus a profit. You've been in this business long enough to know the way the industry works," he replied.

Mr. Steamer pulled back, placing his feet on the desk. "For your own benefit and for the sake of saving time, I'll be as brutally honest with you as possible. Your last book only lasted three weeks on the top twenty, and the one before that wasn't anything to get excited about either," he stated in a raw tone.

David adjusted his chair to the side. "You're telling me things I already know."

Mr. Steamer frowned. "Then you should also know that there are no more bestsellers in you. Be man enough to admit it. It's better for me and less painful for you."

Ignoring facts, rumors regarding his inability to write as he once did had surfaced for the past few years, yet he refused to acknowledge this reality, least of all to himself.

"Writer's block is like one of those silly but treacherous computer games," Mr. Steamer continued. "They pick and tear at the very discipline required to write until the attraction of reaching a million points overpowers the will to write a difficult paragraph. After that it's never the same."

"You don't have a clue what you're talking about," he quickly replied, taking into account that Mr. Steamer might have hacked into his computer and discovered his habit of playing games rather than writing. In spite of that he felt Mr. Steamer had no right to complain about anything. "My writing has made you a lot of money over the years, and now it's not making you as much. Things have a way of balancing themselves out," he reasoned.

"You also made yourself a lot of money from me. What's the name of that six figure car you drive again, David?" he asked.

David never cursed and wasn't about to begin now. He was angry for placing himself in this awkward position. Many other authors who lost verbal battles with Mr. Steamer were never heard of again. He needed to regain some badly needed confidence, to reach a certain level of self-esteem before it was too late.

"Now that we both agree that you can't write any longer …"

"I didn't agree to anything," David barked back.

Mr. Steamer ignored him, rolled his eyes upward like a bored teenager and said, "Now that we both agree that you can't write any longer, there is nowhere for you to go but downward. This doesn't have to be the case. Adult literature is a proven winner with mass appeal. You can be as repetitive as you wish with those brainless storylines. Lock yourself in a room and create new seductive characters, and the books will sell by the millions. It's a win-win situation for the both of us, and you can still maintain your lifestyle. The moment I get my money back, you can spend the rest of your life playing computer games."

"I'm not capable of writing things I'm not familiar with. The coarse language associated with that filth is not, nor was it ever, part of my vocabulary. It wouldn't work even if I tried."

"I'm trying to work with you, David, but all I'm getting is excuses."

Frustrated beyond words, David tried for the impossible—to reason with this man. "You know for yourself the basic commandment for any writer. We only write of things that we feel comfortable and familiar with. I don't have the offensive terminology to make this work; I haven't practiced any of the sexual exhibitions needed to write those stories, and you know that."

"That can easily be fixed. I'll get you the most skilled porno stars to sit beside you as you write. Those people will think it's a step up the ladder in their miserable careers and will do it for a discount. Throw an adventurous editor into the mix, and the problem is solved."

David gritted his teeth. "I'm not going to write those kinds of books for you!" he shouted.

Mr. Steamer was not the kind of man to be screamed at and when angered he wanted the whole world to know. His eyes appeared as if they would catch on fire. The veins in his neck seemed to expand, ready to explode. If David hadn't caught on that Mr. Steamer was infuriated before, he knew now.

"Let's both get one thing straight, David," he growled. "You are through writing boy meets girl, girl loves boy, girl's mother hates boy until he saves a cat from a fire. Those days are long gone."

"I'm still capable of writing honorable novels."

"No, you're not!" he screamed back slamming his fist onto the table. "You can only fool people for so long before they become sick and tired of reading your same stories." He took a deep breath, saving the worst insult for last. "You writers are all alike. I see it all the time. Why don't you admit that you're washed up and help me recover some of the advanced monies you conned me out of?" When the best David could come up with was a blank stare, Mr. Steamer let loose, resembling a lunatic, "I want my money back! Do you hear me? I want my money back!"

The screaming part was expected. David didn't think for a moment that any meeting with him would not involve shouting at some point. His insults were predictable, but he didn't think the truth would hurt him as much as it did. Perhaps Mr. Steamer was correct in his assumption that his career had peaked years ago. Regardless, he could not bring himself to write filth.

"I will give you the benefit of the doubt and assume you didn't hear me the first time, but as I told you before, I will not write those kinds of books. I wouldn't have much of a fan base if my career took that direction."

Mr. Steamer did something extremely rare. He smiled. "What fan base, David? Haven't you noticed? You're an intelligent man. If you opened your eyes you would see that your most loyal fans have deserted you a long time ago. The remaining few are either dead or dying of boredom from reading your last book."

David was clearly struggling. There was some truth to what was said. He brought his hand up and pinched his ear lobe out of frustration.

"Give yourself credit, David. You persisted and endured longer than most, but all writers eventually become yesterday's news.

There will always be only one Shakespeare, but if you cooperate, I can arrange it so that A&E will do a biography on your life. Celebrities love that. It will give you a start for the speech circuit that awaits you. In exchange you write what you are told to write."

David sprang up and pointed his finger at him. "Listen to me good, Steamer, I do not, nor will I ever, write porn—not for you or for anyone else!"

"You meant Mr. Steamer, didn't you?"

David had reached his limitations, surpassing his ability to reason. He needed to get out of that office, march directly to his accountant's office and find out where he stood financially. With some luck, he would be told that he had earned enough money and could take a few years off, find a new publisher, and, if need be, embark on a new career if he had to. When he reached the door, to his horror, it was locked. He shook the door handle vigorously, but it wouldn't budge. He began to breathe loud and heavy, knowing all too well that he was now panicking. He angrily turned to face Mr. Steamer and saw him resting calmly in his chair, pointing his index finger in an upward position.

"Do you see this finger, David?" he softly asked.

"Open the door or you'll be getting a call from my lawyer."

"There is no need to make the lawyers any richer than they already are, so enough with the dramatics. Now do as you are told and answer my question. Do you see this finger?" he repeated, holding it up higher.

"You know I do!" he yelled back.

"This finger can unlock that door. All I need to do is to press a button under my desk. Once that happens, you'll be free to go wherever you wish, but you can never return for as long as I live. That can be for a very, very long time, so think carefully, and heed my words when I tell you that tomorrow morning there will be a press conference introducing another hungry writer who would be more than happy to work for me and all the possible wealth that goes along with it." He lowered his finger under the desk. A clicking sound was heard. "The door is now open. Leave if you must," he dared him.

David checked the door. It was unlocked. Mr. Steamer was serious. His body wanted to leave, but his mind wouldn't permit it. He suddenly felt like he was being cast aside, thrown on a rowboat in the middle of the ocean to fend for himself with only a can of beans to survive.

Mr. Steamer rubbed his chin, calmly advising. "It's in your best interest to listen to your heartbeat. I can hear it pounding from here," he told him.

David had tumbled into Mr. Steamer's sticky web and was helpless to do anything about it.

"Close the door and sit back down before I have you escorted out once and for all."

David did what he was told.

The two-story community centre was literally packed as expected for a holiday Monday morning. Downstairs were six evenly divided squash courts, all being used by older men determined to excel in a younger man's game. Across the hall, inside the exercise room, a Frank Sinatra song blasted from four powerful speakers as overweight ladies in skintight leotards were stretching their thighs farther than they should have. At the end of the hallway, two maintenance workers took turns looking out for their superior while the other was inside the mechanical room smoking a cigarette.

On the second floor, stressed mothers wearing stylish jeans were chasing after their misbehaving children trying to calm the little horrors down with a promise of treats. Beside the snack bar and all along a line of arcade games was a massive glass partition, separating that area from the Olympic-sized swimming pool on the opposite side. If one were to look down at the pool they could see thirty to thirty-five kids mixed in with a handful of teenage lifeguards, who were constantly walking back and forth with eyes carefully fixed on the children. The atmosphere was exciting, the water warm, and the yelling plentiful. The children were having a good time, mindful of the ten rules that numerous red signs surrounding the pool area declared they must follow.

A loud siren was heard throughout the swimming pool area, a siren that set off automatically, twice a day, seven days a week. It was only a drill, yet all the kids inside the pool were ushered out by the well-trained lifeguards. Within minutes, the pool was empty, and the kids carefully counted and standing obediently against the wall. Two other lifeguards walked along the edge, cautiously inspecting the pool while the head lifeguard shouted out safety drills, preaching the importance and reason for each one.

This pause gave Cathy and Tracie time to simultaneously look up at Jackie, who was sitting upstairs on the other side of the glass. She waved down at them, they up at her. Smiles were plentiful between the three; a moment of contentment that could be abruptly crushed if Jackie's red cell phone rang. All indications were that she could possibly receive a critical call, which she could ill afford to miss and which would change David's life forever.

Hanging half way up the wall was a large mirror, approximately two feet by four. What made this mirror different from others was that whoever stood at the opposite side could see into Mr. Steamer's office without being seen themselves. Department stores used these effective two-way mirrors to entrap unsuspecting shoplifters.

Sitting and watching from the other side, Lora had been instructed by Mr. Steamer what symptoms to look for. Her job was to carefully monitor David's behavior, study his reaction to the coming events. From what she saw already, things were not going in David's favour, and as Mr. Steamer pointed a remote control towards a bare wall, she knew things could only get worse. When Mr. Steamer pressed down on a red button, a huge white screen automatically began to lower from the top of the ceiling, working its way down, and stopping inches from the floor.

"What's that all about?" David asked nervously, wondering what he was up to.

Mr. Steamer stepped back, aimed the control slightly to his left and pressed another button.

"It'll take a second to load," he said as though he was getting ready to watch an epic. He then sat down, waiting for the figures to appear, and when they did, David stared at the screen, unsure what all those numbers had to do with him. It took him a while to actually absorb the fact that he was looking at his personal financial statement. It was all there: his banking records, everything from basic monthly bills to the receipts from flowers he had delivered to Diane's tombstone. The most personal information was copies of his charitable donations. That sensitive list included, but was not restricted to, the Children of Africa Fund, the Red Cross, and, most delicate of all, the ten percent of his earnings dedicated to his church. In total, twenty-five thousand dollars each and every month was automatically deducted from David's bank account. At the very bottom right hand corner of this statement was a negative figure of two hundred and forty-eight thousand dollars and sixty-two cents flashing on and off. That number represented the accumulated debt David found himself buried in as of this morning.

"I thought I'd save you the trip to your accountant's office," Mr. Steamer said casually.

"Where did you get those from?" he cried out.

"A person in my position, with my wealth, can acquire sensitive information from more important people than you, David. Don't flatter yourself."

"Where did you get them from?" screamed David, so loud that tiny portions of saliva sprayed on Mr. Steamer's desk.

Mr. Steamer calmly pulled a tissue out of a box and carefully wiped the saliva off his desk. "Who cares, David? The truth is that you are knee deep in debt, and if I shut off your financial tap you won't even have money to eat."

"You son of a b—!" he continued to scream.

Mr. Steamer threw the damp tissue into a garbage bin. "Is that a compliment or an insult, David? It really doesn't matter to me. Both are flattering and appreciated." He looked back up at the screen, notably at the charitable donations. "Based on all the money you're giving away, I take it you were trying to play God, but then again, you should have known that playing the role of God is very costly."

"What I do with my money is of no concern to you!"

David was aware of Mr. Steamer's legendary tantrums and fits since the first day they had met. He had seen him verbally tear people into shreds and convert them into emotional zombies. He turned proud people into shameless fools, had them agreeing with everything he said when moments earlier they had thought the opposite. Deep down inside, he was frightened of what was to come, frightened of being seduced and terrified of the outcome.

"You don't own me!" he cried out, jumping to his feet, but when his knees shook, making it impossible to stand upright, he quickly sat back down.

Mr. Steamer found him irresistible. At times like this, he was at his best, or to some poor souls, his worst. Pulling his chair back, standing up to show David that his knees didn't shake, he was now ready to unleash his version of hell upon him. Like a predator ready to feast on injured prey, Mr. Steamer walked around him, flaunting his poise and taking a deep breath to appear larger than he really was. He placed his mouth near David's ear. "You should have realized that things don't last forever," he whispered taking time to lean back. "The money train couldn't keep up with you. There were no more bestsellers left in you to keep fueling your gravy train any longer, and if you're foolishly thinking of changing publishers, think again. Between you and me, I control the industry. If I don't already own that publishing house, then the person who does fears me as they would fear the devil. If I so much as hint to them that I am not pleased with you, they won't even allow you to enter their parking lot."

David remained perfectly still, his hatred for that man intensifying with every passing second.

"Can you imagine a world with no money, David? No more fresh flowers. No more taking Cathy to Disneyland, and, most of all, no more trips to your beloved Scotland. A whole new wretched lifestyle awaits you, my dear friend." He stepped away, placing himself in front of the mirror. "Did you really think all the money you gave away was appreciated?" he continued knowing full well that Lora was staring back at him from the other side of the mirror. "The moment you stop giving is the moment they all call you a cheap miser." He turned to face David once again. "Are you man enough to walk out of here for the sake of some outdated morals that your father forced upon you, or will you write what I demand you to write?"

"I still own all the movie rights to my work!" David shouted out for no other reason than simply to respond.

"True, David. That you do." He smiled, both men knowing full well that it could take years to negotiate any movie deal. Mr. Steamer then ruthlessly added, "I don't think you have the backbone to walk out of here." When David didn't challenge him any further, the fight was over. Mr. Steamer had won.

David rubbed his face with both hands. "Why are you doing this to me?"

Mr. Steamer didn't have to respond, and he didn't; rather he walked back to his desk, sat down, and immediately slid his hand inside his jacket, pulling out a small key. He unlocked the top drawer, removing a document and slapping it on top of the desk.

"It's a new five-book deal. That's all you need to know for now other than the story lines need to be vulgar. The rest is straightforward, and just so you don't think of me as being unreasonable, if you don't sign it in the next five minutes, I have a vacant receptionist job available here for you. You can start tomorrow morning at a thousand a week with a half-hour lunch. The first coffee is on the house. After that bring change with you."

David was a heartbeat away from losing his lifestyle and all that went with it. Based on his sound upbringing, he knew he should walk away from this madness never to return rather than surrender to something he didn't believe in. His father had taught him never to give in to temptation: "*One must never do things against their will or what they don't believe in,*" his father had preached. "*The moment they do, they lose a part of their soul.*" He sadly looked up at Mr. Steamer and asked, "What would Cathy think of me if she found out?"

"That's not my problem. I'm not her father. You are," he replied.

David lowered his head at the contract in compliance. "I think I should go through it with my lawyer before signing."

"That would be a waste of time. Since nine thirty this morning your lawyer is not your lawyer anymore. Your lawyer is now my lawyer. It would place him in a conflict of interest to represent you any longer."

"That's impossible," he replied in disbelief.

"You always had this horrible habit of overrating loyalty. You squandered away all your money on hopeless issues. I bought loyalty with mine," he stated, grabbing a gold pen and lightly tapping it on his desk.

An exhausted David rightfully concluded that if Mr. Steamer successfully hijacked his lawyer, then he would stop at nothing to get his signature on that contract. That man had more money than he could ever hope to spend. He could do without his advance monies back, but David was in no position to question anything anymore. If Mr. Steamer carried out his threat, his financial lifeline would be cut off, as would his lifestyle.

"I need time to think this over," he pleaded, knowing it was something Mr. Steamer would not give.

The tapping from the gold pen got louder, in tune with David's pounding headache.

"You are testing my patience, David," Mr. Steamer growled.

The last thing David wanted to do was to sign that contract, yet he found himself prepared to do just that.

"Can I at least ask you for one favor before I sign?"

"You are in no position to ask for anything."

"You said earlier that you were a fair man."

"I'm always a fair man, but people must believe me when I insist that two plus two equals five." He then paused. "You do agree, don't you, David, that two plus two equal five? I have earned the right to insist on that."

David understood his mind games well. Agreeing was just another form of humiliation, but at this point he didn't care.

"Yes. It equals five," he agreed, giving him his small victory.

Mr. Steamer laughed out loud.

"You have to learn that there are certain things that should not be agreed to for the sake of a favour. They tend to come back to haunt you."

David didn't understand what he meant, nor did he care. He needed that favour.

"I can't allow my family or my church to ever find out. These books have to be accredited to an anonymous writer. I'll deny I ever wrote them," he insisted.

Mr. Steamer paused, taking his time to consider his request before saying. "I need a favour from you as well. I need you to sign a one-page letter confirming you were of sound mind when signing this contract and that you did so at your own free will. If you agree, then the author of these five books can be known as Judas for all I care."

It was a fitting name, David thought. The name of an historical betrayer suited him well, for he would be betraying his own family values the moment he signed that deal. He was about to ask another question, but Mr. Steamer cut in, angrily throwing the pen in front of him and bitterly crying out, "No more questions! I have given you more time than you merit! I will give you no more of it! Sign the bloody contract, or get out of my office!"

On the other side of the wall, Lora placed her horrified face inches from the two-way mirror. Regardless of the number of times these betrayals continued, she still found it difficult to cope with. She felt for Mr. Steamer, knowing of the respect he felt for

David and now that respect was about to be slashed. When she saw David pick up the pen, she wanted to bang on the window, yell out his name, and beg him to reconsider. If only he knew of the severe consequences and the darkness that awaited him the moment he signed. But it was too late. With the stroke of that gold pen, David was now legally obligated to write five new books, all of a sexual nature. She caught a gloomy Mr. Steamer staring at her, an indication that heartbreaking as this was, the time for her to act and show strength was now. She had to block all personal feelings and to set in motion a rapid chain of events, the first of which was to call Jackie.

The moment Jackie answered the call, she asked. "Is this to inform me that Mr. Turner has signed the contract?" with the faint hope that it was not.

"It is," Lora told her.

Jackie paused. "I do hope Mr. Steamer took it well."

Lora glanced back inside the room, noting Mr. Steamer was standing above David with his finger running along the contract, explaining certain aspects of a paragraph with him. "I wish I could say he did, but at this very moment his pain is being hidden by his responsibilities."

A long pause was needed, each woman searching for the correct terminology before Lora added, "I am optimistic that the children will perform their duties as well as expected."

"They are as prepared as I am, and we will proceed at the opportune time."

The deal was now inked and legal. David didn't need the gold pen any longer, throwing it back on top of the desk. That pen represented everything disgusting and unethical, and yet he had just signed a deal with it, which he never should have. Mr. Steamer opened the contract to page ten and singled out a paragraph in the middle of the page: "This states that the pen does not belong to me any longer. You own it now. I can't take it back even if I wanted to. That pen is now contractually yours."

"I have enough pens at home, I don't need any more."

"It's worth a lot of money."

If only to bring his nightmare to a merciful end, David stood up, grabbed the pen, and slid it inside his shirt pocket.

"We all have to live with the decisions we make, David. You have to live with yours, and I have to live with mine. Don't think for one moment that I am the wretched miser you think I am. I am not as sinister as you might think."

"Yes, you are, Mr. Steamer, and much, much more."

"Think what you will, but it would surprise you what others think of me."

"Without a doubt," replied David, longing to leave and to lick his wounds in private.

Mr. Steamer placed his copy neatly inside the top drawer and pushed David's copy towards him. "You need not worry when your phone rings anymore. It won't be me, and I would appreciate if you don't call me for the next while. Lora will get in touch with you in four months. The first of the five books is due at that time as stipulated by our written agreement."

David grabbed his copy and stormed out of the office, slamming the door behind him. If he never saw Mr. Steamer again, it would be too soon. He marched down the long hallway, in desperate need of fresh air; the sooner he breathed it, the better. He felt contaminated, in desperate need of a shower. It was essential that he wash off the deception smothering his body, and if he could pull his heart out, he would cleanse that organ as well. When he turned the corner and saw Lynda Steward standing above the reception desk, throwing her sparse belongings into a small box, he didn't stop. Rather, he felt himself picking up his pace.

"Thank you for getting me fired," he heard Lynda snarl at him, yet he acted as though she wasn't there. "I only read half of your last book before I had to throw it away; it bored me to death."

David continued his exasperating pace, walking directly inside the elevator and not bothering to turn around when the two doors automatically shut. The ride down the forty floors, though quick, seemed like it was taking forever, stirring his thoughts and unleashing a series of strange visions. Was this elevator actually taking him straight down to hell as the form of punishment for what he had just done? If so, it would be a fitting end. When the elevator stopped and the doors re-opened, he didn't find himself stepping out into a gorge of fire but in the main lobby of the first floor. He got out as quickly as possible, pushing the main door of the building with such force that the lower protective hinge almost flew out. Once outside, he pitched the gold pen into the air, hitting a lamppost and ricocheting back down onto a parked car.

What have I done! he scornfully thought.

Driving aimlessly for the next ten minutes, David pulled over to the curb and parked his car. Amazingly he found himself in front of a pet shop, the same place where he had purchased Mr. Rogers. Shoving aside the nightmare he had just endured inside Mr. Steamer's office, having Cathy step into the house and seeing a new bird would be the perfect solution—the magic wand to right all wrongs. He was not that naïve. He had created a huge setback for himself that had to be dealt with, but at this moment in time, nothing could drag him out of his depression quicker than seeing that smile on Cathy's face.

He entered the store to the sounds of various feathered species, mostly imported from South America, some rare ones from Asia, and some of the less expensive local ones thrown into the mix. The change of scenery helped relax him; although every so often the images of Mr. Steamer's face would appear out of nowhere, waving the contract before him like he was waving a flag and laughing at his cowardliness. Despite the irritating images, he stopped at that identical spot where Mr. Rogers was bought years earlier, surprised that the same cage was still there. The birds inside expanded their chests and flapped their wings for him, battling each other for his attention and anxious to impress him. Not sure which of the dozen or so that would make a good companion for Mr. Rogers, he sought and received assistance from the first available clerk, a young female.

"We call that one Lucy," she said pointing to one of the birds.

"I'll take her," he replied, still finding it difficult to shake the visions of Mr. Steamer from his mind, so much so that he didn't even notice the clerk had charmed him into buying a wooden nest with a concave circle at the bottom of the nesting box.

While the clerk assembled a box to place Lucy in, an unanticipated calmness overcame David. He didn't know how or why, suspecting it had something to do with the bird, but suddenly the vicious meeting with Mr. Steamer seemed so long ago, including the issues that went along with it. If a twenty-dollar budgie had the power to override any consequence associated with signing that contract, then why be afraid of it? A signature on a contract was just that, his name on a piece of paper. Granted, there were many legal obstacles attached to it, but then again, that's all it was, "David Turner" on a dotted line.

"Not to worry, she will be perfectly comfortable inside this box," reassured the clerk, helping the protesting and anxious Lucy into the box.

David paid no attention to her. His mind was now focused on Cathy and the loss of respect for him if she discovered that he had signed that contract. She would forgive him. That he was sure of, but things would never be the same after. He would live the rest of his life with that dark cloud hanging over his head, never able to look at her the same way.

An Andean parakeet flew over his head, somewhat surprising him and perched itself on top of a cage.

"That one goes by the name of Gringo," the clerk told him. "He's been with us so long that we just let him out of his cage to fly about. He's not for sale," she continued as though he was about to ask if he was. He watched it fly away again and felt envious of the little creature. It seemed so full of life, so content, having the freedom to fly from one spot to another as it wished. If only he had that freedom to just fly away, him and Cathy, away from all this madness.

It was at that precise moment, that instant when David made up his mind.

"I'm not going to go through with it," he whispered beneath his breath. Suddenly Mr. Steamer's threats to end the lifestyle that he was accustomed to didn't appear as drastic as it once had. A Jaguar's glitter could not outshine a father and daughter relationship. No one could force him to become someone he was not and could never be. If he walked away from this deal, his charities would suffer, but then again, what association, including his church, would want to be affiliated with a porn writer? They had all survived without him before, and they would have to learn to survive without him now.

When Jackie saw that Cathy and Tracie were playing at a secluded corner near the shallow end of the pool, she knew this was the ideal time to proceed. Cathy was lying stomach down on a long rubber raft, Tracie next to her, knee deep and towing her cousin in circles.

"Please, Father," she whispered, "give us the strength that is required to see this through." She then opened one of the many glass partition doors and stepped into the swimming pool area, immediately smelling chlorine, mixed with tropical warmth generated by the heated pool. She welcomed the calming warm environment, even if only for a mere second before locating an empty seat below and sitting down where the children could easily see her. She waved at them; they in turn smiled and waved back, but when Jackie pulled the cell phone from her purse, there was nothing more to smile about. Both children understood, sadly aware that David had signed; it was now their turn to act.

Up until that moment, Jackie had every intention of staying, but things of this nature were never easy to be a part of. It was left up to her discretion to watch what was about to unfold; she opted not to, preferring to leave, understanding that her peers would not recognize her actions as cowardly. She placed both hands together, as one would when ready to pray, looked in Cathy's direction and bowed her head as a show of respect. Cathy returned the gesture. Jackie was now free to go, quickly climbing back up the stairs, fighting through the crowd and walking directly into the ladies' washroom. Once inside, she stood in front of a mirror, holding back tears and wondering why it always had to end this way. She placed her hands over her ears and shut her eyes, hoping it would soon be over.

With Cathy still lying on the rubber raft, Tracie pushed her towards the deep end as far as she could. When water began surrounding her neck and threatening to enter her mouth, she was forced to stop.

"I cannot go any farther," she told her cousin.

Cathy paddled her arms in a circular motion, turning the raft around to face her. "I think it now best that you thrust me off before anyone takes notice," she said suspecting that a lifeguard may have already done so. "Will you do me the smallest of favours while I am gone?"

"You need only ask."

"I believe Mr. Turner's intention was to purchase another budgie to keep Mr. Rogers company. Would you be kind enough to look after them?"

"It would be my pleasure."

The children faced each other in silence; the brave smile on Tracie's face slowly fading. She ran her finger along Cathy's forehead, down her cheek, and rested it on her chin—a custom of parting ways.

"You are so brave," she softly whispered.

"And you," replied Cathy, grinning.

The children kissed each other on the cheek for the last time before Tracie pulled the air plug off the raft. She gave it a final thrust into the deep end and swam back towards the shallow side. The rubber raft stayed afloat for a number of seconds before it ultimately sank, bringing Cathy down with it to her death.

With Lucy safely inside, the clerk placed the box on the counter. "There are enough holes. She won't suffocate." She laughed, implying that the box's ventilation was a standard concern from all customers. David wasn't bothered by the amount of holes the box had. This pet store had sold many birds before and knew what they were doing. His thoughts went back to Cathy and a wish to snap his finger and wash away all the craziness that faced him. An uplifting vision flashed before him, so sudden that his body twitched from the excitement, embarrassing the clerk. *Why not simply escape from all this madness and return back to Scotland with Cathy and never come back? Why not fly back to his birthplace, a country where two hundred year old items were still regarded as new?* True, he had lost his desire to write, but at the same time he should give himself more credit. He was an experienced writer and could always make a comfortable living in this field. Though Mr. Steamer scoffed at him, claiming he'd end up teaching in some university along with the title of Professor of Literature, what was wrong with that? Employment in a Scottish university was more attractive than being branded a washed-up writer who had ended his career writing dirty books, he thought.

"I'll be right back," said the clerk. "I'm going to add in a month's worth of food at no extra cost."

David's enlightened visions continued. He saw himself with Cathy back in Scotland, preparing a picnic, with sandwiches and juice. He saw himself walking hand in hand, climbing one of the many Scottish mountains, enjoying lunch, and staring at the magnificent ageless castles below. When climbing back down, they would see hundreds of sheep, covering the hillsides, each with their colored markings, identifying them to their rightful owners. They would stop and chat to everyone and friendly hikers, along with herdsmen, would make a fuss over Cathy. They could also spend quality time visiting historic sites, absorbing Scotland's long and rich history, and wouldn't it be miraculous if they actually saw the Loch Ness Monster?

Jackie heard the siren go off, followed by children crying and adults shouting to one another. This time it was not a test. What was supposed to happen did. She volunteered for this assignment, and now it was time to see it through. She couldn't stay hidden inside the washroom forever. Opening her eyes and staring at her reflection, she mumbled a few chosen words to boost her confidence and splashed cold water on her face. She stepped out into the coffee shop area, finding it deserted. No one was behind the snack bar counter minding the shop. There were no children waiting in line for their turn to play the arcade games. She saw that everyone was now standing at the partition, hands firmly pressed on the glass and anxiously glaring down at the swimming pool. Something terrible happened and every so often she heard parents shout out, "Oh my God!" to each other.

Jackie struggled to find a gap between the crowds and managed to catch a glimpse down below where she saw chaos. Teenage lifeguards in sheer panic were running from one side of the pool to the other, whisking startled children inside the change rooms while other lifeguards were pulling the remaining few out of the pool. Near the exit door, she saw Cathy lay motionless over a towel, a frantic lifeguard giving her mouth-to-mouth resuscitation. Standing beside Cathy was Tracie, weeping and being questioned by another lifeguard.

The heavy entrance doors swung open with two medics dashing in, carrying a stretcher while a third medic ran behind them carrying a medical bag. They forced the lifeguard away from Cathy and attempted to bring her back to life failing in their attempt. Cathy would breathe no more.

It was Jackie's turn to enter the second and most important stage of her mission: taking over the role of an actor. She had to excel. She had to become as believable as an academy award winner. She pushed away whoever was in her path, opened the door, ran down the steps, and madly screamed Cathy's name loud enough for all to hear. David had left Cathy in her care, and she would partially be responsible for her death. She needed everyone to see for themselves how distraught she was.

David hoped the clerk would take her time returning with the birdseed. He was in a midst of another phenomenal fantasy and didn't want it to end, finding himself and Cathy back in Scotland. The day was as windy as a Scottish day could be, with the two of them standing on the middle of the Stirling Bridge, a site where battles were fought, where history was made. Absorbing that brief time in history, they could then take a walk to a small village named *Cambuskenneth*. There, they would find the *Cambuskenneth* Abbey where the first Scottish Parliament had been held and where a fourteenth century evil king was still tucked away inside a tomb, four feet above ground for all to marvel at.

When leaving, they could look down the narrow road, South Street, where they would see a tiny white cottage that once housed the man who ferried people across the River Forth. The present resident, Siobhan McGuire, lived there now with her two lovely children, Scott and Kelly. The last time he visited that area, she welcomed him into the front courtyard for a cup of tea, a chat, and was introduced to her Italian fiancé from Canada. Around the corner was the Abbey Inn Pub.

Unlike America, a village pub in Scotland was a special meeting place for regulars, such as the McMillan brothers, Jimmy and Rab. The rest of the neighbors would sooner or later "nip in," have a drink or two, and catch up on all the latest gossip.

"That's twenty dollars. The food was free," the clerk made known for the second time.

David walked out of the pet shop, carrying Lucy by his side. He thought it ironic how this morning began as the most miserable day of his life and now, only a few hours later, he felt this overwhelming hope.

I'll need a few weeks to get things organized, he thought. He would have to sell his house, all his belongings, and transfer as much money that could be raised from the sales back to Scotland before Mr. Steamer's lawyers got their hands on it.

His phone rang. It was the police. They weren't specific, only that he should rush to the community centre.

CHAPTER SIX

The Italian-made monument with Cathy's name engraved on it stood side by side with that of her mother. Though hardly noticeable, it was a bit heavier and thicker than Diane's, but not by much. The architects and carvers of the monument did their best to appease David's request at matching the exact dimensions of his late wife's, but with such short notice, they were rushed and wouldn't be blamed for being slightly off. No one expected a healthy seven-year-old to die so suddenly, least of all her devastated father. He had been merely going through the motions since that phone call from the police, too occupied with funeral arrangements to fully accept or recognize that Cathy was no longer part of his life.

The list of invitees was kept to a minimum. Only close friends and family members were invited, twenty at the most. David feared huge crowds could be interpreted as a celebration. There wasn't anything to celebrate about here, and as Jackie firmly held onto his hand, every so often she would feel a nervous twitch filter down to the tips of his fingers.

Next to David stood a weeping and heartbroken Lee, holding hands with Tracie, who in turn held Nick's hand. Others were standing around the tiny grave with the same thoughts in mind—the cruel and unfortunate set of circumstances that had befallen David yet again. First his wife, and now his baby, both so loved yet both dead, neither one of them ever to return. How could he be expected to start over again? Where would he go from here?

Father Mark did his best to explain why this lovely and adorable little girl had been taken away by God, but as difficult as it was, he managed to mumble a good many reasons, speaking more clearly when repeating that Cathy was now safely in his hands.

David respected Father Mark, an admiration going back to when he was his altar boy, but Cathy was his daughter, his miracle baby whom God had allowed to live against all the odds. What right did he have to take her away at such a tender age?

Compassionate spirits didn't do these spiteful things, yet God had decided to do this to him. He now needed to know why and would demand an answer from the priest. He needed him to explain things on a one-on-one basis but not here, not now, and not in front of all these people.

At the edge of the cemetery a black limousine arrived, driving as close as possible before being forced to come to a stop by the chain linked fence surrounding the graveyard. A tall, muscular chauffeur with a neatly trimmed goatee and dark brown eyes that seemed to overpower his face stepped out from the car. He appeared programmed, ignoring everyone and everything around him while opening the back door. Lora stepped out, carrying a large envelope. She thanked him and stood aside while he closed the door before the two of them exchanged a few words. The back window automatically opened. Mr. Steamer could clearly be seen sitting in the back. In his hand was a single rose. Lora took it from him and made her way towards the crowd of mourners. Finding a tree fifty yards away, she thought it best to stay hidden until the sermon was over.

Father Mark didn't have much more to say, instead focused on the loving relationship Cathy shared with her father, consciously feeling guilty about the whole sad affair since he was the man representing God. When completed, he bent down, telling Cathy to rest in peace, concluding the sermon by crossing and blessing the casket. A single line formed before David, with people extending their final condolences. Each offering him various counseling, ending with scores of warm and lengthy hugs. Ignoring Jackie altogether, they all invited him for supper in the not too distant future, something both parties knew would never happen, and then giving David one last pat on the back before departing. Nick and his family were last. The brother felt awkward yet blessed at the same time. Beside him were his wife and daughter, two of the most beloved and precious beings in his life. David had lost both of his. He could not begin to imagine his brother's pain. When David stared directly into his eyes, seemingly asking why, he fidgeted back and forth, finding it next to impossible to keep eye contact.

"Why don't you and Jackie spend the next few days with us?" he finally told him.

"I appreciate the offer, but I think I need to be alone for a while."

"You will call if you need anything?"

"I will, and thank you both for the support," he said, glancing quickly at Lee and then at Tracie.

"Daddy told me that Cathy is in heaven," said Tracie, who strangely did not shed a tear for Cathy, something that didn't go unnoticed by both her parents.

David wanted to tell his niece that things were fine as they were. There was no reason for God to take Cathy away like he did, no reason whatsoever for her to be in heaven, but his dispute was with God, not Tracie.

"Yes, sweetie, Cathy is in heaven," he replied, satisfying her.

Following a final hug from Nick and Tracie and a nod from Lee, all three departed, leaving David, Jackie, and Father Mark, the only ones remaining.

"Do you remember when I was your altar boy?" David asked, surprising the priest, "when we would huddle in the back room and count the money from the collection box?"

"Yes, of course I do. You were one of the few that could be trusted," smiled Father Mark.

David paused for a moment. "One time you looked away. I didn't have much time to think, and I stole a dollar. I never stole again. That was my one and only time. Next time you talk to God can you ask him if that was the reason he took my child away from me? Was her life worth only a dollar? To be honest with you, I can't think of any other reason."

The warm smile vanished from the priest's face. He couldn't answer his question, nor was he foolish enough to even try but understood why such a thing would be asked from him. Lowering his head, he thought it best to leave. That was the sign needed for the two maintenance workers to prepare for the next stage, to lower the casket and fill the grave with earth. Both laborers silently walked to the backhoe machine; one climbed up and sat down, wisely waiting for David to leave before turning the engine on.

A lengthy silence ensued between David and Jackie. Although he held back the obvious, others close to him were not as kind, whispering behind Jackie's back, accusing her of negligence. The fact she was inside a washroom when the child drowned and not sitting by the poolside watching the girls made it difficult for David to argue the point. A little girl died while under her supervision, and, as time went by, these rumors would change into accusations and later into full-blown resentment towards her. He didn't blame her, but his daughter did drown while in her care. A life was gone, and there was no telling how he would feel later towards her regarding this whole tragedy. He concluded that perhaps it would be best for the both of them to take a break.

"I don't know what to say, David," Jackie said, reading his face. When he didn't reply she added, "I'm thinking of visiting my parents for a few days. They haven't been very well, but I can stay with you if you like."

"I'll be fine. Go to your parents," he replied, feeling a sense of relief.

"My condolences, Mr. Turner," he heard a voice behind him say. A few feet away stood Lora, holding in her hand the single rose, in the other, an envelope.

David looked behind her, noticing the chauffeur standing next to the limousine, arms folded, and waiting for his next order. To his right, sitting in the backseat, was Mr. Steamer, and though he wore dark sunglasses, he appeared to be staring directly at him.

"Mr. Steamer sends you this rose as a sign of his deepest condolences," Lora continued. "He would also like you to have this," she said, handing him the large envelope. "Inside you will find a monetary gift from Mr. Steamer for the amount of ten thousand dollars. He would appreciate it if you would donate it to any charity you choose in Cathy's memory."

David took the rose and envelope. "Convey to him my thanks."

"There is something else inside. It's a discharge, relieving you of your contractual obligation from the recent deal signed with the publishing house. Mr. Steamer wants you to know that he has destroyed his copy, and you are more than welcome to destroy yours."

David didn't see a need to thank her a second time and did not. He was in no frame of mind to ask her why Mr. Steamer would do such a thing after all the pain and grief he put him through to sign the contract in the first place.

"Feel free to contact Mr. Steamer at any time," she concluded before turning around and walking back to the waiting limousine. The chauffeur swung open the back door, permitting Lora to get inside, and seconds later they slowly drove away, disappearing from view when the car turned around the bend.

Jackie gave David a piece of paper with a number written on it. "That's my parent's phone number. I can be reached there if you need me." She kissed him delicately on the cheek and, with a half smile, walked away. He didn't say a word, nor did he attempt to stop her from leaving.

"Excuse me, Mr. Turner," he heard another voice call out, noting one of the maintenance workers with a shovel in his hand while the other was sitting patiently on top of the backhoe, both anxiously waiting to do what they were paid to do, to refill a hole with dirt. "Can I start the machine?"

It was difficult to come to terms with the fact that the instant he gave them his blessing, tons of soil would be dumped on his fifty pounds of joy.

"Can I please start this machine?" repeated the man.

David didn't give him the permission he asked for; rather he walked away. The moment he stepped off the grounds and entered the parking lot, he heard the machine roar behind him. He froze on the spot and remained in that position for the longest time, unable to move. Eventually he turned around and watched them burying his baby. He covered his face with both hands. It was his turn to cry, and cry he did.

The clock hanging on the wall was purchased years ago, yet this was the first time he had actually heard it tick; every second that came and went sounding like a sledge hammer smashing through a car window. The humming noise behind the refrigerator, a noise he wouldn't have given a thought to before, now felt as if it vibrated the entire floor. Even the budgies annoyed him. More than once David seriously considered setting them free to fend for themselves because their singing reminded him of melodies he sang to Cathy when she was months old.

His original intent was to lie down on the sofa for a few minutes to gather his thoughts. Ultimately the few minutes had stretched into six hours of tossing, turning, and uncertainty. He rarely sat up, only to reach for the painkillers, but when they did little to restrain his massive headache, he resorted to alcohol. Half a bottle of vodka later, nothing had changed. He sensed that a terrible mistake had been made. With dusk approaching and darkness inevitable, he didn't want to be on his own after all. Not on this, the first night without Cathy.

Ignoring the caution written on the container—no more than eight tablets within a twenty-four hour period—he swallowed a further handful, washing them down with another two ounces of straight vodka. His body was not accustomed to this sort of abuse, and he spat everything back out. Feeling abandoned, scared, and unsure of what to do next, he sprung up and dialed the phone number Jackie had given him. An elderly lady answered, most likely Jackie's mother, or so he thought.

"May I speak to Jackie?" he asked.

There was a slight pause.

"Who?"

"Jackie. Jackie Ulliman," repeated David, hoping the mention of a last name would help.

There was another slight hesitation from the other side.

"There is no one by the name of Jackie that lives here," the elderly lady insisted. The phone went dead prompting him to angrily try again, and when it went unanswered for the third time, he didn't bother with a fourth attempt.

Maybe Jackie purposely gave him a fictitious number. It didn't matter to him as to why, not at this stage; it only meant that he would not have anyone to talk to. In shear panic, he called his brother Nick, but an automatic message cut in after a few rings, apologizing that the system was experiencing technical difficulties with no guarantees that the line would be back to normal within the next twenty-four hours.

David never set time aside to get to know or befriend anyone. Years ago he did have a few friends whose company he had enjoyed, but they were Diane's friends whom he'd met through their marriage. After her death he'd allowed them all to fade away, not returning their phone calls. Those selfish incidents were much too late to regret. Companionship and friends were two luxuries that simply weren't there for him at this, his greatest time of need.

He backed up, feeling the sofa touching his calf muscles. If he sat back down, chances were he would not get up for another six hours, consume more pills, and be terrorized by new noises. He thought of trying Jackie again or perhaps Nick, but the lure of the vodka caught his attention again. If he couldn't find someone to talk to, then he would do the talking. He was going to ask the one person who was responsible for all the misery in his life. He was going to visit God on his own turf.

With sixteen ounces of liquor circulating inside in his body and the remaining ten in the bottle resting on the passenger seat, David parked in front of the church. As to how he had got there or how many red lights he had gone through, he didn't know. The important thing was that he now found himself in front of God's house, and he had better be inside and not hiding behind his Son, Jesus. He reached for the bottle, got out of the Jag, and struggled up the stairs, needing the railing to help reach the door.

This chapel had been chosen by David's father as their place of worship within days of arriving to America. He, himself had spent a good part of his younger years inside this holy place and had become a faithful follower throughout his adult life, but it didn't matter to him. He was now entering the church in a foul and offensive mood. Not bothering with the Catholic tradition of dipping his fingers into the holy water and crossing himself before entering, he shut the door behind him. Other than a few lit candles that were almost burnt out, the building was dim, too dark to see it if anyone was inside praying.

"I want these lights on," he screamed, slamming his hand on the light switches next to him. The lights came on. The church was empty, disappointing him. Even at this time of the night, a few elderly ladies could always be seen scattered on each side of the centre aisle holding on to their rosary beads and mumbling a prayer for a long departed relative. His intention was to warn them not to light any more candles for their loved ones. He had done that more times than he cared to remember and was rewarded for it with the death of his wife and child. He needed to tell these old delusional women that this place was a house of lies and deception and that their money would be better spent elsewhere.

Barely able to maintain his balance, he took another drink, missing his lips and spilling a good portion of the spirit down his chin. Unfazed by it all, he managed to remain on his feet long enough to examine the church's windows. The magnificent mosaics of angels stepping on snakes, protecting the good from evil, with their swords held high in their hands, now resembled characters from *Alice in Wonderland*. Where he once saw statues of saints and disciples, he now saw pieces of stone with a series of meaningless bearded men carved into them. He then focused straight ahead at the altar. Behind the glamorous platform, up above, was Catholicism's most sacred symbol of them all: a huge wooden crucifix of Christ nailed to the cross.

"I thought I'd find you here!" he shouted sarcastically at Jesus Christ. "I need to have a word with you!"

Weaving along the aisles, he swayed from side to side, holding on to the back of the wooden benches for support, ultimately reaching the front pew. He raised his head and pointed at Jesus, notably at the spike penetrating his right hand.

"That had to hurt." He bitterly laughed. "Did your Father enjoy watching the pain on your face when they did that to you? Is he enjoying the same pain on my face now?" he cried out before falling back on the bench.

"Are you deaf? I asked you a question!" he yelled, but Christ didn't answer back. Drinking greedily, he took another gulp from the bottle and looked at the statue's feet. One was placed behind the other with only a single spike piercing through both, leaving him to wonder how a Father, with supposedly incredible powers, would permit such a brutal thing to happen to his own Son.

"You don't have much of a Father do you? The coward hid behind clouds watching them do that to you." He tried to take yet another gulp but spilled most of the liquor down his neck, spreading onto his chest. "What I find remarkable is him wanting us to believe that you died for our sins. My hat goes off to your Father for coming up with that phrase. My compliments to his imagination. Mr. Steamer would hire him on the spot." He laughed so vigorously that the bottle of vodka slipped out of his hand, bounced off the bench and exploded upon hitting the floor. The noise didn't register with him at all; rather he rested his head backwards, mumbling, "You were never a Son of God. There is no God. You were buried in a cave and turned into dust. My wife and child were buried six feet under. The real tragedy is that all three of your desperate souls are lost somewhere with nowhere to go because there is no bloody heaven." He then closed his eyes and soon after, fell into a deep sleep.

It was the snoring that awakened David. The noise wasn't nause-ating, but more a gentle whistle. As far as he was aware, he didn't snore. There had to be someone sitting next to him. With eyes still shut and smelling the liquor spilled on him from the night before, he turned to his side, opened his eyes and saw Father Mark sleep-ing peacefully next to him. A soft, warm blanket, which was not there before, now covered his body. Guessing that the priest had placed it on him while he slept, he leaned forward. The blanket slid down his body, his legs, and came to a rest on a damp floor. He wasn't positive but suspected that the bottle of vodka might have slipped out of his hands and shattered on that same spot the night before. If so, then most likely Father Mark had cleaned it up. Looking straight ahead at the crucifix, he couldn't recall much, only that he had shouted harsh words at Christ.

David was grateful to Father Mark for his care but felt an urge to get out of there, a place he always considered a safe haven but now felt damp and dreary. Glancing at Father Mark's watch, he was surprised to discover that it was now one o'clock in the after-noon. Other than to thank him for not calling the police, there was no reason to wake up the holy man; there was nothing to talk about, least of all to listen to his routine lecture on faith and hope. Sliding along the bench, upon reaching the end, he stood up and was ready to walk away when the snoring stopped. Father Mark had awoken.

"Good afternoon," smiled Father Mark.

He looked back at him, not as God's representative but as a befuddled old man who was squandering his life and living a lie while all along preaching that same lie to others. *Such a shame,* he thought, since Father Mark's intelligence was above par, and he was skilled in so many other ways. He was a master handyman with the knowledge to electrically wire an entire house and knew the ins and outs of plumbing. He was forever fixing things around the church by himself rather than to call a tradesman. If only he hadn't chosen to be a slave to a phony icon, he might well have been a very successful businessman in the construction field. Instead he chose to dress in a dull robe day in, day out, wasting his life away.

Although he may have lost all respect for the old man as a priest, he would always respect him as a man.

"I had no right being in here last night; not in my condition," he apologized.

Father Mark picked up the blanket and neatly folded it into four perfect squares. David wasn't the first intoxicated member of this church to insult the statues, nor would he be the last. Sooner or later they would all end up inside the confession room a few days later to express regret, yet David's irate state told the priest that he wouldn't be entering a confession room for a very long time to come.

"Is there anything you wish to discuss with me?" he asked.

David smirked, expecting that very question and was ready for it. "You mean that 'priest to troubled soul speech' where you make excuses for God's behavior? As your altar boy I have heard you recite those same nine words many times to many people. No disrespect, but have you ever considered a new approach?"

"It's a shame you think this way."

David pointed at the crucifix. "The shame is that I wasted my life worshiping that man's Father. He couldn't save his own Son, and I foolishly believed he would protect my family. That's the real shame, Father Mark, nothing else."

"Don't lose faith in God, David."

"You ask too much of me." He hesitated for a moment before adding. "Mr. Steamer was never shy to admit that he was a miserable employer, but God is two-faced. His arms are always wide open, but when you need him most, he disappears and leaves people like you to clean up his mess. If the truth be known, your employer is even more ruthless than mine."

Father Mark rose up. "Please stop this."

"From the first day that my family entered this church, I loved serving God. There were times when I kneeled before him until my knees hurt, just staring at every painting of him for hours, hoping he would at least smile at me, and though he never did, I never doubted his existence. Before mass I would sneak in here alone and touch the crucifix's feet because it energized me; it made me feel so good, so pure. I would have done anything for Father and Son." He paused, taking in a breath of air. "I don't have to tell you what the both of them did to me. You were there for both funerals," he reminded him.

David was half way out, stopping abruptly when he heard the priest shout, "I saw you steal that dollar from the collection box."

He stopped at once, giving Father Mark the opportunity to finish. "There was a small mirror hanging on the opposite side of the wall, so small it was barely visible, but I could still see you behind me. You were not the only altar boy to have stolen money. Others filled their pockets so deep that they almost tripped over them when they ran out of the church, but you were the only one who put that stolen dollar back the very next day. Actions speak much louder than words. What you did back then made you unique, different from the rest. God is not blind. He saw you as clearly as I did."

"So I saved God a dollar. Big deal," he replied before heading for the exit once more.

Before leaving the building he heard Father Mark cry out, "It's not the agonizing journey, David, but what God leaves for you with at the end of it that will amaze you."

"My journey ends here today, and I see nothing that amazes me!" he shouted back before walking out of that place of worship with the intention of never returning.

Though the medical building was a four-story structure with plenty of spacious offices, the doctor's office was one of the smaller ones, offering a very personal setting. It was clean, with all the traditional amenities, including artificial plants, which appeared so real that one had to gouge a leaf with a fingernail to see if it was authentic. In the middle of the room rested a polished table with a variety of magazines for the young, the old, and the bored. Unlike other medical offices, these magazines were current, not worn out, dated ones with yesterday's news. Every so often the phone would ring; the secretary politely answering it, canceling or making new appointments and generally doing some accounting work in between calls. The odd time Nick's eyes met hers and was followed by a quick polite smile from the both of them. She would then move on with her work; he would search for another magazine to break the boredom. The headline "Riots at the Junction" caught his attention. He picked up the weekly journal, read a few paragraphs, and discovered that an unnamed source had leaked sensitive information, stating that a future development called Woodbridge Estates was proposed for that slum section of the city. The informer implied that all existing homes would be demolished, replaced with upscale condos. The poverty-stricken residents who lived there were furious, so incensed that they had smashed windows and upturned police cars, injuring countless. He read on and noticed a picture of Mike Longo, a powerful politician, insisting that something had to be done to help these people and that the federal government should provide new subsidized housings at another location before the whole area "caught in flames." He wondered if David's prediction had come true, that the unnamed source was in on the scheme, giving this Mike Longo the excuse he needed to clear that area for the group of investors, the group Nick was thinking of being part of.

"She's been in there for a long time," said Lee, snapping him out of his trance.

"The doctor did say to give him time alone with her," he replied, throwing the journal face down on the table and finding another he thought might interest Lee. "Look at that," he said offering it to her. "There's an article in there about the benefit of vitamins."

Lee took it but was not prepared to read it; rather she took it from him and cast it aside onto an empty chair beside her. Vitamins didn't interest her. Tracie's reaction to Cathy's death did. She had yet to cry over it, which she considered abnormal, and she needed to find the reason why. She had her suspicions. Unbeknownst to Nick, she was beginning to secretly suspect that David somehow had something to do with the way Tracie was reacting to it all. Not fully believing that he was directly responsible with Cathy or Diane's death, losing two of his loved ones was too coincidental for her to accept. Was God punishing David for doing something that was so evil? Did he commit an act so venomous that God saw fit to take away his wife and daughter as punishment?

"Did you get a hold of David?" she asked.

"Not yet. I'll give him another day, and if he still doesn't answer his phone, I'll pay him a visit."

"I find it strange that he would disappear like this so soon after Cathy's death."

Her distrust of David went over his head, and when the doctor's door opened, they both watched Tracie timidly walk out with the doctor close behind her.

"I want to go home," was the first thing she said.

Nick knelt down and tenderly rubbed her checks with the back of his fingers. "How about we pass by the mini-putt centre first?"

"Can't we just go home?"

Bewildered, he stood up. He had never known her to turn down a game of mini-putt. He looked at Lee. She did not appear pleased and for some odd reason, he felt he was to blame. "Why don't we stop off at McDonald's then," he asked Lee loud enough for Tracie to hear.

"Tracie wants to go home," she insisted without asking the child. She took her by the hand and walked out of the office, leaving him behind to talk to the doctor alone.

The ride back home was a quiet one, so quiet that within minutes of leaving the medical building, Tracie was fast asleep in the backseat.

"The psychiatrist reassured me that her lack of emotions is only a temporary thing and must be allowed to run its course. According to his analysis, if she didn't acknowledge Cathy's death, then she wouldn't have to deal with it. As far as not crying, she would in time, but for now she has to go through the grieving process in her own time and in her own way," Nick told her.

Lee wasn't impressed. She believed the doctor was telling them only what they wanted to hear. Her thoughts went back to David while Nick's thoughts drifted back to the Junction riots.

The moment Nick drove into the driveway, he could not believe the change. David's house was in shambles. Weeds and overgrown hedges created an eyesore, not to mention patches of dead leaves that blanketed the entire property, giving it a haunted appearance. He stepped out of the car and saw the beginnings of fading circular dry patches on the once immaculate lawn, guessing it had not been watered in some time. He wanted to scream in anger when recalling how David, his father, and himself had sweated laying down that turf the week after his brother moved in. Disgusted, but maintaining his composure, he shut the car door, shaking his head at the filth littering the driveway. As he walked towards the house, he picked up as much of the trash as he could hold and neatly piled it at a corner of the garage.

"I don't believe this," he muttered to himself.

The pathway leading to the front door was clogged with unread newspapers and advertising flyers. Sickened by the debris, he placed his face against the glass portion of the door window.

"Open the door, David. I know you're in there!" he cried out, originally knocking but eventually kicking the bottom of the door without any thoughts of damaging it.

Frustrated at being ignored, he made his way to the rear and wondered how long it had been since the fruit trees were watered. They were once David's pride and joy, and already the top leaves showed signs of drying up. Cursing beneath his breath, he rolled out the water hose, placed the sprinkler in the middle of the trees and turned the water on.

He then peeked through the rear sliding doors. The kitchen was a mess. Fast food wrappers, empty beer cans, and half a dozen empty wine bottles lay scattered in every corner. One end of the kitchen table had paper plates containing half-eaten food; on the other side a dozen or so flies were swarming around it waiting for the opportune time to feast on the remaining crust. The dining room table was filled with empty Chinese food boxes, some not even opened. It was a gruesome sight, one that would never have been acceptable to a Turner. He slammed his knuckles on the window, determined not to leave until David either made his presence known or the window shattered, not bothered which came first.

"I know you are in there. Now open the door!" he yelled.

"Go away!" he heard David scream back through the second floor window.

Nick backed away and looked up, "Will you just look at those fruit trees? They're going to die!" he screamed.

"Leave me alone!"

"You know I can't do that. If that was me up there and you down here, would you leave me?" he asked. "No, you wouldn't. Now meet me at the front."

He made his way back around to the front, stood patiently facing the door and waited until he heard it unlock. Calmly, he gave it a soft push. It opened the maximum two inches allowed before the safety chain inside prevented it from opening any farther. Seconds later he noticed David's bare feet on the other side.

"Your feet are filthy," he told him.

David quickly stepped back, hiding his feet again.

There was a long pause between the brothers before Nick asked, "Do you remember when we were kids back in Scotland, the day I deserted you at Herman's Barn and went home?"

"I think so."

"When I got home Dad asked where you were. I told him you had upset me, and I left you there. If I ever needed a beating it was then, but I don't have to tell you that Dad never beat us. He just gave us that look, that silent, wide-eyed glare that was not threatening but at the same time said a thousand words."

"I remember his look."

"Good. Now I hope you understand why I can't leave you in this condition, not now, not ever. I know he's watching, and I know he's got that look on his face as we speak. I could never disappoint him like that again. Now remove that chain, and let me in."

"You'll not like what you see."

"I know that."

There was a slight hesitation before David began to weep. "I don't know what to do anymore. It's so quiet in this house without Cathy, so painfully silent."

Nick was relieved upon hearing him cry. He took it to mean as a cry for help. "I won't lie to you. I don't know how you feel. At times like this, family is what's needed. Now, please let me in."

When he heard David slide the chain off, he pressed on the door and cautiously stepped inside. Nothing could have prepared him for what he saw next. David was in ruins, unshaven and reeking from the repulsive smell of stale alcohol and a nauseating foul stench of body odor. He looked pitiful, wearing urine-stained boxers, no socks, and a tee shirt that was once white but was now spotted with dried ketchup, gravy stains, and long dark smears of God knows what. His eyes were bloodshot with dark bags underneath that were not there before, and his hair was so greasy that most of his locks were in clusters.

"Oh my God, David, what have you done to yourself?" Nick said in disbelief.

"I did warn you," he replied, walking away without as much as another word. He made his way to the kitchen, sitting down on the first chair he found and stared at the wall. Nick followed, forced to come to an abrupt halt when entering the kitchen. It was an appalling mess. David sadly looked at him.

"I did warn you," he repeated.

At once, Nick made his way to the sink, opened the drawer below, and immediately pulled out a plastic garbage bag. He didn't have to move far to fill it, starting with the trash that littered the counter, and by the time he worked his way from one end to the other, the bag was filled with empty pizza boxes, paper plates, and plastic wine glasses. He then soaked a sponge and concentrated on scrubbing the stubborn stains that smeared the top but soon was interrupted by the loud bickering coming from the two budgies.

"When was the last time you fed the birds?" he asked throwing the greasy sponge back inside the sink and removing another garbage bag from the drawer.

"I don't remember."

"Tracie asked me to check up on them while I was here."

"They don't mean that much to me anymore. Do you think she'd want to take care of them?"

"I think she'd love to," replied Nick, quickly filling the second bag.

Not much was discussed until Nick reached for the third bag.

"Thanks for watering the fruit trees," David told him, reinstating their importance to the Turners.

"No need to thank me. It had to be done. It would be unforgivable if they died," Nick claimed and then pointed to an unopened box of Chinese spare ribs. "Can you pass me those?"

David handed him the box. Nick opened it, sniffed inside, and said, "They still smell good. Are you hungry?" When David shook his head, Nick stripped the rib with a half dozen bites and threw the bone inside the garbage bag. "They're still good. I won't throw them away in case you get hungry later," he said wiping his sticky fingers on the table cloth.

That display of affection relaxed David to some degree; enough for him to say,

"My heart aches, Nick."

Nick sat down next to him, pulling the chair closer. "And it should ache. That's the price we pay for loving the way we do."

David lowered his head. "I remember when Cathy was born. I was in the waiting room knowing the doctors were performing a caesarian on whatever was left of Diane's body," he recalled, tears forming in his eyes. "The doctors later told me she should not have survived, but she did. She cried right there in the nurse's arms Nick. She defied all odds and cried as if to tell me not to worry because she would pull through." He picked up a dirty tissue from the table, wiping his eyes. "I must have cursed and thanked God a million times that night. He gave me my child, and at the same time took my wife away. I didn't agree with what God did, but I forgave him."

Nick refrained from provoking him. This was not the time to make sense of God's behavior but a time to grant David the freedom to express his feelings, to let out his frustrations.

"I'm just so tired of all this." David wept. "Why did he pick me? Why not do that to a person more deserving? I just want to go back to bed and never wake up again."

Nick took his hand. It trembled and felt so cold that he could have been holding on to an ice cube. He leaned his body closer to him. "As long as there is one person left in this world that loves you, then you owe it to that person to live as long as you can. I read that sentence in a book years ago. I thought it was one of the greatest lines I ever read. The author of that book was you, David." He allowed him to cry, watching his tears drip and land on his filthy toes. They were plentiful, loud, and heavy, but at the same time, prayed that they released some of David's pain. He finally let go of his hand, stood up, pulled him close, and then wrapped his arms around him, giving him a soft kiss on the cheek.

"You owe it to, Cathy, Diane, and yourself to keep and cherish those happy moments the three of you had. If you can do that, then you will never be alone my little brother," he whispered.

David broke into a full-fledged cry, tightly hugging him back. "What am I going to do now, Nick? I miss them both so much, so, so much."

Nick swayed David's trembling body back and forth like a parent would do to his terrified child on their first day of school.

Lora was on her way for a meeting with Mr. Steamer. She carried with her two large folders. In those folders were black-and-white professional photos of two men—one a minister, the other a supermarket manager. Stapled to those photographs were twenty pages of documents containing a long and accurate history of those two individuals. All their achievements and highlights were documented, from the day they were born to present day. If these two men gave to charity, the file stated that fact. If they faithfully practiced religion, it was written in capital letters, and if they cursed or were ever on the verge of falling into temptation, it was further highlighted in red.

Lora reached the meeting room she was looking for—Mr. Steamer's private sauna. She wiped the tiny-fogged window, barely able to see that he was sitting on the cedar wood bench, wrapped in a long red robe and with his face inches from the sweltering rocks. She watched him pull onto the lever, releasing cold water onto the white hot rocks and chase the mist, inhaling as much as he could and keeping it deep into his lungs for as long as possible. It didn't shock her that he could do that. As his assistant, she had seen him do it many times before and knew this pattern. She knocked on the door before he had the opportunity to pull on the lever again. He got up, walked to the window, and wiped it, nodding his head in acknowledgement upon seeing Lora on the other side. With the red robe firmly around his body, he politely opened the door and stepped outside.

"Show me what you have found," he said, staring at the folders.

"Two potentials," she replied, spreading the folders and placing them in front of him. "One is a minister and the other a supermarket manager," she continued, positioning the two black-and-white photos on his lap. He was not interested in their facial features; rather he took the written biographies attached to the photos and pulled them off. He took his time, carefully studying the supermarket manager's past.

"It reads well. This is a good man," he said until reaching a paragraph that was highlighted in red. "It states here that when he was nineteen, he kicked his dog in anger."

Lora was prepared for all highlighted questions. "It was more of an accusation. He claimed that the dog got in his way as he was walking."

The supermarket manager didn't interest him any longer. He returned the file to her and began carefully scrutinizing the minister's life for traces of wrongdoings. He found none.

"This poor man and his wife have attempted to adopt a child for over five years. I believe this minister would be a wiser choice." He returned the minister's file. "Proceed with the minister. Though, I doubt that he could match Mr. Turner's performance, he is the obvious choice," he said.

Lora attached the photos back to the paperwork and walked away. Mr. Steamer went back inside the sauna.

This classic car was parked in front of a church. Planted firmly on the back chrome bumper of this old black 1957 Plymouth was half a dozen religious stickers. One stood out from the rest. It was a sixteen-by-three-inch sign with the slogan "JESUS IS FOREVER." With its two rear wings arching upwards and its push button gearshift, this car was meant to look like it could fly. It burst onto the auto scene in the late fifties, the decade of the "Fifty-Foot Woman" and the "Incredible Shrinking Man," a time when anything was possible, a trip to the moon included. Wishing to capitalize on this ideal opportunity, General Motors built this futuristic looking automobile. It was presumed to be the long-awaited breakthrough of technological wizardry, but when they duplicated this same model in 1958, it became obvious that consumers were not buying into that concept any longer. With only a handful still left, joggers, pet walkers, and car buffs would always stop to inspect it, marveling at how well maintained it continued to be and amazed that it was still running. The body shone, the upholstery inside was absolutely spotless, and everything about the car was still in good working order.

The owner of that distinctive auto was a minister named John Parker. He was a funny-looking man. His face drew attention due to his slightly pushed in forehead, smaller than normal eyes, followed by his thick cheeks, and topping off his features was a ski-slopped nose. One would think him to be the last person to own such an automobile. But the Plymouth had a history. It had been passed down by his father, and John Parker adored that car, spending as much money needed to keep it road worthy and purposely forgetting the times it left him stranded in the middle of nowhere. Besides driving it, his other joy was watching the milometer and marveling at the amount of miles it had reached, predicting a million more. His wife, Florence, was and would forever remain his faithful and devoted wife. Brought up by strict God-fearing parents, she was happy and felt privileged to be married to a man of the cloth. With hair always pulled back into a bun, she was very plain and never flashy, preferring to cover most of her toned body rather than flaunt it. Many considered her personality boring, which was just fine with her.

The Parkers had returned from shopping earlier than anticipated that particular day. The department stores were not as bustling as one would have thought for a Saturday afternoon; as a result they found themselves sitting in front of the television, watching an episode from their collection of DVDs of the popular series *Little House on a Prairie*. With their charitable functions and volunteer work consuming most their time, this was a rare afternoon treat. Both enjoyed this peace, sipping on their tea, and praising Michael Landon, the producer of the series for his great vision.

"It's incredible the way he got those children to act so professionally. They can't be more than three years old," remarked Florence. John agreed, not wanting to remind her that she repeated this observation every time they watched this particular episode.

Deciding to take a break, Florence refilled the teapot while John took this opportunity to check the mailbox.

"I'll be right back," he said before walking out of the house and to the wooden mailbox. Shoving his hand inside, he pulled out a handful of papers, some bills but mostly advertising informing consumers of the never to be repeated sale on everything from sofas to microwaves. Mixed with this junk mail was a letter. What made this letter unique was the small blue symbol of a dove at the top corner.

"Oh my God," he whispered, recognizing this emblem only too well. It belonged to the adoption agency. They both prayed for this day, longing for such a letter, never giving up hope.

"Oh my God," he repeated.

Florence wondered what was delaying her husband. She looked out of the window and saw him, on his knees, in deep prayer, with that letter firmly held in his hand.

"What is it?" she cried out.

John raised his trembling arm for her to see.

"From the agency," was all he had to say for her to fall on her knees and thank the Lord.

John Parker took extra care on grooming himself this morning, placing every single hair properly in place and dressing in his finest suit. On the comical side, he even trimmed the hair on his ears and nose, making Florence laugh when she caught him. She was not as bold. Playing it safe, she went with her characteristic style, well aware that one is never given a second chance at first impressions. Some would gape at her lifeless attire, arguing it was genuinely homely, almost costume-like, a combination of what an Amish woman would wear and how a child would dress her rag doll. But to her, it was the most flattering dress she owned and was extremely proud of it, especially the multi-designs sown along the bottom hem. She relented on one item, which she considered extravagant. She used makeup this morning. Tiny traces were noticeable on her face. Embarrassed by it all but feeling it necessary to add a glow about her, she broke with tradition and dusted her cheeks with borrowed rouge.

A week had gone by since they had received that letter, and now they found themselves seated inside the adoption office, both eyeing the small clock resting on the nearby table. Their appointment was for 9:00 a.m., yet they had arrived an hour earlier, sitting in the same chairs since 8:00 a.m. They would jump up from their seat whenever a staff member walked by, finding it essential to hold on to each other's hand. Their edgy behavior was within their rights, for this was the end of their five-year struggle. The aggravation, disappointments, and sky-high legal fees were all but a distant memory, for all their waiting was now paying dividends. This was the day the Parkers were going home with their adopted daughter.

All the legal documents that required signing were signed; all background checks were positive with no sign of any criminal activity whatsoever between the two. Without question, the Parkers were, as Mr. Steamer stated, the obvious choice.

The door behind the desk opened. The Parkers barely found the strength to stand up. An administrator walked out. Beside her, a gorgeous little girl with long, blonde, curly hair appeared.

"That's her," Florence whispered in awe. The child possessed the smile of a princess, lighting up the entire room, and though they had seen countless pictures and read the descriptions, they didn't do this child justice, for she resembled an angel.

"I'm Jackie Ulliman," announced the administer, introducing herself as she shook the Parker's hands. "And I'm sure you know who this sweetheart is," she added, placing a child before them. This child practically melted them with her set of deep blue eyes and rosy cheeks. Captivated by this little darling, the Parkers were too stunned to answer back prompting the girl to take the lead,

"Hello, Mr. and Mrs. Parker. I'm Cathy."

CHAPTER SEVEN

One year later ...

It was a gorgeous day, not a cloud in the sky; warm but not hot thanks to the cool breeze blowing from the northwest. This magnificent weather added to David's spirits. A bit nervous when originally asked to join Nick and his family for a picnic, it surprised him that as the weekend approached he was actually looking forward to it. With a half-hour drive still ahead of him, he had time to reflect on the many personal changes over the past twelve months. The return of his confidence and self-respect were two major items, but two other events stood out as well: making peace with God and reviving his career as an author. Both, he thought, were lost forever, both slowly finding their way back into his life. As far as God was concerned, he eventually sought and received Father Mark's delicate guidance. He hadn't fully thrown his faith behind God as he once had, but with time he hoped he would. Quite simply he missed him and was willing to trust him all over again, but at his own pace.

David's relationship with Mr. Steamer over the past year had been semi warm at best; although he had to give him credit where credit was due. Mr. Steamer hadn't cut off his financial life line after all and generously gave him the time he required to recover from his personal tragedies, but Mr. Steamer was forever all business, and he expected a new novel from him, sooner rather than later. Even though writing was still an uphill battle, he felt capable of meeting a deadline. In the past eight months got more deeply involved with the fictional characters he'd developed, caring and nurturing them, allowing them to interest and challenge him. He had revisited the basic writing rules, which in the past had made for stronger and more interesting novels. He even dared entertain the thought of having a bestseller once again.

The conservation area came into view. With its very own recreational complex, this unique establishment was more than a picnic site. Bordering on its edges were a string of cafés and stylish antique shops offering tourists a perfect place to enjoy a beverage or perhaps discover a bargain or two. The teens considered it a trendy place to meet, the baby boomers loved to take their grandchildren there for the day, and the newlyweds could spend a romantic day with each other promising that one day they would bring their own children here. This park was also covered with lush bushes, trees, bike trails, and had a shallow manmade lake in the shape of a heart right in the centre of its two hundred odd acres. If swimming, fishing, or an old fashioned barbeque were things one was looking for, this park had it all.

The Jag came to a full stop at the front gate, and immediately the park ranger came out of her hut. She was a sight to behold, having a ring pieced through her upper lip and a mop of multicolored, short spiked hair. He did his best to ignore the half dozen earrings on each ear and the one she had dangling from her eyebrow, but when she opened her mouth and he noticed a piercing on her tongue as well, he had to hold his breath.

"You don't have anyone hidden in the trunk by any chance," she teased peeking inside the car. He was tempted to ask if it was painful when she talked due to her piercings but decided it really wasn't any of his business.

"Other than a spare tire and a cooler, the trunk is empty," he joked back.

She stepped back and glanced at the trunk as though she had X-ray vision and could see that he was telling the truth.

"That will be five dollars, sir."

He gave her the money. "Can you tell me where I might find the Turners?" he asked her.

The young lady checked her clipboard, found the Turner's site, and pointed to one of three dirt roads leading inside the park. "If you follow that road it will take you to the bottom of a hill where you make a sharp right and look for area 3A. You should be able to spot them somewhere there," she said, pressing on a remote control, which lifted the gate.

He drove cautiously, following the ranger's instructions, passing families, kids chasing other kids with water spray guns, old men sleeping under the cover of a shaded tree, and teenagers holding hands. It would be fitting if Jackie could have been sitting next to him at moments like this, he thought. Unfortunately she was turning into a distant memory. He had not heard from her since the day she walked away from him at the cemetery, and though he did dial her number one last time, it became obvious she had purposely given him an incorrect number. She'd had ample time to contact him since then and elected not to do so. It seemed like she had disappeared from the face of the earth. He was confused as to her reasons, though suspecting that she was still guilt ridden over Cathy's death. He hoped that one day she would contact him just to hear her voice again and give him the opportunity to tell her that all was fine and not to feel responsible any longer.

Upon reaching the bottom of the hill, he slowed down, anticipating that sharp turn that the park ranger had spoke of. Finding section 3A exactly where she said it would be, he drove into the adjacent parking lot, got out of the car, and took a deep breath, enjoying the scent of freshly cut grass. It was time to enjoy other odors as well, such as broiling hamburgers, a scent he had missed and was glad to be smelling again. Looking around, he immediately found his family; not at all surprised that the spot they chose was a secluded corner, an area where others would avoid but where someone with Lee's condition found ideal. The fewer people around her, the more at ease she felt.

Tracie saw David first, prompting her to run towards him. Before he had the chance to haul a cooler out from the trunk, she was standing next to him.

"Hi, Uncle David!" she shouted. "We're over there." He lifted the cooler from the trunk. "Lead the way, sweetheart."

Tracie could contain her enthusiasm for only so long before running ahead of him. He laughed at her passion and had to repeat to himself that she was Nick and Lee's daughter, not his. There were times during the past year where he felt he had over stepped his boundaries, volunteering to take her to the movies, showering her with gifts and phoning her in the evenings just to say good night. If there was no school the next day, they would talk late into the night, mostly about the budgies. He recalled one such night when she called him, crying that the single egg Mr. Rogers and Lucy had together mysteriously disappeared from the nest.

"They'll have more," was the only comforting advice he could give her. These lengthy conversations with his niece would only end when Lee grabbed the phone from Tracie, insisting that she had to go to bed and then hanging up on him immediately after.

"Uncle David is here," announced Tracie.

Lee saw the huge cooler David was carrying.

"We'll need another table," she complained to Nick, locating an unused one approximately fifty feet away. "There's one over there."

Nick looked over at the table she was referring to. There was no need for an additional one. The existing one was spacious enough to have catered for more than four people, but he either didn't think it was worth arguing about or didn't get the chance to because David had arrived.

"Where should I put the cooler?" he asked.

"Slide it under this table," replied Lee, spreading the tablecloth neatly around the edges.

"Don't get comfortable. We need another one of these tables," said Nick walking past his brother. David didn't argue either; he only followed him.

Tracie removed the cover off David's cooler and peeked inside. "Uncle David brought my favorite juice, Mommy."

"You don't need to take one from Uncle David's cooler. I brought the same kind. If you're thirsty, take one from our cooler."

Nick grabbed one side of the table, David the other. Taking small strides, they labored their way back.

"Did you know the circus was passing by next week?" David asked as a passing thought. "I could get four tickets, and we could all go."

Nick laughed. "You would never get Lee to go. Clowns and crowds would eat her up, and I hate the smell of elephants."

"Would it be okay if I took Tracie then?"

Nick hesitated as he always did when his brother requested such outings with his daughter, replying in the same manner. "Let me talk to Lee about it."

At times David wished his brother would be more assertive as a husband, rather than always having to twist Lee's arm for permission when it involved Tracie. He realized he might have been a bit on the selfish side for always asking to have Tracie for the day, but if he didn't ask, it would never happen.

When they got back, they placed the second table parallel to the first, both standing back to admire a job well done, or so they thought. Lee complained that it wasn't level enough, and if not correctly positioned, the drinks would spill. David found a piece of wood and forced it under one of the legs. It seemed to do the trick. The brothers could finally relax, but Lee was relentless, wanting to get this picnic over with as soon as possible, then leave.

"You might as well start barbecuing."

"We just got here," complained Nick.

Lee disregarded his remark, removing drinks, hot dogs, and hamburgers from their own cooler. She didn't stop there, continuing to slice the bums in half, laying the relish, mayonnaise, and finally the bottle of ketchup on top of the table.

"Where's the mustard?" asked Tracie.

"You will have to do without mustard this time," Lee replied without looking to see if the mustard was actually missing.

Tracie sat at the edge of the bench with a look about her, wanting the whole world to know that life was not fair, leading David to examine the commercial stretch of the park. He saw what appeared to be a small logged hut that was now converted into a convenience store.

"They should have some there," he pointed.

"She can live without the mustard," snapped Lee, forcing him to quickly retreat and regret his decision to butt in.

Embarrassed by her sharp statement, Nick blamed it on the group of noisy teenagers playing football nearby, possibly closing in on Lee's comfort zone and setting her off. It had happened before.

"If you are going to pay for it, then we can't lose," he told his brother, easing the situation.

"I think I can afford it," replied David, quickly forgetting his earlier regret to not get involved.

With her father and uncle on her side, Tracie found the courage to ask, "Can I go with you, Uncle David?"

"Of course you can." he agreed before Lee had time to intervene.

They walked a short distance before Lee shouted, "Don't buy her any junk food!"

True, it was only mustard, but David was unsure as to which one to buy. He could only pace up and down the aisle so many times before Tracie would put two and two together and realize that her uncle didn't have a clue as to which jar was the brand choice.

Playing it safe, he selected the most expensive one, placing his hand behind the row of jars and choosing the one from the back. This habit had originated while Diane was alive. When shopping together, she warned him to always be aware that the freshest foods were hidden at the back. Though she meant it to be applied only to vegetables and fruits, he soon associated this practice to all foods, whether it was a tin of beans or a container of mustard. It made him feel sharp knowing he'd got the upper hand on the shifty merchants. With mustard in hand, he made his way to the next passageway, finding Tracie standing in front of the candy section. She seemed hypnotized by the endless selection of chocolate bars, bubble gum, and the dozen selections of potato chips. He crept behind her, placing his mouth near her ear.

"If I bought you that chocolate would you be able to finish it before we got back?" he whispered.

"I could, but I don't think it would be a good idea, Uncle David. Mommy said no junk food."

David pointed to some wrapped gum. "That is junk food whereas chocolate is filled with nourishment."

She nervously looked behind her, imagining her mother might be spying and after a slight pause she quickly snapped the treat off the shelf as though it was a hot iron and passed it on to him.

"Should I tell Mommy?"

Her question seemed innocent enough, but in reality was much more complicated in the Turner's household. To lie was not an option. It wouldn't do, and David knew that as well as her. He'd have to think of something witty, a comfort zone for the child.

"If she asks, then you have to tell her, but if she doesn't, then when you get back, whisper that I bought you a chocolate bar into your dad's ear." Her guilty expression disappeared, replaced with a slight grin. She found this acceptable.

The melody was faint at first, barely noticeable, but as the seconds ticked by, the tune got louder and unmistakable. It was the seductive rhyme that all ice cream trucks belted out from their loud speakers, stirring and exciting neighborhood kids. Those folksy notes would spark children into scrabbling to find their parents, begging and pleading for only a few dollars to buy ice cream before the truck moved on to the next neighborhood and no telling when he'd be back in this area again. When alive, Cathy was no different from other kids her age. Regardless where she found herself, no matter which section of the house she was in, when that melody played, it captivated her. She simply had to have a scoop or two of her favorite vanilla ice cream, dipped in chocolate, and sprinkled with almond chips on top.

As anticipated, the ice cream truck softly applied its brakes and came to a complete stop in front of the convenience store window. Having a pied piper effect, a long line of children ran to it, shamelessly waving their money in midair and struggling for a better position in line. Each and every one of those kids were troubled, thinking the worst, that all the ice cream would be gone by the time it was their turn, but when the friendly man dressed in a white uniform slid open the side window and reassured them that there would be enough for everyone, they calmed down.

David looked out, captivated by a child who stood out from the rest. She was third in line. This little girl possessed long, curly, blonde hair, resting elegantly down her back, so beautifully, so enchanting it reminded him of his daughter's golden locks. What made it more coincidental was the way she held on to her money. Cathy used to hold her money in the exact same manner, delicately between index finger and thumb so as not to put pressure on the bill. In her own adorable way, she theorized that people who held on too tightly suffocated whichever president was pictured on the bill. He felt a tuck on his sleeve shirt, snapping him out of his trance. Tracie was trying to get his attention, reminding him that it was his turn to pay.

"I'm sorry. I wasn't paying attention. How much is it?" he asked.

"Four dollars and seventy cents please," said the cashier.

He placed a ten-dollar bill on the counter, quickly finding himself drawn back outside, towards that little blonde girl. She was next, handing over her money and politely waiting for her ice cream. For the strangest reason, he felt a sudden urge to see her face. He wasn't clear as to why he even cared about her appearance, assuming it was more of a curiosity than anything else. When the man handed this little girl her ice cream, to his amazement, it was vanilla with chocolate dip and sprinkled with almond chips on top. His curiosity intensified. He didn't need a reason any longer. He now felt a strong impulse to see her face.

"Uncle David, your change is ready," said Tracie, pointing to the cashier, who by this time rolled his eyes upwards at David's lack of respect for the customers behind him.

"She said that I have your change, sir," he told David, slapping a five-dollar bill along with some loose coins onto the counter.

Embarrassed, by the whole episode and to the relief of the customers behind him, he took the mustard, chocolate bar, and grabbed his change off the counter. When glancing outside again the truck had disappeared as well as that intriguing child. It suddenly occurred to him, he was recklessly allowing his vivid imagination to run wild. That girl was not Cathy. His daughter was dead and buried, he bitterly reminded himself. He had to bring his emotions under control or risked taking a step backwards. He was at a family picnic, and if he didn't get his act together the day would be ruined. Nick and Father Mark had laboured long hours the past year to help him overcome his emotional meltdown. It would devastate them if he caved in and crumpled, especially on this gorgeous day and in the presence of Tracie.

"What were you staring at, Uncle David?" Tracie wanted to know.

"Your Uncle David was foolishly day dreaming."

"Can I have my chocolate bar please?"

He laughed. "Let's get out of this store first."

Once outside, he gave her the bar, selected the smoothest part of the logged wall to rest his back on, and took pleasure in watching his niece wolf down the treat.

"Slow down or you'll choke."

With half the bar shoved inside her mouth and the other half waiting for the same fate, she nodded her head and giggled.

Surprised, he heard the melody again, demanding his attention. He looked at the end of the dirt road and saw the truck come to a stop roughly one hundred feet ahead of him. To his astonishment, he also spotted that same child strolling out from behind a tree, chatting and laughing with a boy close to her age. A few licks of her ice cream later she turned around. David finally got what he wanted: a clear view of her face.

The bag containing the mustard fell from his hand, smashing onto the pavement and shattering the jar into countless pieces. Tracie jumped back, startled by the noise, looking down at the mess and then back up at her uncle. He had his eyes and mouth wide open, a confused and shocked expression on his face. This frightened her. She turned to see what he was staring at, and, like him, reacted and though she had just seen a ghost. She immediately let out a faint cry, strangely lowering her head, not daring to move.

A chilling horror discharged throughout David's body and seconds later, a new contradicting warm sensation blended uncontested with that same fear; two potently charged emotions battling for control of his senses, yet both refusing to overpower one another. They complimented each other, creating a natural high, a sentiment that no drug known to man could ever hope to generate. His body stiffened, and he swallowed continuously until his mouth was completely dry and he could swallow no more.

"Tracie," he managed to utter, pointing to that child. "Look over there."

She would not reply, choosing instead to keep her head down.

"Tracie," he repeated louder, "look at that little blonde girl."

She would neither look up at him or at the girl in question, and when he shouted at her for the third time it only upset her further.

"I know who stole the bird egg, Uncle David," she cried out.

"Not now, Tracie! Not now! Take a look at that girl, and tell me who she is!"

Rattled, she looked up at him. "I was sitting on the staircase and saw mommy throw the egg out of the window," she confessed hoping that her startling revelation would take priority.

"Never mind the egg. Look at her, and tell me who she is!" he yelled unaware that he was shouting at an eight-year-old, oblivious that strangers were now taking notice.

Tracie stepped onto the dirt road, taking quick backward steps, away from him. "I don't like this. I want to go to my daddy," she cried, uncaring that a car was approaching and was forced to slam on the brakes in order to avoid hitting her.

"Don't go, Tracie!" cried David, ignoring the fact that the driver was cursing at him for intimidating her onto the road. When she reached the other side, she looked at that blonde girl in horror one last time before running back to her parents.

People were taking notice, listening to David's shouting and staring in amazement at his behavior. He was in a world of his own; his primary focus was on that child who, at this point, had her eyes locked onto his.

No one else mattered. David was deaf to the angry threats being shouted at him by strangers, asking him what his problem was and that someone should call the police. As far as he was concerned, there was no one in this park but him and that child, standing fifty feet away. He recognized her. There was no mistake; there was neither logic nor rational supporting what he saw, but it was definitely her. He knew that girl better than anyone else, standing there, gaping at him with eyes and mouth wide open in wonder, more so than he was gaping at her. Without a doubt, that was Cathy.

A million questions screamed to be asked. David sought none, unconcerned of the answers. It didn't matter at this point. That was her, and she was very much alive. Whoever were involved with her fictitious death were of no concern to him, not now. As God was his witness, those responsible would be dealt with later. As of now, he needed to move slowly so as not to startle the child. He moved forward in even paces, not too aggressively, and when she saw him advancing, she appeared frightened, taking a few backward steps before turning away from him and breaking into a brisk stride.

"Please, wait, don't go!" he shouted, matching her stride for stride, eventually trotting assertively towards her but every time he got nearer, she ran faster.

"I bought Mr. Rogers another bird!" he cried out in desperation.

She abruptly stopped, as did David, placing him only a few feet behind her. If ever there was a doubt before to her true identity, it vanished with those words. Only a child named Cathy Turner would know of a bird named Mr. Rogers.

"Her name is Lucy, and you were right all along. She has made a fine companion for Mr. Rogers," he told her. The girl lowered her head in submission, just as Tracie had earlier, giving him the freedom to take one more step. "Listen to me, baby. I know this is all crazy for the both of us, but I'm not going to ask you anything now, and you don't have to explain anything to me. You know who I am, and I know who you are. This is all real, Cathy, so please turn around and face your father." She continued to stare at the ground, offering him no sign of recognition. Stunned by her reaction, he wondered if brainwashing had played a role in her behavior, tormenting him further as to what other harm she may have been subjected to over the past three hundred and sixty-five days.

"I'm going to take you by the hand, and we will leave this place together," he said as calmly as could be.

"Please don't touch me," she begged him.

He slowly moved beside her, and although he told her he wouldn't ask anything further, there was one question he felt compelled to ask: "Did anybody hurt you in any way, baby?" She would not respond. "It's okay. You don't have to answer, just give me your hand."

"Get away from her," cried out an anxious woman behind him. She was not alone; an angry crowd had assembled behind him, many of whom were unwilling to get involved at this point.

Ignoring everyone, David put out his hand. Cathy panicked, sprinting away, but before he could give chase, he felt someone holding him back. A man from the crowd had taken a hold of his shirttail, preventing him from chasing after her. Enraged, he swung his arm in between, forcing the man's hand loose and tearing off a piece of his shirt.

"She's my daughter for heaven's sake!" he yelled, intimidating the crowd away. When he looked back at the child she was standing next to a classic black 1957 Plymouth, frantically talking to two adults, John and Florence Parker. John eyed David from head to toe before calmly escorting his wife and the girl safely inside the car, at all times aware of the group of angry men encircling David whereas David's main focus was on memorizing the license plate off the Plymouth.

"The cops are on their way!" someone shouted.

John Parker bravely made his way towards David, not displaying any sign of animosity, hinting that he sought dialogue, not altercation. David didn't move. He didn't want trouble either; he only wanted his child back. It didn't matter that he had seen her lifeless body lying on a cold trolley at the coroner's laboratory, nor the fact that her eyes were firmly shut and her entire body was stiff and pale. He didn't want to remember that he stood side-by-side with a doctor when identifying her body. The reality of it all didn't register with him, and he wanted this funny-looking man approaching him to understand that Cathy was going home with him.

"Hello. I'm Reverend John Parker." He pointed back at the car. "And that's my wife, Florence."

David didn't say anything, noting that despite Florence's persistence, Cathy had unlocked the car door and was now standing beside the car bumper and staring at him.

John placed his hand out, offering to shake his. "And you are?"

"I'm the father of that little girl," he replied pointing at Cathy.

John quickly lowered his hand. "I beg your pardon?"

David looked behind him once more, watching Florence get out of the Plymouth and waving both arms at an arriving policeman. "You heard me. That little girl is my daughter."

"What makes you say that?"

"Every father knows his daughter," he shot back as though the reverend had just insulted his intelligence.

John remained reserved. If he thought David was a crazed lunatic, then he didn't show it.

"This is such an unnatural predicament to find ourselves in." He nervously laughed.

"I'm taking her home with me."

John didn't laugh anymore. "To be honest with you, I was told her parents were dead."

David spread his legs and clenched his fists, the first sign of potential violence. "Do I look dead to you?" he angrily replied.

John was a minister, not a hoodlum. A physical confrontation with David was the last thing on his mind. "I suppose not. So what do we do now?" he asked.

"Simple. Get yourself a good lawyer, and give me back my daughter."

Taking a quick glance behind and seeing a young police officer talking to Florence, John felt more secure, yet at the same time felt David was a troubled soul and didn't want him to get hurt.

"There is a police officer here, and soon there will be more," he tried to reason. "Why don't we walk back and talk to him before this all gets out of hand. This has all been a terrible misunderstanding. I'm sure there's an explanation."

The sight of the police officer also encouraged the crowd, instilling courage into them as a whole. Two well-built, middle-aged men stood out from the crowd, both with a set look on their faces and inching closer to David, ready to pounce on him at any moment.

"Don't get any closer!" he yelled at them.

With his finger pointing at David and his other hand resting on his gun holster, the officer cried out, "Stay right there, sir."

"This man has my daughter!" he screamed back.

The policeman snapped the clip off his holster. "I said don't move!"

"Please, mister, give yourself up. I promise to get you the help you need," pleaded John Parker.

David felt the aggressive mob ready to rush him, and with the officer threatening to escalate the situation, he had to quickly think. In seconds he could very well be handcuffed and on his way to jail. Being dragged into a police car with hands behind his back was not the way he wanted his daughter to see him.

"Tell them who I am, Cathy!" he shouted before feeling two huge arms wrapped around his body, another two draped around his legs, trying to wrestle him onto the ground.

"Hold on to him," cried the officer, dashing towards them.

David elbowed and kicked the two men, hurling them both onto the ground and made his escape. A veteran officer with experience would know not to draw a weapon at a park filled with children, but David's sudden dash caught the inexperienced officer by surprise. He did withdraw the weapon, got down on one knee, and pointed the gun at the bolting David with every intention of shooting him down. Petrified, John placed himself between David and the officer, savagely waving his arms at him.

"No!" he screamed.

David ran blindly, finally coming to his senses and stopping behind a string of shops. He caught his breath and looked behind. No one was following, but the sound of multiple police sirens told him it would only be a matter of time before he was apprehended. He was desperate and needed a place to hide, a safe haven where he could get lost in a crowd until things settled down. Beside him was a rear door. He immediately opened it, stepped inside, and when the door shut, he stood at the foot of a long dim hallway, which led into a fashionable coffee shop. Though dark, he could see the walls covered with pictures of James Dean, at his handsomest, cigarette dangling from the corner of his mouth and eyes squinted. On the other side of the wall hung photos of the Rat Pack in their glory days, playing billiards, drinking, and each one with an arm wrapped around a Vegas showgirl. The men's washroom door had a photo of John Wayne holding a Winchester over his shoulder, daring anyone to mess with him, while on the female's washroom door hung that ever glamorous picture of Marilyn Monroe standing over a windy subway air duct in her loose white dress, making a weak but famous attempt at holding it down.

He walked through the narrow corridor and entered the main café. The place was filled with younger adults, some with the latest two-hundred-dollar sunglasses and others chatting into their Blackberries. He searched for a single table but found none; however, there was one empty seat facing the window. A red-haired teenager, sipping on a four-dollar cappuccino and nibbling on a low fat muffin was seated there. He walked over and calmly asked if the seat was taken. She shook her head. He thanked her, sat down, and grabbed a forgotten newspaper, pretending to be interested in the baseball scores.

Firstly, the teen kept to herself, ignoring him, but he soon became aware that she was staring. It was one of those celebrity stares he had loathed throughout his writing career. These fans were the opportunist kind who had no reservation at hounding him at every chance, demanding his autograph; these ones were the harassing foul-mouthed bluffs who believed he owed them not only compensation but his uncontested time since they had bought his books.

"I know you. You're a writer!" shouted the girl unexpectedly, displaying a mouthful of braces.

Remaining reserved, David lowered the newspaper, making light of the situation,

"You have the wrong person." He laughed, but what he saw outside the coffee shop was not a laughing matter. Not only was that same police officer standing in the middle of the road, but other officers now stood in a semicircle around him, listening to what the excited rookie had to say. A slim, mid-forties, attractive female detective had joined them. With her long dark hair and a pair of matching dark eyes, she didn't waste time showing that she was in charge, taking control at once, and delegating different areas for each officer to search.

"David Turner!" she shouted out reciting his name and adding, "My mom buys all your books."

He brushed the rude teen aside, continuing to watch the rookie officer explain for a second time the sequence of events as they happened to the detective. He wasn't a lip reader, but he was certain that the words "child predator" were mouthed to describe him. Other witnesses came forward offering their version of events, most likely telling the detective that he chased a little girl, howling madly how he wanted to take her away. The determined look on her face told him that she wanted him off the street, and he couldn't blame her. She had no way of knowing that he was actually chasing after his own daughter.

"I want your autograph," the teen demanded, shoving a pen and paper beneath his nose.

"I'm not who you think I am," he lied.

"Yes, you are."

He ignored her, looked back outside, and saw no one. They were all gone. Relieved for a moment, he buried his face into the newspaper.

"That lady who was talking to the police just walked in. She's at the door staring at you, David Turner," the teen said, giggling

His heart beat faster. He slowly looked towards the front entrance. The detective was indeed staring directly at him.

"Say cheese," the girl yelled out.

To his dismay, the teen was using her cell phone to take photos of him at random. "My mom won't believe this," she continued as though he was a freak of nature.

"I'm not this Turner guy!" he angrily snapped, looking back at the entrance and uneasy that the detective still had her eyes glued to him.

"Whatever." She guffawed, backing up against the wall and relentlessly taking snap shots of him from every angle.

He threw the newspaper down, got up, and with his head hung low made his way towards the rear entrance. He took one last look inside and saw that the detective was making her way towards the teen.

The Jag was parked in Nick's driveway, idling for the past five minutes. Sooner or later David would have to shut off the ignition and face them. He would need to explain why he had deserted Tracie back at the conservation area. Based on Lee's emotional state, no explanation on earth could justify abandoning Tracie the way he had. He wouldn't contest it if they thought less of him because of what he did, yet he remained optimistic that the amazing news about Cathy would overshadow everything else.

Will they think I have gone mad? Will they deem me insane when I break the startling revelation she is alive?

At first, yes, but Tracie was the key. She had seen Cathy with her own eyes. True, she was only a child, but she couldn't deny what she saw. She was there and had seen what he had seen. The moment she verified his version of the story, he and Nick would immediately alert the authorities, followed by hiring a dream team of lawyers. Before long the two cousins would be playing together again, and, as a homecoming gift, he would build his daughter her very own tree house.

Hiding inside, behind the curtained window, Nick and Lee were watching David. Behind them stood Tracie, still speechless from the whole ordeal. In spite of the vigorous questioning by Lee to tell her side, the child had not uttered one single word since returning back alone from the convenience store.

"Try to stay calm. Let me do the talking," said Nick, reaching for Lee's hand.

She drew her hand back. She wanted answers, not his affection. "I just don't understand all this. What possible grounds could there be for him to leave her like he did?" she snapped.

"David wouldn't leave her alone without good reason."

Lee pointed at Tracie's blank expression. "I can't think of any reasons for that," she shouted, "God help him if he …"

NICK MARCIANO

"If he what?" Nick cut in, stopping her from completing her ugly accusation in front of Tracie. "That's my brother out there, not some stranger, so whatever poison you have building up inside your head, get rid of it now!"

What neither Nick nor Lee could understand was that David had changed, not so much physically, but mentally. The tragedies in his life had left him with inner scars. Throughout the past seven years, the combination of Diane and Cathy's death had placed him on the threshold of losing his mind, and now the sight of Cathy, whether real or fantasy, had plunged him into a twilight zone. It was now more convenient to overlook harsh realities such as the ashen look on Cathy's face as she rested peacefully inside her tiny coffin. His reasoning was now replaced by illogical thoughts. The sighting of his child had altered his mind to a point where common sense was, not only swept under the carpet, but it didn't even exist. Some would deem this the spark that would ultimately lead to insanity. To David, it was his daughter he saw; there wasn't anything crazy about him or what he saw.

"Oh my God, he is getting out of the car. I don't want him in my house!" cried Lee, grabbing hold of Tracie as though David was about to kidnap her.

"Stay put," ordered Nick when he saw his brother walking towards the patio. He swung the door open, and before David had a chance to walk in, cried out, "What's the matter with you? What were you thinking?"

Lee dashed out of the house. She angrily pointed her trembling finger at him. "How could you leave Tracie alone like that?" David reacted as though their outrage towards him was a secondary issue and that they would be better off yelling at the wall.

"She's alive." He smiled.

"What are you talking about?" cried Nick.

"Where's Tracie?" David asked, looking behind them, tempted to go inside the house to get her.

"Why?" Lee wanted to know, blocking his entrance.

Tracie appeared at the door. David looked directly at her. "Tracie," he softly said, "tell them who we saw."

Tracie took Lee's hand, lowered her head and ever so slightly moaned.

"Come on, sweetheart! Tell them!"

Nick tenderly placed his hand under her chin, attempting to raise her head, but she resisted, opting to maintain her stiff posture. Taken aback somewhat, Nick asked, "Who did you see? What is Uncle David talking about?"

"I don't like this," she murmured.

"Please don't do this to me, Tracie. We both saw her. You know it was her. Tell them, sweetheart," David pleaded.

Lee cringed when she heard him call her "sweetheart."

"Stop this!"

David quickly pointed at her in a rude and juvenile gesture. "I'm talking to Tracie, not you."

"What is Uncle David talking about? Baby, tell us," begged Nick.

"Both of you leave her alone!" Lee continued to shout.

Things were getting out of hand. Maybe David was asking too much, assuming that a youngster of Tracie's age would admit that she saw her dead cousin. He should have known better, perhaps chosen a better strategy than simply expecting her to admit to anything.

"It's all right, Tracie, no need to tell them. I will," he said before rubbing his face a number of times. "We saw my Cathy. She's not dead at all," he beamed, face glowing and waiting for their just response.

Nick backed away, shocked and with a bitter taste in his mouth, while Lee grabbed Tracie by the arm, pulled her inside the house, and slammed the door shut.

When Detective Wood finished her coffee, she didn't ask for a refill. Her day was long and formidable. Another cup would give her heartburn. It could have been worse had the Parkers been difficult. The detective found them to be the perfect witnesses, answering every question in detail, making it clear that they held no resentment but rather sought medical help for the man who chased after their child.

"Thank you for the coffee," she courteously said.

"Perhaps the other officer would like a coffee?" asked Florence, referring to the uniformed policeman standing by the door.

The policeman let the detective do his talking for him.

"I'm sure he's fine," she assured them.

"We heard that a young teenager may have taken photos of him inside the café." John said.

The detective explained, "It's not as easy as it sounds. Times have changed. You would think the teen would be anxious to give them to us, but apparently the man we are looking for is some sort of celebrity. At this moment the photos are in the care of that girl's lawyer who in turn is negotiating a deal with a trash magazine to sell them for God knows how much."

"Can they do that?"

"I'm afraid so, but it shouldn't make a difference. By the time we can legally retrieve them we should have our man. There were enough witnesses who saw his face. Soon a sketch of his face will appear on all the media outlets and make front page on all three major newspapers," she concluded before getting ready to leave.

Though Cathy had been through a chilling experience, the detective had to ask her one last time, "Are you sure you have never seen that man before?"

She got the same response, which was no comment, not a shake of a head, not a display of emotion, no reaction whatsoever.

"I think it best that she goes to bed now," suggested Florence.

"Yes, of course," agreed the detective. "You all have a good night, and not to worry. We will get this celebrity.

Tracie should have been in bed sleeping, but instead she was sitting halfway up the staircase. With pajamas on and a teddy bear taking the place of a pillow, she was resting her head on the step above, listening to the squabbling downstairs. She hoped that David would not mention anything about the missing egg, understanding that she had panicked and foolishly admitted that she saw Lee throwing it out. She quietly asked God to forgive her for being so weak when the time called for her to be so strong.

"That was her, I tell you. It was her. Everything about her was Cathy: the almonds on top of the ice cream cone, the way she ran, and the way she held on to her money. That was my Cathy!" cried David.

"And I'm telling you that they're going to lock you up!" Nick cried back, matching his brother's intensity.

"Why can't you believe me?" cried David. He was not known to be a violent man, but at this instant he felt like thrusting his fist through the wall.

"Cathy is dead!" Lee yelled back at him.

David swung his head at Lee and shot back. "Go and get Tracie! She'll tell you otherwise!"

"I told you to leave her out of this!"

The shouting was intense. Sentiments and hot tempers were demoralizing the prized respect this family held dearly for so long, and no one understood this better than Nick. He needed to put an end to this before damaging statements and cruel accusations slipped out, things that simply couldn't be taken back or forgiven.

"Stop it. Both of you!" he shouted.

"Oh my God!" continued Lee, pointing to the miniature television set, which was strapped under the kitchen cupboard. "David is on this channel too."

The three of them stared at the tiny screen, eyes glued on a handsome reporter holding on to a microphone and standing in front of the same trendy café that David was hiding in.

"It was inside that café"—he pointed—"that the child predator was last seen. Unfortunately, when the police gave chase he escaped through the back door and disappeared."

An artist's conception of David's face flashed on screen. Other than a few exaggerated features, such as the beginnings of a craggy beard and a dangerous frown, the resemblance was staggering. "Should you come across anyone who bears a likeness to this man, do not approach him. Contact the police immediately. He is considered armed and dangerous."

"That's nonsense," cried David, staring at Nick. "You know that's not true."

Lee removed the television remote control off its stand, turned off the television, and slammed the remote back onto the counter with such rage that the two batteries flew out. One battery struck Nick harmlessly on his shoulder and fell to the floor, the other bouncing off the wall and coming to a rolling stop next to David's feet.

"I can't deal with this. I'm going to bed." She wept, marching out of the kitchen and coming to a sudden stop at the bottom of the staircase when she saw Tracie. She placed her arms on her hips, glanced back at the brothers, and screamed, "I would like the both of you to know that she heard everything!" Enraged beyond reason, she sprinted up the staircase, took her child by the arm, dragged the poor girl up the remaining steps, and led her directly into her bedroom.

David picked up one of the batteries and gave it to Nick. "I'm sorry for getting Tracie involved like this," he apologized, "but she was there. If only she'd talk. If only she would tell you what she saw."

Nick fitted the batteries back into the remote control and placed it back on its stand. He then delicately rubbed the sides of his temples in an effort to sooth his pounding headache. "David," he calmly said, "Cathy is dead. We both saw her lying in the casket. We were both there when they lowered it into the ground. She is dead, and if Dad taught us anything, he made it known that no one ever really dies. Accept that she is gone from this world and is now in heaven with Diane." He took a needed breath. "Please don't take this the wrong way, but I know this really good psychiatrist. He's been helping Tracie to deal with Cathy's death. I think it would be in our best interests if I set a few appointments for you before things get out of hand. Think about it. It can't hurt, and following that we could all go on a vacation together."

David thought for a moment. "When were you thinking of going?"

Nick was unexpectedly surprised that he agreed so soon. "In a month, possibly two," he told him but secretly understood it would take longer before he could get David out of the legal entanglement he had got himself into. Between court appearances and psychiatric evaluations, he couldn't consider any realistic estimation.

"That might be too early, but I can see us going away in about eight to ten months," he predicted. "It will take at least that long before I'd want Cathy to be going anywhere."

It was a paralyzing and stunning reply, one which all but confirmed that Nick faced a much more complicated problem, one which could not be denied any longer. His much beloved little brother may have already entered the world of insanity.

CHAPTER EIGHT

David had been up since the crack of dawn and was now sitting in a familiar chair, inside a familiar waiting room. He needed to ask a favor from the only man that could help him. An appointment had not been requested, but he felt he didn't require one, not after his long association with this firm. He knew Mr. Steamer was available to see him now and was most likely sitting back in his black leather sofa with a brutish smirk on his face, making him wait for no reason other than for his own amusement. He wanted that new book from David and made it known he would not take his calls or see him until he brought in the fresh manuscript. Making him stew and sweat in the lobby was Mr. Steamer's payback.

Frustrated by the disrespect, David jumped up, startling the receptionist. "I need to go and see him now," he said firmly and would not accept no for an answer.

The woman cringed at being placed in this awkward position. She had heard of David, respecting his work, but on the other hand, she was told never to let anyone in without permission. "I'm sorry, Mr. Turner. He knows that you're here. You will just have to wait until he is ready to see you."

Ignoring her, David rushed past her desk and marched along the shiny hallway, the receptionist rapidly pacing behind, pleading with him to stop. His assumptions were correct. Mr. Steamer was not busy at all. When he swung the door open, he found him sitting comfortably on the sofa, next to his massive desk reading *Forbes Magazine*. Lora was not too far away, standing by the window ledge, watering the roses with an old rusty water pot. Mr. Steamer didn't seem disturbed by the interruption, rather he anticipated

David storming into his office as he did. Without removing his eyes from the magazine, he nonchalantly said, "Did you know that Bill Gates is no longer the richest man in the world? According to this magazine he isn't." He then looked up at David. "If he had asked for my advice, I can guarantee you that he wouldn't be a poor second," he added, as though this bit of news was a national catastrophe.

The receptionist stood by David's side, stressed and troubled, foreseeing retribution for not properly doing her job.

"I'm so sorry, Mr. Steamer. I told him to wait, but he just passed by me."

"No need to apologize, Miss Anderson. I know how rude this man can be. You can leave now."

Thankful of his understanding, she nervously smiled at everyone before shutting the door.

"Fire her immediately, and call security to keep an eye on her when she packs her belongings. I have always suspected that she was stealing pencils anyways," he told Lora.

"Yes, Mr. Steamer," she replied, resting the water pot on the floor, warmly smiling at David as she made her way out of the room.

"You, sir, have to be a receptionist's worst nightmare," Mr. Steamer joked, and as an afterthought added, "And don't waste my time telling me that I shouldn't have fired her. It's your fault that lady has no job." He threw the magazine on the table and sat down behind his desk."

David walked in, slow enough to catch a glimpse of the morning newspaper which lay next to the *Forbes Magazine*. On the front page was the artist's conception of David's face and in block letters asking, "DO YOU KNOW THIS MAN?" If Mr. Steamer suspected that he was that fugitive, as of yet, he kept it to himself.

"I need a favor. It's very important to me," he said, standing in front of his desk.

Mr. Steamer laughed heartily. "I can be so naïve at times. Here I thought you had come to surprise me with at least the first draft of a new manuscript, but instead you march into my office like a madman asking me for a favour. You've got some backbone on you, my dear friend, and since we are on that subject, when am I going to get my new book from you?"

The desire to write again had just barely returned and then vanished altogether the moment he saw Cathy again. At this moment he was not mentally capable of writing a sentence. "I will personally deliver the first draft when I can," he claimed, which in the publishing business could mean anywhere from an hour to never.

"Give me a date."

"As soon as I can is my date."

"Why do you insist of pushing me to the edge?" he asked.

"Will you do me this favour or not?"

Mr. Steamer stood up, grabbed the newspaper from the table, and sat back down. "What do you want from me now?" he asked, carefully studying the artist's conception of David.

He's teasing me. He knows that's me, David thought, but it didn't stop him from pulling a piece of paper from his shirt pocket and throwing it on the desk. "There's a license plate number written on there. I need the name and address that goes along with it. I know you can get it for me."

Mr. Steamer spread the newspaper wide open, flashing the front page in front of him. "I'm surprised. I would have thought you'd be asking me for a different favor."

Feeling it best not to challenge his openhanded overtones, David did not reply.

"The ears are all wrong. They are a bit too pointy, making this fugitive look like Mr. Spock," he said, engulfed by his own wit. "If I was this wanted man, I'd sue him, whoever drew this."

David could feel his belittling, which was not satisfying enough for him; now Mr. Steamer was toying with him much like a cat would with an injured mouse before devouring it. It shouldn't have surprised him. After all, this was a man who feasted on other's agonies, possessing the haunting skill to predict events before they even happened.

"If I was that wanted man I would sue him as well," said David, continuing with his game.

"Of course you would," he replied, picking up the phone. Whomever he called was on speed dial, answering immediately. He shouted out the license plate number, ending with, "Give me everything you have on the owner of these plates," then hung up and turned to David. "It will take a few minutes."

"Thank you."

"Did you know that the phrase *thank you* was invented by the insecure?" he seriously asked, adding, "One weakens oneself by saying those two pitiful words."

David expected that from him. It wasn't anything new. His only wish was that the phone would ring with the name and address he yearned for and then to leave.

"No need to be so restless. You will get what you need in minutes. In the meantime sit down. I have something to share with you."

"I can hear you standing up just as well."

"I would prefer for you to sit down," he insisted.

David convinced himself that it wasn't intimidation that made him sit, but rather blamed it on the forth-coming information he had to have. He didn't want to give him any excuse to change his mind. In all honesty, he didn't care what Mr. Steamer needed to share with him. Most likely it would be more of his sarcasm or his ranting and raving regarding matters that only made sense to him.

Using his feet, Mr. Steamer wheeled his chair close to the out-side window and stretched his neck down below. "Have you ever noticed the neon sign on top of the four-story brick building?"

"The street is filled with buildings and neon signs."

"The neon sign I'm referring to is over twenty feet by four feet. Day and night, twenty-four hours a day, that billboard never stops flashing."

David knew the one. It was the advertising sign coming from *The National Gossip Magazine* building, notorious for harassing and writing trash on celebrities. Immoral by all standards, anyone with a decent intelligence level despised that magazine for its sensationalism since it only published half-truths and outright lies. They didn't employ proper reporters. Basically anyone who walked into that office was considered part of the staff, but only if they had gossip to sell. The editors depended on those desperados to harass celebrities and bring back with them all compromising photos along with any associated filth. These human parasites made the paparazzi appear tame in comparison.

"You mean the gossip place?" he replied distastefully.

"Call it what you will, but I call it my money-making machine," Mr. Steamer said turning away from the window and facing David. "I own that magazine, and it makes me a disgusting fortune. Three million copies faithfully go out each and every week. Every person from trailer trash to the rich, including bored housewives read it. Even the president of the United States was rumored to be caught reading it on Air force One," he bragged as though his magazine was an addictive drug.

David wasn't surprised that he owned that magazine as well. It wouldn't shock him if he owned the whole block, including the sewers and the rats that infested them. His wealth and prosperity didn't interest him at all. He was more interested in the phone call, which suddenly came. He jerked forward, anticipating that Mr. Steamer would readily answer it.

"That's not the call you're waiting for," claimed Mr. Steamer, calmly allowing it to ring.

"It has to be somebody," snapped David, tempted to pick it up.

"It wasn't your call," insisted Mr. Steamer after it stopped ringing.

David had the urge to ask him how he knew, but in a strange and unconventional way, he believed him.

Mr. Steamer focused his attention back outside at the *National Gossip Magazine* building. "You wouldn't believe what goes on in that building. As early as four in the morning the lineup starts, sometimes reaching two blocks by nine. They all claim to have the latest on celebrity breast implants gone badly or any other cosmetic surgery that could possibly backfire on a human body. Most is not worth a penny," he continued, grinning when recalling a certain case. "One time a college kid took a photo of a well-known actor, air brushed his shirt, and tattooed a monstrous swastika on his back. The little weasel then tried to convince us that this actor was financing skinheads. It was done so well that he almost had us convinced, but once in a while some prime scandal finds its way in. So moneyed that it becomes a problem for me. How ironic is that?"

"Why are you telling me these things? They have nothing to do with me."

Mr. Steamer sneered. "I didn't say they did, so if you would stop interrupting and get rid of that attitude, I could finish." Wheeling himself back to his desk and placing his hands back on top, he whispered, "Thirty minutes ago, a teenager, her mother, and their lawyer negotiated a hefty fee with my chief editor for some damaging photos taken of a wanted celebrity inside a café."

David's body tensed. *Stay calm, stay calm. He didn't identify you as the fugitive,* he thought over and over, ironically wanting to thank him for not doing so.

"The cost was high, but I bought all the photos, including the phone she used to take them. I would have bought the girl herself if I had to."

David rubbed his face. Mr. Steamer was highly intelligent. He knew what he was doing and had his reason for purchasing the photos. "I still don't know what this has to do with me," he insisted.

Mr. Steamer chuckled at his remark, "The photos are of a once very successful man who now has allegations hanging over his head that he may be a child predator. We both know it's you on the front page, David."

"I am not a child predator!" he angrily replied, slamming his fist on the desk and knocking over a small silver trophy that paid tribute to Mr. Steamer.

Mr. Steamer stared at the toppled trophy. "That trophy was given to me by a dear friend, and if I told you his name, it would amaze you," he said before flipping it back on its stand.

Uneasy and not thinking rationally, David wondered how far Mr. Steamer was going to take this. They both knew that if he so desired, he would be locked up by now. Perhaps he had already contacted the police, this frustrating chatter only a ploy to keep him there until they stormed through that door.

"We have had our ups and downs in the past, but you have to know that what they say about me is all lies."

"I am in the media business, David, where the truth is boring, and where sensationalism makes money. Honesty can't even buy me a cup of coffee. I have the power to sell your pictures and make a killing. Before you know it, a panel of experts will be interviewed by Larry King on CNN. He would pull on his suspenders before asking them to give the viewers their professional opinion as to how a once successful man could possibly transform into a monster that preys on children." He paused, rested back on his chair; then, either as an afterthought or to flaunt his ego, he stated, "You would be surprised by the amount of dirty little secrets I have accumulated over the years from people like you."

David swallowed, pausing before asking. "What are you going to do with the photos of me?"

Mr. Steamer rested his head back on the chair. "It's too early to tell," he replied. "What do you think I should do?"

"Would it matter what I think?"

"Not one bit," he smiled.

The phone rang. "That's your call," he confirmed before answering it. Words were not exchanged; rather he wrote down a name and address on David's piece of paper, hanging up immediately after. "The person you're looking for is a minister by the name of John Parker. He lives in a house adjacent to his church," he said, sluggishly dragging the piece of paper in circles towards David before leaving it at the edge of his desk.

David picked it up, turned around, and walked away.

"If you get caught I will have a computer sent to you. You might as well finish my book or two while serving time," Mr. Steamer smirked, relishing the last word, as he always liked to do.

David walked out of his office and eventually reached the lobby. When he passed Miss Anderson's desk, he couldn't help but notice two muscular security guards standing behind her, arms folded, watching her every move while she packed her belongings. It was safe to say that Mr. Steamer would not lose any pencils due to employee theft. Not today.

This aging church had a dual purpose. It served as a place of worship, also having the distinction of being the home to three generations of the Parker family. Jacob Parker originally built it from ground up in the Depression era—the infamous dirty thirties with practically no resources and very little money. He bartered, giving the homeless and the poor a meal in the evening in exchange for them mixing cement in the day.

When he passed away, his son Mark had the church extended, adding a playroom for the children. Following a long awaited government grant, he then cleared approximately two acres of the land next to the church and transformed it into a small cemetery. When he died, the church was then willed to his son, John Parker, who had lived there ever since.

Over time John's reputation was one of honor and trust. If a troublesome teenager was swaying towards the wrong direction, John would be there in a heartbeat, steering the teen back towards the righteous path. Whether members of his congregation or just a neighbor of a different faith, everyone generally agreed that John Parker retained an enormous gift: the ability to persuade and to prevent tormented souls from crossing that line—that evil world of temptation, a place the devil himself created.

This minister had the talent to triumph over the troubled, capturing their ears, and persuading them that his way was the Lord's way. He had been credited with saving the marriage of many after they had confessed their lustful intentions to him. That was John Parker, a good, decent man.

Twenty-four hours had passed since the Parkers experienced that bizarre incident at the conservation area. They talked about it in great length, both concluding that it shouldn't have any bearing on their lifestyle, not now nor in the future. Despite police warnings to always be aware of their surroundings, they courageously refused to permit the actions of a sick man to disrupt their everyday life, and in spite of Detective Wood's insistence, they declined the police protection the family was entitled to. A police car stationed in front of the church twenty-four hours a day did not sit well with the Parkers. It was one obstruction they didn't want their members to be subjected to.

At any rate, this was Friday night and would be spent as all other Friday nights had been in the past. Police cautions and other warnings needed to take a backseat. This evening was reserved for eating out and spending the night at one of the few remaining outdoor drive-in theaters still in existence in all of California. This special evening was a Parker tradition started with their own daughter, but when she became a victim to cancer, Friday nights became just another night. Only when Cathy entered the household did they resume this practice, to spend five hours at an old fashioned drive-in theatre. Under the stars, a family with small children could enjoy a relatively inexpensive meal and at the same time watch two films on the mammoth white screen. There was never a dull moment with these kids. The constant back and forth trips to the washroom, the begging for more popcorn, and the inevitable bickering between kids at the end of the night. Most of them fell asleep before the film ended, but this was all part of the charm.

Florence and Cathy were inside the car waiting for John to lock all the doors before leaving. "Watch him closely," Florence grinned.

Cathy kept her eyes fastened on the front door of the building, anticipating John's appearance at any moment. She wanted to see for herself the habit Florence claimed he had developed over the years. When he did emerge, Florence turned to Cathy. "Watch closely, or you'll miss it," she repeated. As she predicted, the moment he reached the bottom of the stairs, he stopped, paused for a second or two and then in his own unique way twisted his body around and faced the garage.

"I don't think he even realizes he's doing that." Florence laughed.

Cathy stopped giggling long enough to say, "That was so funny."

The church came with seven doors. John locked six, always forgetting to lock the seventh door leading from the garage into the house. He either had to go back inside the building to secure it shut or enter the garage to lock it from the inside. He didn't need reminding of just how difficult it had become to raise the garage's sliding door. It was practically falling apart. The wheels had rusted over the years; the uneven track was forever seizing up, requiring physical strength to lift.

A month didn't go by without him cutting his hand on the handle when hauling it up. His dried bloodstains on the ground just below the handle were a testament to that. He had already put in a good day's work, first by cutting the grass and then by digging up a portion of the garden. The thought of lifting the garage door in order to lock that door inside didn't sit well with him; therefore, he decided to leave it unlocked for this night. He walked to the car but didn't enter.

Before each and every trip he would calmly stroll around the Plymouth, proudly giving it that "good for another five years" look and at the same time kick the tires. He would also look under the car, always finding an oil spot or two on the ground and convincing himself it originated from another vehicle.

"We're going to be late," cried out Florence.

He quickly got up, clapped the dust off his hands, and walked around to the driver's window. "There's a spot of oil on the ground, but I don't think it's coming from the Plymouth," he said, entering the car.

It didn't occur to either one to check what film was showing at the drive-in theatre. If it wasn't *Little Mermaid*, then *The Lion King* or *Shrek* would do. Most likely they already had the same animated movie on DVD, collecting dust somewhere inside the house.

David had been hiding inside the ravine since leaving Mr. Steamer's office and would continue to do so until dusk. He couldn't think of a better place to hide. Though million-dollar homes, including his own, surrounded this forested grove, it had also become a haven for men like those two eyeing him from across the shallow creek. The intimidating drifters sat on a rock, side-by-side, mumbling to each other from the corner of their mouths and smirking at him. These two were not the harmless kind that one might find on a street corner with a tin can in hand and a sign around their neck reading, "Need money to eat" in big block letters. These two thugs belonged in a mental institution, not outside meddling with the general public. The present leftists politicians with their sixties mentality still intact had passed a series of thoughtless acts. They believed everyone could be rehabilitated and released back into society, and with a bit of understanding even those two deranged men staring back at David were curable. They were wrong.

Sitting on a dry patch of grass, David was staring back at them. Though he was a good seventy-five feet away, it was simple to detect that one had a face covered with scars. He suspected it was due to years of hostility mixed with the lack of basic nourishments. The other one had a larger than normal reddish nose, covered with blisters, some so large that they could have been mistaken for warts. He recalled his father warning him that that physical defect was due to excessive alcohol drinking.

Feeling more uneasy than frightened, he wished they would stop scrutinizing him and leave. He had too many things on his mind, and these two were just adding to them.

The drifters finally jumped off the rock and aggressively waved at him, giving a shaky performance as two amicable neighbors, kindly offering their friendship. When he didn't wave back, the scarred one yelled something at him, his speech so slurred that David wasn't sure what was howled at him. When the drifter ran his finger across his own throat, he realized it was a threat. The other one stopped at the edge of the creek, pointing at David's feet and yelling, "Nice shoes, mister."

Sheltered throughout his life and inexperienced at potential dangers similar to the one he faced now, he wasn't sure of his next move.

"Thank you," he shouted back at them, prompting the scarred one to unleash a mouthful of damning words, half of which he never knew existed. And then, for no apparent reason, it all ended. They simply turned around and disappeared into a wall of thick bush.

David breathed a sigh of relief and sat down at his original spot. He was hungry and tired, forgetting the last time he had eaten or slept. He couldn't go back home because by now Mr. Steamer would be screaming at his printers to get his photo out as quickly as possible. With his face plastered on the front page of every newspaper, going back home was like walking into the arms of the law.

The cell phone rang. He pulled it out of his top shirt pocket, checked the screen and noticed it was Nick. He knew what to expect from him and was prepared.

"Hi, Nick," he softly answered.

Nick didn't waste time. He got right to the point. "First of all keep in mind that others may be listening to this conversation," he pointed out in reference that the call might be bugged. "Secondly, are you all right?"

"I'm fine. No need to worry."

Nick chose his words carefully. "A Detective Wood was here."

David guessed it was the female detective he saw in the café. "What did she want?"

Nick cringed. Whoever was listening would ask how David knew Detective Wood was female, unless it was actually him who was inside that café. At this point David was his own worst enemy. Nick needed to keep this conversation brief. "Listen to me. I just called to make sure you were all right and to tell you not to worry. Things are getting taken care of. I need you to call me tomorrow morning and let me know where you are. I'll pick you up and take you to the nearest police station. I already called my lawyer, and he will meet us there to make sure the correct things are said."

David had made plans for tonight. As far as where he would end up tomorrow, he had no idea. "I want you to know that I appreciate everything you're trying to do for me, but I'm not sick. That was Cathy, and if anybody is listening, I want them to know that as well."

To his credit, Nick remained calm. He was already ahead of the game in case things took a turn for the worst and David was charged with any offence. Earlier that morning he had met with a doctor and his lawyer. In short, it was agreed by the three that the doctor would claim that David was suffering from severe depression. That's when the lawyer would take over to negotiate the best possible deal with the prosecutor. With a bit of luck, the two would conclude that since David had no criminal record, he might have to spend a month or two in a hospital with six to twelve months probation added at the end.

"You have to work with me, David. This is no good," explained Nick, biting his lip.

David didn't want his brother to get into any more trouble than he may already be in. Lee would never survive without him. This was his problem, his crisis, and he would handle it as he saw fit.

"I believe it's better for the both of us if you didn't contact me anymore. Go back to your family. I will be fine, and never forget that I love you."

"Don't do this to me," replied Nick before his phone went dead.

David walked at the creek's bank, pitched the cell phone as far as he could, and watched it submerge into the river. He took out the piece of paper with John Parker's address written on it, needing to remind himself that he was not doing anything he considered illegal. His only desire was for things to be the way they once were. No one was going to get hurt.

His next step would be considered unthinkable a year ago. But that was then. This was now.

At times Mr. Steamer's actions resembled a chess game: what would he do? What should his next move be? Would his final choice be the correct one, or would he regret it later? Regarding the Turners, things were moving quickly, and time was running out. Without any tangible decision yet made, Mr. Steamer remained calm, lying on the sofa, deep in thought, eyes wide open.

For the past hour he had scrutinized and dissected every option made available to him, confident he had made the right choice only then to think it was a ridiculous idea two minutes later. Something about the minister bothered him, but he couldn't put his finger on it, and now found himself second-guessing his earlier decision at placing Cathy in the minister's care.

If experience had taught him anything, he had learned that each personality could be compared to a fingerprint; there were no two alike. Each soul reacted differently when confronted with temptation, each one possessed certain limitations; the frail ones were predictable, while the strong ones flourished. It was a matter of record that over time the Turners were exceptional and did well, but what of John Parker? He hoped these feelings he had about him were wrong, but should John prematurely fail, would he allow the child to be adopted out again? She was fast approaching that age, that borderline phase in her development that was most sensitive. David schooled her well, and, up to this point, so had the Parkers, but was it enough? Was the child ready to move forward? Did she really need to be adopted again if John Parker failed or was she now ready to be moved forward onto her next stage of her development?

Such was the life of Mr. Steamer and would forever be. He had been down this road many times before; so many that if it were to be tallied, the final number would even astound a mathematician. His responsibilities were like no other, and it was moments like this when he felt weighed down and lonely. He wished that perhaps the Creator would one day amend the procedure, permitting him to fill a boardroom with elders, and together they would advise him of the positives and negatives of his decisions. But such was not the case, nor would it ever be. Since lives and the future of many could be affected, the final verdict had to come from him. He had never known the Almighty to be upset if he blundered, but it would leave a bitter taste in his mouth if God were disappointed in him.

Lora stepped into the office carrying with her a briefcase. Mr. Steamer sprang up from the sofa. The sole purpose of their meeting was for her to log and document his thoughts and his pending decisions into the Book of Records. This book was sanctified and read only by the Almighty himself; although rumors persisted that occasionally he would ask one of his elderly advisers to read it alongside him as well.

Upon exchanging smiles she sat in the opposite chair, placing her briefcase down, removing the Book of Records and opening it at the appropriate page. With pen in hand she asked, "I take it a decision has been reached?"

"Yes," he replied with a troubled look on his face. "My decision is to hold off making a decision for the time being."

A slight pause followed from the both of them; Lora, not quite certain if she was to log anything down; he in turn studying her face for any reaction. He found none.

"Shall I document your non decision?" she asked.

"I would think not. I cannot think of a more boring read for our Father."

She closed the sacred book and carefully placed it back into the briefcase.

"Do you agree, or do you think of it as cowardly of me to play it safe?" he asked.

She felt honored for simply being asked. Mr. Steamer had been known to do such unexpected things, to show a side of him that others didn't know existed. "I believe that things should not be documented until it is felt that they should be. I do not consider that cowardly at all."

With this stalemate temporarily out of his way, he had another problem that could not wait: "As far as David is concerned, can you kindly get me Detective Wood on the phone?" he asked.

"Will she need the twins?"

"Yes. I think it would be wise. She may need their help."

The twins were two young police officers whose age was difficult to determine. They seemed to be in their late twenties but were easily thousands of years older. Only Mr. Steamer knew of their true age. Their appearance was a throwback in time and could best be identified with the athletes pictured on an old fifties National Football League collecting card. Both sported old-fashioned crew cuts and possessed broad shoulders, but they could also be mistaken for modern day wrestling heroes. Underneath all that strength and threatening looks, they loved to laugh, and when they did, the gentle side of them became evident.

David took a final glance at the church as his Jag passed it for the fourth time. He saw no need to bypass it a fifth, coming to a stop roughly two hundred feet away. He parked parallel to the adjacent cemetery that was filled with crosses and aged headstones from the past, a far cry from the impeccable cemetery where Diane rested.

To his relief, the Parkers were not home. All the church lights were off except for the sole bulb hanging from the garage door, and even that was dim, barely bright enough to light a small portion of the driveway. There was another minor source of light: a small bulb inside a plastic advertising sign, directly in front of the building. On that sign were written the times and dates of the regular services, the next bingo session, and the future bake sales that were not to be missed.

He noticed an elm tree that had long branches dangling down, touching the pavement and thought it a good place to hide the car.

He drove underneath it; the sound of leaves dragging along the roof was of no concern to him. Shutting off the ignition, he studied the church, counting doors, windows, sizing them up, imagining himself inside and that when the time came to leave, he would be carrying Cathy out with him.

The half a dozen homes surrounding the church were far and few between; the silence welcomed with only the distance whistle of a train and the sound of illusive crickets, the only noises of the night.

He got out of the car, parted some of the branches away from his face and began to inspect the building; his primary goal was finding Cathy's bedroom and hide inside until the Parkers got home. The serious consequences he'd be faced with for breaking and entering never dawned on him.

Such thoughts were far from his mind. He had never broken the law in his life, and did not consider this to be illegal now. He had tried the civilized and rational way to get his daughter back, but no one would listen. Breaking into a stranger's home to get her back was, not only justified, but it was also something that any father would do.

Rather than go directly to the front door, he cut to the side and walked along the cemetery, bumping into the odd headstone along the way. Following his instincts, he tried the rear doors and windows first but discovered they were much more solid than they appeared.

The church may have been built decades ago, but it was constructed like a fortress. Only one door remained: the front door.

Suffering another setback when he found that door to be as rigid as the rest, he walked back to the right side and wondered if there was an entrance inside the garage that may lead to the house.

Since leaving the drive-in, John Parker had tried to avoid all bumps on the highway, but occasionally he would hit a stretch of road that was rough, sending the Plymouth into a jet like turbulence. Sometimes it shook so violently that John had to slow the car down to twenty miles an hour in order to regain control.

"When are you going to get that fixed?" asked Florence.

He knew that question was coming and was prepared to give her the same answer as always. "It's almost impossible to find shock absorbers for this model anymore. But I'm still looking."

The next few miles of road were recently paved and smooth, affording him the time to check up on Cathy. He looked in the rearview mirror and wasn't surprised to see that she was in a deep sleep. With her arms wrapped around her half-eaten bag of precious popcorn, and her head slanted slightly to the side; she appeared heavenly.

He poked Florence on the arm. "Just look at her."

Florence momentarily unstrapped her seatbelt and turned around to see the same endearing sight; a lovely little girl holding on to her popcorn as though it was the last meal she had left to eat for months to come. She watched Cathy sway back and forth to the rhythm of the Plymouth, took a deep breath and said, "It makes me want to go in the back, sit close to her, and rest her head on my shoulder."

John smiled, "Please put your seatbelt back on."

For the next minute or so, not much was discussed between husband and wife until John said, "I'll have to visit Mrs. Stonestreet Sunday evening. Her son, Dean, has agreed to replace the garage door."

John Parker's house of prayer was forever in constant need of repair, but he had devised a somewhat similar concept as his grandfather had before him. His followers would volunteer their time and skill at repairing the church. In return he would contribute his time, making house calls and conducting private sermons for their families, just as he was doing with Mrs. Stonestreet. This simple understanding between members of the church and its minister was a win-win situation for both parties.

"Thank God. I was always fearful that one day you would lose a finger on that handle."

"Mrs. Stonestreet loves your carrot cake. If you bake some I'll take it with me on Sunday evening."

"Cathy and I can bake it Sunday afternoon after the service."

"I shouldn't be too long. Perhaps an hour or two," he assured her and then added, "That poor woman is not doing so well."

"You might have to have a talk with her family about placing her in a home."

"Dean is stubborn, but you have to respect him. He told me that the only time she will ever be put in a home is when she doesn't recognize she's in a home."

"Sooner or later they will have to hire a live-in nanny to look after her," Florence added.

Florence peeled back the bed sheet and adjusted the pillow. She was adamant at perfecting the small cushy bundle in the middle, just the way Cathy liked it. Within seconds, John would be carrying her up the stairs and placing her in bed, God willing, without awaking her. She then lowered her hand inside a miniature trunk, which stood next to the bed, pulled out Cathy's favorite plaything, a stuffed doll, and rested it next to the pillow.

John came in, carrying Cathy in his arms, one soft step at a time, never in a wave but more of a floating motion. "She's still in a deep sleep," he whispered, proud of the fact that he had carried her all the way up from the car without waking her. He lowered her tiny body onto the bed, tenderly bringing down her legs and arms first before lowering her head in the middle of the pillow.

"Don't worry about her clothes," Florence told him, removing Cathy's shoes and quickly swinging the sheets over her body before tucking the ends firmly underneath the mattress.

The two of them stood back, admiring her and mumbling the Lord's Prayer together, thanking God for the precious child he had blessed them with and took turns kissing her good night before leaving the room. When they reached their own bedroom, John recalled that the garage door was left unlocked.

"I'll be right back," he said making his way back downstairs.

They were insignificant, almost unnoticeable at first, but as John got closer to the garage entrance, they became apparent; there were indeed bloodstains on the floor.

Ultimately they became more obvious, some larger than others, some in a perfect circle while others formed an irregular pattern. The sight was disturbing, but it didn't frighten him. Not until they turned into small puddles did he become alarmed. More of an instinctive reaction than anything else, he raised both arms and checked underneath to see if he was bleeding, realizing it was next to impossible since he came in through the front door. He knew of a family of rabbits just behind the church, always trying to escape the jaws of roaming wild coyotes and wondered if one of them had been injured, somehow finding its way into the garage.

"*It has happened before*," he thought, convincing himself this was the case.

Unsure of what to expect next, he cautiously opened the garage door, switched the light on, and stepped inside. The trail of blood ended under the overhead door handle. He briefly considered calling the police and would do so if he hadn't noticed rabbit droppings along the concrete floor.

It had to be a rabbit, he thought, dismissing this whole thing as a sporadic incident. He was on all fours, scrubbing the stains off the floor when he heard Florence shout out, "When are you coming to bed?"

It might have sounded like a peaceful night, but if someone with acute hearing was inside Cathy's room, standing next to the closet, they would hear heavy inhaling, a pause, and then prolonged exhaling. This noise was caused by repeated breaths of stale air. Those sounds and the wheezing that followed belonged to David Turner.

The closet was tight to begin with, and with a shelf installed midway for Cathy's shoes, it made it more agonizing for a grown man to hide in. On several occasions he had tried to stretch his arm inside this limited place only to wince in pain when pulling back. The soreness he had to endure did not hurt as much as overhearing the Parkers talk about his baby in the loving manner in which they did.

He ran his fingers up along the door's edge until they reached the horizontal handle, raising it just enough to hear a clicking sound. It unlocked. Holding his stomach in, he squeezed out the hurt and stiffness adding resentment towards the Parkers. Adding to his woes, the towel wrapped around his injured hand was soaked in blood. There was no pain when he cut it on the garage door handle, but now it was pounding, evenly matched by the pounding beat of his heart.

Standing only a few feet from Cathy made him forget his pains. She came across as the most startling child on the face of this earth. Watching her sleep in that peaceful way practically made him cry when realizing just how much he had missed her. He took a few steps towards the bed and lowered his face near hers, grateful that she appeared unhurt.

"I'm never going to leave you again, sweetheart," he thought, bringing his hand near her face, barely touching her, yet yearning to hug her. A year was a long time; there was so much he wanted to say to her, so much that she needed to pass on to him. He then noticed a pair of scissors lying on top of the table. Next to the scissors was a tube of glue, half used crayons and a series of small pictures that had been cut out from a science magazine. It appeared she had been working on a school project in relation to the stars in heaven; so typical of his princess. With fingers barely sticking out of the bloody towel, he picked up the scissors, carefully rotating them. They were of the small dull kind, designed especially for children. It didn't matter. They would do what he needed them to do, to cut a tiny lock off her hair and shove the strands deep inside his pocket where no one could find them.

Detective Wood loathed riding in a speeding cruiser but was aware of cases where a second either way could make all the difference between a tragic or peaceful ending. She feared that David Turner, the suspect, might panic if placed in a desperate position, the most unpredictable and dangerous of situations facing them.

"How much longer?" she asked one of the twins next to her, never losing her cool.

"Four more blocks," he replied turning the corner at such speed that the two outside wheels practically tipped off the ground, sliding the detective against the passenger door. When the car leveled off, she picked up the microphone, looked behind at the other twin that followed, and firmly ordered, "Look for that black Jaguar. When found, box it in. We will take the rear. If the suspect is inside his car, do not approach him. If David Turner is not in the car, do not go into the church. I repeat, do not go inside the church."

With the last right hand turn completed, the detective was surprised to find the Jag parked right there for them to see, under an elm tree, approximately two hundred feet from the church. As ordered, the driver slammed on the brakes a mere foot from the Jag's rear while the other cruiser stopped in front, boxing the Jag in. If David was inside the car, he wasn't going anywhere.

"Do not draw your weapons," the detective cried out. "He may have the girl with him." She swung open the car door, quickly leading the way while the twin officers followed closely, with hands on their guns, none drawn, as the detective had ordered. Displaying poise, she pointed the flashlight inside the Jag. Neither the suspect nor the child was inside. She then walked to the hood of the car and placed her hand on top. It was cold, signifying that the car had been parked at that same spot for a long time.

"He's inside the church," she said displaying the first sign of uneasiness.

The trunk of the cruiser was opened. One of the twins removed the door slammer, a slang term used for the four-inch, reinforced steel pipe used to smash locked doors open.

David placed every single picture that was cut out of the magazine inside Cathy's pink purse, including the bottle of glue, the scissors, and crayons. Her school project would be completed, at her rightful home, not here at a stranger's home.

It began as a very low toned moan, but he was aware of it immediately. He heard that whimper many times before, and it meant only one thing. His daughter was waking up, and he couldn't be more pleased. Her eyes opened, slightly at first, just enough to see him staring back down at her. She remained motionless and calm, not at all startled by his presence.

"Hello, baby," he beamed in utter delight.

Why didn't she spring up, take hold of his neck, and pull him down to kiss him as she had done many times before? Why did she look at him as though he was alien, not blinking, not grinning, just a blank expression on her face?

"Cathy. It's me, Daddy. Don't you recognize me, baby?"

She would not acknowledge him, choosing to remain still.

"I've come to take you home," he told her, lifting her purse but failing to remember that his hand was wrapped in the blood-soaked towel. The sight of blood was enough to stir up her emotions, her blue eyes wide with fright. He quickly shifted the purse to his other hand, hiding the injured one behind his back. "My hand got cut on a silly garage door. It's nothing," he told her, hoping that would put her at ease. It didn't. She still looked frightened by the sight of his wound. "You can finish your school project at home," he quickly added, infuriated by his own stupidity.

The child gradually removed the covers, ready to get out of the bed. Offering his hand, he warmly said. "Give me your hand. Daddy will help you get up."

She was unreceptive, not willing to accept it, making him wonder if he was expecting too much, too soon. He gave her added breathing room by taking two steps backwards. It seemed to help. She moved one leg towards the edge of the bed and paused, waiting for him to move farther away before getting completely off and planting her feet firmly onto the floor.

"That's it, love. Let's get out of here. We can go to Uncle Nick's house. It doesn't matter how late it is. I will convince Aunt Lee to wake up Tracie so you two can play."

The need to touch his daughter was overwhelming, too difficult to resist. Moving forward, he erased the progress made so far when she quickly lowered her head in submission.

He stopped at once. "No, baby. Don't do that. Lift up your head, and look at me. It's your daddy. Don't be frightened," he pleaded. She wouldn't compromise; rather she backed up to the extreme corner of the room. When her back touched the wall, she slid down, placing herself into a semi-fetal pose by lifting her knees and wrapping her arms around them. She then buried her head into her knees and remained that position.

Watching her in that state horrified David.

Oh my God, he thought in disbelief. *What have they done to her?*

Convinced that his daughter needed to be rushed to the hospital, he moved forward, stopping at her feet. When lowering his hand to help her up, she appeared frightened of the possible contact, and though her head remained buried between her knees, the moment she felt the heat from his hand, she began to shake at the prospect that the two may actually touch. He never got the opportunity, for at the doorway stood Florence and John Parker.

"Get away from her!" shouted Florence.

David immediately recognized the two, despising them for brainwashing Cathy the way they had. He was so enraged by the sheer sight of them that for the first time in his life he felt an urge to punish, to hurt, to seek revenge.

"What did you do to my daughter?" he screamed back with clenched fists.

Florence noticed his blood-soaked towel and thought of the worst.

"Oh my God!" she yelled at the top of her lungs. "Oh my God, John! Look at his hand!"

Unaccustomed to violence, John did what came naturally. He shielded his wife, placing himself in front of her, and with a powerful voice never used before in his entire life shouted, "Get away from our daughter!"

"She's my daughter!" David quickly shot back.

They both moved forward. A confrontation was inevitable. Two normally peaceful men finding themselves a violet circumstance, ready to fight, not able to resist a father's instinct to protect their loved one. David grabbed a small chair next to him, raised it over his head, in turn John was ready to thrust himself at him, but it all came to an abrupt end with the sound of a thunderous boom directly below the bedroom, shaking the entire house. Loud yelling, followed by rapid footsteps racing up the stairs were heard. Florence ran to the top of the stairs, saw the two burly officers climbing towards her, two steps at a time, and pointed towards Cathy's room.

"He's in there. Please hurry!" she cried out.

Before David could even react, the twins shoved John aside and darted straight at him. He was about to explain his side of the story but didn't get the opportunity. It all ended in seconds. The officers easily overpowered him, first tackling him to the ground, forcing his arms behind his back, and then slapping a set of handcuffs on him.

"You're arresting the wrong man!" he yelled, but they didn't want to hear anything he said. The fact that the towel fell off his injured hand and the bleeding began again did not stop them. They each took one elbow, harshly lifted him off the floor and brutally forced his face against the wall.

"Cathy! For God's sake, tell them who I am!"

Cathy raised her head, staring at the twins aggressively manhandling him. Her heart ached. She reacted the only way she was allowed to. She wept for him and for everything that had happened.

Detective Wood appeared at the door's entrance. She analyzed the situation. David was subdued and no longer a threat, the Parkers, though horrified, where unhurt. She then focused her attention to the little girl, thankful that she appeared unhurt.

"Are you two all right?" she asked the Parkers.

Florence held on to her husband, bitterly pointing at David.

"That's the same man from the conservation area!" she firmly cried out, ready to run to Cathy but was held back by the Detective.

"Can I please just have a few words with her first?" asked Detective Wood.

Florence faced John, still visibly shaken and seeking his guidance. He wrapped his arm around her shoulder to calm her down and slowly pulled her away, giving the detective access to Cathy.

"Hello there," the detective said, smiling at Cathy.

Cathy took her time. When she eventually raised her head, the detective asked, "Can you tell me something that is very important to me?"

Cathy slowly nodded.

"Did that man over there hurt you?" she softly asked. "Did he hurt you in any way?"

Cathy shook her head, indicating no.

"I'm going to ask you one more question, and then you can go to your mommy. Is that all right with you?"

Cathy nodded yes.

"Have you ever seen that man before?" she asked pointing at David.

"Tell the lady who I am," David pleaded, knowing full well that she had never lied before.

The annoyed detective looked back at him. "You're blowing your one and only chance, Mr. Turner. I would suggest you be quiet. I'll be there soon enough." She faced Cathy again. "Have you, sweetie? Have you ever seen that man before?"

Although the question was a straightforward one, it totally frustrated her and when she opened her mouth to speak, she stared at David and shut it again without uttering a word. Overwhelmed by it all, she once again lowered her head onto her knees and wept louder.

"She can't lie!" screamed David. "That's why she's crying! Can't you see that? Can't you all see that!"

The Parkers had seen enough and were not prepared to see Cathy tormented any longer.

"No more questions," insisted John. His wife then ran to the child and helped her to her feet.

"Get away from her!" David yelled but was left helpless to watch in agony as one of the twins escorted Florence and Cathy out of the room. He looked at the detective and asked, "Why are you doing this to me?" before emotionally caving in and repeatedly moaning Cathy's name.

"Read him his rights," the detective told the officer before he took David away.

"Why does that man insist that Cathy is his daughter?" John Parker asked.

"I'm not sure, but I will find out."

CHAPTER NINE

It was a beautiful Saturday morning, typical of a June day when the sun's rays finally reached the upper window and shone inside David's cell. Every so often he would move his body, a few inches at a time, following the rays and absorbing their soothing warmth on his face.

When they past him and began climbing the concrete wall next to the bed, it told him that morning was coming to an end, but he still didn't get up, preferring to stay as he was, lying in bed with his healthy hand used as a pillow. The pillow that came with the cell, although appearing clean, still had a repulsive smell to it, and the thought of how many heads had rested on it before him bothered him. Eventually his hand became numb from the weight of his head, so he sat up and rubbed his face. No one occupied the bed on the cell to his left; on his right was an elderly man, an harmless drunk who was sleeping it off.

The jail in itself was surprisingly peaceful, not at all as portrayed on television or in films. He didn't see the lineup of drug addicts or half-dressed hookers being led away as he first envisioned. With this dead time, he reminded himself that mistakes were foolishly made. He had to learn to keep his imagination at bay and not let it wander freely as it was accustomed to. It would be dangerous and unwise to allow that to happen again, not now, not if he was ever to get Cathy back.

One thing that non-writers could never understand was that fiction writers were born with incredible visions used to create stories. Tragedies, dramas, feel-good tales, epics—it didn't matter. Novelists like him had the discipline to construct characters from scratch and build on them in any way that their mind desired. They had the ability to put words into their mouths and could decide whether the characters were good or evil, black or white, or whether they lived or died. It was a talent many were envious of, especially those who had trouble even writing a paragraph, but this gift also came with a dark side and if not properly controlled, could very well become a hideous curse. The stronger writers managed well and enjoyed a successful career, but the weak-minded novelists usually had bad endings, most notable being Ernest Hemingway, who sadly resorted to alcohol as a way to shield himself from his lurid visions. He shot himself on July 1961.

Though not as extreme, David did find that at times his imagination would take a hold of him, like a hungry virus, bringing with it cruel and unimaginable thoughts. Most of the mental pictures dealt with loved ones, and at this particular moment he found himself fighting to block the image of the Parkers taking turns at abusing Cathy. He had to, or he would go insane. He also had to think of a new strategy and learn from his errors, to analyze and to weigh his options. Eventually Nick would succeed at getting his release; that he was certain of. Once out of jail he would have to be more foresighted and calculating. He couldn't continue screaming and yelling that she was his daughter because no one would listen. He would have to be more secretive, learn to be more polished and not so obvious. This thing was much more complicated. It went beyond a minister and his wife. It had to be much more complicated than that to alter his daughter's mind in such a way that she couldn't even acknowledge him.

David heard the sound of the main gate unlock, followed by chatting and laughter. Soon afterwards two sets of footsteps were coming his way, hopefully it was Nick and his lawyer. Since the police sergeant was a "fan" of his, he had kept him updated, confirming that Nick and his attorney were on their way to finalize his release. He couldn't be more thankful to his older brother, recalling what his father had preached: "*When in time of need, family finds strength within itself,"* he would proudly proclaim in his distinguished voice.

He stood up, walked to the gate and took hold of the freshly painted bars, placing his face tightly against the cold steel in order to catch a glimpse at who was approaching. Since one of the voices was female, he realized it wasn't Nick. It belonged to Detective Wood. Seconds later she came into view carrying a folder under her arm, chaperoned by a muscular bald-headed guard. They both stopped in front of his cell.

The guard pointed upwards, at a video camera. "When you're ready to leave, or if you need me for anything, just wave. I can be back here in seconds."

"I'll be fine," she reassured him. The guard left. "Good morning, Mr. Turner," she said, not wasting time.

He pulled away from the bars, stepping backwards and sitting back onto the bed, opting to be rude.

She pointed to his bandaged hand. "How's your hand?"

"It hurts," he sarcastically replied.

She ignored his reply, coming back with, "So what gives? Why the Dr. Jekyll and Mr. Hyde thing? Why the sudden change?" she asked, blending a bit of humor by adding, "A full moon maybe?"

"You would make a bad comedian, Detective."

"I thought it was funny," she laughed, opening the folder and putting on her reading glasses. She mumbled a few paragraphs before looking back at him. "You're a difficult man to figure out, Mr. Turner," she said, removing another letter from the folder. "I did a bit of homework this morning and found nothing but good things about you. You're a successful writer, no criminal record; you give to charity and to your church. You are so pure and so wholesome as to be boring. No offence meant."

"We live with the net and Google; everybody can find out anything about anybody. If you think that surprised me, then you will be disappointed."

"True, we do, but I want to take it one step further. You see, I'm a very nosey person. What I want to know can't be found inside a computer." She paused before asking. "So tell me, what in the world makes you think Cathy Parker is your daughter?"

A nerve had been hit, and it hurt. Though he had promised himself not to get infuriated anymore, he could not contain himself. "You didn't do your homework very well, Detective Wood. I don't know where you got Parker from. Her last name is Turner."

"You seem to be the only person in the world who believes that."

She was upsetting him, ironically by being pleasant. Perhaps he had said too much as it was. "I'd prefer that you leave and wait in the front until my lawyer arrives. Then you can return with all your folders and ask all the questions you want. He would be happy to answer them for me."

"To be perfectly honest, I don't blame you. It's just that lawyers get on my nerves, and I'll tell you why. They never smile. When they get involved, it's not personal any longer, nor do they believe that it should be personal. I'm giving you the opportunity to get explain yourself before they put a muzzle around your mouth. In other words, Mr. Turner, this conversation never took place. It's just between me and you and no one else."

"That video camera up there tells me different. It tells me that this conversation is being taped."

She swept her long dark hair away from her ear. "Whisper to me then," she challenged.

"Into a recorder taped onto your body?"

"Mr. Turner," she said firmly, "no matter what outfit I put on in the morning, I always feel that it makes me look fat. I would never have a tape recorder taped to my body for that same reason. If I didn't think you had something to say, I wouldn't be here giving you this opportunity."

"Why the generosity?"

"Because so far no one got hurt. If that little girl so much as had a scratch on her, I would not be here right now." When he didn't react, she finally ran out of patience. She neatly placed everything back into the folder. "It appears that I have overestimated you, but then again I have been wrong about people before," she added, gearing up to wave at the guard to come and usher her out.

Though he didn't fully trust her, there was an unexplained glow about her that he couldn't quite put his finger on. He felt a strange urge to trust her and to tell her of the hell he had been put through. Maybe she might understand a father's agony, knowing strangers have his daughter and that no one believes him.

"Are you a subscriber to the animal channel?" he sincerely asked her.

Somewhat surprised by his odd question, she replied, "I'm afraid I don't have much time for television. Why do you ask?"

"Because it's the closest comparison I can make to my situation. You can watch that program at any time and see any animal, large or small, protecting their offspring to their death if necessary. It's an impulse that they are born with. We're not animals. We're civilized. Laws state that we can't kill to protect our children, but the instinct in us is just as strong as any animal."

She smiled at him. "Unfortunately I have never been blessed with children, Mr. Turner. I chose this line of work over a family, so I wouldn't understand that feeling you speak of. Help me understand."

"You can't explain the bond. It's tattooed in a parent from the day our child is born and remains with us until the day we die. If I didn't try to get my daughter back then I would have no reason to live," he concluded.

The detective paused for a moment before removing what appeared to be a birth certificate from her folder. "Can you come closer please?" she asked.

He hesitated for a moment or two and then eventually got up and walked back to the bars.

"Do you see the name on this certificate?" she asked, holding it in front of him. "Let me read it to you so that there can be no misunderstanding." She cleared her throat before continuing, "Cathy Henderson was born to a Jessica Henderson and given up for adoption more or less eight years ago. No one really knows her true age. Since then, this poor child has been raised by one family after another. Approximately one year ago she was adopted by John and Florence Parker who had her last name legally changed to Parker." She placed the document back into the folder. "I am the first to admit that this little girl bears a remarkable resemblance to your Cathy. Amazingly they even share the same name, but simply put, she is not your daughter, and you must face up to that fact."

The detective read his face. He was not listening. She pulled another certificate from the folder; the death certificate that David knew only too well. "This may be uncomfortable," she warned.

"No need to explain that one to me. I know it word for word," he mumbled back.

She hesitated before placing the death certificate back inside the folder. "I visited the coroner's office this morning before coming here and had a lengthy conversation with the gentleman who signed this. Please forgive me if I sound insensitive, but your daughter was very dead when she got there. Her lungs were completely filled with water." She paused for a moment when he lowered his head. "I apologize for reviving that memory, but facts are facts. Your daughter died and was buried next to your wife. It may be easy for me to say let it go, but you do have to let it go," she made clear, placing the folder back under her arm and waving at the video camera above her. "You have many good things going for you, Mr. Turner. First of all, the girl was not harmed. Secondly, the minister and his wife hold no resentment against you. Third of all, it appears that you have a very caring brother who's on his way here as we speak. You should be released within hours. But I have to remind you, if you go near that little girl again; well, you are an intelligent man. You can fill in the blanks."

The main entrance door unlocked. She looked at the end of the hallway and saw the guard approaching to escort her back out. She glanced at him one last time,

"Sometimes things appear much worse than they are, Mr. Turner. By the way," she grinned, "I loved your third book. My personal all-time favorite."

It took until mid-afternoon to finally secure David's release. Like a juvenile who got caught shoplifting and was now being driven home by his angry parent, he was seated beside Nick, picking at the remaining ink stains from the fingerprinting that was now entrenched underneath his fingernails. He had been scraping at the stubborn fragments from the moment they had left the station. His injured hand was still pounding, but it didn't stop him from trying to remove the stains from there as well. Those ink stains were disturbing. He felt as though they were screaming at him, accusing him of being guilty when he wasn't guilty of anything. He believed he would be contaminated and diseased until the time he soaked them in detergent and washed them away.

Nick would occasionally take his eyes off the road and look over at his brother, finding it difficult to grasp that a member of his family actually had fingerprints taken and possibly a criminal record that went along with it. It added to the tension making this ride home appear dragged out and longer than it actually was. Even as children, they would remain tight lipped if they found themselves in the midst of a crisis such as they were in now. In times like these, silence was golden. Silence was safe.

A hotheaded driver behind Nick's car sounded its horn, an offensive reminder that Nick wasn't aware that the light had turned green. Caught off guard, he pressed the gas pedal and waited for the inevitable, for the driver behind to quickly pass and give him the finger, which was exactly what happened. When the brothers realized it was an elderly lady who was most likely late for her early bird bingo game that zoomed by them, they looked at one another and softly chuckled.

"Thank you for everything," said David. "I would still be locked up if it wasn't for you."

"Brothers don't thank each other for these sorts of things," smiled Nick. "All parties involved wanted to settle. That's not to say that you won't end up back in there unless you honor the deal that Sam negotiated on your behalf."

Sam Balvati, the new lawyer Nick had been using for the past while, befriended him when they first met at a business seminar. Sam was the one who introduced him to the Woodbridge Estates deal. Since then they had established a social friendship, with Sam enjoying dinner at his home many times.

"He's a good lawyer. I'm going to have to buy him a gift," said David.

"You don't have to buy him anything. What he did back there was his job. The best gift you can give us is to abide by the conditions he negotiated on your behalf."

"What are they?" he asked, expecting anything and everything.

"Just standard guidelines, such as getting medical help and to lay low for a while until all this blows over. In six months a psychiatrist will review your progress, prepare a report for the powers that be, and we will take it from there." Nick hesitated. There was more. "They insisted on one additional restriction and were very adamant about it."

"Which is?"

Nick knew he would be upset when it was made known to him. "Let me take this turn," he said, making a left and delaying the bad news for a few seconds. "They insisted that you stay at least a mile away from that little girl at all times."

David bitterly mumbled Christ's name beneath his breath. "How am I supposed to know if I'm a mile away?" he snapped. "Am I supposed to carry a tape measure with me at all times?"

"If you have to, yes, but don't step within an inch of that mile."

"That's a lot of nonsense," David snapped back.

It troubled Nick that his brother still didn't fully comprehend the seriousness of his actions. If he were someone other than David Turner, he never would have even been granted bail.

"All you need is time. Time has a way of curing everything," he told him.

"I don't need that much time to do what has to be done."

Nick quickly pulled the car over to the side of the road and stopped. Something wasn't right. "What are you thinking? What's going on inside that bloody head of yours?" he asked him point blank.

"I'd rather you didn't get involved."

Nick did something that he rarely did. He raised his voice. "You can't act noble and then be selfish at the same time. If you haven't noticed yet, I'm already involved!"

David relented. His brother was right. He was being selfish. Taking a deep breath, he shoved his hand deep into his pocket and pulled out a dozen strands of blonde hair, parading them back and forth as though they were a winning lottery ticket. "They searched me over and over again but didn't find these. This is all I need. Nothing more than these strands of hair," he announced and then boldly smirked. "These came from Cathy."

Nick wanted to scream as loud as he could, drive to the nearest mental institution, and throw him in or, better still, back into the police station, but he had to remain composed. That was his brother sitting next to him, his own flesh and blood, not a stranger, and if he himself had gone through the same tragedies as David had, who was to say he would react any differently.

"I suppose you're going to get a lab to extract DNA from them?"

"First chance I get."

"What if it returns negative? What if she is not Cathy?"

David didn't reply. Nick didn't take it any further. Memories of them playing as kids back in Scotland flashed through Nick's mind. He was the big brother, always watching over him. On occasions he would suffer a thumping from hooligans rather than allow any harm to come to his brother, and now, years later, David sat beside him of unsound mind, going mad before his very eyes. He began to cry, not out of weakness, but because of the love he felt for him, and, in a true sense, betrayed by his own feelings—that he had failed not only his brother but also his late father.

"Please don't do that, Nick."

"I can't help it. I love you, and it just breaks my heart to see you this way."

"And my love for you is mutual, but no one can feel what I feel inside. I have no choice but to see this through my way. If I don't, what will happen to me, Nick? What will I become? Not now, but in twenty or thirty years from now knowing she is out there somewhere and possibly with grandchildren I don't even know of?" He held up the strands of hair. "These are the only things that I have left of my family. These strands of hair are my heart, my soul, and the air that I breathe."

Nick was exhausted. David had made up his mind and neither he nor anybody else could change it. "I need you to understand something that is very dear to me," he sniffed before continuing, "No matter where this flight of yours takes you or where you may end up, I will be there for you. That's the way Dad taught us, and that's the way it will continue to be."

David searched out the box of tissues, finding it laying on the backseat of the car. He pulled out a handful and gave them to him.

John Parker removed the carrot cake from the microwave, tested it with his finger, and satisfied that it was warm enough for Mrs. Stonestreet to nibble on. With luck, she would only take twenty minutes or so to consume the small slice, therefore fulfilling his end of the bargain. In turn, Dean, Mrs. Stonestreet's oldest son, would repair the garage door as per their bartered agreement.

Lowering the wheelchair's tray, he positioned the warm plate close to her, and, though she was frail and partially senile, the smell of the cake ignited the old woman. He separated a small piece with a fork and placed it inches from her lips. She opened her mouth, but not wide enough.

"You're going to have to open a bit wider," he told her, unconvinced that her hearing was completely gone. Displaying patience, he touched her lips with the cake. It worked. She opened wide enough so that he could tenderly plant the cake inside, laughing out loud when she suddenly placed her lips together with the plastic fork still inside her mouth. He gently pulled it out.

There was a knock on the door.

"Were you expecting anyone?" he asked, but she was too occupied with the food, sliding the cake from one side of her mouth to the other.

When he heard a second tap at the door, he placed the fork down. "I'll be right back."

John opened the front door. Standing outside was a lady holding two suitcases, a captivating red-haired, blue-eyed goddess that could make any happily married man wish he was a bachelor again.

"Dean Stonestreet?" she asked.

John Parker's jaw dropped, for her beauty was immediate. The thick, bright red lipstick painted on her lips was the ideal tantalizer, one that could make a man's fantasies come true, and it didn't end there. Her high cheekbones were comparable to those of a high-priced supermodel, and her legs were not too thin, just perfect. The tight blue dress she wore was just short enough to show off her perfect shape, and the white sweater gave her the "look but don't touch" tease. Caught off guard and intimidated, John saw in her a bewitching quality that was both inviting and dangerous. A man of the cloth like himself should not have felt this way, yet he did.

"No, I'm not Dean Stonestreet. I'm the family's minister," he uttered.

"I was to meet a Dean Stonestreet at this address."

Perhaps it was her perfume or the clothes she wore, or perhaps it was her large oval earrings that seemed to sway back and forth in slow motion, but she besieged him and clouded his mind. Embarrassed by his reaction, he desperately attempted to pull himself together. "He should be home in twenty minutes," he managed to say, mortified that a man of God, a married one at that, would entertain such repulsive thoughts.

She placed the suitcases down and offered him her hand. "Nice to meet you," she said without giving her name. "I was hired by

Dean Stonestreet as the live-in nanny to look after his mother." She looked at her watch. "I'm a bit early. I can come back."

"I'm John Parker," he responded shaking her hand, prolonging their touch longer than he had a right to before she had to let go.

Becoming mentally and physically paralyzed by her mere presence should have been John Parker's first warning. The unexpected and sudden lewd and indecent thoughts were the second. These were the dangerous and corrupt thoughts he had preached against and was respected and noted for helping to stamp out of others before they destroyed entire families. He should have recognized these symptoms and he should have agreed with her to leave and to return later. He should have prayed for forgiveness for his sliding into the lustful side and not being quick enough to slide back out. All these things he should have done, but he did none of them.

"You are more than welcome to come in and wait if you like," he said.

"Are you sure I am not intruding?"

Yes, you are intruding and you frighten me! he wanted to shout at her, but he mindlessly stuttered the opposite, "You are not intruding at all. Please come in."

Before the woman had the opportunity to lift up her suitcases, he was out of the door. "I'll get them," he eagerly volunteered, purposely brushing his shoulder with hers in the process.

She followed John into the house, shutting the door behind her and stood politely by the doorway, scanning the insides of the hundred-year-old home until she saw Mrs. Stonestreet sitting in the wheelchair.

"Mrs. Stonestreet, I assume?"

John placed the suitcases against the wall. "Yes, that is Mrs. Stonestreet. Please allow me to do the introduction," he said ushering her before Mrs. Stonestreet's wheelchair. The old lady lifted her head at the two but could only maintain it at that level for a short time.

"This lady will be taking care of you, Mrs. Stonestreet," he said moments before her neck muscles let go and her head slumped down again.

The nanny knelt down before her. "Hello, Mrs. Stonestreet. I am your new nanny."

"No one is certain if she can hear or not. Not even her doctor. She has been known to react when things are written in capital letters."

"Do you have a pad and paper by any chance?"

Within seconds, he brought her the things she had asked for. She thanked him and wrote her name in huge capital letters, placing the pad in front of Mrs. Stonestreet's face. "This is my name."

John positioned himself behind the wheelchair to see the name. It read, "LYNDA STEWARD."

The morning was a wet one, but not windy. In a matter of hours the clouds would all disappear and the sun would shine. David knew this by the number of earthworms that were urgently crawling away from the driveway and heading towards the grassy area before it became too late for them. He had to sidestep a few of them in order to get at the morning newspaper expecting to find his picture on the front page for all the wrong reasons.

It had been a while since Mr. Steamer was in possession of those photos. Sooner or later he would cash in on his prize, sit back, and enjoy watching David squirm just as those worms are doing now. He had thought long and hard about the consequences that came along with the scandalous headlines and would somehow have to deal with the untruths and the deception head on.

Even without the photos, rumors about him circulated the moment he was released from jail. Though Nick and Sam Balvati had done their best to keep it hushed, someone had leaked out that he'd been in jail. David could only think it was the guard who befriended him when he was locked up. As with all hearsay, this particular one had developed a life of its own; the latest rumor being that he was now in prison and getting exactly what he deserved from other bigger, meaner inmates. Some of his fans were shocked by what had been written about him on the Internet, especially on other writers' blogs and chat rooms. His few remaining supporters refused to believe that their beloved author was in reality a monster.

David picked up the newspaper, expecting the worst. To his surprise, today was not the day either. For some reason Mr. Steamer was still holding out. He folded the paper and upon walking back he noticed Mrs. Robinson, his nosy neighbor, staring down on him from the second floor window. Perhaps she presumed the rumors to be true and believed that she had been living next door to a predator all these years. She didn't give him time to smile at her as was customary; instead she vanished from the window. "*It's not true!*" he wanted to shout at her before making his way back inside. He sat down and made an effort at reading the paper but found he was only glancing through it rather than reading it. There was a reason for his edginess. In fifteen minutes he would be placing the most important phone call of his life, a call that would bring his princess back home by dinner time. The anticipation was unbearable, the wait agonizing, but following that phone call he would need to get in touch with Detective Wood and bring to her the evidence she needed—Cathy's DNA results. With proof in hand, they would rush to the Parkers' church to get his daughter. It was as simple as that. He would not show any ill feelings towards the detective for doubting him; on the contrary, he liked her. She was just doing her job and could easily be forgiven. As for the Parkers, the justice system would see to it that they and all the others who were involved would be dealt with.

At nine fifteen he made the call.

"Appolez Labs," answered a voice.

"May I speak to Andrew?" David asked.

"One moment please."

During this tense pause his hand shook, and though the thought never crossed his mind before, he asked himself, *Where do I go from here if it isn't Cathy?* Would he grieve all over again as he had done the day she was supposed to have drowned? Would he ultimately wise up to the fact that he was indeed insane and all this had been brought on by a madman's hallucinations? If this was just a dismal fantasy, then he deserved to be put away for his own safety and that of others he concluded.

"Andrew speaking."

"This is Mario Hernandez," David lied, not certain how or where he got that fictional name from, suspecting it might have been the name of a baseball player who defected from Cuba which he had read about years ago. "I was told to speak to you regarding the paternity DNA I submitted. I'm calling for the results." Following a slight hesitation from Andrew, he was positive he heard mumbling on the other side of the line, sounding as though a hand had covered the receiver. It was not something that was anticipated. All he wanted was the results and nothing else. "Are you still there?" he asked.

"Mr. Hernandez," asked a raspy older voice that didn't belong to Andrew. "This is Mr. Wright from Salt Lake University in Utah. I have been waiting for your call, sir."

This setback unsettled David. He didn't know this man, and he had no right to be speaking to him at all. "I don't understand. I was told to speak to Andrew and only Andrew; something about confidentially."

"Well, yes, but every rule has an exception, Mr. Hernandez. Let me explain if you will. Andrew is a dear friend of mine. He contacts me when things cannot be explained."

Confidentiality in these matters was a must, which meant Andrew had no right to involve this other man. There were legal complications that Appolez Laboratories risked by involving a third party.

"What do you want from me?" he quickly asked.

"Please forgive me. It's a bit complicated, but I will do my best to explain. You see, Mr. Hernandez, this lab could not extract a DNA from the sample you brought in."

David wasn't a scientific forensic expert but was educated enough to understand that what this man was implying was impracticable. "That's impossible," he declared.

"I agree, but the lab did that test several times, and the results came back the same—no DNA. Andrew was kind enough to contact me yesterday morning with this incredible news, and I took the first available flight here to wait for your call."

Who is this Mr. Wright, he thought, *and what is his true role?* His suspicion was that Mr. Steamer may have had something to do with this. Perhaps the café photos he had were not enough and he needed to add this Mr. Wright character to further humiliate him.

"I need to speak to the person in charge."

"That wouldn't be a problem if that's what you really want, but please trust me when I tell you this, eventually you will need my help."

"I want to see the results I paid for. I don't need your help."

"I can personally bring them to you. Tell me where and when."

"Where did you say you were from?"

"From Salt Lake University."

"What interest would someone as far away as Utah have in me?"

"I represent a very small group of spiritual individuals, eleven in total, who are always searching for answers."

"You're crazy," snapped David.

"I am not crazy, Mr. Hernandez. People from our group will attest to that. There are individuals here whom also thought I was mad when I approached them as I'm now approaching you."

"I'm not interested in any group of spiritual individuals you represent," he made known.

"I can appreciate your distrust, but please believe me when I tell you that I have every reason to believe the owner of that hair strand is an ethical force so special that it would be irrational to describe this phenomenon on the phone. It would do this revelation injustice." When David paused, Mr. Wright added, "I think it is in your best interest that we meet."

David wasn't sure why he hung up. He didn't intend to. It just happened. He walked into the living room, sat on the sofa, and stared blankly at the wall.

With hand still held firmly on the receiver, Mr. Wright also stared blankly but at Andrew. "He's in the early stages. He will come around like the rest. It's a shame he didn't tell me who these hair strands belonged to. To actually see 'one of them' would have been the highlight of my life, the equivalent of finding the Holy Grail," he let Andrew know.

Andrew opened his desk drawer and removed a clear plastic bag. Inside that bag was a white envelope. "This is the envelope the sample came in. I can examine it for fingerprints."

"Thank you, but I would prefer to send it to Mark Walsh if you don't mind."

Taking a long drag of his cigarette, the bald, unshaven motel manager watched from his registration office window, studying the vintage car outside as it hesitated back and forth a few feet at a time for no apparent reason. He'd seen this sort of wavering a thousand times before and would continue to see it a thousand more. He couldn't help but laugh at the hypocrisy of it all. The car's back bumper was filled with religious slogans, yet the man driving that old Plymouth was about to have a lewd affair with a prostitute.

Putting out his cigarette and pulling out a fresh one from the pack, he continued to be entertained when, for the third time, the car stopped in front of room eleven, and each time with no one stepping out. The oily manager laughed. He recognized this exhibit as another "indecisive john" who asked if he would live to regret his affair or what if his wife discovered that he was about to use the weekly shopping money for sex. And what of the kids if they discovered what their daddy had been up to? What if he caught a sexually transmitted disease? How could that be explained?

Whether that "john" found the guts to enter that room or chose to drive away was of no concern to him. The room had been previously paid by a stunning redhead, registering under the name of Lynda Steward. The strip motel business needed loose women like her to stay afloat, representing well over 80 percent of his business. Eventually he got bored by it all, took another beer out of the refrigerator, wiped his hands on his dirty shirt, and returned back to his television set where the main wrestling bout was about to begin.

Inside room eleven, Lynda Steward made herself appear lustful for the minister. Dressed in a tight skirt and a matching body hugging sweater, she stood at the window, flaunting herself in front of the Plymouth and puzzled as to why John Parker was reluctant to enter. All signs were that he was having serious doubts about the liaison the two had covertly agreed to earlier. As seconds ticked into minutes, she wondered if perhaps she was trying too hard or maybe hadn't prepared herself as well as she should have.

John Palmer remained inside the car. Highly strung and in an emotional state, he had to rub the top of his leg to stop it from shaking. When another car pulled into the motel driveway, his anxiety intensified. *What if that was a member of his congregation driving that car?* he thought, or worse, *what if Florence knew all along and had sent someone to take photos of him?* The fact that the car harmlessly drove by him, parking itself in front of room twenty-five, didn't settle him down at all. Ultimately he had to come clean and admit that he had made an error in judgment and couldn't go through with it. He eventually backed up, sped to the fringe of the driveway, and, at the first opportunity, the red-faced minister blended his car with the oncoming traffic, quickly disappearing from view.

Lynda didn't shut the blinds as for the slight chance that John would reconsider and find the courage to return. If he didn't, she would be disappointed and had no choice but to try to lure him back at a later date. She moved away from the window, sat at the edge of the bed and checked the wide range of movies the motel had on their list, everything from action movies, dramas, black-and-white classics, and the obvious adult films. She settled on the spiritual fantasy *Ghost*, starring Demi Moore, a feature film that she had seen countless times before, and one that she could have easily relate to. The phone rang. Only John Parker knew she was there. She optimistically answered it. "Hello?" she softly said.

"Looks like your man got a severe case of cold feet," teased the hotel manager "I'll come over for half the price. At least you'll make something."

The mere sound of his hoarse voice staggered her, rendering her speechless at the sullied intensions of that man. Frightened beyond belief she dropped the phone as though it was a hot iron, backing away from it until she reached the wall. "Help me, Father," she whispered.

"I'm coming over," she heard his voice through the receiver.

She quickly stepped around the phone, grabbed her purse, stormed out of the room, and drove away, all in under forty-five seconds.

Every morning he drenched himself with expensive Italian after-shave. It wasn't only the smell of the lotion that made female heads turn when he walked by, it was also his handsome looks. With a body seemingly chiseled from an ancient Greek god, Sam Balvati was the catch all the single ladies were searching for in a man. Standing at over six feet tall, he bent towards the mirror and combed his jet-black hair back, placed on his daylong smile, and scratched at the John Travolta dimple centered just below his lip.

Sam had it all, including a great outlook in life. He wasn't perfect for the simple reason that no one was perfect, having faults, such as being late for meetings. As it stood he was already twenty minutes late, but then again the universe would stand still if Sam Balvati was ever on time. When he did arrive, he would express his opinion on everyday life, rarely giving anyone an opening to express their own.

In an ironic twist, that's what was charming about him, the way he took control of a conversation and kept people's interest. That was his repute, that and his off-the-wall wardrobe. Where others would not dare be seen with bright-colored ties wrapped around their necks, he owned half a dozen. Where checkered pants went out of fashion with the sixties, he would boast about his four pairs and always made sure the creases were ironed exactly in the centre. It didn't bother him that his colleagues laughed at his attire, earning the nickname "the Weatherman." He would laugh along with them, adamant that his clothes were months from becoming fashionable again and that he was one step ahead in the trend game.

Those and other oddball characteristics of his were balanced out by his intelligence, which he kept well hidden and under control. He used his sharp vocabulary only when he felt it was necessary.

"It captures my competitors off guard," he would boast to anyone that would listen.

Nick had never met a man who was as confident and full of energy as Sam. He was always very reasonable with his fees compared to others in his profession, more than once forgetting to invoice altogether. He was also someone who Nick Turner wanted to be but knew he could never be. It was his idea to meet Sam inside this coffee shop, though he knew he shouldn't have. He had a love-hate relationship with coffee, at one time drinking seven to ten cups a day. He already drank three while waiting for Sam and couldn't stomach another refill so soon, but the waitress was staring at the sign just above his head, which read "maximum twenty minutes." If Sam didn't appear soon, he would be obligated to drink another cup or leave; neither of which he wanted to do.

They were to discuss the Woodbridge Estates deal, something he was hesitant to get involved with in the first place. No matter how intriguing or lucrative Sam claimed the deal to be, David was right, the deal smelt illegal. But on the other hand there was a sense of temptation that went along with it, a bit of excitement, a touch of adventure. This business venture was the thrill and stimulant he had never experienced before. For once in his life he would understand how it felt to be a shooter, a player, a person to be envied and admired. The intrigue that came along with the Woodbridge deal was something he always felt he had to experience, at least once in his life. He wanted to feel the way Donald Trump felt, where it had nothing to do with money but the thrill of walking that thin line and succeeding; a sharp contrast from the way he was raised, which was to always be cautious. But there was another reason he wanted to do this, a reason so personal that he would not even dare admit it to himself because of the shame attached to it. Not that Lee would ever leave him, but his mother had left his father because he was too tedious for her. He felt that he inherited that side of his father, and it bothered him.

Sam eventually walked into the coffee shop, carrying his briefcase by his side. He never ceased to amaze Nick, this time by the ridiculous silky white tie he wore. It was wider that anything he had ever seen with red dollars signs in place of the standard polka dots.

Where on earth does he buy those things? Nick thought. He stood up, waved at him, and sat back down laughing.

"What's so funny?" was the first thing Sam said when he took a seat, knowing full well it was his bizarre tie.

"Where do you shop?" he asked, subconsciously forgiving him for being late.

Sam polished the tie as though it was a winner's trophy. "Sorry. Can't tell you that because you'll tell your friends and they'll tell their friends and before you know it, you will all dress like me. Besides, I wore this for a reason."

"You won the lottery?"

"No, but very close," he replied, full of the enthusiasm. He was about to continue, but the waitress suddenly slapped an empty cup on the table, pouring coffee into it without his permission. When she noticed Sam's weird tie, she smirked and in the process spilled a few drops.

"I'm sorry," she laughed, rolling her eyes upward and walking away.

Sam waited until she was a fair distance. "She wouldn't be laughing if she knew McDonald's got sued because someone accidentally spilled hot coffee on themselves. I know it sounds absurd, but it's true. It cost McDonald's a fortune to settle."

"Were you handling that law suit?" Nick asked in jest.

"I wish," he replied, pouring a second teaspoon of sugar into his cup and then proceeding to open his suitcase and placing a file on top of the desk. "I'm going to make this quick and easy to understand. To keep it in perspective, this deal is too good to be true. A money-making machine if you will."

Nick glanced around for the waitress, tempted to order another coffee but decided against it at the last second. "I'm surprised you would say something like that. You're constantly telling me when a deal sounds too good to be true, it is."

"That's the rule of thumb," Sam quickly replied, "but once in a lifetime it does happen."

"So this thing is the real deal then?"

"It's as real as rain drops. All the ingredients are in place." He took a sip of his coffee and spread the file. "I want to show you something," he continued, pointing to a miniature design of the area in question. "This is what that neighborhood looks like now."

Nick was aware of this section of the city. Years ago it was the ultimate middle class area where people enjoyed living the American dream, but throughout the years, horrible decisions by politicians transformed it into one of the most dangerous ghettos imaginable. It had deteriorated to a point that even the police didn't enter without the company of a well-trained SWAT team.

Sam pulled out another file and slid it on top of the first. "And this is what it will look like in two years," he explained.

Nick was impressed. Anybody would be. Gone were all the old buildings, replaced with a theme park on the south side and a huge mall complex on the north side, including a twenty-screen theatre. The east and west sides were lined with trees, and in the centre stood four high-rise condominiums—two were twenty-stories high, the other two were thirty stories. He almost caved in to his addiction by the sight and was tempted to order another cup of coffee but resisted for the second time.

"Incredible," he whispered.

"This is the way it's going to be structured. There'll be twenty of us at a hundred thousand each, which will give us the two million needed to satisfy our friend's thirst. Once this money is secured in the offshore bank account of his choice, he assures us that the zoning will be changed from the current residential to commercial."

"God, that's hard to believe."

"It gets better." He grinned. "A month before the zoning change we put in an additional half a million each and buy the entire block for ten million. Other investors will take us for fools, but the joke will be on them because the moment the zoning changes it will be worth over forty million," he beamed, barely able to contain himself.

"Can you imagine the pollution that will be caused when they tear down those old buildings?" said Nick, immediately realizing it was a dim-witted thing to say, a tribute to his uneasiness about the whole deal.

"That's a construction problem, not ours. Our dilemma is how to hide our profit from the taxman."

"What is going to happen to the people living there now?"

Sam was taken by surprise. "To be perfectly honest with you, I never gave it much thought. Most likely they will be relocated to another area. Who knows?"

"Shipped like cattle," Nick mumbled to himself

"No one ever claimed that life was fair. It's what you make of it, and if we don't move on this, then others will."

"I suppose so," Nick agreed.

"You have to understand something. It's not your fault or mine that those people find themselves in their situation. Democracy gives everyone the opportunity to succeed, but for everyone that makes it, a hundred have to fail. That's the way the system is set up. There is no such thing as the rich if it wasn't for the poor."

It didn't surprise him that Sam switched on his intelligent mode. That was Sam. He then waved at the waitress. He had a sudden urge for a fourth cup of coffee and needed it now.

CHAPTER TEN

FBI agent Mark Walsh had a close relationship with Mr. Wright. That in itself was not illegal, but sharing federal and confidential information with him was. For that reason he thought it best they meet as far away from head office as possible. This park was four blocks away from headquarters, the comfort zone he needed. It also gave him the opportunity to enjoy his favorite past time—feeding nuts to the squirrels. It was a fun and entertaining way to relax and, in a peculiar way, made him feel like he was accomplishing something with his life, unlike Mr. Wright, who was leaving a legacy with his.

Occasionally he felt a bit jealous of his dear friend, but not in a harsh way, rather more in a complimentary way. In the past he attempted to be as spiritual as him but found he could not. Spending the good part of thirty-five years dealing with terrorists, kidnappers, and the worst that life offered had left him little time to understand the value of religion. He finally abandoned it altogether because the entire heaven and earth thing didn't make sense to him anymore; however, he always enjoyed meeting Mr. Wright. It made him feel balanced, a way at offsetting the guilt he held for forsaking a faith that once was so dear to him.

Mr. Wright walked around the last bend. He looked ahead up above a large tree and noticed a half dozen native western squirrels jumping from one branch to another. He would bet a million dollars that his old college friend had something to do with those critters behaving as they did. Sure enough, Mark Walsh was sitting on the bench below, feeding the little pests. Anyone could mistake him for a retired, gentle giant due to his tired eyes and stocky build, yet hidden under that placid layer, he was still one of the bravest and most fearless men Mr. Wright had ever known. Even in his college days, when Mark quarterbacked the school team all the way to the state championship, he showed a competitive edge that few could match.

"Do you know all those squirrels by name?" Mr. Wright asked upon reaching him.

He pointed to a specific one whose tail seemed to be missing spots of fur. "I call that one Patches."

"I recall an old soul song from the Deep South called 'Patches.'"

Mark Walsh cleared his throat, deciding to sing the chorus to show him that his memory was also in intact. "Patches, I'm depending on you, son."

Mr. Wright laughed. "Those were the days of the Temptations, Smokey Robinson, and Benny King."

"To this day whenever I hear Percy Sledge belt out 'When a Man Loves a Woman' I still get a funny feeling just as I did when I heard it for the first time," recalled Mark.

It was charming to watch these two men reminisce like they did, but at the same time there was something sad about it as well. Those days would never return. Perhaps they should have embraced them more respectfully when they had the opportunity to, before their lives went in different directions as they did.

Mark pointed at his friend's encircling belly. "I see you never outgrew your love for ice cream and chocolate."

"It would be a boring world if we all didn't have an Achilles' heel," replied Mr. Wright. "Mine is sweets, and yours is feeding squirrels." He then sat next to his friend and sank his hand inside the jar of nuts, taking out a handful. "I can't begin to tell you how much I appreciate this," he said, picking a specific squirrel out from the rest and throwing food at its direction.

"I discovered a few things that might be of interest to you," Mark began, forgoing Mr. Wright's gratitude and getting down to business as he was trained to do.

"Such as?" replied Mr. Wright, leaning towards him so as not to miss a word.

"There were a series of fingerprints on the envelope Andrew sent me. I had each and every one checked out. Most of them belonged to postal employees. One belonged to a Korean store clerk who most likely sold the envelope. I had him checked out and didn't find anything unusual. Just a typical hard worker with a wife, two kids, and trying to make an honest living; however, another print told a completely different story altogether."

"You must be referring to the Mr. Hernandez I told you about."

Mark scratched an itch on his forehead before answering. "That other print didn't belong to a Mr. Hernandez. It belonged to an author named David Turner."

"Why does that name sound familiar?" asked Mr. Wright staring blankly at him.

"It should. David Turner was at one time one of the bestselling authors in all of California."

Mr. Wright snapped his fingers. "Yes, of course, that's right."

"He seems to have the same qualities as your other students," continued Mark. "He gives to charity, donates to his church. I can go on and on, but bottom line, everything about David Turner makes him the perfect candidate. Other than a recent brush with the law for stalking a little girl, he is dirt free."

"Without ever meeting David Turner, I can tell you this, he is not a stalker of children," stated Mr. Wright.

"If I didn't trust your judgment I would stop right now, but something unusual happened to him a while back. His wife died just over eight years ago in a horrific head-on car accident, which in itself was tragic. People die in car accidents all the time. What I found interesting is that his wife was in the late stages of her pregnancy when it happened, but the baby she was carrying survived the accident. It shouldn't have been possible. Based on our information, Mrs. Turner was not wearing a seat belt due to her condition and without getting too graphic, the steering wheel practically cut her body in half. That unborn child should have died before she did, but it didn't. It lived when it shouldn't have."

Mr. Wright thought for a moment. "It fits the same pattern."

Mark took his time to respond, not at all surprised by Mr. Wright's conclusion. "Do you suppose that child is one of 'those' that you always speak of?"

"If the strands of hair without DNA belonged to that child, then, yes," he sadly concluded. "I always get so close to actually meeting one of them but for one reason or another God won't allow it," he grieved.

Mark placed himself in Mr. Wright's position and shared his heartache but could never understand why his friend continued to chase something that had never been proven to exist, regardless of the DNA's result.

"Perhaps one day God will change his mind," Mark told him, knowing that is exactly what his friend needed to hear. He then stood up, took out a piece of paper from his pocket and offered it to him.

"What's this?"

"David Turner's address."

The Plymouth's beaming headlights penetrated through the motel window, so bright, so direct, and in an awkward way, so exciting. Two days earlier they shone in a similar fashion, but at that time John Parker lacked the valor or the boldness to enter even though Lynda Steward was inside waiting to receive him. His past forty-eight hours had been filled with regret since this candlelight affair was something he had secretly craved for as long as he could remember. Nothing had occupied his mind the last two days other than what it would have been like if he carried this through the first time, to satisfy a lust so well hidden for so long.

In the darkest and deepest corner of his mind, he felt he deserved this affair and would go through with it if only for this one time in his life. He blocked Florence's existence and all possible consequences, including the irony of preaching against the lures of temptation. The urge to see this through was that ruthless, clouding his senses. Since meeting Lynda, he saw himself standing in front of a long tunnel and her waiting for him at the other end. No other thing mattered but to reach her. Getting caught in a scandal of this magnitude was the farthest thing from his mind. Hurting his wife and destroying his reputation were non-issues, replaced now by the unknown pleasures that had eluded him all his life. He even dared place some of the blame on God. *Why would he awaken these impulses inside me that had lain dormant for so long and then expect me to abide by his commandment with such temptation before me?* He thought.

Lynda appeared at the window, looking more appealing than she did two days earlier. She paraded herself, slowly pacing back and forth for him. John's heart feverishly pounded, both fearful and stimulated by the sight. He got out of the car and suddenly felt an unexpected gust of wind blowing onto his face, forcing his eyes shut and leaving him gasping for air.

The blast appeared out of nowhere and with a clear sky bursting with a million stars above, it made that gust all the more unusual. He recaptured his breath, shook the chill from his body, and when he reopened his eyes, Lynda was no longer there. Alarmed, he was tempted to jump back into his car and drive away, but the sound of Lynda unlocking the door from inside acted like a magnet, and he moved closer to the room.

He stole a look through the window, and saw Lynda leaving the doorway and walking to the bed, sitting down at the edge and staring at the television screen. An old episode of *Little House on the Prairie* was on, the family-oriented television series he knew only too well. She looked back, catching him off guard. He smiled at her. She did not smile back, choosing to remain in an unemotional and robotic state. He could sense that something was not right. Perhaps it was the unexpected cold breeze or perhaps the peculiar expression on her face; he just didn't know. He heard a flapping noise coming from behind the car's bumper and saw that one end of the "JESUS IS FOREVER" sticker had come off, the other end barely holding on, swaying back and forth with the wind.

If there ever was a time to reflect, a time to reconsider it was now, but he chose not to, rather he placed his hand on the door handle and opened it, quickly stepping inside the room and shutting the door behind him. The first thing he did was to nervously draw the blinds together, making certain that every inch of the window was concealed. Next, he glided the safety chain inside the socket and pulled the lever horizontally, assuring that both locks were in place. When he turned to face Lynda, her focus was not on him but on the television.

"I own the whole DVD collection of that series," he said because he didn't know of any other way to begin their conversation.

She didn't reply; her eyes still glued to the screen.

An uncomfortable and lengthy pause followed leaving John no choice but to also stare at the program, just in time to watch actor Michael Landon brag to a friend of the love he felt for his wife.

"I also love my wife very much," he informed Lynda.

"I never doubted that," she answered, finally looking at him. She got up, walked towards him, and stopped two feet in front. "Are you positive you want to go through with this, and if so, is it of your own free will?"

"It is of my own free will," he quickly answered back and admitting, "I'm not sure what to do next."

"Do what your will tells you to do."

"Do you mind if I turn off the lights?" he asked.

When she didn't reply, he took it upon himself to dim the lights, the only source of light coming off the television screen. He then moved forward, coming to a standstill a mere inch from her inviting breasts, but never looking directly at them. He raised his arms and gently removed the sweater off her stiff upper body, folding it first and then placing it neatly onto the bed. His next move was to bring his lips close to hers and was surprised when he noticed that her forehead was covered in perspiration. She no longer appeared the confident sexy women she made out to be and now appeared like a frightened and lost juvenile. Devastated, he pulled back and watched in horror as she did the same.

"I'm so sorry," Lynda apologized, quickly grabbing her sweater back from the bed.

Before he had a chance to grasp at what was going on, she was at the door unlocking the bolt and chain. "I'll say a prayer for you, Mr. Parker," she told him before dashing out of the room.

It all ended so abruptly, leaving the minister feeling foolish and stupid. He didn't question why she had acted that way, to bring him to the brink, only to leave him stripped of all his dignity. He was now desperate to get back home to his family and try and forget that this ever happened. He stepped out of the room just in time to see the "JESUS IS FOREVER" label blow away from the Plymouth's bumper, hitting one parked car after another until it made its way onto the road and was carried off by a speeding thirty-four wheeled tractor trailer. Without that sticker, the car somehow lost its dignity and did not appear classic any longer. Now it only looked like the aged auto that it was.

It wasn't a full blown a quarrel. Nick rarely, if ever, argued with his wife; however, on occasions Tracie did hear him raise his voice to make his point, followed by Lee's annoying whispers. Her father had promised to watch a movie with her, but as of yet he was still in the other room arguing with Lee that Tracie was now eight years old and should stay up later. At this moment the outcome wasn't a concern, for Tracie was stretched out on the sofa, fascinated by a special program titled, "Do Angels Actually Exist?" She giggled when interviewed non-believers scoffed at the idea, claiming angels were only a myth, and smiled when others swore they saw images of God's messenger's seconds from a near-death experience. She seemed thrilled when a doctor was interviewed; defending his claim that he returned a sickly woman back from certain death with the guide of an angel. She was so engulfed by the program that she didn't even notice Nick enter the room.

"What are you watching?" he asked, hiding his difficult time with Lee.

"A program about angels."

"I could use one now," he replied.

She was about to laugh at his fitting reply but held back, instead she pointed at the DVD, which rested on top of the television set, a reminder of his promise to watch it with her. "Will you be much longer?"

"I'll try not to."

Lee appeared out of nowhere, relentless and in the same bitter frame of mind. "Either she goes to bed, or I will."

"That's your choice. I promised I'd watch a movie with her, and that's what I intend to do," he told her, this being one of the rare times she was challenged. He then grabbed the remote control so Lee couldn't shut off the television and held it firmly in his hand.

Lee simply walked around Nick and pulled the electrical cord off the wall. "Get to bed!" she boorishly told Tracie before storming out of the room.

Instinctually, Nick shoved the cord back into the electrical socket, reset the television, and when he turned to face Tracie, the first thing she said to him was, "Mommy was right. It's past my bedtime."

Nick had heard stories where over time mothers became jealous of their own children and hated to think this was the case with Lee. She seemed to be getting worse when even the mere mention of Tracie's name would set her off. He felt he had to put a stop to it, to send Lee a signal that he wouldn't allow her selfish tantrums to interfere in his relationship with his daughter. "Load the DVD. We're going to watch that movie tonight," he told her.

Tracie slowly sat down, not fully won over that all this chaos over her was worth watching a movie she had seen before.

"Please, do what I ask," he insisted and then walked out of the room to face up to Lee and demand that she apologize. Moments later Tracie was left alone to once again hear loud angry whispers.

She heard her name mentioned, and while Nick made every effort to be discreet about the whole argument, Lee did not, screaming and accusing him of spoiling their daughter rotten.

Tense situations like this did not sit well with Tracie. Feeling responsible, she thought it best just to go to bed. She got up but stopped the moment a news bulletin flashed on the TV screen. A preppy female reporter appeared with a microphone in one hand and holding on to her flapping silk scarf with the other; behind her stood the Parker's home.

"They say that lightning doesn't strike twice," she began, "but for a minister's wife this was exactly the situation. Minutes after it was revealed that her husband, Minister John Parker, had visited a motel for a planned illicit affair, Cathy Parker, the eight-year-old adopted daughter of John and Florence Parker fatally fell to her death from that second-story window," she reported, pointing up at Cathy's bedroom window and then onto the hard concrete below.

Tracie looked on in disbelief, pressing her hands against her cheeks.

"It can't be," she whispered.

"It's not known at this point if the child's death had anything to do with her father's attempted affair. All indications are that this tragedy is all a bizarre coincidence." A picture of Lynda Steward appeared behind the reporter. "This woman, Lynda Steward, shown here, went public with the incident, stating that she felt remorse at almost having had an affair with the minister and contacted our station."

Tracie lowered her head and silently wept for a moment or two with a sudden urge to go upstairs and lie down on her own bed. As she dragged her feet by the birdcage, she noticed that Mr. Rogers and Lucy were acting peculiar, jumping from one side of the cage to the other, singing as never before. She looked inside at the nest and saw that another egg had been laid, a replacement for the one that Lee threw out. She should have been delighted; she should have called her uncle David and screamed for joy, but she did neither. Instead she gracefully thanked God for trying to cheer her up by the presence of the new egg, made her way up the staircase into her room, and closed the door behind her.

At home, watching the identical channel, David Turner found it unbearable to accept that Cathy had died for the second time. "*My poor baby,*" he painfully thought. "*My poor, sweet baby. Why are they doing this to us?*"

Three days later, David found himself resting his chin on the Jag's steering wheel, staring at the church entrance and waiting for someone inside to swing open the two main doors. No matter how prepared he thought he was, this part was grueling. To see Cathy buried the first time was excruciating enough, now this second time was surreal. How could this be? How could his daughter die twice?

The events that he had been forced to endure shouldn't have been possible, but they did occur, and they were all real. He even dared venture into the supernatural world for possible answers, asking such questions as, would Cathy raise from the dead for the third time, and if so should he be camping by her plot, day in and day out just in case she did? His body tensed when a clear image flashed before him that she was about to be buried alive inside a casket, suffocating unimaginable agony and crying out his name for help.

There had to be answers, he thought, there had to be reasons, and the need to scream at the heavens above to shout out the most heinous foul language for all the saints to hear wouldn't help. God would not come down to salvage the turmoil he had created. The Almighty had made it known in many ways that he was on his own, and he was not only accustomed to God brushing him aside, but he now expected it. His days of begging God for support were over for good, and he preferred it that way.

The church doors finally opened. An arched-back minister—wearing an ancient, over-sized pin stripped suit—was the first of an entourage to wander out. Immediately behind him, six men stepped out in sequence, meticulously carrying a newly con-structed, well-glossed casket down the steps. They were followed by a string of well-behaved children, presumably Cathy's school-mates, all dressed in identical uniforms and on their foremost behavior. Out next were a small number of other people, mostly senior citizens, including Mrs. Stonestreet. They all waited for the casket to be shouldered above the pallbearers so they could begin their exhausting march towards the freshly dug plot.

John Parker appeared, beginning his descent down the steps at a snail's pace with an elderly lady holding on to him, possibly his ailing mother. With the support of two younger men holding on to her elbows, Florence Parker showed herself next, her face con-cealed with a black veil and appearing fragile. If she forgave her husband, she made a poor effort at masking it, purposely waiting until he was a fair distance ahead before she stepped down.

David got out of the car, immediately noticing a large yellow backhoe machine waiting to refill the plot with earth. Hiding behind one of its huge tires, he focused his attention back to the chain of mourners as they followed the old minister who was lead-ing them towards the plot. Their march was consistent and well spaced, lasting over five minutes. Every participant was careful not to pass, taking minuscule steps and bowing their heads. No one uttered a word, respectfully giving Florence the freedom to cry as loud as she desired.

Turning his body a full 180 degrees away from the crowd, he leaned against the back wheel and slid down, covering his face in the process. He would not cry. Tears for Cathy would be a private affair, not before these possible criminals. Upon hearing the min-ister begin his sermon, David pressed his hands onto his ears, not wishing to be part of it. He didn't want to hear the minister claim that Cathy had loving parents and that God had reasons for tak-ing her away. He had heard all that gibberish before from Father Mark and feared he would be sick from the hypocrisy of it all if he would hear it again.

He remained in his position for the longest time. When he removed his hands away from his ears, to his relief, the sermon was over. He slowly rose up and upon looking back at the crowd was stunned to see Detective Wood standing next to and talking with John Parker. He asked himself what she was doing there. Was she in any way related to the Parkers? Was she friend or foe? Or was it simply a matter of a woman who just happened to be a detective paying her respects at a highly profiled funeral?

Her presence could eventually be explained, but there couldn't be any justification as to whom he saw next. It was Lora. She just appeared out of nowhere, but what followed next was, not only abnormal, but eerie. She marched directly towards the detective and shook her hand. They exchanged what appeared to be pleasantries and then Lora leaned over and touched John's shoulder, handing him a single rose and envelope identical to the rose and envelope containing the ten thousand dollars that was given to him the year earlier. John looked confused by Lora's generosity. He attempted to smile but couldn't, politely thanking her and giving the envelope to his mother. Before he could say another word, Lora walked away, followed by the detective.

Both of them came to a complete stop a good hundred feet away, taking turns talking, constantly smiling, and nodding their heads in agreement. Whatever was said came to an end with closing gestures of sheer compassion and understanding for each other. The detective then set off to a waiting police cruiser where the same twin officers that earlier arrested him at Parker's house, were waiting for her. She was about to climb into the cruiser when a long black limousine pulled up, stopping behind her.

It can't be, he thought when the rear window automatically opened and he saw Mr. Steamer sitting in the backseat, wearing his customary fitted sunglasses.

Upon seeing Mr. Steamer, the detective walked over to him. He said something to her, and in turn she peeked inside the backseat and saw someone sitting next to him, reacting as though she had just seen a megastar. She waved to whoever was sitting next to Mr. Steamer, as did the twins.

Stunned by it all, David quickly looked back at the mourners, and then lowered his eyes exclusively at the coffin and thought, *Oh my God … Cathy might not be inside that coffin. She might be sitting next to Mr. Steamer.*"

Bizarre as it all appeared, David believed that at long last things seem to be fitting a pattern; pieces of a puzzle were starting to come together, and more and more it looked as though Mr. Steamer's people all belonged to some sort of a child slavery ring with Cathy just an article for sale, a commodity placed on a podium, auctioned off to the highest bidder. Somehow, someway they perfected the skill to manipulate a child's death, influence DNA results, get rid of whoever stood in their path, and resell these children on the open market.

There could be no other logical explanation, he thought.

The police cruiser pulled away, followed by the limousine. He had no choice but to follow Mr. Steamer. He needed to find out who was sitting between that madman and Lora.

Within five minutes of following them, it began to rain, starting off as light drizzle, almost a mist, but was now pouring so violently that wipers were of little use. The mixture of cold rain drops splashing against the outside window and David's heavy breaths inside the Jag fogged the windows, making it virtually impossible to trail the limousine. He used the back of his hand to wipe the fog, at times making visibility worse and panicked when he was losing ground, practically running over a curb and hitting a street pole before swerving back onto the road.

Somehow he managed to swing his way back onto the street unharmed, squinting his eyes until he saw what appeared to be a black speck up ahead. Weaving in and out of traffic, he caught up to it just in time to see it slow down and park upon reaching the entrance of an apartment building. Stopping a hundred feet behind them, he immediately saw a doorman dash out of the apartment, springing open an umbrella when reaching the limousine's back door, but it wasn't Mr. Steamer or Lora that stepped out first, nor was it Cathy. It was Lynda Steward.

Oh my God, he thought, flabbergasted by her sudden appearance.

Lynda stood aside, allowing Mr. Steamer to come out next. The two of them stood next to each other, giggling at the expense of the doorman in his attempt to keep them dry by swaying the umbrella back and forth between the two.

"Your efforts call for this, dear sir," said Mr. Steamer, handing the doorman a sizeable tip.

"Thank you," he replied, sliding the fifty-dollar bill into his pocket.

Mr. Steamer warmly placed his hand under Lynda's chin, much like an elated father would do to a daughter who excelled in school. Swollen with pride, she bashfully grinned, kissed him on the cheek, and sprinted into the apartment so quickly that the doorman couldn't keep up with her. Mr. Steamer laughed, got back into the limousine and departed.

David entertained the thought of following it once more, but the bad weather, combined with oncoming traffic, would make it impractical. His looming conflict with Mr. Steamer would have to wait. He would do the next best thing: deal with Lynda Steward. He got out of the car and soon found himself outside the apartment's lobby looking in, noticing video cameras spaced every so often on the ceiling.

With all the advanced security systems, it wasn't going to be easy to slip into this stylish building and next to impossible to get into Lynda's apartment, but he wasn't going to let some secretive electronics discourage him from doing so. He placed his hand on the door handle, ready to enter the foyer where the doorman met him head on.

"Can I help you?" he asked David, but before he could answer, the elevator door opened.

Out stepped two middle-aged women. The doorman suddenly ignored him and turned his attention to the tenants, shamelessly thirsty for more tips. Without being asked, he told them that the gloomy weather outside was temporary and that in an hour or so the sun would break through the clouds. Accustomed to his enthusiasm and loving the attention, the women began a conversation with him. David took advantage of the distraction. He entered, undetected, but not for long. One of the ladies took notice of him, first with a series of quick glances and then into a firm stare. He didn't recognize this woman and had no desire to know who she was, putting distance between the both of them by directing his attention at a bulletin board. This didn't stop her from walking straight to him.

"December fourteenth, four years ago, Sear's department store, located at the corner of Claireview and Riverside Street," she told him, raising her eyebrows as though he should be surprised by her memory.

"Sorry. I don't understand?"

"You autographed my book on that date, in that department store. You're David Turner, the author, are you not?" she asked.

Normally he would deny these things but saw this as an unexpected opportunity to get into Lynda's apartment.

"Yes. I am David Turner," he smiled.

"You appear much like your photo."

"Is that a compliment or an insult? I'm never sure," he answered back with this overused line.

"A compliment for sure."

The doorman and the other lady overheard their conversation and joined them, "A pleasure to meet the two of you as well," David said, taking the time to shake their hands.

"When is your next book due?"

He didn't have the response she wanted to hear. There was no other manuscript in the offering for now, and he didn't know if there ever was going to be one. "No official date yet, but I would like to think within the next six months," he lied.

"Publishers always have a way of keeping us in suspense," she laughed.

David made a terrible liar and knew it. If he continued, his face would blush as it always did when placed in an awkward position. He had to think fast. Noticing a pad and a pen hanging off the bulletin board, he quickly scratched his name twice on a piece of paper, ripped it in half and presented each lady with his autograph. They were delighted by his generosity, profusely thanking him. It made an impact on the doorman just as he hoped it would.

A yellow cab appeared at the front of the building, blowing its horn three times to attract the ladies attention inside. They politely thanked David again and patiently waited by the exit for the doorman to accompany them to the taxi.

"I'll be right back, Mr. Turner," he said before swinging his umbrella open and ushering them out from the building.

David looked through the glass wall and noticed one of his lady admirers handing the doorman his tip before entering the backseat and the huge grin on his face afterwards. This man thrived on tips, concluding that he would do anything for a few dollars.

"I believe you have a tenant named Lynda Steward living here?" David asked him the moment he returned.

"Yes, sir," he replied. "She lives on the fifth floor. Did you want me to ring her?"

"She's a dear friend of mine whom I haven't seen in a long time. I'd love to surprise her," he said slipping him a hundred-dollar bill and quickly making him forget the policies governing the building.

Lynda Steward was sitting alone at the table, a warm bowl of vegetable soup to her left and a freshly made salad to her right, mumbling a prayer of gratitude to the Almighty for the food she was about to eat. A soft tap on the door interrupted her. She was not expecting anyone. Understanding that security downstairs would not allow anyone in without her consent, she wasn't alarmed. "*It could only be one person*", she thought: that harmless and comical neighbor three doors down the hallway. He was forever running out of commodities, things like milk and sugar. When she opened the door and saw David standing there, she was more angry than surprised, folding her arms in disgust.

"How did you get in?" she demanded to know.

"Does it matter? I'm here now."

"You're not welcomed here," she coarsely uttered, trying to shut the door, only to be startled when he placed his foot in between to prevent it from closing. She didn't panic, opting to turn around and preparing herself to make a phone call.

"If your intention is to call management, a greedy doorman will get fired."

"He shouldn't have been so greedy."

"All I ask is for ten minutes of your time, and then I'll leave."

Lynda paused for a moment then looked at her watch. "You got five," she said, making her way to the sofa and sitting down.

David entered. The inside was not only gorgeous, but spotless, full of expensive furniture, a wide-screen television more suited for a male couch potato, a huge aquarium packed with exotic fish and scores of plants battling to outgrow each other. The only items out of place, or so he thought, were the religious icons and paintings scattered throughout the apartment.

"You have a lovely place."

The compliment didn't impress her. "Don't waste your remaining four and a half minutes flattering me."

She didn't ask him to sit down, but he did, on a smaller sofa opposite her. "Receptionists must make a lot of money in order for you to afford this place."

"If I had to rely only on my wage I would be living with rodents and cockroaches. It's the fringe benefits that make me the real money. You'd be surprised by the amount if I told you."

"Sleeping with a minister must top that list."

"I'm not that kind of girl. I don't sleep around," she calmly replied.

He didn't ask her the obvious: why lure that poor soul into a sleazy hotel room and not go through with it, but thought better to move on to a more pressing question. "I saw your photo on television the other day."

"And I heard you chase little girls in parks. The things we do in order to achieve our fifteen minutes of fame is staggering."

Her accusation sickened him. "My reasons were justified," he told her, not wanting to take it any further.

"Such a coincidence," she scoffed. "My reasons were also justified."

He swayed from side to side, uneasy by her frame of mind. "Look. I didn't come here to judge you."

"Then why did you come here? You still haven't told me."

"I think you know why I'm here," he stated. When she didn't answer, he moved his body forward. "You need to tell me what you were doing in Mr. Steamer's limousine." She momentarily froze. "He's a very dangerous man."

She paused for a moment, gathering her thoughts and if David thought he had won her over, he was dead wrong. "He is one of the kindest men on earth," she firmly barked back.

"Someone who is both dangerous and kind always has something to hide," he said, angrily trying to make his point clear.

She leaned her body towards him. "You have to realize that he knows you're here. He knows everything. It wouldn't surprise me if he could hear us right now."

"His magic tricks don't interest me. The whereabouts of my daughter does. The fact that you were inside that limousine makes you part of his inner circle. You must know where she is."

She rolled her eyes. "Get over it, David. Your daughter is dead. Everybody knows that."

"Everybody is wrong!" he cried out, the first hint of anger and frustration at not knowing how they forged her death certificate.

"And you're living in a fantasy world," she jeered back.

David relented. Though she reeked from her lies, he didn't want to spend the short time she gave him by yelling back and forth. If only he could make her understand. If only he could place her in his shoes and explain that as a father, nothing would stop him from finding his daughter.

"I was deceived into believing that my Cathy drowned a year ago, only to see her alive and breathing. Hours ago I saw them supposedly bury her again. Help a father who loves his daughter more than life itself. I beg you. "

She leaned forward. "You need help."

Refusing to give up, he didn't want to believe that she was that cruel, continuing with, "The eyes are the gateway to one's soul. I'm sure you heard that phrase before. Whenever I looked into Cathy's eyes, I entered into her inner self; we became one, the same heart beat, we breathed the same air. Surely you have experienced a love so deep."

"What good would it do if I said I did?"

He paused for a second, inspecting the religious paintings that hung on the walls. "I don't believe you are as dreadful as you make out to be, so why don't you just tell me what you know?"

She twisted her wrist and looked at her watch. "You have three minutes remaining."

"Don't do that," he said, referring to her countdown.

She stared at him stone faced. "I want you out of here."

He paid no attention to her, calmly asking, "How much are blonde, blue-eyed little girls going for these days? How much did it cost that minister to buy Cathy, and what was your commission from the sale?"

Lynda firmly glared back. "You don't have any idea of what this is all about. Don't start believing you do, because you're making an idiot out of yourself."

"I know that you got out of that limousine, which makes you a part of all of this. I know that Mr. Steamer is holding her somewhere and most likely is accepting bids on her as we speak, but believe me when I tell you this: he will be caught and will rot in prison for what he is doing, and you, Lora, and everybody else who's involved will be rotting alongside him."

"Two minutes left."

"Stop that!" he screamed, springing up from the sofa, unable to contain himself any longer. "Haven't you caught on yet that Steamer is mad?"

"He's a genius," she quickly countered, trying not to grin at his accusation and looking at her watch once again. "Your time is up," she announced, cheating him out of a full minute. She stood up. "You should have taken my offer. You should have had that coffee with me when we first met. You could have invited me back to your place, and with a couple of glasses of wine in me, who knows? You have no idea what you might have missed," she taunted him before walking to the phone, not to call the manager of the building, but the police. "There is a man in my apartment, and he won't leave when I have asked him to," she said when they answered. "He threatened to harm me."

David was wasting his time. Her soul had been polluted by Mr. Steamer and could not be reasoned with. The sooner he got away from her, the better. He bitterly made his way to the door. On his right, a few feet from the exit, was a small table used to stockpile newspapers and magazines. On top of the magazines was a tightly sealed envelope with a clear red seal stamped on the top left corner. Beside the envelope he was shocked to see a gold pen, the same version that he received from Mr. Steamer when signing the adult book deal. He was not a thief. He had never stolen anything in his entire life, but the contents of that envelope and what may be inside, demanded to be stolen. The gold pen only fueled the importance.

Lynda wasn't paying attention; too busy giving the police directions to her building. If he was going to steal that envelope, it had to be now. Sliding it under his arm, he quickly walked out into the hallway, taking the stairs down, two steps at a time, and out the side entrance. With head hung low and an adrenaline flow that would make blood boil, he marched to the parking lot, coming to a sudden stop ten feet from the Jag were he saw an older, well-fed man with a long white beard, nibbling on a chocolate bar standing there to meet him. He had never seen this man before and was certain that he was just another member of Mr. Steamer's cronies.

"I have been searching for you for a very long time, Mr. Turner. It's a pleasure to finally meet you," the stranger warmly said, shoving the half-eaten bar into his pocket.

Keeping his guard up, David inspected him thoroughly. Though this man seemed polite and harmless, he wouldn't be fooled by his grandfatherly appearance or his placid pose. Lynda, Detective Wood, and Lora were all initially passive and eager to extend a hand, yet all three hid behind their counterfeit smiles before eventually stabbing him in the back. Rightfully paranoid, he could no longer trust anyone, least of all this man.

The old man held out his hand. "My card, Mr. Turner," he said offering him his business card.

David didn't want his card. He didn't want anything to do with him. "If you want an autographed photo, you have to contact my publisher," he snarled as rudely as he could, hoping it would end there.

The man didn't seem insulted by his bad manners; rather he chuckled. "That's kind of you, but that's not what I'm here for," he explained, once again placing his card under David's nose, refusing to take no for an answer.

Ultimately David took his card, suspiciously taking time to inspect it. It was a larger than life form of introduction, two angels flying in midair, pointing to where the name *Mr. Jacob Wright* was clearly printed in bold black letters. Just below his name was an emblem for Salt Lake University.

"You might not remember me, but we spoke on the phone a while back. At that time you went by the name of Mario Hernandez."

David remembered the name. This was Mr. Wright, the same man who unexpectedly came on the phone when he called to inquire about Cathy's DNA. He recalled something about Utah and eleven spiritual individuals but not much more.

Mr. Wright pointed across the street to a coffee shop. "I'm alien to this city, but heard that they make the best coffee there. Perhaps I can buy you one?"

"This is not a good time for me to be talking to anyone."

Mr. Wright had seen that similar anxiety on David's face before, on eleven different faces, the same symptoms, the same phobia that all of his students had faced at one time or another. "I can't think of a better time than now, Mr. Turner. I appreciate what you are going through and know I can help. You just may discover that we share the same interests."

"I'm sorry, but I have to go," he relied, practically pushing the old man aside. He then unlocked his car door and slid inside. Once settled, he opened the window, waiting impatiently for this man to move away.

"I don't think you realize all there is to know about your situation. If you did, then you would realize that you may have been given the ultimate gift from God."

"Please, sir, get away from the car," asked David, short of a threat.

Mr. Wright hastily walked to the side window. "All my students were also given that same gift and went through the same challenges that you are going through now, but if you allow me to explain, I assure you, your anger will be replaced with appreciation."

"Get away from my car, sir," he repeated.

Mr. Wright practically shoved his head inside the car window, forcing David to pull back. "Mr. Turner," he said, doing his best not to sound too harsh or too insensitive. "I have every reason to believe that your child died along with your wife on the day of her accident."

Astonished that a total outsider, a man he had never met before, would take it upon himself to make such an absurd statement added to his suspicions that this Mr. Wright, with his decorative card and simple looks, was just another member of Mr. Steamer's crew.

"You don't know anything about me, old man," he bitterly mumbled beneath his breath. Ironically, meeting this man reinforced his confidence. He felt he was getting closer to the truth and that Mr. Steamer was now desperate, sending this comedian and resorting to hideous lies in an attempt to throw him off. "Tell Mr. Steamer that he should not bother sending any more of you. I am going to him," he threatened. He threw the stolen envelope onto the passenger seat, sped away, and went searching for the man he loathed more than Satan.

CHAPTER ELEVEN

Legend had it that this hellish ritual gave that tycoon the potency he needed in becoming the miserable mogul he felt he needed to be. David knew that demented publishing magnate well. His name was Mr. Steamer, and, though he owned his very own sauna back at his glamorous penthouse, the moment David drove by and saw Mr. Steamer's limousine parked in front of the "Gentlemen's Only Sauna Club" along with his private chauffeur leaning against the hood, he would bet his life that Mr. Steamer was inside. When the smiling chauffeur spotted him, he moved to his side, welcoming David to go inside and pointing at the main doorway as an added enticement. At that instant David knew that Mr. Steamer was expecting him and giving him the conflict that he sought. He got out of the car, went to the trunk, and put on a rain jacket. He was now ready to meet him head on.

"How are you today, Mr. Turner?" the chauffeur asked as David passed him and entered the club.

David walked straight by, barely looked at him, and entered inside the lobby. The sign on the wall instructed him to climb down a set of steps, and as soon as he located the sauna he was greeted with a scorching mist hissing angrily out from the bottom of the sauna door and floating upward towards the ceiling. That eerie sight didn't discourage him at all; however, he did take the next few paces as though walking on a thin pane of glass rather than on a solid tiled floor. It wasn't a case of having second thoughts. At this point he was no longer frightened of anything or anyone, confident that the pointed screwdriver he was hiding under a rain jacket was enough to protect him should things turn violent. Would he actually use that pitiful weapon against that madman? He convinced himself that if he wasn't prepared to use it, he would not have brought it with him.

Discreetly placing one eye at the bottom right hand corner of the door window, David glimpsed inside the sauna room. The fog, mixed with heavy mist, made it difficult to see, but there was no mistake—Mr. Steamer was sitting on a cedar bench with only a towel wrapped around his lower body. He saw him pull on a cord, which in turn sprayed chilled water onto the scorching rocks; unleashing an angry sizzling cloud of vapor that Mr. Steamer treasured. When this heated fizz drifted off the rocks and onto Mr. Steamer's face, he watched in stunned silence as the tycoon shamelessly chased it, capturing it with his nostrils, siphoning all he could, as deep into his body as it would go. With both of his lungs filled to capacity, he then sat back down and held his breath for an unbelievable period of time. A winged dragon could not have mastered this weird technique better, thought David.

Mr. Steamer snapped his head at the window, catching a startled David off guard, but rather than act surprised by his presence, he broke into a malicious grin. Without as much as a single word, Mr. Steamer was daring him to enter his private form of hell. Not to be outdone, David grinned in return, matching his cunning display and showing him that the days of fearing him were over. He momentarily moved away from the window, pinched the screwdriver's handle, and when he looked back inside, Mr. Steamer was standing up and waving him in. He partially opened the door and entered halfway, bringing with him a cool and nasty flow of air behind him. This fresh air contacted Mr. Steamer's legs first, working its way upwards, battering his chest and neck and causing him to shiver by the contrast.

"Do you realize cold air is entering? It takes me a good twenty minutes to get it to this sweltering condition," Mr. Steamer snarled, curling his eyelids.

David was reluctant to let go of the door, holding it wide open.

"Shut the bloody door!" screamed Mr. Steamer, fidgeting back and forth, grinding his teeth when the invading breeze worked its way behind his neck. When David refused, he calmly cautioned, "You may think you have me all figured out, David, but I assure you there is no character like me on this earth. I am one of a kind, an irrational organism, the last person you would want to upset."

David finally entered, letting go of the door, and when it completely shut he rested his back against the opposite wall. Both rivals stared at one another; David consumed with a deep hatred of the evil before him, Mr. Steamer seemingly annoyed and bored by the whole affair. "It's all fun and games until someone loses an eye," Mr. Steamer scowled.

"Is that a threat?" he asked, running his hand along his jacket in search of the screwdriver's handle.

Mr. Steamer's answer was to pull the cord and take pleasure in watching the added hot mist choke the room.

Within seconds, David found the heat unbearable, perspiring from every pore of his body. When the mist worked its way into his lungs, he squirmed, held his breath extensively and fanned the vapours away from his mouth, appalling Mr. Steamer.

"No, no, no, you stupid man. Don't do that. Breathe it in," he implored as though David was foolishly squandering away a bottle of expensive wine. "Treat it with respect; allow its intensity to enter your blood stream, and you will discover a once in a lifetime rush. One could conquer the world with such feelings."

"I asked you if that was a threat."

"That's irrelevant, neither here nor there, but I will tell you something that should be addressed. You must stop harassing my friends and yapping on about ridiculous nonsense such as cults. It plays havoc with my self-esteem that you would think I captain such a bunch of misfits."

"I saw what I saw, and I know you're behind it all," he harshly declared.

"Behind what?" he barked back, ready to squirt more cold water onto the rocks.

"You know what I'm talking about!"

"Trust me when I tell you this, David. You would be better off remaining ignorant. It's safer for you to continue believing that I just sell books," he replied, upset that the hinge, which was used to wrap the cord, had just pulled itself out of the wall, with only one of the two screws still holding it into place. He pushed the damaged hinge back into the wall hoping it would hold. It did, but only barely.

"I think you sell more profitable items than books, things that only a distorted man on par with the Devil would sell," David let him know.

"You seem to be mentioning Satan a lot. What do you want me to tell you? That I can change you into a pig with a snap of my finger? Is that what you want to hear?"

"Well, can you? Can you change me into a pig with a snap of your finger or grow horns on your head? Why don't you put on a display for me, Mr. Steamer? Why don't you twist your head in circles?"

Mr. Steamer looked away in disgust. "You watch too many movies, my friend."

It was David's turn to smirk. "Are you the devil?" he asked as though asking to borrow some tools.

"Don't get arrogant, Mr. Turner," he cautioned. "I just may possess those powers and others that would astonish you."

As far as David could remember, that was the very first time he was referred to as "Mr. Turner." He wasn't sure what it meant, whether Mr. Steamer truly had the supernatural capabilities he warned him of and that was his final warning or whether he was simply being sarcastic.

"My daughter is still alive, isn't she?" he brashly asked.

Mr. Steamer had every intention of pulling on the cord again but thought otherwise when it appeared the hinge couldn't support it any longer.

"Enough of these questions!" he yelled back, more upset at the broken hinge than at David's nagging. "Don't act so heroically,

David, because right about now you are boring me to death. You're all a cluster of reeking hypocrites, all of you. You blame everyone but yourselves rather than accept the responsibly for your own deplorable actions."

He threw the cord against the wall in frustration and seconds later, strangely smiled, enjoying what he was about to admit to next. "At least I am honest enough to tell you that I'm a master salesman. I sell sex. I sell real estate. I sell dirty books that people like you had in the past agreed to write for me."

"You forced me!" David shot back.

Mr. Steamer broke into a hardy laugh. "On the contrary, my greedy friend. It seems to me you have a very poor memory. I have a contract in my safe that confirms you signed it on your own free will. My suspicion is that you were terrified of becoming flat broke, and there is nothing more despicable than selling one's soul over money."

David turned his head sideways. "I made a mistake," he whispered more of a benefit to himself.

Mr. Steamer wasn't interested in his self-confessed blunders. "Mind you, I find selling temptation a much easier undertaking than selling books. It's a foregone conclusion that sooner or later you all fall into that oily pit and like robots all beg for forgiveness immediately after." He paused, removing a drip of condensation from the tip of his nipple. "There are certain things that can't be taken back. Giving in to temptation is one of those things. Surrendering of your principles is a very expensive commodity, David. Eventually debts have to be re-paid in order to balance things out."

"Such as one's daughter?" he asked not fully believing Mr. Steamer was foolish enough to answer it.

"A man who is owed money will accept any collateral."

"You are insane!"

"Don't ask questions if the answers frighten you."

"God help you if she's hurt."

"Let's leave God out of our affairs. He's a demanding spirit as it is and does not have time to meddle in measly affairs like yours and mine."

"I know you're holding her somewhere and that you're going to sell her."

Mr. Steamer roared. "Only a washed up writer with a decaying imagination like yours would conclude such a thing."

"I'll find her, for you sadly miscalculated the power of love. It's a strength like no other. People like you need to be pitied for never having experiencing it."

Mr. Steamer's grimaced. "You stand correct, David. I could do with some sympathy to counteract the tragedies that I have been subjected to in my miserable life. If only you were there to see for yourself how a good man was crucified over a few measly pieces of silver. I was there. I saw that for myself, and if only you were there with me, behind the thick walls, you would have witnessed invading armies smash those walls down and slaughter the thousands of helpless women and children inside. I could go on forever, David. I can tell you that I have seen miles upon miles of impaled men, impaled in such a way that their deaths were measured and their pain beyond belief. For all that treachery, death, and misery, all you people had to show for it was one brief moment of pleasure, one brief moment of dominance. Those are the images that are constantly on my mind, David. That's why I would welcome your pity with open arms."

"You are a sick delusional old man.

"No, David, you are mistaken. I cannot remember the last time I was ill, and I am well aware of my age. As far as calling me delusional, let me tell you that I am a tortured soul who has the most damnable occupation in the universe. It's a job that comes with forever being cursed and knowing that I will continue to be betrayed. You are the fortunate one. You can move on with your life. I have been deprived of a future other than to move about from one double cross to the next."

David had heard enough of his sick fairy tales, his obvious attempt to put out of his mind the real reason as to why he was there. "Where is she?"

Mr. Steamer also had his fill. "You have been very dishonest with yourself, and deep inside you know that. All that people have been hearing from you is the same thing over and over, 'Where is my daughter? I know she is alive,' when all along you know exactly where to find her. You saw for yourself where she was buried. If you want the truth then go and dig her up, open that coffin, and discover for yourself if she is indeed alive," he challenged.

"You know her coffin is empty, and so do I."

Once more Mr. Steamer saved his best for last. "Do you really believe that, David, or is it more spineless of you to stay buried under that rock and never seek the truth?"

David didn't answer; rather he was fearful of where this conversation was heading, afraid that perhaps Mr. Steamer was correct. If he seriously wanted to prove she was still alive then he had to accept his challenge. The actual act of unearthing Cathy's casket wasn't as shocking as it sounded to him, not at this stage, but looking inside was. What would he do if he found the body of a child inside, her crime being that she resembled Cathy and all along he was wrong?

Disappointed, Mr. Steamer gave him additional time to think things over, and when David remained silent and confused, he felt cheated and deprived of a good fight, waving his arm in disgust.

"I thought so," he yelled. "You cowards are a carbon copy of each other. Now get out of here or so help me you will walk out of here with hoofs and a tail on your behind! You will be squealing like a pig and end up hanging upside down on a meat hook, and it will be your head that spins, David, not mine."

All beings were born with it, and so was David—a human safety device hidden deep inside the brain that wisely prevents a rage as intense as to commit murder. In his case, he yearned to lunge at Mr. Steamer and thrust the screwdriver into his heart, but he realized that he was not capable of killing anyone.

"By sheer coincidence, David, would you have a screwdriver on you?" he calmly asked. "I need to fix this thing. It's driving me crazy," he said fiddling with the loose hinge.

Staggered and deflated of all the energy by those words, David needed to leave, and no one knew this better than himself. He slowly opened the door.

"Hurry up!" Mr. Steamer yelled. "It's getting cold again!"

On the verge of collapsing, David hastily walked out, eventually breaking into a semi-trot along the corridor. He came here convinced that Mr. Steamer was a seller of children and was now leaving more mystified than ever. He unhooked the top of his rain jacket and let it slip down off his shoulders. When he got outside he found a garbage bin and hurled the screwdriver inside it, just in time to see Mr. Steamer's chauffeur mocking him. He couldn't face him, choosing to go in the opposite direction, around the entire block in order to avoid him before getting into his Jag and driving away.

His ride home went by in a flash, and the moment he entered his house, he threw the envelope he stole from Lynda's apartment on the kitchen table and immediately took a cold shower.

What now, David? he thought to himself. In a strange twist, his only link to Cathy was Mr. Steamer, but he realized he could never face him again. There was only one thing remaining that was available to him. This required a backhoe machine, guts, and hard labor along with the willpower to actually unearth a grave. The first three items weren't a problem. The last one would involve a lot of soul searching.

When Lee complained that she was feeling nauseated and would retire for the night, Nick couldn't have been more relieved. Not that he had fallen out of love with his wife, on the contrary, he adored her, but he was anxiously waiting for a phone call from that flamboyant lawyer of his, Sam Balvati, in regards to the Woodbridge Estate deal.

If his wife were present, she would hound him about the call, asking for precise details and of the amount of money that had been risked. Eventually it would turn into an all-night chore trying to explain to her the complexity of it all and ending with her assurance that she finally understood when, in reality, both of them knew she wouldn't have a clue.

Lee was many things, but she was far from being an intellectual and would make a horrible businesswoman. She was simply too conservative, over-sensitive, and very emotional, certainly not a gambler. If he decided to go through with the deal, in time he would feed her bits and pieces of information, never forgetting to add: "Not to worry. Sam said it's all legal."

When the phone did ring, Nick answered it in record time.

"Make yourself available tomorrow night," ordered Sam, barely able to control himself. "The deal, for all intent and purposes, is done. All it needs is our endorsement."

"Are you serious?" replied Nick.

"Very serious." He laughed and as an afterthought added, "And bring your cheque book with you."

"That won't be a problem," mumbled Nick, guilt-ridden that he had let himself get as deeply involved as he was.

"You worry me when you mumble like that."

"I just didn't think it would go through so quickly," he explained, troubled that this deal could come back to haunt him.

"You would be surprised how money and greed can speed things up."

"What should I wear?"

"You've got to be kidding," Sam replied, amazed that he would ask such a trivial thing.

Nick was on edge. The enticement and the pull of the deal was taking on a life of its own and getting bigger than him. He was beginning to feel out of place, lost by it all, and perhaps there was nothing wrong with him being tagged "boring" after all.

"Don't laugh. I need to know what to wear, or I won't be there," he insisted in a serious tone.

"I'm making you a ton of money, and all you're worried about is what to wear. You sound like a woman."

"You better find out, Sam," he told him and was adamant about it.

Sam could ill afford to take any chances. If Nick was using "a suit and tie versus jeans and a tee shirt" as an excuse to back off from the deal, he could not allow it to happen. He needed his signature on that dotted line, fixated at making this work.

"Sure. I'll place a few calls and let you know," he reassured him.

"I'll be waiting for your call," Nick replied and hung up without saying good-bye.

Sam wasn't the slightest bit offended. He made inquires on Nick's behalf. It would be an elegant affair. Nothing but tuxedos, caviar, expensive wine, and laughter to celebrate the signing of the Woodbridge Estate deal. Sam called him back, told him what he needed to hear, giving him an address where he could pick up his rented tuxedo, and told him not to worry about the cost. It had all been taken care of, courtesy of Sam Balvati.

The rented school bus parked at the side of the long line up of anxious girl scouts. Kate, the strapping head Scoutmaster was the first to enter, followed by the children and ending with her assistant, a striking longhaired, blonde woman. From the moment the bus driver saw this beauty enter, he found it next to impossible to keep his eyes off her. His longing to touch her and be touched back was not a sexual thing, far from it, but rather a mysterious warm urge.

This assistant went by the name of Angelina. Some would compare her facial features to those of an angel. She had flawless blue eyes, a perfect nose, round cheeks, and an uplifting smile that could cure the sickest of the sick. Though Kate never heard of her before, she hired her on the spot when Angelina presented her with a series of immaculate diplomas, all confirming that she specialized in working with children.

Moments before the bus departed, Angelina chose to sit at the back of the bus, next to Tracie. For most of the journey they politely whispered into each other's ears in what appeared to be a foreign language. Their topic dealt mostly with the Woodbridge Estate deal, each of them merely expressing their personal opinions and their thoughts. Occasionally Tracie would frown at the prospect that Nick would fall into temptation and sign that deal; Angelina was there to quickly boost her spirits in any way she could. She reminded her that they must have faith in Nick, at all times holding on to her hand for comfort. Tracie thanked her for her kind words of encouragement but at the same time not wishing to express her true feelings, that Nick might soon become another sad statistic.

Midway through their destination, Kate led the singing of "Three Blind Mice," bursting into a lasting roar when some of the Girl Scouts sang the incorrect lyrics. This was understandable. The children were excited about the field trip, overjoyed that this gorgeous day wouldn't be spent at home but deep inside the unspoiled and lush forest known as Indian Pass Hills. This National Park served as a stopover where people could park their cars and enjoy all that nature had to offer before heading into the bustling metropolis. The same could be said about hardened city dwellers who simply wanted to get out of the muggy city and lose themselves inside nature itself.

The excitement inside the bus intensified when the top of a dome came into view. That rooftop confirmed that they were minutes from reaching their destination, a domed bus station, which stood at the foot of the park. As the bus entered, it was at a slow pace so that the children inside could plaster their faces against the window and see for themselves that the station was filled to capacity. There were other groups of schoolchildren like them and flocks of Asian tourists with their expensive cameras dangling around their necks. Added to the hustle were cries from hotdog venders trying to shout louder than their opposition, each vowing that their food was superior, bigger, and healthier than their competitors who stood a few feet away.

The bus came to a stop. Angelina's work was to begin, but she felt the need to offer Tracie one more word of advice before leaving her: "You have been well prepared and should it turn for the worst, know that we are all proud of you, my sweet child," she told her, lightly squeezing her hand in the process.

"I am ready," Tracie bravely replied, squeezing her hand in return.

Angelina stood up and walked to the front of the bus. Her responsibilities included being the first one out and to count the kids as they stepped off. "Thank you," she kindly told the bus driver, meaning every word. She stepped down onto the platform, resting a clipboard on her hip and ran check marks as each girl stepped down, then carefully steering them against the nearest wall.

"All the children are accounted for," she told Kate when she stepped off.

Kate took over. She paired the children in twos, instructing them never to let go of each other's hand. "Does anyone need to use the washroom before we head off?" she asked. No one spoke. No child wanted to be the first to raise a hand. The experienced guide had been down this familiar path more than once. She recognized the symptoms, uncomfortably crossing of their legs and too self-conscious to confess that they had to go. "Keep in mind that it'll be more embarrassing if you have to pee in the woods." At first, only one courageous child raised her hand, but eventually half a dozen more found the will to admit that they too needed the restroom. Kate and Angelina laughed.

The investors could easily have been mistaken for a collection of intoxicated penguins, all clothed with the identical black tuxedos, white starched shirts and patting themselves on the back in jest. With their lawyers sitting beside them, acting more like bodyguards than attorneys, they all sat around the expensive oak desk. In the middle of this desk stood an impressive full-scale model of the Woodbridge Estate project, standing three feet high and seven feet wide. Whoever was responsible for creating this scaled version was skilled beyond means, for if one inspected it thoroughly, they could even see tiny human faces looking out of the miniature windows.

The mood was a festive one. The wisecracks and humor over the top, and when the man that had made this all possible, Mike Longo, stepped onto the stage, followed by his four-man entourage, the investors clapped their hands, giving him the welcome and respect reserved for foreign diplomats.

Mike Longo lightly tapped on the microphone, testing it, and at the same time pointing his finger at some of the more well-known investors in acknowledgment while ignoring the ones he should have known but couldn't remember. This was the extravagant man with the perfect tan who made the Woodbridge Estate deal a reality, the fraudulent official. In his late sixties and trying to pass as much younger, his dyed black hair was slickly combed back with the customary touch of trimmed grey on each of his sideburns and a matching moustache over the top of his stylish goatee. This man was the perfect model of a corrupt politician. He drank a glass of the purest water in front of the crowd, yet in his back pocket hid a tiny silver hipflask filled with rare cognac. When presenting his written speech, he wisely kept his unsettling smile to a minimum, due to cosmetic surgery gone badly and when forced to smile, his unblemished white false teeth gave him a cartoonish look.

Sam Balvati leaned towards Nick. "I just love that guy."

Nick wasn't impressed. He had seen that politician's face on television several times over the years and also in that magazine article he read last year when he was at the doctor's office. It made him uncomfortable then, and seeing him in person for the first time made him just as uneasy to look at.

"Tell me why that man's face reminds me of Jack Nicholson when he played the role of the Joker."

Sam laughed. "Be kind to Mr. Longo. He's the ultimate survivor. He is rich, powerful, and a very imposing figure. "

"He must be powerful to change zoning by-laws and throw entire families onto the streets."

"This is America, not a third-world country. Warts and all, people here don't starve to death."

If David was to add up the time he had actually slept, it may have equaled two hours. All night he tossed, turned, and sweated. He got up in the middle of the night, took another shower and went back to bed only to agonize all over again. If Mr. Steamer's words were not haunting him, then Lynda Stewart's actions did. He asked why she took so long giving the police instructions to her place unless she was giving him the time he needed to steal the envelope. He had avoided it as though the evils of Pandora's box would be unleashed once opened, but sooner or later he'd have to deal with its contents, and no one knew this better than him.

It wasn't until midday that he finally sat down, picked it up, and ran his fingers up and down with the ridiculous assumption that he might very well feel the words written inside. Finally he tore away at it and removed the document inside. On the cover page, "Investor's Copy" was stamped in blue. He recognized it to be a contract of some sort, carefully reading the first three pages and confused somewhat by the numbers and percentages, including Nick's name repeatedly mentioned along with "Woodbridge Estates." At the bottom left of the final last page was the name and signature from a representative of the Estates. To the right he saw a dotted line, waiting to be signed by his brother Nick and below was an additional line that was to be signed by a witness. That witness was Sam Balvati. The moment Nick and Sam wrote their names, this contract would be binding. It became clear as to what he had stolen: a copy of the contract pertaining to the Woodbridge Estates proposal, the same deal that his brother had sought his opinion on.

What was this doing at her apartment? he thought.

As far as he knew, Nick had never met her nor did she socialize with him. He threw the contract back onto the table and immediately called Nick's home, but no one answered, which meant only one thing—he was out, and Lee was afraid to pick up the phone. He then tried his cell phone, but it was turned off. Wherever his brother was, he didn't want to be disturbed.

David had his own demons to deal with, and now his brother's contract added to it. He just didn't know where to begin, who to go to, and what his next step should be. With a list of problems a mile long and each one fighting to be addressed first, he was so overwhelmed that he simply sat down on the sofa, in front of the television set. A movie was about to begin: *Hang 'Em High*, starring Clint Eastwood, a revenge film from days gone by when westerns were all the rage and one that he was familiar with.

Lying back, he stretched his feet and convinced himself that eventually things would work out, but he wasn't fooling anyone, least of all himself. Weighed down by all his troubles, he thought of better times in his life as a means to offset the turbulence he felt now. He recalled people calling him and Nick the "Righteous Brothers," not for their singing ability, but for their charitable work.

"Your two boys are just too good to be true," employees of his late father's construction company would swear of the Turner brothers.

He remembered his father's face lighting up when anyone complimented his sons. On one occasion, when David was only fourteen, his father taught him to operate a backhoe machine as a reward for bringing home an unblemished report card.

David focused his attention back to the western, to the part of the feature where a group of cowboys inaccurately accused Clint Eastwood of cattle rustling and were preparing to hang him from the nearest tree. That scene was intense and should have been enough to keep his interest, but seconds later his thoughts flowed elsewhere.

He envisioned Mr. Wright standing between him and the television set, telling him that he didn't truly understand his situation and that he had been given the ultimate gift from God. He shook his head, trying to make him disappear, confused as to why Mr. Wright appeared before him in the first place. He blamed it on the conversation he had with Mr. Wright, the part where he was told that his child died in the same car crash that killed Diane.

The ruthless cowboys forced Clint Eastwood on top of a horse, placed a rope around his neck and despite his pleas of innocence, they slapped the animal's behind, frightening it away and leaving him to dangle in midair, feet shaking and choking to death. True, it was only a movie, but just as Clint Eastwood struggled to breathe, so did David.

That sudden gasp for air sparked the image of the unborn Tracie, herself choking with the umbilical cord wrapped around her throat. Continuing to find it difficult to breathe, he loosened his shirt collar even though the two top buttons were already undone. Clint Eastwood's character survived because the writer of the movie script wanted it that way, but Tracie had no such scriptwriter. She should have died that night, but, like Cathy, she lived. "It's a miracle that both babies survived," were the actual words spoken by the doctor that night.

But did Cathy really survive the impact of a head on collision? And did Tracie actually live through her choking ordeal? he was finally forced to ask himself.

David couldn't bring himself to believe Mr. Wright's account. Things of that nature did not happen in the real world. The idea was too farfetched, too unbelievable. If anything, his first assumption of what was happening was more realistic and believable. A children's market did exist, and people would pay large sums of money if desperate enough to get their hands on a child like Cathy, as he suspected the Parkers might have done.

But then again, what was Mr. Steamer's role? His dirty handprints were all over this. He was forever going out of his way to come across as the devil's replica, threatening to unleash supernatural powers. Was he actually the leader of a cult influenced by Satan in order to lure people into temptation and in turn force

God to take these children away? Was this whole thing really that farfetched? Was it just a coincidence that the moment he had signed that book deal and the moment John Parker's would-be affair with Lynda was made known, Cathy died both times?

Out of the blue, another thought came to mind. It was the spiritual myth that Father Mark once told him in front of Jackie: "I can't think of any pair in the world who God would trust to tutor His children, to school them properly of earthly ethics and morals than the Turner brothers," he told him and then went on to warn that the chosen few had to prevail against the evil urges of the dark side, or God would have no choice but to take his children back.

It took a few gruesome scenes from an old western for David to grasp that Tracie should have not survived at birth and a few more moments to suddenly realize that Nick was about to make the same mistake that he and John Parker had made, to submit to temptation by signing that disgusting Woodbridge deal and lose his daughter for it.

Kate marched upward, turning around every so often to check the orderly line of children following her up the well-travelled trail. She was pleased with the way things were progressing and delighted at the way Angelina carefully watched over them.

Up ahead, the trail took a sharp right. On the left hand side were vertical and hazardous cliffs with sharp rocks and deafening rapids below. It was well known that suicidal people had been recorded jumping to their death from that high point, but since the last fatality two chained fences, ten feet apart, were installed at the edge of the cliffs. The first fence was a boundary marker, one where travelers could watch the furious river below in safety. Between fences was a ten-foot buffer zone marked with large red caution signs spaced every forty feet along the fence, reminding climbers that this area was not to be entered. The last fence stood a few feet away from the dangers below. Clear signs warned careless hikers that if caught anywhere near this fence, this last form of defense against the rapids below, they would be banned from ever returning to Indian Pass Hills along with a hefty fine.

Kate was experienced. She was seasoned enough to expect the unexpected; the safety courses she had taken over the years attested to that. She was also trained to be aware of hazardous areas where others wouldn't ever notice; hence no one would be allowed to go anywhere near the first fence.

"Stay to the right," she cried out as they passed that dangerous bend, thankful when they passed that spot and the sounds of the furious torrents below couldn't be heard any longer. Raising her hand, she brought the children to a halt.

"Time to drink and rest," she announced to a welcomed cheer, pointing to a series of benches that stood next to the trail. "Pick a bench, and sit down."

The children ran towards the benches as though their lives depended on it, and soon afterwards Angelina removed a wrapped bundle of small orange juice containers from her backpack. She handed them out, each and every child thanking her in the process. When she got to the end, she gave one to Tracie and sat next to her, away from the others. She opened her purse. Inside was a cell phone that she wished would not ring for the duration of this trip but was prepared to answer it if it did.

"We have to have faith and believe that it will not ring today," she told Tracie.

"I am well prepared for either," was the child's courageous reply.

Most of the children chatted with each other while others simply drank their juice and looked deep inside the forest hoping to see the friendly Bigfoot from the Henderson's television fame, and when the furry monster chose not to make an appearance, they made believe that they did.

"Answer the phone, Lee!" shouted David after his fourth try at reaching his sister-in-law. The last three attempts rang six times before the answering machine kicked in and this, his fourth effort, seemed to be heading for the same ending. "Pick up the phone, Lee!" he shouted louder as if expecting to be heard.

She finally answered it.

"Lee, it's me. I need to speak to Nick," he said calmly so as not to set her off on one of her panic attacks.

Lee knew who it was. The screen on the phone told her it was him the first three times he called, and, though she would steadily deny it, she never forgot or forgave him for deserting Tracie at the picnic. She had lost all respect for him, and it was no secret that their relationship had never been the same since. To make matters worse, she had become very wary of him and no longer perceived him as a celebrity to boast about but a man who was vulgar to look at, a man who made her nervous whenever he looked at Tracie. She couldn't let go of the accusations against him, of the finger pointing and the constant whispering by others that he might be a predator.

"I need to speak to Nick," he repeated.

"He went to a meeting with Sam. Something about a real estate deal and won't be home for a while."

He wanted to scream and tear the phone off the wall but did neither. Keeping his poise he asked, "Did he leave you a number where he could be reached?"

"What's this all about? I want to know."

"Give me the number, Lee. Give me the number now," he asked more firmly.

"436–6785."

He wrote the number on top of the envelope. "Is Tracie home with you?"

His mere mention of Tracie's name sent shivers up her spine. "Why do you want to know where Tracie is?" she snapped.

He couldn't remain composed any longer. "Just tell me where she is!" he yelled into her ear.

"She went out hiking with the Girl Scouts!" she cried back.

"Where?"

"That's none of your business."

"Tell me where she is for God's sake!"

"Don't scream at me!"

Settle down, David, he thought, aimlessly walking around in circles with the phone pressed tightly to his ear. "Sorry, Lee. I didn't mean to raise my voice. You don't have to tell me where she is, but you need to go and get her. Bring her back home with you. I don't mean in an hour. I don't mean in five minutes. I mean now!"

The inevitable happened. She panicked and hung up. Most likely she would now lock herself inside the washroom to call Nick, thought David, but he was mistaken. Instead of calling her husband, she marched to the birdcage, picked it up, startling the budgies and slammed it down next to the open window. She angrily unfastened the gate, shaking it so violently that the shocked birds escaped into the open air. She wasn't finished. She needed to hurt David the way he had hurt her. She had no reservations about doing what she did next. This was her second time grabbing the newly laid egg and hurling it outside, waiting long enough to hear the faint sound of it hitting the ground before shutting the window.

"Can I speak to Nick Turner?" David asked after dialing the number Lee had given him.

"I'm sorry, sir, but he is in the middle of a meeting and can't be disturbed."

"This is his brother, David. I need to speak to him about an urgent family matter. I need to speak to him now," he repeated louder at the risk of losing his temper again.

"One moment please," she said, placing him on hold and directing his call from the offices of the investor's meeting directly to Mr. Steamer's headquarters.

"How are you, David?" answered a female voice.

He lowered the receiver, holding it on to his chest in utter dismay. He thought he recognized the voice and hoped he was wrong. "Dear God," he whispered. "Please don't let it be her." He slowly raised the phone back onto his ear.

"David, are you still there?"

"Is that you, Jackie?" he asked in a shattered tone.

"Yes, this is Jackie. It's so very nice to hear your voice again."

"But, but what are you doing there?" he shuddered.

"That's not important right now."

He was furious at being so naïve. He should have known something wasn't right when Jackie disappeared immediately after Cathy drowned. He should have known that she was one of Mr. Steamer's puppets and most likely he arranged their relationship in order to spy on him. In spite of her betrayal, he still held on to the slightest hope that their past affiliation was not all deceitful. "I know you can contact my brother. It's extremely imperative that I talk to him. I can't stress how much this means to me."

"There is nothing I can do for you, David. I am truly sorry."

"I know you are part of this, Jackie. You know Tracie is in grave danger. She's only a child," he struggled to remind her. "You met her, you talked to her, and you ate at the same table as her. That little girl is my niece for God's sake. Please get me Nick," he implored, short of weeping.

"I wish I could help you, David, but what you ask of me is impossible."

"Don't let him sign that deal. You know what I'm talking about. You have to know it means Tracie's death. Don't be like them. Don't be that evil."

"Bye, David," were her final two words before the phone went dead.

The two waiters dressed in neatly pressed black tuxedos stood by the swinging doors like programmed robots, eyes fixed on the stage at Mike Longo, anxiously waiting for his blessing before launching the evening's extravaganza. That politician's egotistic character brought out the worst in him. He was the ultimate manipulator of words, at times giving the waiters every indication that he was about to begin, only to break into a long drawn-out speech about his accomplishments and the prosperity during his reign in office. When it appeared that he was repeating his dialogue and that his yapping might turn into an embarrassing exhibit, his aide whispered into his ear. It worked. Mike Longo snapped out of his ongoing ranting and nodded at the waiters to begin, much to the delight of the investors.

The doors swung open, and seconds later a butler, who appeared to be in his late sixties, made his presence known. He looked so elegant, wearing a black-tailed tuxedo and crisp white gloves, which held a silver box. This box contained twenty contracts, all four pages long, each accompanied with a gold pen tied with a thin gold chain to a ring on the bottom right hand corner. The butler placed the box on the table next to the model representation of the Woodbridge Estate.

"The contracts, gentlemen," he announced in the most perfect, upper-lipped British accent this side of the Atlantic Ocean. Some investors couldn't wait to sign it. Overcome with voracity, the greedy ones made a mad dash for them, almost tilting the Woodbridge sculpture over while others quickly snapped them out of their lawyer's hands.

Unsettled by their pitiful behavior, Nick turned away, wishing he was somewhere else, but he wasn't. He was in a room filled with hollow and miserly people, fat cats who only cared about themselves. People he despised and yet found himself in the midst of.

He yanked the gold pen off the contract, placed it in front of him and spun it in circles.

"That pen is worth fifteen hundred at least," Sam told him.

"It doesn't seem right to spend that much on a pen."

"I'll keep it after you sign the contract if it bothers you that much," said Sam, snatching the pen from his hand.

The ownership of a pen was the last thing on Nick's mind. "I don't understand this entire showmanship. It reminds me of a game show."

"Loosen up, Nick. You won the lottery with this deal. Start behaving like it."

The exhibition didn't end with the butler passing out contracts and gold pens; it was only the beginning of the shameful display to come. Seconds later the back doors swung open, and out came a busty model dressed in a sparkling long gown, pushing a silver tray crammed with fresh seafood. There was cooked salmon, crab, octopus, shark fin, squid, and, as one would expect, as much caviar as could be consumed. Included in that mix was some of the largest shrimp ever caught, all buried in chopped ice. From the third and last rear entrance, another identically clothed model wheeled out another tray, filled with meats, fruit, mini-sausages wrapped in bacon, every cheese imaginable, homemade bread that was still warm, and, as a form of decoration, were forty bottles of twenty-year-old wine, which were imported directly from France, two for each investor.

All components were in place—wine, food, lovely ladies, an imported butler, and twenty contracts. It was now time to get down to business.

"Demolition will begin as soon as possible," claimed Mike Longo. "Within twenty months, rising from the ashes will appear Woodbridge Estates; no longer a vision but a reality made possible by you gentlemen," and as an afterthought he mentioned that the removal of the old, the sick, and the poor living there was now a federal government problem, not theirs.

"You can add that to your accomplishments," heckled an investor, followed by a roar from his partners.

"That I will," Mike Longo cried back, grinning and blind to the fact that it was more of a sarcastic remark than a compliment.

Some investors signed the minute they could, while others were overheard saying, "I don't sign anything unless my lawyer reads it first," more as a formality and to appear more refined than they actually were. Walking around the table was the butler, picking up the endorsed contracts and placing them back into the silver box, at all times carefully moving out of the investors way as they hustled towards the seafood tray. There they huddled together, dipping the shrimp into the spicy sauces and focusing on the model's eye-catching cleavage before shoving the food into their mouths. Only one contract remained unsigned—Nick's.

Despite the racket, a tapping could be heard. It was Sam, tapping the table with the gold pen much as Mr. Steamer did with David when he was waiting for him to sign his book deal.

"Do you have to do that?" snapped Nick, staring at the pen and then at Sam.

Sam stopped. He placed the pen down. "I'm sorry. It's a habit I inherited from an old boss of mine," he explained, watching Nick examining the contract for the third time. "I went over it a dozen times and know it word for word. Why are you making me look incompetent in front of all these people?" he asked.

"There's not a single paragraph in here about the relocation of those residents, only that they will all be gone when construction begins," he said, angrily slapping the contract with the back of his hand.

"Like our Mr. Longo said, it's a federal government problem, not yours or mine."

"I don't see that written in here."

"Why don't you let them stay at your place then?" Sam laughed.

Nick wasn't amused. "You make it sound like it's a crime to care."

"I'm sorry. I didn't mean to get out of line, but I'm not going to apologize to anybody for my success or my lifestyle, and neither should you. Let the washed up rock bands throw free concerts to raise money for the poor so they can increase their record sales. At least we don't hide who we are."

Unbeknownst to Sam, one of the two models approached his end of the table with a dish of food. "Would you care for some cheese?" she asked.

He turned to her just in time to see her bend down and place the dish in front of his face, at the same time revealing the top portion of her breasts. Sam was ridiculously handsome. One would think he enjoyed and was accustomed to these clear flirtations, but strangely the opposite was true. He unexpectedly blushed like a small child and quickly lowered his head. Sensing that she may have offended him or that he might be married, she walked away.

"I still feel uncomfortable with this sentence," said Nick, not noticing that Sam had his head hung low. When he didn't look up, he asked, "Are you all right?"

"I don't know," he replied, raising his head.

"You're all red. What happened?"

Sam held on to his stomach, giving every indication he was about to vomit. Suddenly the butler appeared out of nowhere, coming to Sam's rescue and stood behind Nick, practically shoving the silver box in front of his face. "Yours is the only one left, sir. If your intention is to sanction it, I will give you more time. If not, I will submit the rest, minus yours," he made known.

"Please sign it," Sam managed to utter.

"Are you sure you're okay?" he asked him again, and when he nodded his head, Nick looked around and felt that every person, including Sam and the butler, were sickened by his gutless indecision. He alone was to blame for putting himself in this position, wanting to "add zing" to his life, not them, and the fault was his and only his.

Sensing that he was at last ready to sign, Sam cleared his throat. He needed Nick to understand something before going through with it. "The last thing I want to do is put pressure on you, but keep in mind that when you sign it, it will be of your own free will."

Nick flipped the contract to the last page and stared at the dotted line.

As video cameras went, not only was it one of the smallest, but for its intelligence capabilities, was unsurpassed. With its dark green glass shield, it mixed well with the other ceiling fixtures, such as the lights and air conditioning jackets. Normally a camera of such stature could be installed anywhere on the ceiling. This particular one was set up at the extreme corner of the investor's room. The sole purpose was to track Nick's every move. No one but the butler or Sam paid much attention to it; with both taking the occasional glance at it.

Back at the Steamer's Publishing, Inc. building, inside one of his many penthouse offices and sitting behind a huge TV screen were Lora, Jackie, and Mr. Steamer, all three spying on the investors through this camera. Beside them sat young Sean, the director of this camera's control system. Mr. Steamer asked for his assistance due to his expertise in operating such surveillance equipment. This youngster had in front of him a wealth of controls at the tip of his fingers that he could choose from, but basically used only four of its multiple functions available to him—to zoom in and out, rotate the actual lens a full three hundred and sixty degrees, pause it on and off, and make use of the instant replay. With this technology at his command, he could point that camera at any person or object, zoom in on anything as small as a penny, and if Mr. Steamer so desired, bring it in so close for him that he would be able to see the beard on Abraham Lincoln.

For the past twenty minutes, not much on the screen was of interest to Mr. Steamer. Sean roamed as freely as he wished from Sam to the butler and then back to Nick until something caught Mr. Steamer's eye. He suddenly sat up and placed himself behind Sean. "Can you please focus on Nick Turner's hand and enlarge it?" he politely asked.

Lora and Jackie stood up and huddled around Mr. Steamer. All three stared at the video screen, and when Nick moved his hand away from the contract, there was no mistake—he had signed on the dotted line, making him the twentieth investor.

"Do you want me to bring it any closer, sir?" asked Sean.

"No, thank you," Mr. Steamer replied, turning his attention behind him to Lora and Jackie. "He did it. He signed the contract."

The women were understandably disheartened. Not so much for themselves, but for Mr. Steamer. "If Lora can forgive me for speaking on her behalf, we both want to express our deepest sympathy, Mr. Steamer," moaned Jackie.

"You need not feel badly for me. I have been subjected to these disappointments countless times before and will continue to be for eternity. One would think that I would be accustomed to these things, but I admit that losing both the Turner brothers in one year is difficult to accept." He weakly smiled at the women and then at Sean, putting on his bravest front, but Lora knew this time was different. This time he was hurt more than other times, and it showed. He regarded the Turner brothers as exceptional, and he loved them for all they stood for.

Lora had not seen a sincere grin on Mr. Steamer's face for centuries, one that he could call his own. She knew that he could enlighten any situation if he so desired because God saw fit to trust him with powers beyond anyone's imagination. He was not allowed to amend what the Turner brothers did. He could not tamper with history, but he could amend the Turner tragedies, adjust them, and turn them into something that was uplifting, to take a wrong and make it easier to bear. After all his years of faithful service, Mr. Steamer deserved to be happy, and why not tell him now?

"Mr. Steamer," Lora began, ready to pour out what was on her mind.

"Please make the call to Angelina now," he stopped her as though reading her thoughts.

Forming a single line, the children looked on in wonder when Kate pointed down below at the nest resting on the edge of a tree branch. Two tiny spotted bird eggs could be clearly seen from above, adding to the youngsters' fascination. Pleased by the children's keenness, she reassured them that they all would be given the opportunity to see the eggs up close. It would have to be one child at a time and warned the girls that there was to be absolutely no touching of the nest or the eggs. "If the mother bird knows that they have been touched, she will abandon them," she told them, not really sure if this was true or not.

Standing forth from the front, Tracie appeared restless, sporadically looking back at Angelina, hoping her cell phone would not ring, but this time it did. She saw her whispering into the receiver. Her facial features told the little girl the news was not good. Without giving a thought to losing her turn in line she walked to the back, stopped before Angelina and softly asked, "I presume Mr. Turner signed the contract."

Heartbroken, Angelina lowered the phone, "I am afraid he did," she confirmed, adding, "It would not be right for the rest of these children to see the bird eggs and not you. We can wait until you see them before we carry on."

"I think that I would rather proceed with what is expected of me. I am ready now," she replied.

Angelina placed the phone back to her ear in time to hear Lora say, "Mr. Steamer's thoughts are with you both." And with those final words, Angelina dropped the cell phone back into her backpack.

"Mr. Steamer wanted it known that his thoughts are with you," she let Tracie know.

"And I will not disappoint him."

Angelina glimpsed at Kate, satisfied that the Scoutmaster was too occupied with the other children to be aware of what was to come. She then raised her index finger, tenderly running it along Tracie's forehead, continuing down her cheeks and bringing it to an end at the bottom of her chin. "May your journey be a sound one."

"I trust that our Father will see to it," grinned Tracie, kissing her on her forehead.

It began with a few backward steps until Tracie simply turned around and walked away from the rest and coming to a stop at the main trail. She placed her feet together,

and suddenly felt an enticing warm wind blowing on her face. It felt good and reassuring. It came unexpectedly, and if she was at all nervous before, that warm gust of air blew away with it away any remaining fear.

"Thank you, Father," she said, knowing God was responsible. Feeling confident, she spread her arms as though about to escalate upwards, towards the skies, and began to sing a beautiful harmonious song, one whose words were not of this world. Seconds later she stopped singing, held on to her chest and collapsed to her death.

CHAPTER TWELVE

Tracie was gone, and the four of them were forced to deal with this tragedy in their own way. Young Sean had already excused himself. He was the least experienced and was permitted to go to the next room to grieve in private. When his sobbing became unbearable, Jackie saw fit to comfort him, leaving Lora and Mr. Steamer alone.

"Shall I go and search the files for prospective parents the both children?" she asked.

Mr. Steamer scratched his ear and ran his hand down to his chin. "Do we have anyone on record that could better Cathy's education?"

Lora thought it unusual that he would ask that question. He knew just as well as she did that David Turner, in his own unique way was a sacred oddity.

"The world is filled with many wonderful people, with many outstanding and moral standards. Our files hold the names of such potentials, but all would be hard pressed to teach Cathy any more than Mr. Turner had already taught her."

"If I understand you correctly, you are suggesting that Cathy has reached her potential?"

Once again Lora was confused by his question. On more than one occasion, Mr. Steamer told her in confidence of how pleased he was with Cathy's incredible advancement and that it was all due to David Turner. He thought of the times Cathy had waited for the opportune time to call Mr. Steamer and tell him of the wonderful things she and David talked about that particular day and how pleased he was by Cathy's passion. He paced in circles, a number of times, deep in thought, and then suddenly stopped and looked at Lora. There was something about his expression that excited her. Something about the way he unexpectedly warmed up, saying nothing but actually telling her many things.

"Shall I go and search the records? Shall I bring you files of prospective parents?" she asked again as a lure to expose his thoughts into the open.

Mr. Steamer took an elated breath and with a sparkle in his eyes and a genuine smile that Lora hadn't seen for centuries and said, "Yes. Bring me the files. But not now. Tomorrow would be a better time and when you do, bring back with you the Book of Records as well for I have made a decision, and it must be documented. To put it mildly, I think Cathy is as ready as she can be. She has no need for further tutoring, only a gathering with our friends to celebrate her graduation," he said and with a sparkle in his eye, added, "For I think it time that she enter the next stage of her development."

Stunned by the joyous turn of events, if she heard him correctly, then Cathy's days of living with mortals were over. A metamorphose awaited her, one so extravagant that God himself would put everything on hold to watch. She couldn't but enhance the admiration she held for Mr. Steamer. This was him at his very best, the true gentle warrior who did proper things at the proper time.

"I take it that the files of potential parents are only for Tracie then?" she asked him.

He paused for a moment. "It could be written that Nick Turner was equal to David in his tutoring methods but due to Lee's influence, I feel there is still more that Tracie can learn from new noble parents."

Lora could not agree with him more. It was unfortunate, but Tracie was not quite as ready as Cathy. "Do you have a time and date in mind for Cathy's celebration?"

"Tonight," he answered without reservation and then looked at his watch. "In three hours."

Lora couldn't help but giggle at his audacity. To arrange such a celebration and for it to take place within that short time frame was a monstrous task. To invite other spirits who live thousands of miles away and to get the white mansion ready for the occasion would be even more of a challenge and undertaking, but she knew that he would get his way. Though his decision was a hasty one, there was no doubt in her mind that everything would be ready, and it would be a smashing success.

Lynda Steward got Jackie's call only minutes ago with the news of that night's celebration. Since then she had already showered and washed her hair. Missing from the washroom counter was the expensive lipstick, the one that cost the manufacture pennies to produce, yet sold for over ten dollars. As far as additional beauty products one would expect to be spread across the basin counter from a young woman preparing for a night out, there were none. Other than a can of unscented deodorant and a bottle of inexpensive weak perfume, there was no eyeliner, no rouge, no hair products, and no hair dryer.

She stepped out from the washroom and stood in front of the mirror, not convinced the plain blue gown was the correct choice. True, it was one of her favorites, considered slightly more conservative because of its length, but she could not be sure. The thought of contacting Angelina for her opinion had crossed her mind, but she quickly dismissed it, since she would be busy preparing Cathy for tonight. On the other hand, these festivities were special. She wanted to be as sure as could be, not wanting to spend all night self-conscious about her attire. She was confident that Lora would be more than pleased to offer her opinion. She would call her.

The receptionist found she had to hold the phone away from her ear, disturbed by his earsplitting voice. The man on the other side of the receiver was not only rude but on the verge of threatening her. She explained that Mr. Steamer could not and would not be disturbed, but the man in question would not take no for an answer.

"I will keep on calling and calling until you get him on the line," growled David.

On the threshold of hanging up, she finally relented. "One moment please."

Mr. Steamer was in the midst of removing the protective wrapping from his tuxedo when the call came in. "I'm very sorry to disturb you, Mr. Steamer, but David Turner insists on talking to you. Shall I direct his call to security?"

He still had to shower, shave, and do all the little things, such as polishing his shoes in order to look as respectable as he needed to be for tonight's festivities, but it was David Turner on the line. He had more than one reason to take the call and to deal with him.

"Let him through," he told the receptionist. "I'm very busy, David. Be quick. What do you want?" he sneered at him the second David got through.

"She's only a child. I'm begging you not to hurt her."

Mr. Steamer looked back at the video screen. Nick didn't appear comfortable; however, he did hand his contract to the butler, sealing his fate and that of Tracie's.

"I'm afraid it's too late for that. Just like you, your older brother got greedy. I'm watching him now as we speak. He just signed a contract, which he should not have, and it cost him a daughter."

"What does a signature on a piece of paper have to do with the life of two innocent little girls?" he screamed back.

"It is because of that innocence. The both of you should have known better. You both should have held on to the values that your father taught you," he reasoned.

"No one made you God!"

"And I am thankful of that, for he is much more forgiving and resilient to the actions of so many. I am not that strong. I would make a pathetic God. But kind as our Father is, he must be answered to. There was nothing I could have done for your brother. He wrote his own script. He sealed his own fate with the help of a gold pen, out of his own free will, and now Tracie is gone from this earth because of it, so why don't we leave it at that, David?"

"You miserable, miserable old man!" sobbed David.

"You sound pitiful in your preposterous attempt at name calling."

"But why?" he started to weep.

"Because the penalty of plunging into that temptation pit is an expensive one, my dear friend. There are no second chances, no possible way to turn back the hand of time."

"I'll find you. No man is invincible!"

"Get your facts straight, David. You are forever calling me a man. I never once claimed to be one."

"You don't fool me. I know who and what you are," cried David. "I will find you and do everything in my power to keep you caged in hell."

"Don't be so dramatic, David, and hear me well. Unlike you, dying is a luxury I don't have, and I am envious of those that can," he made known before hanging up the phone. He looked back at Lora. "I think Mr. Turner is reaching his end. We may need the services of Detective Wood again."

"I was speaking to her only moments ago. She and the twins were preparing for tonight's festivities."

"Can you please call her back? There is one more thing she has to do for me."

"Yes, Mr. Steamer."

Before Lora had the opportunity to call the detective, the phone rang. It was Lynda Steward seeking Lora's advice and wishing to know if her blue plain dress was conservative enough for the evening's celebrations. Lora told her she would look lovely in it and then made the call to the detective.

It had been a while since Sam excused himself from the table and went looking for the butler to request some effervescent antacid, complaining about his stomach cramps. He placed the blame on that extra mouthful of caviar. Nick found his excuse weak since others in the room filled their stomachs with the same expensive seafood and showed no similar symptoms. Regardless of his reason, neither Sam nor the butler had been seen since.

With Sam gone, Nick felt lost and alone even though he was surrounded by the obnoxious lawyers and investors. He had nothing in common with them other than he was now in an uneasy partnership with this group of greedy men. When he caught Mike Longo slipping a hundred-dollar bill between the model's breasts and whispering into her ear, he had reached his limit and wanted to get out of this mad asylum he found himself in. He couldn't think of anything better to do than to stop by a video store on his way home and choose a new release to surprise Tracie. He stood up and looked for Sam one last time, wanting to tell him to keep all paperwork pertaining to the deal at his office, away from Lee. He shivered at the thought that she might discover it.

Out of nowhere, a state trooper walked into the convention hall. Nick had no way of knowing it was the same man who eight years earlier knocked on David's door to inform him of Diane's car accident. That man had aged and not well. With his bushy eyebrows, thin mustache, and thick-rimmed glasses, his once-round face was now thin, haggard, and covered with wrinkles.

If Nick needed an ironic twist in his life, the sight of a state trooper was it. He envisioned that their real estate scheme had been exposed and that this officer was the beginning of a police raid, ready to swarm the room at any moment. He quickly sat back down when he saw Mike Longo shove the lady model aside and greet the trooper. They recognized each other, shaking hands and talking when suddenly Mike Longo pointed him out to the trooper.

Why me? he bitterly thought. *There are other people in here who are just as guilty.*

Uneasy, though not sure why, he grabbed a cluster of grapes and picked at them one at a time, tossing them inside his mouth and chewing them as though they represented his last meal.

The trooper stopped before him and removed his hat, placing it horizontally against his chest, four inches above his belt, as was his custom. When Nick turned to face him, he found something odd about this officer. Though his eyebrows were a grayish color, almost white, he had a full head of thick, black curly hair. The man was obviously wearing a hairpiece, a bad one at that.

"Mr. Nick Turner?" asked the trooper.

"Yes. I am Nick Turner," he replied, caught with one single grape stuck between his index finger and thumb.

"Do you have a daughter named Tracie?"

Nick didn't want to ask why, and he didn't.

"Sorry, Mr. Turner, but do you have a daughter named Tracie?" he asked again, running his hand along his false head of hair.

"I do."

"I'm sorry, sir, but I have to inform you that your daughter passed away."

Nick squeezed the grape, spewing its liquids all over the table.

David's eyes had been fastened on the phone receiver for the past hour, expecting it to ring at any moment, and when it did, he couldn't help but to jump away from it. The incoming number on the call display screen was not telling him something he didn't already know. David anticipated his brother would be looking for him. By now he would have received the disastrous news that Tracie was dead, something he already knew.

He didn't answer, ashamed and embarrassed by his gutless decision not to do so. It rang until the message machine kicked in. He owed it to his brother to at least listen to it.

A weeping Nick, scarcely able to talk, begged him to get over to his house. David listened in agony as the devastated and broken-hearted man shamelessly cried, "She's dead, David. My little Tracie just dropped dead. Oh God! Oh God, David!"

He continued to wail, at times not making any sense and often repeating that the doctors were confused by her sudden death. Although exceptionally rare in children of her age, they think she might have died from a heart attack most likely caused from a heart spasm that briefly cut off her blood supply.

From the background, David heard a turbulent Lee cursing his name, demanding to know how he knew Tracie was in trouble before anyone else. He was stunned to hear her grab the phone off Nick and yell at the top of her lungs, "They also told us that a healthy eight year old just doesn't drop dead like she did unless extremely stressed. What did you do to her?"

He heard Nick grab the phone away from her and try to calm her down when she threatened to call the police, flatly charge David of being involved in Tracie's death and accusing him of being the ringleader of a child molesting ring. The agonizing message ended with Nick pleading that he needed his brother and with Lee calling David names he never imagined were part of her vocabulary.

David took a few steps backward and sat down, thinking that Cathy couldn't be a victim of a child slavery ring like he first thought; it wasn't that simple, yet how could he possibly explain to his brother or to anyone else that Mr. Steamer possessed super-natural powers and was directly responsible, for not only Tracie's death, but also Cathy's resurrection.

Should he tell Nick to begin searching the streets for Tracie and by chance find her like he found Cathy? He himself would not believe it. It was all too uncanny, too weird, yet all true. The past incidents, bizarre and unnatural as they were, did actually happen and were not found in chapters from a Stephen King novel.

With his emotions in shambles, he laid his head back, the opportune time for his imagination to show its ugly face and harass him as never before. He imagined a smirking Mr. Steamer saying, "You didn't even have the guts to talk to your own brother, yet he was there for you at all times. You are beyond being a coward. You are a waste of a life."

His visions continued to spin out of control, coming to an end when Mr. Steamer dared him to dig up his daughter's grave. He wondered if that madman's challenge was in effect a ploy in order to frighten him to do the exact opposite. Didn't that man have his fill of ruining him? Did he now want to completely destroy whatever was left of his miserable future as well?

It was at this moment that he understood that in order to come to terms with all that had happened, the unthinkable not only had to be considered, but had to be acted upon. The act was so hideous and barbaric that if caught it would place distance between him and his brother, possibly forever. Tragically, if wrong he would also be found guilty of a more repulsive felony: the squandering of a once promising life—his own.

David grabbed the Jag's keys. He was going to a cemetery to dig up a grave. Cathy's grave.

CHAPTER THIRTEEN

What distinguished this black crow from his equals was its beak. While most of his feathered peers were all born with normal downward beaks, this crow was born with its bill upward. In spite of this birth defect, the bird adapted well, choosing well-aged road kill to survive on, not the fresh kill where it would have to tear at the hard torso.

It flew in well-spaced circles for a number of times. With its head lurched downward, the big black bird was searching for a place to land, a lookout post. From there it could rummage for scraps of food or better, dead rabbits that other prey may have deserted. It landed on the tombstone next to the one that read Cathy Parker. There it perched, turning its head effortlessly from left to right. When no food was found, it seemed bored, and within seconds sprung up into the air, landing on a yellow backhoe parked at the edge of the cemetery.

The bird had been there before, finding forgotten sandwiches behind the seat. As luck would have it, a large slice of dried ham was stuck between the seat and the leathered edge. The bird plucked at it and quickly launched itself up in the sky, eventually becoming a tiny speck.

This particular evening was murky, and the lack of wind made it worse. Across the street, David was sweating inside the Jag, waiting for darkness. Taking a long slow drink from a warm bottle of water, he studied the graveyard and then looked up at the fading horizon, estimating another hour before it would be dark enough for him to do what had to be done. He took hold of the steering wheel and pulled himself forward.

When tears rolled down his face, it surprised him. He hadn't anticipated them; they just formed on their own, most likely due to what he had become. Recognizing that he had reached the point of no return, he wiped the tears away and wondered how it had all got this demented, this surreal, a horror film coming to life.

Only eight short years ago he was a successful writer with a beautiful wife and a child on the way. Those were the best years of his life, a time when invitation after invitation poured in, requesting his attendance anywhere, from universities to dinners with international diplomats. Everyone wanted to be seen with David Turner. Everybody wanted to be photographed with the handsome man who seemed too good to be true.

At times it got so chaotic that Diane seriously considered hiring a publicist for him. He laughed it off claiming that a representative was only a poorly disguised excuse for an egotistic celebrity, something he just couldn't understand.

Now David found himself perspiring heavily inside a car that suddenly seemed too expensive and he was minutes away from unearthing a casket

This is shear madness, he told himself, yet seconds later thought he heard Cathy screaming out his name from six feet under.

He looked back at the church, with its single light bulb on top of a post doing its best to light up as much of the area as possible. There was a depressing feeling about the Parker home.

The whole property looked as if was deserted. The signpost announcing the times and dates of services, including upcoming events, had vanished. Someone went through the trouble of yanking it completely out off the ground. It appeared that the Parkers had moved out, perhaps separately, or probably didn't want to live there any longer. It didn't matter to him if Florence had left John Parker or not; he had his own crisis that had to be dealt with.

He leaned over to the side, opening the glove compartment, and took out a flashlight, screwdriver, and a pair of pliers along with a crowbar, which rested on the floor of the passenger seat. Before getting out of the car, he placed his hands together in prayer, "If you do exist, God, and you are as good as your reputation attests, then find it in your heart to forgive me for what I am about to do. If you don't exist, then I need not fear the fires of hell."

David stepped out of the car, determined to see this through and not to stop until the casket was opened or until he was caught in the process. He turned the flashlight on and quickly and decisively marched towards the backhoe. Throwing the crowbar in the back, he jumped onto the driver's seat, not expecting the keys to be there waiting for him, and they weren't. His late father had taught him that most machines didn't need keys to start if one understood what made them work.

He lowered his head under the ignition box, pointed the flashlight under its cover, and within seconds had it unscrewed. Pliers in hand, he sliced off the correct wires, crossed them in a certain way, and the machine gave every indication it was about to roar. Along the side ran a long galvanized muffler, and when a black mushroom cloud sputtered out, the backhoe was under his control.

He immediately switched on the two huge upper headlights, angling their powerful beams towards Cathy's tombstone. Sitting back on the weather-beaten leather seat, he shifted it into gear. With the machine swaying back and forth, he only stopped once before reaching the grave and that was to hold on to his stomach while he vomited.

Tonight would be Sean's first attendance at such a celebration, so it was understandable that he should ask Jackie if he looked proper in his tuxedo; and when she told him he came across as a younger version of Mr. Steamer, he first blushed and then burst with pride at the compliment. The ladies themselves looked absolutely stunning, wearing long white dresses that reached their ankles, white shoes, and beige shawls that were wrapped around their shoulders.

"Tonight's celebration is a highly-spirited event, my young man. Absorb from it all that you can," Mr. Steamer advised Sean as the youngster walked past him, thankful and privileged for his guidance.

When Sean disappeared down the hallway, Jackie stepped forward. "In retrospect, Mr. Steamer, Sean's self-consciousness reminds me when I attended my first celebration."

Mr. Steamer had just recently showered and shaved. He didn't have to ask the ladies how his pressed tuxedo fitted because he felt confident. Along with his silk scarf loosely wrapped around his neck and his long, thin beige overcoat, he appeared unquestionably distinctive, resembling and acting like a celebrity about to present the best actor award. A veteran of these celebrations, having attended or orchestrated them since the beginning of time, they never lost their sparkle or their importance.

"I always compare these nights with giving a decisive thrashing to the demon." He laughed, the ladies giggling along with him. "May I study the guest list?" he asked, giving Lora time to recoup, and when she did, a directory of the evening's guests was given to him. He studied it. "I see that Miss Wheeler has confirmed her attendance."

"She did," Lora replied, suspecting Mr. Steamer had invited her with the outside chance that she would regrettably decline due to other commitments.

The last thing he wanted to do was to imply any disrespect towards Miss Wheeler, who was Mr. Steamer's spiritual equal. There was always a sense of harmless banter between the two higher messengers at these functions, and this evening would most likely be no different. It was well understood by everyone that Miss Wheeler and Mr. Steamer had always respected each other's celebrations and considered their featherlike lampooning as a tool to encourage and strive for better things.

"It would only be proper that she was present. She did invite us to hers," Lora reminded him.

"And when was that?" he asked.

"One hundred and twenty-four years ago, in the charming little village of Caledon East, just north of Toronto, Canada."

Mr. Steamer hesitated, pretending to be struggling to recollect, but he didn't fool Lora. She knew that he remembered every detail of every celebration that had ever taken place. "Yes, yes, I remember now."

"Would you think it out of line if I asked why you appear troubled by her presence?"

He took his time, searching for an answer and, following a short pause, decided it would be best not to give her one. He had his reasons for being concerned; worried somewhat that Miss Wheeler was too conservative for the plans he had in mind for this evening. Not that she could prevent him from carrying out those plans, since he didn't have anyone to answer to but God himself.

Lora didn't ask a second time. It wasn't her place to do so. If he wished to share things with her, he had a habit of momentarily scratching the back of his ear. When he showed no signs that he would, Lora asked, "Shall we go?"

He glanced at his gold pocket watch and then at the two women. "Yes, it is that time." He took a few steps out of the door, suddenly stopped, and began scratching the back of his ear. "Regardless of how awkward Miss Wheeler may feel or by some of our Father's elderly advisers' reactions, I have come to the conclusion that David Turner should be in attendance as well."

The women looked at one another and grinned ever so slightly.

"I trust that you are both in agreement," he replied, causing them to broaden their grins into full-blown smiles.

The ground was more solid than David had thought it would be, compressed and rugged. The iron chains were responsible for the cuts and scratches on the back of both his hands and the upper part of his arms. The slash on his right inner arm was not in need of stitches but was bleeding as was his elbow. All these injuries and too many bruises to mention were caused at sliding two chains under the coffin before the backhoe could hoist it up.

He finally managed to clip the ends to the machine's extended arm and secured them onto the thick, welded iron hook. Testing them numerous times and confident they would hold, he struggled to climb back out of the six foot hole. He slipped and plummeted back in, landing head first on the coffin's surface and adding yet another injury, a gash to his cheekbone.

Undaunted, he struggled back up, kicked the edge, creating a small foothold so he could fit the tip of his toes inside and hauled his battered body out. Continuing with sheer adrenaline, he jumped back onto the backhoe and sat down behind the controls. The chain held well, and he hoisted the coffin up, swung it to the side of the pit and lowered it four feet away from the machine's front wheels. Shutting it off, he leaped from the seat, positioned the two upper headlights directly at the casket, grabbed the crowbar, and jumped down, landing both feet beside the coffin.

Kneeling down, he used both hands to wipe the loose soil off the top and repeatedly chanted, "I'm so sorry," not certain to whom he was apologizing to or why; the words just flowed out of his mouth. He then pressed the tip of the screwdriver into the coffin's slit with his left hand and, using the palm of his other, hammered it in as far as it would go. This forced the lid to open just enough for the end of the crowbar to fit.

What if Mr. Steamer was just a strange old devil worshiper and it's not my Cathy, but a child whose only crime was that they shared a resemblance? he thought in absolute terror as he turned around to pick up the crowbar.

It fit perfectly, and though the lid was solid, it was no match for the one-inch piece of iron, a foot and a half long and with one strong-minded man at the end of it. He jerked it up, a bit at a time, encircling the top every two feet and repeating the procedure until the only thing left was to swing it up and look inside.

His arms weakened, and he felt light-headed. Too frightened to open it, too frightened not to, he cast the crowbar away and placed his hand under the overlapping handle. As he raised the lid, it squeaked, adding to the eeriness and the temptation to let it go, but he held on and opened it wide enough to see a surrounding silky lining. Then it suddenly jammed, refusing to open any wider.

"No! No! No!" he screamed, jumping onto his feet and placing both hands under the handle. With every ounce of strength left in him, he wiggled it until it snapped open, losing his balance in the process and falling backwards. Slowly crawling back towards it on his hands and knees, he looked inside and other than a shiny sheet and a soft milky white pillow—it was empty.

David did not move a muscle for the best part of the next few minutes except to stare inside; then strangely enough, he began to laugh. He started with minor chuckles, which eventually turned into a loud hysterical laughter that seemed like it could go on forever. Doubling up until his sides hurt, he walked away, leaned his back against the machine's tire and sat down.

"Nicely done, Mr. Turner," he whispered, swaying back and forth, but he wanted the world to hear what he had to say next him and screamed, "I was right all along. My baby is alive!" he repeated until it became a pitiful mumble.

Unexpectedly, the casket's lid shut on its own, making a haunting echoing sound that snapped David out of his hellish spell. There was no need to reopen it. He knew of its contents and stared at it for the next few minutes before realizing that he was now crying just as loud as he had been laughing.

It was simply a remarkable feat, one that would be deemed impossible to achieve, given the short time frame, but despite having only three hours to prepare, things were flowing nicely. Lora and Jackie had invited everyone on Mr. Steamer's list; unbelievably each and every one confirmed that they would be more than happy to attend. These "special" guests arrived from all corners of the world, chosen hastily, but carefully by Mr. Steamer himself. They were all so different and yet so alike, of all race and colour with one thing in common: they all had a responsibility to their own Devine Icon and were all angels of their own faith.

Representatives from the Buddhism, Hinduism, Islam, Judaism, and Sikhism faiths were present along with many more from different religions that Mr. Steamer saw fit to invite. They all shared the most basic value: to love others as they would want to be loved.

This was an exciting time, an opportunity for all beliefs to "catch up" and not to preach whose ideological principals had more merit. It was a time to share and try to understand Mr. Steamer's values as he would when invited to their celebrations. It made this evening's gathering wide reaching and confirmed that the universe was vast enough for all faiths to enjoy and to share.

The lineup of stretch limousines took turns stopping in front of 999 Paradise Avenue, giving their guests time to get out and then drive away to make room for the next one to take its place. As the visitors stepped out, the butler, the same one who was present at the investor's meeting, announced into a microphone their names and the faith they represented. Handshakes and warm welcomes were in the offering first, exchanging pleasantries and complimenting on each other's attire was next. They smiled and were attentive to one another's charming tales of goodness mixed with reminiscence of past celebrations; and when the initial conversations ended, they strolled up at a neatly trimmed path, which brought them to a huge white mansion.

This massive building was a marvel of engineering design. With its two dozen huge pillars surrounding the outer building and its glossed stonewalls, people entering would assume they were entering an ancient Roman building where toga-garbed senators planned their expanding empire. What added to the splendor was a powerful beam of light originating from the skies above and penetrating through the mansion's roof—a glowing cylinder of light with its beginnings in paradise and the ends on earth.

Sooner or later, David believed that he would be caught and dragged away from the cemetery, placed in front of a judge as a formality, and then locked away for life. It didn't matter that the coffin was empty. He had a "history" of chasing little girls. He was fingerprinted because of it, and when the proper authorities asked him what he did with the missing body, they would assume the most hideous crime of him, but at least he'd awake every morning knowing that Cathy was out there somewhere. The price of spending limitless years in prison would be well worth it. She would one day grow up, marry, and have children of her own.

It could be fun, he tried to convinced himself of his imminent prison time. While locked up he could meditate for hours upon hours and take advantage of his writer's imagination for a change rather than fight it. His mind would be free to roam wherever he wanted it to like never before. There would be no barriers, no issues, no Mr. Steamers. In this fantasy world he could easily put himself and Cathy back in Scotland to live the life that had eluded him since Diane died.

At last, he thought. *At last I can be part of those illusive fairy tale endings that I wrote about.*

The red light revolving from the police cruiser's roof eventually found its way to David, flashing on and off on his face. He didn't react when the cruiser parked in front of the cemetery, and the fact that someone was now holding on to a flashlight and calling out his name didn't unsettle him at all. He wouldn't jump up in a cowardly attempt at escaping no matter how many came to arrest him. In an ironic twist, he felt a caring blanket of calmness protecting him, a feeling of contentment, and he welcomed it. Still resting against the backhoe's tire, he watched the police approach. Emotionally drained and with no drive left in him, this peacefulness was earned, and he would demand a few more minutes of it before they took him away.

He couldn't make out how many police officers were approaching; two, maybe three shadowy and vague images, all taking small steps with commanding voices telling him to stay put. When he heard a female's voice, he recognized it as Detective Wood's.

"Where are you, Mr. Turner?" she shouted.

David tried to locate her, but the powerful flashlights pointing in his face irritated his eyes to the point of stinging.

"Get those lights off my face," he cried out, placing his arm in front of him to block the beams.

"Stay where you are, Mr. Turner. We're not in the mood to chase you in the dark!" warned another officer.

"I said get those flashlights off my face!" he screamed. "I'm not going anywhere!"

The detective located him. He was telling her the truth. He didn't behave like he was about to run anywhere. She then turned to her right, saw the mound of dirt next to the freshly dug grave, and shone the light downward, into the hole.

"Amazing," she said.

Approximately five feet behind her stood the twins. "Not only is he an author, but he can also operate machines," said one officer to the other.

Beside the heap of soil was the exposed coffin. Detective Wood pointed her flashlight at it, carefully inching next to it and without reservation, opened the cover and looked inside. "Simply amazing," she repeated, shaking her head then pointing the flashlight at David's bloodied hands and arms. "I can see that you had a busy night, Mr. Turner."

"It would appear that way, Detective Wood, but well worth it," he declared, letting out a loud laugh. "You saw for yourself. It is empty. My daughter is alive, but then again don't take me for an idiot and pretend to be surprised. I saw you and your twins with Mr. Steamer." He stopped laughing. "You are all a piece of work, especially you, detective. The way you paraded that death certificate before me was a performance to be proud of. Whatever Steamer is paying you is not enough."

"Nothing has changed. You still are as unyielding as ever, or should I say pig headed?"

"Forgive me if I sound insensitive, but it doesn't matter to me who you are or what you all represent anymore. It just feels so good knowing I am sane after all."

"I'm Paul," said the first officer. "And this is my brother Peter."

David wasn't interested. The last thing he was going to remember were the names of these phony police officers.

"Why do you two remind me of the Smother Brothers?" He laughed.

The detective grinned, as did the twins. "I have to remember to tell Mr. Steamer that. He would find it so charming."

David stopped laughing. "Seems like everyone I talk to finds Mr. Steamer charismatic. Give him my regards and wish him well for me because I really don't care who or what he is anymore. If he should ask you, tell him that my journey ended tonight. It ended the moment I opened that coffin."

"Not true, Mr. Turner," she told him and then leaned into Paul's ear, whispering instructions. He nodded and walked away.

David was puzzled as to why she would send him away and assumed that it was to call the real police. "I'm enjoying this calmness. If you could wait and talk with me for a few more minutes, I would appreciate it. If what I heard about prison is true, I'll never get the chance to feel this way again."

"Prison is a place where the dangerous and the disorderly are held. I never thought of you as dangerous or disorderly when we first met, and I don't think that of you now."

"Thank you for the compliment, but it's a bit too late for praises. A judge will think differently."

The detective shook her head in wonder. "You do have a way with words, Mr. Turner, but we didn't come here to call the police.

There was no logic as to what David did next, but he laughed again, not knowing why he did so. "If Mr. Steamer didn't send you to spy on me or to call the police, then why are you here? I have been stripped of a daughter and of a life. There is nothing left that I can give you."

The detective paused. "Can I ask you a ridiculous question?" she eventually asked.

"No question is ridiculous to me anymore."

She hesitated for the second time, seemingly worried that he would laugh at her again. "Why not bring God back into your life?" she asked, surprised by his reaction. It was a settled one, one that made her suspect he was forever waiting to be asked.

Perhaps it was the loneliness or the unknown that awaited him, or it could very well have been his craving to love and in return to be loved, but the mere mention of God sounded pleasant. For the past year he had forgotten what the sound of the Almighty's name could do to one's soul. It felt good, and he missed the feeling.

"Can you, Mr. Turner?" she asked him for the second time.

Detective Wood originally presented herself as a law officer and then he thought of her as one of Mr. Steamer's cronies, and now she was portraying herself as a saint. Her suggestion that he should believe in God as he once did, admittedly stirred something inside him, but he couldn't help ask himself if this was all just a hoax. Was it just another story she could tell Mr. Steamer as a way to amuse him?

"I'm afraid you are asking too much of me, Miss Wood. At this moment I'm the happiest I've been in a very long time. Bringing God back into my life would only complicate things," he lied. "Maybe it's best to leave things as they are."

"But you do believe that Cathy is alive?"

"Of course she's alive."

"Don't be so green, Mr. Turner. You can't believe she is still alive and not believe in God. It doesn't work that way."

The detective was correct. He was selfish. His bitterness towards God was so strong that he only saw what he wanted to see and feel what he wanted to feel. His drunken rampage inside Father Mark's church flashed before him. Rubbing his face and fighting back tears, he whispered, "I was inside a church a while back, drunk and ignorant, and said some unforgivable things of him and of his son. I doubt he would want me back."

"Don't be so judgmental, Mr. Turner. Forgiveness is what makes God who he is."

David attempted to hold back but could not. He wiped his nose. "I do miss God," he softly admitted, expecting her to laugh and expose this spiritual conversation as a practical joke, a cunning scheme to mock him.

"It does tend to get lonely without him. Doesn't it, Mr. Turner?" she softly said.

"That it does," he sobbed, removing a huge burden off his shoulder. He then paused before asking the inevitable. "You know where Cathy is, don't you?"

"Yes, I do," smiled the detective.

"Will you take me to her?" he meekly asked.

"That's why I came here."

David let out a quiet moan. "Thank you."

This powerful spirit went by the name of Miss Wheeler, and she had canceled all other scheduled meetings to attend tonight. She would be hard pressed to miss any celebration that Mr. Steamer was in charge of and would certainly not miss this one. Her hair was silver-grey and shaped into a perfect bun on top of her head; her complexion was smooth and unblemished. Because of her height, standing barely five feet, and her plump figure, she needed the helpful hand of the butler to step out of the limousine. When he announced her name, it caused a commotion, clearly indicating that she was a woman of influence. She enjoyed the warm welcome, the display of respect shown towards her, feeling she had earned it over time. When the fuss came to an end, she found a moment to herself, stood up straight, and pulled on her dark blue dress, removing a wrinkle that irritated her from the moment she left home.

An electrifying outburst from the crowd was heard next as the guests noted Mr. Steamer's limousine was next in line, and after it parked at its designated spot, Lora stepped out, followed by Jackie. Mr. Steamer took his time, teasing his guests. When he finally came out, he smiled and waved at all his associates, some of whom he hadn't seen for centuries.

On his left was Mr. Moto, a friend of his from the Shinto faith whom he last saw in the year 1586 when he was invited to be a part of a Shinto celebration. Behind him was Mr. Steinberg of the Jewish faith. How could he ever forget how Mr. Steinberg went out of his way to get him to attend a recent Jewish celebration only a mere three hundred years ago. On it went as other high profile guests acknowledged him and a humble Mr. Steamer taking pride at all the attention his presence generated. It reinforced what he hoped for, that he would be respected by his equals.

Following a few acknowledgments of their own, Lora and Jackie chose to stroll up the path towards the white mansion. Mr. Steamer, on the other hand, felt he deserved to bask in his glory for just a bit longer. The fact that Miss Wheeler was nearby and staring at him might have had something with his desire to prolong his triumphal moment.

"So very nice to see you again, Mr. Steamer," she cried out to him, meaning every word.

"The pleasure is all mine," he replied, walking to her. "I must apologize for the short notice."

"Short notices are what we thrive on," she stated with no hint of resentment in that she had to travel eight time zones to get there.

"So true," agreed Mr. Steamer, courteously offering her his elbow. "May I escort you up the path?"

"I could not think of a more proper gentleman to accompany me," she told him, placing her arm through his and beginning their short trip up the path at a comfortable and relaxing pace. "Is the child getting ready?"

"As we speak."

"The little darling must be excited."

"It is an exciting evening for all of us," he said before pausing and, with a twinkle in his eye, added, "I have a surprise or two in store for tonight."

Uneasy and very well aware of his unorthodox reputation to do the opposite of what was expected of a man with such powers, she stopped and asked, "Let us hope those surprises do not displease our Father."

"If I displeased our Father in the past, he has yet to let it be known, Miss Wheeler, but thank you for your kind concern."

Paul returned, carrying with him a plastic bag. Inside was a bottle containing a clear liquid. He gave the contents to the detective, and in turn she faced David.

"You can't see Cathy in your condition. She has changed. Please drink this. It will help to keep you calm."

"You want to drug me?"

The detective laughed. "You make it sound much worse than it is. This liquid is soothing and harmless. I leave it up to you to drink it or not."

He stared at the bottle, concluding that he didn't have anything to lose. His life would never be the same as it once had been no matter what happened from this point onward. Either they were going to take him to see his daughter or this final potential betrayal would push him over the edge for good. "I would give you permission to take my soul in exchange for seeing my baby again."

"All souls eventually have to leave a body, Mr. Turner; however, now is not the time to give up yours," she made clear before removing the bottle from the bag and offering it to him.

David cautiously took it from her and removed the lid. He sniffed it. It had no odor and when he took a small gulp realized it had no taste other than being on the sweet side.

"A small amount is enough," she assured him, and she was correct. If the liquid's purpose was to relax him, it performed its function immediately and to perfection. His arms felt heavy and clumsy. He found it difficult to keep his head upright, drooping to the side. His eyes suddenly became heavy and tired, difficult to keep open, and when he was about to slide onto the ground, the twins quickly intercepted, placing their hands under his arms, preventing him from falling over. The fluid didn't give him time to reason, rather he felt clouded and in a pleasing frame of mind. All felt good, all felt right.

"Enjoy the mood you now find yourself in, Mr. Turner. You are safe and in good thoughtful hands with three guardians to watch over you," the detective claimed.

David felt the twins lifting him up and gently dragging his body away from the gravesite. From that point onward, all visions appeared in either slow motion or fast forward, a human remote control dictating his every movement. The cruiser seemed so far away, but in a flash the car door opened, by who, he wasn't sure, only that he was now sitting in the backseat with the detective sitting next to him.

"Though our destination is not far, it will seem like decades away. Make yourself comfortable, for I give you my word, you will not be deceived," he heard her promise.

His head slanted, resting on the car window, just enough of an angle to look back at Cathy's tombstone. Perhaps it was the trickery of the night or the aftermath from the few drops of liquid, but the coffin and the stack of dirt he had dug up earlier had disappeared. He also saw the landscape back to its original state. Even the backhoe was returned to its initial spot at the edge of the cemetery. No one would ever suspect that the grave had been tampered with.

It could have been seconds after leaving the cemetery, or it could have been hours; David was not clear which, nor did he recognize any of his surroundings. The houses and street signs were not familiar; only quick fuzzy images with shadowy people and neon signs flashing abruptly by.

He should have recognized something, a building, a restaurant, a landmark, but all was foreign to him. When the police cruiser came to a sudden stop, his head jerked back and forth, finally resting in a downward position.

At this point he lost all control of his neck muscles and found he could no longer hold his head upright. He thought he heard one of the twins apologize for stopping so suddenly then felt the detective's warm hand lifting up his chin and directing his head towards her. She talked to him, but his hearing was subdued. He thought he heard her say that they would be there within minutes. They could already have taken him to a different state or different country for all he knew.

When reaching the massive doors of the white mansion, Lora and Jackie caught a glimpse of Sam Balvati and Lynda Steward standing in front of the building, blending in among the crowd. With glass of punch in hand, Sam was in the midst of sharing a funny story with Lynda and Sean. He always had time to share a silly tale with anyone who would listen.

"She looks exquisite," Jackie said of Lynda.

"And Sam looks absolutely handsome," added Lora.

Before they had the opportunity to enter, Sean went to them. "There is plenty of milk, juice, fruits, and biscuits along with every imaginable vegetable inside." The youngster grinned, overwhelmed by the abundance.

"Thank you," they replied, smiling at his passion.

Upon entering the white mansion, it became clear that Mr. Steamer spared little for tonight's gala, and the evidence was everywhere, borrowing some of the most renowned masterpieces known to the Catholic faith. He had the walls covered with spiritual Renaissance paintings from history's most celebrated artists.

Leonardo Da Vinci's original painting "The Last Supper" hung next to his unfinished "St. Jerome in the Wilderness." True, Da Vinci never completed that magnum opus in his day; however, Mr. Steamer discovered a way to have it completed, telling Lora to return it back to its original unfinished state following the festivities. He also arranged to have a segment of the Sistine Chapel with Michelangelo's iconic image of the "Hand of God" giving life to Adam cover a section of the mansion's ceiling. Perhaps the most tour de force was Michelangelo's two other works of art. The first was "Pieta," a sculpture of the body of Jesus resting on top the lap of His Mother Mary after he was mercifully removed from the cross. The other was the statue of David. These two masterpieces were so massive they needed an entire room to themselves in order to be appreciated.

A huge, shiny oak table was situated in the middle of the lobby, and on that table rested endless trays filled with exceptional fruits and imported vegetables that Sean spoke of. Found only at exotic specialty food outlets, those spreads themselves would show anyone that this evening was one to be forever remembered.

Standing at the base of a spiral staircase, Mr. Steamer was chatting with Mr. Sader, his spiritual equal from the Hindu faith, about a specific celebration he was invited to by Mr. Sader ages ago. That night Mr. Steamer enjoyed a night of music, dance, and feasting at a Hindu temple. At that specific celebration, statues of Mahabharata and Ramayana were everywhere to be enjoyed along with paintings of the most fundamental icons to Hinduism, the trinity of Brahma, Vishnu and Shiva the creator.

A sign carved in stone above the entrance stated, "Hurt not others in ways that you yourself would find hurtful," a phrase that bonded all beliefs. At that time, Mr. Sader never placed his faith ahead of Mr. Steamer's beliefs just as Mr. Steamer would not put Catholicism ahead of Hinduism tonight. Things of that nature were inconceivable between religions; however, tonight was Catholicism's turn to showcase itself just as the other faiths showcased themselves at their celebrations.

When Mr. Steamer completed his conversation with Mr. Sader, he turned to other guests, doing his very best to shine, to be the perfect host, to be everything to everybody. He was always conscious when spreading his time equally among his guests and would do his utmost to be gracious before moving on to the next. They all wanted to share their accounts with him and were elated to be seen in his company.

In fairness, Mr. Steamer was very meticulous when the need called for it, cautious not to offend, but when he stole a glimpse up the spiral staircase and saw Lora stepping out of the master bedroom he could not concentrate on his fellow guests any longer. He needed to know about the goings-on inside that room, something only Lora could tell him. He politely excused himself from the circle of friends, took one step up, and waited for Lora to come down.

"You are once again behaving like an anxious child, Mr. Steamer," she told him.

His childlike, yet amiable behavior didn't go unnoticed, but Mr. Steamer was not the kind to blush. To put it in perspective, he was simply proud of his volunteer's endless work ethics at making tonight a success.

"We must all reflect and understand that it was and will always be a team effort," he replied gracefully.

"I can anticipate the next question you will ask." Lora laughed. "It would only serve to spoil things if I disclosed too much, but I will tell you that Cathy comes across as a child of God should."

Bursting with pride, Mr. Steamer faced the guests, confidently proclaiming, "In case you didn't hear, she said that Cathy comes across as a child of God should."

The police cruiser may have travelled a million miles, or it may have travelled only one; David was in no condition to determine neither the actual distance nor the amount of time he spent in the backseat. Occasionally, he felt his stamina returning only to have his head slump in any direction it chose to. He wanted to ask questions but was not certain if he had forever lost the power of speech or if it would ever return again. His entire face, down to his chin felt frozen, and he was unable to move a single muscle.

"Mr. Steamer has a treaty with the devil," he said, not sure if his mouth actually uttered those words or if they were only thoughts.

Detective Wood seemed amazed that David could talk at all and could not help but laugh at his accusation, catching the attention of the twins up front.

"What did Mr. Turner say?" asked Peter.

She stopped laughing. "Mr. Turner thinks that Mr. Steamer made a deal with the devil."

The brothers laughed as well. "For you to think along those lines is a tribute to Mr. Steamer's acting abilities, Mr. Turner," said Peter.

The detective raised her hand, making them aware that they may be offending David. She then placed that same hand under David's chin. "We are not allowed to lie to you nor anyone else. Some special verbal provisions are made available to us in order to carry out our duties, but we are not capable of lying. As far as portraying Mr. Steamer as an associate of evil, nothing could be further from the truth. He is not one to be envied either, having a thankless profession and executing it well, statistically analyzing his every move before acting upon it. If the devil had someone like Mr. Steamer on his side, the entire universe would have reason to be troubled."

She removed a tissue from her purse and gently dabbed the drooping saliva from the corner of his mouth and said no more.

Mr. Steamer trusted Angelina with the ultimate undertaking: to prepare Cathy for tonight's gala. It was the most prestigious and honorable responsibility she could ever ask for; the opportunity to stand out and demonstrate not only to him, but to everyone that his confidence in her was warranted. She was upstairs, inside the master bedroom alone with the child, constantly lifting up their spirits. She urged Cathy to remain calm and groomed her, setting every strand of hair in place and at the same time answering any questions she asked of her. This was a once in a lifetime occurrence; when Cathy had no more questions, Angelina reminded her of what to expect and what was expected of her since the invited guests were all spirits in their own right and had come from far distances in such a short time to honor her.

Angelina took a backward step, eyeing Cathy from head to toe. She looked adorable and dazzling. On top of her head was a wreath made out of the brightest flowers intertwined with a white ribbon. She wore an ankle-length, sleeveless white dress, matching thin, white belt and a long scarf around her neck. Her shoes were beige with a tiny silver belt at the side to secure them onto her feet. Adding to her charming appearance, her small purse also had a tiny silver buckle to match the shoes.

One piece of clothing remained: a silky, light-brown shawl, which lay on the bed. Cathy carefully picked it up and wrapped it around herself, needing Angelina's assistance to tie the front ends in a knot. In her eagerness, she moved before Angelina had the opportunity to properly tie it. She uttered a sound, not of pain but out of surprise and when she stepped to the side, a short feather fell down from her back. Both fixed their eyes on it as it swayed delicately back and forth in midair until it touched the floor.

"There is no need to worry. Things like that are bound to happen. It will soon grow back," Angelina explained.

CHAPTER FOURTEEN

When the police cruiser came to a stop in front of 999 Paradise Avenue, David's face was still slouched to the side and his eyes completely shut. All the limousines had come and gone and parked at the edge of the property where the chauffeurs were grouped together and staring at the lights up above in awe. Most of the guests were already inside with only a handful of the latecomers quickly scrambling towards the main doorway. It was a good sign, an indication that the festivities had not yet begun. It would be unfortunate if they had missed the child making her grand entrance.

"We're here, Mr. Turner," the detective whispered into David's ear. Suspecting he was in a deep sleep, she shook his elbow a number of times. "Wake up, Mr. Turner. We're here."

David struggled to lift his head. Though the liquid did not take away his ability to think or reason, it worked well in restricting the rest of his body from functioning properly. He rolled his eyes upwards and saw the white mansion. With the powerful white light shining down from up above and blanketing the entire rooftop, the sight was too breathtaking for him to appreciate in his condition. Regardless of the spectacular view, his one and only thought went back to Cathy and if she was inside that building waiting for him, but his lips wouldn't move.

"Look, Mr. Turner," cried out Paul, pointing at the sparkling cylinder, "If you were to follow that beam to its source, you would see our Father and the elders huddled around its perimeter and looking down on us. Historians have written countless books of it and modern musicians have dedicated songs to it. Many thought it a myth, deliberating its very existence, but as you can see for yourself, Mr. Turner, that it is the elusive stairway to heaven."

Detective Wood deliberately cleared her throat, a notion that perhaps they were disclosing too much, too soon. If she was disappointed by their loose tongues, she didn't harp on it. It was clearly the excitement of the moment and of what was to come that got the best of them. Not wishing to appear offended, nor wanting to offend back, she brushed it aside. "Would you gentlemen be kind enough to help Mr. Turner out of the car?" she asked and then faced David. "It would be wise to not question, but enjoy whatever wonders may come your way," she explained, taking his hand and squeezing it. "Keep an open mind; expect the unexpected; be prepared to be amazed at the things you will see, things that only belong in righteous dreams and for those who have a deep sense of moral principles such as yourself."

Peter opened the back door. With Paul standing beside him, they cautiously lifted David up and helped him onto his feet. His arms were then wrapped around their shoulders and with his chin still slouched down to his chest; they slowly made their way up the path. The detective followed behind, overseeing and offering her advice as to how to best support him.

Miss Hafsa, an elegant, olive-skinned lady from Nigeria and of the Muslim faith was the first to greet them. She stood in front of the enormous doors sipping on her glass of orange juice, nibbling on a biscuit and anxiously ready to receive them. "Welcome, Detective Wood. It is a pleasure to see you after all these years."

"Far too long I'm afraid," she replied, proceeding to hug her.

"And it is a pleasure to see the both of you as well," she told the twins.

The twins simultaneously nodded at her in appreciation, giving the detective time to poke her head inside the white mansion. "A full attendance I see."

"It would be unconceivable for invited messengers of other faiths not to attend this celebration," she said and then faced

David. "Welcome, Mr. Turner. I have heard many wonderful things about you."

David remained with head hung low, leaving Miss Hafsa confused.

"Detective Wood thought it best to have Mr. Turner sedated," explained Paul.

"With his permission, of course," the detective hastily cut in so there could be no misunderstanding that David's rights were not violated.

"I would not have thought otherwise," she replied. "Please come in." She pointed inside to a cushioned chair resting against a wall. "You might consider sitting Mr. Turner in that chair."

Detective Wood inspected the chair in question. It appeared comfortable, also offering David an ideal view of the spiral staircase, the best location for him to see the child make her grand presence.

"That will do just fine."

The moment they walked in, the Brandenburg concertos from Bach, followed by the *Missa Solemnis* from Beethoven was playing softly throughout the house. At times this classical music was faintly heard, and at other times it would be completely drowned out by the enthusiasm and constant chatter generated by the well-mannered guests. Some of them drank milk while others preferred juice or water, with the most adventurous enjoying a very small glass of champagne. Not ordinary champagne, but six of the original bottles developed by the Benedictine monk Dom Perignon from the Abbey of Hautvillers in France where he served as cellar master from 1668 to 1715. A few strolled casually from one guest to another; the topic of their conversation was how proud the Catholic faith should be of Cathy just as they proudly told comparable tales of children from their own faiths. Some took notice of the detective, waving at her and realizing she was pre-occupied with David but made a mental note to greet her properly later on in the evening.

"Would you be kind enough to sit Mr. Turner down?" asked the detective upon reaching the chair. The twins slowly slid him into the chair, anchoring pillows around him and behind his head for added support. It worked. David was secured into the chair, giving the three of them time to see the jubilant Mr. Steamer standing at the extreme corner of the lobby surrounded by a semicircle of guests. At that particular moment he was enlightening them with a harmless joke and laughing childishly at his own ridiculous punch lines, punch lines everyone knew only too well.

"He's in a positive mood," observed Paul, wanting to be a part of that entourage that followed Mr. Steamer around. His eagerness and that of his brother's to mingle with the invitees didn't go unnoticed by the detective.

"Mr. Turner is fine now. You are both free to go and intermingle with the guests if you wish."

The twins resembled adolescents who had just been relieved of their homework responsibilities and immediately walked away. Seconds later, the detective heard David moan. She knelt before him. His lips were dry, a sign of his unyielding thirst.

"I will bring back a drink to quench your thirst, Mr. Turner," she said before walking away.

Left alone, David was terrified. He feared that the detective may have grown weary and would not return as she promised. Panic set in. He did his best to move about, but it only served to frustrate him further when he couldn't. With his head still crouched downward he faintly saw his hand resting on his knee, the sight of his bloodied scars left by the backhoe's chains still evident. "I want my strength back!" he cried out in rage knowing that he couldn't be heard.

Unexpectedly, he saw a fuzzy image of a female hand placed on top of his bruised hand, covering his wounds. From the tip of his fingers, running throughout his entire body, warm jabs of sensation pierced into his flesh and shaking the core of his soul with ecstasy and warmth. The touch was soothing, and when the mysterious hand moved away, it took away with it the wounds that once scarred his arms and hands. All injuries suffered at the graveyard had miraculously disappeared, giving doubts as to whether they were really gone or if this miracle was only a hallucination. He then saw the bottom of a long white gown and a female kneeling down to face him.

"Hello, David," the voice said. He recognized the voice. He knew that face. They both belonged to Jackie. It was her hand that seemingly nursed his injuries back to health. "Mr. Steamer thought it best that I nurtured your wounds."

David moved his head inches to the left and the same distance to the right; all the maneuvering he was capable of. *This can't be real,* he thought, but it was, very real.

"I pray you hold no resentment towards me, Mr. Turner. I did what was expected of me and sincerely love you now as much as I did the first day we met," she admitted. His blank expression persuaded her to explain further. "Please understand that the false phone number I gave you when we last saw each other was necessary but never out of spite." She sympathetically stroked his face with the back of her fingers a number of times, got up onto her feet and disappeared from his limited view.

Moments later another blurry image came into sight.

"Hello, Mr. Turner," greeted Lynda Steward, hastily apologizing as did Jackie before her. "It will be a sad day if you hold any hostility towards me. All prior conversations with you were well rehearsed. All my words were fictitious, carefully written between me and Mr. Steamer and used only to assist me in my duties. I trust you will find it in your heart to dismiss any ill feelings you hold towards me. Should you wonder whether I actually read your novels, the answer is an indisputable yes and spiritually rewarded for doing so." Before departing, she blissfully made reference to Cathy. He wasn't certain of her exact words, but she sounded excited for him.

On his own again, David made every effort at twitching his thumb; it moved, sending a signal to the rest of his fingers to do likewise, but his contentment was short lived. He still couldn't move any other part of his body other than that single thumb, and when he tried to lick his dry lips, he discovered he couldn't move his tongue. Feeling an excruciating thrust, he slowly began to slide off the chair. An arm pulled him back up. He then felt the rim of a cool glass come into contact with the bottom portion of his lip.

"This beverage came from far away. A small number of drops will be sufficient to satisfy your thirst and sharpen your senses much more quickly," claimed the detective.

David selfishly swallowed half a dozen drops, feeling each individual drop slowly glide down his course throat, satisfying his thirst and gratifying every other part of his body. This mellow sensation was so calm and welcoming that he felt a need to show the detective his appreciation with the only means available to him, by grunting.

"No need to try and thank me. It is us who should thank you. Where others have faltered, you have excelled beyond our expectations." She then sadly paused. "We had such high hopes for John Parker, but he submitted to temptation much too quickly whereas you raised one of God's children for seven years, an extraordinary stretch and a compliment to your kind and loving father." She placed a reassuring hand on his shoulder. "The child will be down shortly. Now it is time to enjoy your reward. Mr. Steamer saw to that. He made your presence possible, and, should his strategy go in your favour, you will be more than enriched. Try to remain poised throughout the sights to come, sights that not even a skilled writer such as you could have pictured." She stepped aside, giving others the opportunity to speak to him. She was not only anxious, but eager to answer any questions they asked of David.

David heard unfamiliar voices speaking well of him, all polite and flattering, often comparing him with other worthy humans of their own faith who faced the same challenges as he had. Mr. Eaglefeather, a Native American and spiritually equivalent to Mr. Steamer, also shared a short story with David. He told him of a young brave who lived long ago and was so treasured for his honorable accomplishments that his face was carved on trees for centuries. Other guests knew of Diane and Cathy, mentioning the two in the same sentence, completing their conversation by declaring that all would end well. A few of the timid ones only shook his hand for the Catholic hero that he was, and when an elderly lady stepped forward claiming she once played bridge with his late father, his heart beat faster at the sheer thought.

"Hello, Mr. Turner," welcomed Lora, inserting her head in front of his. "You would not believe the amount of diplomacy and annoying pestering Mr. Steamer has had to resort to, not to mention a string of future considerations he will owe to the elders, but eventually they saw his reasoning and unanimously agreed that you should be part of the festivities tonight."

"I would not have it any other way," interrupted Mr. Steamer, placing his harmonious face next to Lora's and lowering his voice to a murmur when adding, "Though I believe Miss Wheeler is a bit weary by your presence, but that was to be expected."

"Miss Wheeler is adorable and demands admiration, but is very traditional and set in her ways," Lora added, matching his low tone.

It might have been his returning senses, or it could just as easily have been the sudden appearance of Mr. Steamer, but David jolted backwards. He spluttered a series of words, resembling an intoxicated drunk, not having any idea as to what he said. Whatever he slurred, it surprised both Mr. Steamer and Lora. Both found it amusing.

"No, Mr. Turner," Lora continued to giggle. "No one here will release photos of you to gossip magazines. Mr. Steamer purchased them only to have them destroyed."

The noise from the guests intensified. Something was about to happen. "Keep your eyes on the top of the staircase, David. A very difficult chapter in your life will soon come to an end," Mr. Steamer promised before both he and Lora suddenly walked away.

With Lora matching his every step, Mr. Steamer stopped at the bottom of the staircase, looked up towards the master bedroom, and took the role of an experienced master of ceremony.

"I believe that the child is ready!" he cried out.

The guests graciously positioned themselves closer to him and looked up in anticipation that something wonderful was about to unfold.

The detective playfully pinched David's shoulder. "Did you hear the intensity in Mr. Steamer's voice? Can you feel his energy?" she asked, feeling it was her duty to patch up any hostility between the two. "Do away with any ill feelings you hold against him, Mr. Turner. He personally had nothing against you. His occupation is and always will be to test and to tempt. I am certain you can understand that only the purest of souls can raise God's children."

David attempted to move his head sideways to face her, and to his relief found that he finally could. When he raised his hand and barely touched the tip of his chin, he hoped that the fluid he drank may have reached its potency and was now entering its final stages. He called out her name, but there was no sound coming from his mouth. Determined to get her attention, he took hold of her elbow and shook it, but she was too infatuated by Mr. Steamer's exhilarated behavior. Finally she turned to him and said, "Just look at him, Mr. Turner. Have you ever seen such sincere euphoria?"

A female guest cried out, proclaiming that the door from the master bedroom was opening. This announcement brought a group of the guests closer to the staircase. They began to congratulate Mr. Steamer, prematurely shaking his hand, praising him for being a tower of strength and a pillar to his faith.

Overwhelmed by it all, he weakly objected to their flattering remarks and stating that his team of volunteers was to be equally credited.

The detective was aware that David's ability to speak was approaching. It was essential to clarify as much as possible before the festivities began, to clarify matters and not be haunted by the signing of the contract. His signature was merely one piece of a long and complicated puzzle that only a handful of spiritual volunteers, such as herself, played a role in.

"Both you and your brother came with spotless reputations," she began to make clear. "Two loving and faithful husbands who were successful yet never forgetting the less privileged. Two perfect candidates to nurture and educate a child of God. When Diane died, so did your unborn child. No one could have survived such an impact. Lee's child also died that night."

The sound of laughter and toasting of glasses from the crowd got louder, but it didn't prevent the detective from continuing. There were more astonishing disclosures to come, things that defied all logic, news that would stagger even the most religious zealots.

"Listen carefully, Mr. Turner, and please judge us by what you see and what you have been through. It was Mr. Steamer's decision to make the necessary arrangements, for only God and he can sanction such miracles, but in an instant that cannot be measured by time. The child you have always assumed survived the accident was replaced with one from above and given life, as was Lee's dead child. You chose to name that child Cathy; your brother chose to name his Tracie, but they were and always will be God's children. They were never a part of you or your brother."

David trembled at the startling revelations; his entire body shook from head to toe, and he was helpless to stop it. He made every attempt to get up, to grab her, and to shout in her ear that she was insane as were the rest of the people here.

"Your reaction is understandable, Mr. Turner," she granted. "But you must understand that a child of God is just that—a child of God who was temporarily placed on earth, and what better way for them to learn of your ways than from the very honorable people whom they will one day protect? Surely you can understand that only the purest can raise these children. Those who fall into temptation, even once, even if perceived as unfairly seduced, are not pure any longer, and God will take His children back. It is left to higher spirits such as Mr. Steamer to locate new parents for them until he feels they can learn no more. You forfeited your right to Cathy the day you signed that contract, as did your brother with Tracie. Perhaps you find that to be too harsh of a price to pay for one mistake, but then that is God's way."

David refused to believe her and tried to shake his head.

"We have the power to do many astonishing things for wonderful people such as you, Mr. Turner. We ask not much in return only that they have faith in us and choose the noble path set forth by the Commandments. To have the strength that you had, to have remained faithful to your beliefs, morals, and to all that God stands for made you a leader amongst other men. Plunging into Mr. Steamer's seducement and signing that document is now part of your history. There is no reason to feel shame."

Upstairs, the door completely opened, sending a hush down below. No one dared blink. No one dared talk. The detective was no different, caught in the excitement as were the rest and barely able to contain herself.

"You will have to excuse me," she whispered. "It is my time to join the rest of the guests and your time to see embodied all that righteousness has to offer."

He didn't want her to leave, but she did, positioning herself next to Sam Balvati, who was standing just below the staircase and when Sam moved away, he saw the only child inside the white mansion. That child was Tracie.

Despite the repetitive insinuation of wonders to come, despite of all the revelations confessed by the detective, the sight of his niece, alive and breathing, astonished David. Only a short time earlier he was pleading for her life, yet there she stood, smiling and waving at him.

Tracie!" he yelled, forgetting that no one could hear him, least of all, her. His eyes shifted to his left, at a telephone, which stood on top of a small table. He longed to call his brother, to tell him that his daughter was not dead and to also tell Lee that she was wrong to accuse him of being involved in Tracie's death; for in spite of all that had happened, their child was alive.

Tracie acted timid about the whole affair as any eight-year-old would be. She placed her hand on the chain wrapped around her neck and ran her fingers along the tooth that rested on her chest. She then pulled on the detective's arm; when the detective looked down, Tracie whispered into her ear. An agreement seemed to have been made between the two and moments later, Tracie walked towards David and stood before him. Forever grinning she removed the chain. "Shortly new parents will be found for me. I will have no need for this any longer Mr. Turner. Please accept this gift as my display of affection for all the love any uncle could have given a niece."

Tracie calmly placed the chain inside his shirt pocket, gave him a warm hug and walked away, re- joining the crowd below the staircase.

Although he tried to call her back, things were moving in such a rapid pace that he didn't know where to focus next, however one thing did beg his attention. At the top of the staircase, just above the bedroom ceiling he saw two shadowy figures shifting back and forth. Before long a child stepped forward and placed her hands on the balcony railing, arousing the crowd below. Reserved at first, she eventually acknowledged them, and they immediately took to her. This child was Cathy.

Earlier the sight of Tracie stunned him, but the sight of his own daughter took his breath away. Regardless of the number of times he claimed she was still alive, nothing could have prepared him for the thing he craved most—to come face-to-face with his beloved Cathy.

"Someone help me!" he pleaded, squirming to free himself, but when no one took notice, his next reaction was to call out her name. "Cathy! I'm over here, baby!"

His cries were only frustrated thoughts, painful to no one but to himself.

Angelina appeared behind Cathy, resting a hand on the child's shoulder, a heavenly sight to behold, a breathtaking manifestation that could wake up a fifteenth century renaissance genius from his grave shouting for paintbrushes and brilliant oil paints in order to capture this moment so he could transform it into an instant masterpiece. Angelina stepped down to the sound of clapping hands; and when Cathy followed, the applause intensified. Every step was carefully orchestrated by the two, virtually in slow motion so as to allow the guests to swallow as much of the enchanted descent as possible.

Mr. Steamer, forever the clever opportunist at selecting a proper moment, rushed to the bottom of the stairs, climbed the first step, and turned around. "Ladies and gentlemen," he announced bursting with buoyancy, "I once again want to express my gratitude for your presence at this joyous and most extraordinary occasion, for this is the day when all our labor bears fruits. This is the day when we are rewarded for all our efforts; when one of our own Father's children converts into His immaculate messengers."

Cathy was midway down the staircase when David thought they may have had made eye contact. For that split second, he anticipated that she would run down the remaining steps and into his arms to the likes he was accustomed to, but when she looked back down at the guests and showed no recognition of him whatsoever, he was utterly demoralized.

Please don't do this to me again, sweetheart. Don't act like you don't know me. Please, please, please! he begged.

His aggravation turned into bitter rage. With both hands on the edge of the chair, he made every attempt to shake himself loose, to fall down if need be in order to get her attention. He was not successful, further deepening into a fury, a brewing wrath that was entrenched deep within.

Angelina held back, allowing Cathy to reach the last step and into Mr. Steamer's arms. He readily accepted her as a kindly grandfather who had not seen his grandchild in ages, caressing her hair, and, as was the practice, running his index finger along the girl's forehead.

"You look so enchanting," he declared; then, raising his head up at Angelina told her, "Your assignment was well coordinated. My compliments to a well-executed entrance." She coyly lowered her head, surprising him. "No, no, no," he repeated. "No need to be reserved. You earned my respect and merit the acclaim that's due to you. Please recognize your achievement as a feat well done."

Receiving praise from a higher spirit got the best of her. She blushed, much to the appeal of not only him but to all the guests as well.

"Thank you," she replied, adding a well-earned giggle.

"You are very welcome, my sweet child," he let her know, urging others to surround and pamper her as well. He then took Cathy by the hand and ushered her to the centre of the room. "Tonight is an evening to forget all our disappointments and to bow to our successes," he stated graciously. "Today is a day of rest, a day when we need not battle evil forces but to show them what all our faiths combined stand for, to make the sinful understand the everlasting dominance of each other's spiritual leaders." He bent down to Cathy's level and whispered, "Not to worry. Everything will be fine," before taking two backward steps; watchful not to block anyone's view. "Please remove your shawl and show our guests your spiritual conversion." In a perfect flow, Cathy untied the shawl that was wrapped around her petite body, allowing the cloth to slide down onto the floor. Attached onto her back were the first early stages of tiny white feathers, vague at spots but unmistakably destined to one day ultimately broaden and blossom into pure wings.

Civilized and unpretentious up to that magical point, the guests erupted into a boisterous roar, forgetting for a moment who they were and where they were. A glance around the lobby could see Lora and Jackie hugging and as though sharing a million-dollar lottery bonanza, plunging themselves in sheer ecstasy. Detective Wood was seen breathing a huge sigh, laughing along with Tracie and at the same time trying, but failing to maintain her dignified poise while Sam Balvati and Linda Stewart covered their faces in jubilation. Those were only a handful of reactions with each individual spirit absorbing this incredible transformation in the manner they chose.

This was an exceptional moment when they could come out of their conservative shell and enjoy this exception. Caught in the moment, Cathy stretched her neck to the side, eyeing the tip of her wings. Underdeveloped as they were, she couldn't resist to mischievously flutter them for the very first time, not quite certain of the outcome. Their flapping amazingly produced a slight breeze;

just enough to set a napkin flying off the food table and unbelievably land on Mr. Steamer's head.

"I am so sorry Mr. Steamer," she apologized, covering her mouth in a weak effort at shielding her hilarity.

Mr. Steamer laughed, removing the napkin from the top of his head and waving it back and forth at Cathy in humorous surrender.

The screaming was high pitched and could easily have been mistaken for a pair of clawed alley cats eager to battle over a mate, but as the ceremonial rejoicing dwindled, it became apparent that the stretching cries came from within, not from outside creatures. As the crowd hushed, the cries became noticeably louder. The guests turned their attention to the source of this ungodly howl, including a rattled Mr. Steamer. It was David. He was responsible.

Trying to squirm free from his chair and with no sense of self-respect or dignity, he came across as a lunatic, wobbling his body like a chained animal and shamelessly hollering out Cathy's name. Though half of his body still remained seated, the other half became twisted, with his arms awkwardly swaying in midair. It turned into a bizarre and pathetic occurrence to witness before he suddenly stopped when he realized that all eyes were upon on him and that his voice had returned.

The stunned guests looked at him with sympathy, and then they quickly searched for Mr. Steamer for guidance; when all eyes found him, he too appeared to be at a loss. David's obnoxious behavior seemed to have shocked him into silence. His responsibility was to maintain order, and a spirit with his experience should have stepped forward and taken control of this unexpected tragedy, but sadly the opposite was true. Direction was needed, and strangely enough Mr. Steamer could not or would not provide it, coming across as though he would rather be somewhere else and distancing himself from this whole chaotic incident.

"Cathy!" echoed David. "I'm over here, baby." Perspiration dripped off his forehead as he wrestled for control of his own body, coming close to falling off the chair in the process. "Look at me for God's sake!"

When it appeared that Cathy was about to run to him, she was held back by the detective, "You cannot," she was reminded.

Confused by her sudden urge to run to David, Cathy turned her attention at Mr. Steamer. "Please offer me your wisdom and guidance, Mr. Steamer. I do not know what I should do. My heart begs me to comfort, Mr. Turner, not as his daughter, but purely out of compassion."

Mr. Steamer wouldn't interfere, and when it appeared that there was no end in sight to David's howling and no one to stop him, a few brave guests surrounded Mr. Steamer, waiting for answers without asking any questions. Incredibly he lowered his head in submission. A horrified detective took two paces backwards, baffled by his lack of leadership; however, Miss Wheeler rose up to the occasion.

If he would not put an end to this, then she was obligated to do so. Without reservation, she made it known what was on her mind, not concerned by who was present or who was at the end of her scolding.

"Mr. Turner's behavior needs attending to," she slowly but firmly told Mr. Steamer.

Mr. Steamer's refusal to take action left her a pre-authorized right to take over, and she didn't waste any time, taking it upon herself to whisper directions in Detective Wood's ear. The detective seemed stunned by her instructions, glancing at Mr. Steamer for any sign of strength, wondering when he would take his rightful place and override Miss Wheeler. But she was wasting her time. Mr. Steamer didn't seem interested at all in regaining his lawful jurisdiction; worse, the detective was bound by God's own rules to give Miss Wheeler her unconditional cooperation. She was not to question, but to carry on with Miss Wheeler's orders as anyone with a lower rank would do.

The detective called out Paul's name. He came to her, and when she whispered Miss Wheeler's instructions to him, he was taken aback. He asked if she might repeat herself since Miss Wheeler's wishes seemed so extreme, feeling that he may not have understood them the first time. His orders were unchanged. In disbelief, Paul felt it necessary to express his personal opinion. "I truly and honestly believe that not enough time has elapsed. It's simply not sensible," he let it be known loud enough for all to hear, then switching his attention from Detective Wood to Miss Wheeler and then back to the detective in dismay.

"If I can speak for Mr. Turner, he would let you know that he appreciates the concern you have for his well-being. Now can you please do what is asked of you?" Miss Wheeler interrupted and watched as Paul dragged his feet out of the white mansion to do what he was told to do.

"David scornfully pointed at Mr. Steamer. "Prove to me that you are who they say you are! Show me that you are the semi-god these followers of yours claim you are, or are you only a second rate impersonation of who you want to be?"

When Mr. Steamer chose not to challenge him, David snarled, "You are more pathetic than I am, Steamer."

David's heartbreaking actions were taking a toll on the ones who understood and loved him, including Jackie and Lora, who at this time were so tormented by what they saw that they huddled together and prayed for Father to intervene, to raise his powerful arm and restore calm. Sam Balvati was another. Distressed by the whole messy affair, he was boldly willing to accept whatever discipline Miss Wheeler saw fit to bestow.

"May I have your permission to sit Mr. Turner back onto the chair?" he asked her. She didn't owe him a reply and didn't give him one.

You stay where you are, sweetheart. I'll come to you," David shouted.

His speech may have returned, but the capacity to carry his own weight did not. The moment he tried to get up, he came crashing down onto the floor, landing on his stomach and hitting his chin on the hard marble floor. The sting upon contact was real, but he felt nothing. His mind was only on one thing—to get to his child—and was immune to anything else. Extending his arms as far as he could, he dug his fingernails inside the tiny gaps between the floor titles and pulled himself closer to her, each inch agonizing.

Paul returned, stopping at the door's entrance. All eyes were not so much on him, but on the plastic bag hanging down from his right hand, the same bag containing the sedative liquid that was used on David earlier. Miss Wheeler quickly waved him inside. Paul searched for any indication that she might have had a change of heart. None was found.

Everyone was now clearly aware of Miss Wheeler's intention, everyone except David. He blindly continued to crawl forward but was forced to stop at Paul's feet. He helplessly looked up and saw Detective Wood standing next to him.

"I'm so tired, Miss Wood." He sighed between breaths. "Too tired to crawl anymore. Please help me. I beg of you." When she didn't respond, he looked up at Paul, oblivious to the fact that he was holding that same plastic bag he carried earlier at the grave-site. "I don't know if you are Peter or Paul, but, whoever you are, please find it in your heart to drag me to my baby. I'm just so tired."

Paul moved to the side. The bag swung back and forth. Needing a few seconds to grasp at their true intention, to further settle him down, he screamed and savagely grabbed at Paul's ankles, aiming to slither under his legs to get to his child. "You can't do this to me! Not now!"

Detective Wood knelt before David, gently removing his clenched fists off Paul's ankles, and once free of David's hold, Paul gave her the bag and immediately backed away.

"Don't touch me!" cried David.

The detective's sense of duty required her to do otherwise. She took the clear liquid out of the bag.

David stared at it as though he was staring at a hot iron, "You told me you were not allowed to lie, but you did! You told me that I would not be deceived! The detective is a liar!" he shouted at the guests.

Detective Wood was devastated by his claim and when she heard Miss Wheeler breathing heavily behind her back, she became overwhelmed at being placed in this position. She froze and could not continue.

Upset, Miss Wheeler turned to the guests. "Mr. Turner's claim is a ridiculous outburst brought on by his unpredictable behavior. We all know that we don't lie. It only strengthens my position to have him sedated," she argued.

The sense of duty overpowered all else. The detective had no choice but to proceed as ordered. "Please drink this, Mr. Turner," she pleaded.

"No!" he snapped back.

Other than Mr. Steamer, Miss Wheeler was the only other privileged spirit who didn't require David's permission. She looked down at him. "God put trust in me to take precedence over any consent, Mr. Turner. I will exercise that right if need be. In your condition, I truly believe it to be in everyone's best interest as well as your own that my wishes are respected."

"Please, Mr. Turner," implored the detective, holding back tears."

David looked beyond the detective at Cathy, finding her and Tracie holding on to each other, weeping and staring back at him like two terrified kittens. It broke his heart that his daughter had to see him in his pitiful state, howling like a cowardly convict heading to the gallows.

A short time ago he was her hero, a champion that did no wrong, her idol, and now she saw him for what he had become—brittle and unable to even crawl to her. His fear wasn't from the looming sedative but that they would never meet again and her last impression of him would be that of a frail and beaten man. The one remaining symbol, the final gesture that represented his life with Cathy, was to wink at her, a symbolic show of dignity that his love for her was as strong now as it ever was. She didn't wink back, but it didn't bother him, convinced that if she were allowed to, she would have.

"Whoever or whatever you are, please look after my princess," he asked of the detective, finally surrendering to her.

Laying flat on his stomach and cheek pressed onto the cool hard surface, he raised his arm to reach for the bottle as a sign of compliance and an admission of defeat.

"I doubt that it will be necessary!" wailed an overriding voice echoing from one side of the room to the other with such intensity it rattled the crystal glasses that stood on the table.

That verbal explosion could only have belonged to one individual and only one: Mr. Steamer. With arms folded tightly, feet firmly entrenched on the marble floor and bursting with dominance, he issued a command so powerful, it would make the strongest armies lay down their weapons.

"I believe Mr. Turner has suffered enough," he said with a sudden self-assured sparkle glowing off his entire body, not at all like the fragile old spirit he portrayed minutes earlier.

Shaken, Detective Wood immediately stopped, longing for what she and others had prayed for: strength and leadership that had given Mr. Steamer his legendary repute. She saw Cathy and Tracie, along with all other guests instantly rejuvenated and enjoying the remaining tones of Mr. Steamer's voice, which still bounced from wall to wall.

"You do agree with me, do you not Detective Wood?" he asked.

The detective placed the bottle back into the bag, stood up, looked at Miss Wheeler, and, sounding more arrogant than she should have, proclaimed, "That I do Mr. Steamer."

"As I'm positive that the rest of the guests do as well?" said Mr. Steamer, surveying the guests for any negative response and when he saw none he ended his rigid glare directly at Miss Wheeler. "I value your input Miss Wheeler. Would you care to tell all in this room if you think that Mr. Turner has suffered enough?"

Miss Wheeler wisely refrained from giving her option too willingly, opting instead to evaluate the situation, but that didn't stop Mr. Steamer.

"Our Father has trusted the judgment of higher spirits such as Miss Wheeler and me to give his children to unblemished mortals such as Mr. Turner so they can absorb their proper values," he began. Coming to a stop below the painting of Michelangelo's "Hand of God" he raised his own hand, purposely matching the masterpiece's hand gesture above him.

Miss Wheeler was undaunted by his unexpected resurgence. "Forgive me if I sound uncivil, Mr. Steamer, but please lower your hand. I find it unnecessary that you should raise it in the same manner as our God did when he created Adam. I, myself, would never conceive it as a misinterpretation, but others here may read it differently. They may wrongly accuse you of demeaning one of our Father's greatest accomplishments for your own personal agenda."

Mr. Steamer studied his hand's position with that of the painting from the ceiling. Both arms were in line, just as she had claimed they were. "I agree. The coincidence is there, but we all know that I am not God. I cannot create man as he did. I am only one of his superior messengers who have the right to cross forbidden borders where others could not. I chose to exercise that right tonight by having Mr. Turner join us. My grounds were well warranted. That man raised one of God's children to perfection, and for that reason I saw fit to reward him. His presence here tonight serves to counterbalance the suffering he has endured since the day we took the child back."

When he failed to impress her, he realized that he was dealing with Miss Wheeler, a veteran spirit equal to him who came with the same timeless experience as his. Placing himself behind a masterpiece and raising his hand to capture its symbolism may have electrified the guests; it would take far more to intimidate her.

Though Miss Wheeler would not admit to it, it became apparent by her silence that she would not continue unless he lowered his hand, which he did.

"Thank you," she said, anxious for her turn to speak. "Your point is well taken. I will not dispute Mr. Turner's presence here tonight, but his position should have been one of a spectator, not a rude guest."

"We all have eyes, Miss Wheeler. We all saw for ourselves a desperate man's reaction to the love of his life. Your willingness to further induce Mr. Turner would only add to his pain and suffering, something that I find unacceptable. However, like you, I too feel that he needs to be medicated, but not with sedatives." He then pointed to David. "I feel that this man has earned the antidote of my choice, and it comes in the form of the ultimate gift."

Detective Wood suddenly understood why Mr. Steamer had remained indecisive, appearing lost and in doubt only a few moments earlier. If her suspicions were correct, then he merited the title given to him by God and in future celebrations, they would boast of his intelligence, adding to his already unblemished reputation. It all made sense to her now, and she felt embarrassed of her previous doubts about him when in fact he scrutinized, not only his next move, but that of Miss Wheeler's as well.

His carefully planned meltdown was in reality an intelligently orchestrated maneuver with one purpose in mind: to give him the excuse he needed in allowing David to see things reserved for the very few. Mr. Steamer loved David to that extent.

That astonishing news stunned the guests and, at the same token, caused Miss Wheeler to smirk as though his remarks were all in jest. Surely he was joking. It was one thing to permit Mr. Turner into the white mansion, a place she deemed only suitable for spirits of all faiths, but to allow him to enter the *beyond*, where only a handful were ever permitted, was unthinkable. Such actions carried with it consequences that she herself would never venture in.

"You risk displeasing our Father with such actions, Mr. Steamer. Perhaps we should go outside for a short stroll so you can gather your thoughts. You may discover that it is in your best interest to reconsider," she cited when it appeared to her that he might have been serious after all.

"I understand the risks involved and have never been more confident of my decision," he firmly let her know.

Miss Wheeler looked at the many faces surrounding her, seeking alliance, but saw none. She was alone and without support, had no choice but to relent. "This is your night Mr. Steamer. Whatever decision you set forth will be the final one, as it would be mine if this were my jurisdiction. My only concern is if Mr. Turner is rewarded in such a way, it may diminish its value. A gift like yours should not be given so freely."

"I know the value of my gift, Miss Wheeler, and I thank you for your kind concern, but it will be I who must answer for my actions. I believe that our Father will agree that if we cannot reveal the ultimate miracle to people like Mr. Turner then what motivation will his worshipers have to believe in him?"

"They should believe in our Father because the Bible tells them so."

"And they should be allowed to experience the beyond because it exists for the chosen few and should not to be perceived as a myth," he replied quickly.

She thought deep and hard, analyzing what would be said of her at future ceremonies, choosing her words very carefully. "It would be out of line for me to disagree with anything. If your decision is to give Mr. Turner this most precious of gifts as a way to offset what I have done, then our Father will praise you for your decree. If God feels your decision was not the correct one, then you will have disappointed him. Let us all hope that Mr. Turner can come to terms with what he is about to see," she warned, seeming satisfied that she got the last word in.

That part was true. If Mr. Steamer were serious, the David Turner who entered the *beyond* would not be the same man when stepping back out. Would he go insane because of it? Perhaps. Was Mr. Steamer 100 percent certain he was doing the right thing? Absolutely not. But at this precise moment, taking into account all that David had been through and based on his strong character and the love he held for his family, Mr. Steamer was willing to gamble both on David's sanity and that of his very own demotion. God would be the judge of his actions and no one else.

Graciously giving Miss Wheeler time to unwind, Mr. Steamer said, "If you would kindly excuse me, Miss Wheeler, I have things that need to be attended to." Offering her a final grin, combined with a quick nod of his head as a measure that he held no ill feelings towards her, he looked back at David. "I believe Mr. Turner will require assistance."

His words were barely out of his mouth when the twins jumped forward and raised David onto his feet, helping him sit back into the chair.

The man David always suspected of being comparable to the devil was in fact the opposite, and if he was to digest all that had just happened, then Mr. Steamer had risked a spiritual repercussion for helping him.

"I always had high regards for you, David, and your actions here tonight demonstrated that," said Mr. Steamer. With those gratifying remarks, Mr. Steamer finally came across to David as being the kind and thoughtful spirit that he was. His sincerity and that twinkle in his eyes at long last proved to him that he deserved the title of "higher spirit," an angel so far ahead of the rest that God faithful trusted him with his own personal judgement.

David looked at the wings attached to Cathy's back. No matter how surreal it may have been for him to digest, those wings were genuine. She was indisputably, an actual angel, and she happened to be his daughter.

He replied with the first thought that came into his mind, "I'm sorry for letting God, you, and Cathy down by signing that contract, sir."

Mr. Steamer laughed. "Your reply must be sincere, David, for this is the first time you have addressed me as 'sir.' Not to demean your apology, but your signature on that contract is old news. The day you signed that contract was documented and is now part of your past and a part of our written chronicles from where others can learn from. History would lose its importance if it could be changed."

"I will learn from it."

"That, I am certain of. You are a good man, David. You have been all your life. People such as yourself are worthy of exceptional gifts, and I cannot think of a better honour I can bestow on you than the one you are about to receive."

David looked to Mr. Steamer's left, at Cathy, as a means to let him know that if his gift, as a mere mortal, was to be able to talk to an angel, then he could understand why Miss Wheeler was so against it.

"If I am not mistaken, I presume Mr. Turner would like a word with you," Mr. Steamer said to Cathy, urging the child on.

Hesitant at first, only to catch her breath, Cathy did not need to be asked twice. She made their way towards David and said, "Hello, Mr. Turner," the moment she reached him.

It may have been the pressure of the crowd staring directly at him or that David at last found himself a footstep away from his illusive fantasy—to be actually able speak to his daughter—but as he silently fixed his eyes into Cathy's blue eyes, he could not mutter a sound. He feared that she would simply disappear if he spoke or the thought of his own voice waking him up to find that this was all just a dream.

If he was disappointed that Cathy called him Mr. Turner rather than Daddy, he didn't show it. He was captivated by it all, in such a delicate position that words were difficult to come by, yet tears were not. They formed at the corner of his eyes, linked at his chin, and fell lazily down onto the floor. He felt no shame in crying; it went beyond tears, beyond appearing fragile, for there could be no more denying, no more second-guessing. He was now with his daughter and felt he had earned the right to shed tears, choosing not to stop them but permitting them to flow as they wished.

Always thinking, always steps ahead of others, Mr. Steamer had placed himself in David's shoes and realized his moment had arrived, the time to actually speak to Cathy was now, and David needed privacy.

He addressed the guests. "May I suggest we allow Mr. Turner time with the child?" he told them, and with those wise words he soothed the surrounding atmosphere.

The guests agreed, giving the two of them the space they needed. Other than Miss Wheeler, who parked herself at the extreme corner of the room with Mr. Sader, who was attempting to raise her morale, all the others were elated that the turmoil was over.

"Please don't cry, " Cathy told him.

"It has been such a confusing journey to finally reach you and be able to talk to you like this and to have you talk back to me. I never realized that crying could be so wonderful." He sobbed.

"Do you like my wings?"

"They look magnificent," he smiled, bravely asking Cathy, "May I touch them?"

"You may," she replied, turning sideways, giving him the freedom to do so and adding, "One has already fallen off but I felt no pain."

"I'll be careful," he told her, vigilantly stroking them, amazed by the softness and silky texture, not at all as a bird's feather.

"Daddy missed you," he tenderly told her."

The sparkle abruptly disappeared from Cathy's eyes. A nerve had been hit, and when the crowd hushed and turned to stare at them, he was aware of it, quickly understanding the impact. He regretted it, but at the same time he couldn't take it back, and it had to be dealt with.

Not surprisingly, Mr. Steamer appeared out of nowhere. He didn't deal with the situation as David hoped; rather he conveniently changed the sensitive subject by cheerfully announcing, "I think it is time to move forward, David, time to enter the next level."

David didn't want to go anywhere if it meant leaving Cathy. "Can my daughter come with us?" he asked.

"It would be only fitting," Mr. Steamer agreed, turning to the detective and adding, "Mr. Turner will require a shoulder to rest on. Would you be kind enough to join us?"

She was ecstatic at being asked, conscious of the things to come and thrilled that she was going to be a part of it. "Absolutely," she told him.

David had no concept as to what the next "level" was, but if the excitement in her voice was any indication, then it had to be somewhere special.

Wouldn't it be incredible if Mr. Steamer was asking her to chaperone me back outside to a waiting chauffeur to take me and the children back home? he thought.

Mr. Steamer took Cathy by the hand. "Let us go then," he said and immediately the guests parted, leaving a pathway out of the lobby and into a hidden section of the white mansion.

"Place your arm around me, Mr. Turner," Detective Wood told him. "I am not the most robust woman in the world, but I think I can manage."

"Where are you taking me?"

"An exceptional person wants to meet you. ."

"Not outside to a waiting chauffeur?" He replied sadly.

"Not outside to a waiting chauffeur." She laughed.

David wrapped his arm around her shoulder and, with her help, pulled himself up. A few steps later, to his surprise, the crowd began to clap and cheer them on. Jackie sprang forward and caressed his face, kissing him on the forehead. "I am so happy for you, Mr. Turner." She beamed before stepping back.

Lora and Lynda were next, softly touching him on the back. Even the butler and Angelina appeared excited, touching his free hand as he passed them by, appearing privileged for being given the rare opportunity. It seemed everyone wanted to touch him, to feel him.

"Why are they touching me?" he asked.

The detective stopped momentarily. "Simply put, they miss the radiance that a body gives, a body that is still attached to a soul, if only to be reminded how it once felt. You will understand this feeling one day."

"You mean when I die."

"When God gives life, it is forever," she reminded him.

They reached the end of the lobby and entered a long wide hallway where Mr. Steamer and Cathy were waiting for them. The corridor's walls were constructed with mirror panes, fitted neatly side by side. Approximately thirty feet from where they stood, at the end of the long corridor, was a unique door, which led into another room. Unique because of the dazzling beams of every imaginable colour, mixed with mist, could be seen escaping from the half-inch gap below the door.

The brilliant rays worked their way upward, bouncing from one mirror to the next and lightening Cathy's face. True, she was an angel but she was also a child and at times would act as such. This was one of those times. She skipped up and down the corridor, playfully attempting to capture the beams of light with her hand, much to Mr. Steamer's glee.

"Come child," he said, urging her on.

With her shoulder supporting David, the detective followed, and, when a beam of light shone on his face, she felt him apply more pressure on her, a result of his uneasiness by such radiance.

"Hold on to me tighter if you feel it necessary Mr. Turner, but there is nothing to be nervous about."

The colorful beams that continuously flashed from under the door were of an assortment of colors David had never seen before. Initially giving him the impression that they might burn flesh upon contact, the opposite was true, feeling their warmth when skimming off his face. They should have dried his eyes yet filled them with warm moisture, and the small amount of mist sailing throughout the corridor should have been uncomfortable and damp but felt relaxing. When he saw Mr. Steamer and Cathy waiting for them by the door, he stopped.

"What lies on the other side?" he asked the detective.

"It is a small segment of the holiest place imaginable, accessible only by souls of goodness and faith. Behind that door is a single grain of fine sand from an endless beach, a fraction of an eternal universe and beyond and an unblemished locale where God the Almighty calls home."

He knew of only one place that fit her description. It was the afterlife plane of existence, a final resting place where life was forever spent in eternal peace, a space of undying beings, where generation of families could hold hands and create a line that stretched forever. If she was to be believed, she was in fact telling him that they were about to enter heaven. "It can't be," he uttered, stunned by the sheer thought.

"It can be, and it is." She laughed. "But only a tiny fraction."

When they reached the door, Mr. Steamer said, "Remove your arm from her shoulder, David. Even those with impaired mobility will be able to walk upright the moment they step inside," he claimed, removing a handkerchief from his pocket and passing it to the detective. "Cover his eyes. They will need time to adjust."

She took the handkerchief and tied it around his eyes. Once blinded, David felt Cathy's tiny hand take a hold of his.

"Hold on to me, Mr. Turner," she urged him.

David did what he was told, and the moment he heard the door open he sensed a mist spewing over his entire face, each microscopic pellet exploding on his skin, releasing an amazing consciousness straight to his brain. His veins felt as if they were being used as tiny rivers, spreading this consciousness equally throughout his whole body before climaxing the moment it reached his heart.

He felt his hair fly backwards and for a split second felt a need to shut his mouth, yet at the same time longing to inhale any air that came his way. He selfishly kept this magical mist deep inside his lungs for as long as he could before exhaling it back out; the sensitivity left behind was one beyond words.

This must be heaven, he thought, ironically troubled by the thought of being left alone in such a place.

"Are you there, Cathy?" he asked, forgetting that his sweaty hand was still tightly wrapped around hers.

"Yes, Mr. Turner. We are all here," she replied, squeezing his hand.

"Don't let go of my hand, baby. Don't you ever let go of my hand," he pleaded.

"I won't," she promised, gently pulling him onward until he heard the door behind him close.

"We are approaching a downward step," cautioned the detective, taking his other hand.

He was carefully ushered down, and as he lowered his right foot he could not feel a solid footing.

Fearing he would plunge into an abyss, he uttered, "There is no floor below me."

"This floating surface does not need a firm foundation to be walked on, David," Mr. Steamer said. "Trust that a cloud could support you, and it will."

"Just a few more steps, Mr. Turner," he heard Cathy say, and true to her word, they came to a stop five steps later. The detective let go of his hand. He heard whispering exchanged between her and Mr. Steamer mixed in occasionally with that of Cathy.

"I may be expecting too much of you, David," said Mr. Steamer, "but when the handkerchief is removed, I must ask you to be patient once again. The room you entered comes with wonderments and sights that will astonish you. Remain as collected as you can. Absorb the wonders of God's quarters."

"Keep your eyes shut, Mr. Turner. You will know when it's safe to open them," advised the Detective while untangling the knot behind his head.

He braced himself, not sure what it all meant, only that he felt safe and prepared for anything. When the handkerchief was completely taken off, he kept his eyes firmly shut as was told, but a bright light pierced through his eyelids. He moaned from the unexpected stabs, quickly releasing Cathy's hand and covering his face, further insulating his eyes.

"Take your time, David. What you feel originates from above and is foreign to your eyes. Give them the time to adjust," suggested Mr. Steamer.

He eventually lowered his hands, only to quickly cover his face due to the persistent stinging that still managed to penetrate through his eyelids. He shifted his eyes, testing to see how much they could absorb before opening them slightly enough to see a cloud-like mist floating counterclockwise. He could not see the lower part of his legs. They were buried inside the clouds, which encircled him below the knees.

Despite the bright lights, he saw no furniture, no phones, and no pictures on the walls, only a massive glass partition in front of them. Beyond that was a raised marble platform, so polished that it could have been mistaken for a mirror. At the centre of this platform was a dazzling, cylinder-shaped light, slowly cascading vertically from the above.

He guessed it was the same beam of light he saw earlier descending from the heavens above, recalling one of the twins telling him that it was the artery to their home and wondered if God was really looking down on them this very moment.

"Someone is longing to see you again, Mr. Turner," said Cathy.

The vibration was barely noticeable, but very much real. It originated from the core of the marble platform, working its way towards David's legs, shaking them and his body along with them. When the rumble stopped, an overjoyed Cathy unknowingly flapped her wings. It wasn't something she had planned but more an emotional reaction caused by what was to come. Clearly something extraordinary was about to unfold. Everyone present knew what was to be, except David.

"You must believe and try to accept where you are and what you are about to see, Mr. Turner," the detective made it known.

He focused his attention on the platform, hearing soft mumbling, not certain as to where it originated from, though suspecting it was from the left side. The mist made it difficult to see, but it sounded like two people, perhaps three people whispering to each other. One was definitely a female voice, the other that of a child, and then the mumbling stopped. He fanned the fog around him, but it was replaced with a thicker mist.

Heart pounding and confused, but not afraid, he admitted, "I can't see," and then promptly asked, "Who is it?"

"Someone you have not seen for a very long time, David. Someone you loved like no other and in turn loved you like no other," teased Mr. Steamer.

Soft footsteps were heard next, and when David looked back at the platform, he saw a vague outline of a woman walking towards the centre. Her stride was familiar as was the shape of her body, and when she reached midpoint she turned forward to face him.

Obstructed somewhat by the lights, he once again asked, "Who is she?" but Mr. Steamer completely ignored him.

Besides Cathy, he had only loved someone like no other once in his life, and her name was Diane. But she died a long time ago.

"Who is she?" David cried out for the third time, neither bold enough nor foolish enough to think it was her, to believe the unbelievable.

"Look closely, Mr. Turner, and you can easily identify with this woman," the detective whispered at him.

The gap between her two front teeth was unmistakable, and though the left side of her face was still partially camouflaged by the haze, her piercing blue eyes cut through it. David knew of only one person whose eyes were capable of doing that. He adored her when she was alive and had loved her as much since her death.

"Hello, Mrs. Turner," Cathy cried out, waving her arm at the platform.

David stiffened, and his mind went blank, too petrified to accept the fact that he was standing only a few feet away from Diane. He opened his mouth, only to raise his hands to cover it again. Though he held many wonderful recollections of his beloved wife, the final memory of her was that of a body and face mangled beyond recognition. "Oh, my dear God!" he cried out, choking and shivering when she stepped into a better-lit area. Her face was not as he remembered when he saw her last. She was now as beautiful as she was the morning before the accident.

"Welcome, Mrs. Turner," greeted the detective.

Diane took two more paces forward, positioning herself at the very front of the platform. Grinning, she thanked the detective in their language, politely acknowledged Mr. Steamer and Cathy, and finally sank her eyes into David's.

David felt his blood rushing, his heart rate doubling, and his head on the verge of exploding. Without doubt it was her. Only she could make his body react this way.

"Hello, David," she said, and with those two simple words he collapsed onto his knees and began to cry as a baby would. His hands trembled, but, at the same time, his arms were stiff.

"Is this all real? Is she really Diane? Please be honest with me, Mr. Steamer," he asked, struggling to recapture his breath and purposely avoiding the platform.

"To make anything real, one must believe, David."

Possessing the will, yet lacking the courage to actually acknowledge her existence, he wiped the steady stream of tears away, occasionally taking rapid glimpses at her through the glass partition only to look away just as quickly. Collecting himself as best he could, his glances towards her eventually worked themselves into a series of timed steady gazes. Her beauty could not be questioned and neither could her presence. That was Diane standing there, breathing and talking.

"Can I talk to her?" he humbly asked.

"To endure all you had to endure and not talk to her would be unproductive, David. Of course you can talk to her," Mr. Steamer replied.

He soon understood that speaking to her wasn't that simple. Where could he possibly begin? What if she remarried? Was that permissible in heaven? Would he let her know how much he missed her? Of course he would. How could that irresponsible question even enter his mind? And so it went, his thoughts furiously spinning in all different directions searching for the first appropriate words to begin with. Precious seconds ticked away, prompting Mr. Steamer to interfere.

"You must keep in mind where you are, David. Your soul is still a branch of your body, and for that reason you are only permitted a limited amount of time here. It would be wise to make good use of it."

The detective placed her hand on his shoulder. "Perhaps you should get off your knees, Mr. Turner. It would make it easier to talk to your wife if you were standing."

With her guidance, he at long last rose to his feet and faced the marble platform. Diane came across as stunning as ever, wearing a long white evening gown covering her entire body and with a long, silky white scarf loosely wrapped around her neck with both ends resting loosely on her back. Her hair was conservatively folded in an upward position, the way he had always liked it.

"You look beautiful," he stuttered.

"And you as handsome as ever," she kindly complimented him.

"I miss you," he made clear.

"I am fortunate enough to see you every day. It is your touch that I terribly miss, but I know that I will hold you again someday."

Lost in the moment and forgetting where he was, including the complexity of it all, he courageously asked. "Can we hold each other? Can I kiss you?"

Visibly shaken by his requests, Diane had only two options and seized them both, not replying and seeking direction from Mr. Steamer.

"Can I kiss my wife?" he pleaded directly at the detective, hoping that she could persuade Mr. Steamer into granting him his wish. The detective also directed her attention at Mr. Steamer, confirming David's suspicion that she didn't have the authority.

"That would be impossible," Mr. Steamer explained. "With a sense of regret, you have seen for yourself that I have earned a reputation of bending our Father's laws as much as I see fit, but I cannot grant you this. He would never allow it, of that I'm certain and with his utmost regret."

Disappointed, David really didn't expect a different answer than the one he got. Diane was a spirit. He was not. Mr. Steamer was right. To hold and kiss her, though a wonderful thought, would not be practical, but he would not apologize for at least asking.

"Do you remember the last time we saw each other, David?" asked Diane.

"Like it was yesterday. You walked out of the house and told me you would return in an hour. But you didn't. You—" he moaned, unable to complete his sentence.

"Died," she replied, completing his sentence for him.

He cleared his throat. "I should have never let you go out alone that morning. I should have been with you."

Mr. Steamer moved forward. "One's life is planned from the day they are conceived, David. You were not supposed to be with her that morning, and you were not. There was nothing you could have done to change things," he explained.

"I want you to know that I was never in any pain," Diane said to her husband as a means to ease him. "Following the accident, Mr. Steamer was there to pull my soul out of the car and bring it to this hallowed place. What was left behind was only my body."

Mr. Steamer smiled. "It is not the amount of life that God provides one with but how they conduct themselves within that period that is of importance to him. Diane is with us because she chose to spend her given time with righteousness. Every day of her life overflowed with benevolence, and for those reasons, she belongs here. A place in heaven is for all to have or to lose, David. When you get back, continue as before, and one day you will once again be standing next to your wife."

David took Cathy by the hand. "Did you hear, Mr. Steamer? One day the three of us will be united as a family again," he ecstatically told her.

Cathy's reaction was not what he had expected. He was puzzled as to why she had a sudden frown and then proceeded to do something he painfully understood only too well, a gesture he was subjected to many times before: the lowering of her head in submission. At a complete loss, he faced Mr. Steamer.

"Why would she do that?" he needed to know.

Mr. Steamer rubbed his elbow a number of times before answering, "As mentioned earlier, your time here is brief. I think it best you meet someone else before time runs out." He faced Diane and asked, "Would you please bring the little girl out?"

Diane began to walk away from the platform. Fearing she would not return, David panicked. "No! Don't go," he pleaded, but he was too late. She disappeared to the side, engulfed by clouds and mist. "Will she be back?"

"Mrs. Turner will return with a child of my age who wishes to meet you Mr. Turner," explained Cathy.

Confused, he swung his head away from Cathy and looked back at the detective. "When will she be back?" He moaned, paying little, if any, attention to the other child Cathy spoke of.

"Be patient, Mr. Turner." She smiled. "Be patient, and listen carefully."

As he was about to ask her another question, she hushed him long enough to hear the spirited giggle of a little girl's voice coming from the side of the platform. Occasionally, Diane's whispering was also heard filling the soundless gaps left by the little girl and then, as sudden as it began, complete silence.

"I believe your life would forever have a void, never to become whole or inclusive unless you meet this child," said Mr. Steamer. "I may have made an error in judgment for allowing you to know of her very existence, but time and God will judge me for my actions."

"The empty space in my life that you speak of has been fulfilled. My daughter and my wife are my very existence. I know of no other void."

"You have recently learned to trust me, David. Continue to trust me."

Someone was returning to the platform, and it was more than one person. The sound of multiple footsteps confirmed this. David was fearful that it might not be Diane; however, his doubts were short-lived when she stepped back out holding a little girl by the hand.

"Hello," said this unfamiliar child, respectfully greeting him first.

"Hello," he replied back, not certain who she was, only that this little beauty's resemblance to Diane was uncanny.

She had the same color of hair, same facial structure, same flaw-lessly shaped nose, and, most of all, the signature tiny gap between her two front teeth. She was all Diane. Before long he found him-self mesmerized by her sheer presence, notably in the way she was courteously inspecting him, wanting to talk but too shy to do so. From the corner of his eye he spotted Cathy waving at her; in return, this little girl offered her short, reserved hand motions.

"I constantly tease her that she shares your chin, Mr. Turner," Cathy was quick to tell him.

"My opinion is that she inherited your cheekbones," added the detective.

Mr. Steamer was not as kind. "Say what you will, but personally I think she is all her mother," he remarked, turning to David and laughing. "No offence meant." He then moved behind him, placed his hands on his shoulders and pronounced, "May I have the pleas-ure of introducing David's Child."

All attention was on David, but he didn't react.

"That sweet child is your rightful daughter, Mr. Turner," the detective stated, supporting Mr. Steamer's revelation.

The little girl anxiously waited for David's reaction, which wasn't coming. Confused by his lack of acknowledgment, she uneasily turned to Mr. Steamer who took a step forward and cleared his throat.

"I have never known you to be a discourteous man, David. It puzzles me that you would start now when meeting with your daughter for the first time."

The pounding in David's head returned with a vengeance, brought on by this astonishing disclosure. He pressed behind his neck, trying to find those illusive blood vessels that if pressed a certain way, were reputed to stop the vicious hammering, but the throbbing still persisted with no intention of stopping.

He refused to look back at this child, convinced that if he did, her resemblance to Diane would be more obvious than the first time and that they might be telling him the truth. An undeniable conversation with Mr. Wright painfully slithered through—the one where he told him that he believed his daughter had died along with Diane eight years ago. Staggered that he should accept a reality so incredible that it would make the ultimate miracle appear standard, he shouted, "No more, please, no more!"

"No, no, no, David, you mustn't!" Mr. Steamer cried out. "Do not challenge it but accept it. You must believe; you must have faith and embrace this divine openness."

If David thought Mr. Steamer's interruption would put an end to the haunting voices he heard, he was mistaken. They returned, stronger and louder than ever. He recalled Detective Wood telling him that no one could have survived such an impact, least of all an eight-and-a-half-month-old fetus and that Mr. Steamer made the necessary arrangements in replacing his dead child with one of God's.

All men have limitations; David having reached his by the sheer thought that Cathy was not part of him after all, and now they expected him to wash away all the memories of her as his daughter and accept this new child, whom he had never seen before, as his true child.

He spread his rigid arms over his head, clenched his fists. "Oh my God!" he relentlessly repeated.

"Yes, David. He is your God, as he is our Father, and he has given you a privilege that others would not even dare dream of!" cried Mr. Steamer.

"That child before you is your true daughter, Mr. Turner," shouted the detective in a desperate attempt to salvage David's miracle from turning into his nightmare.

Others might have faltered, others might have collapsed, and if David didn't feel the comforting touch of a cloth wiping the perspiration off his forehead, the same fate may have possibly awaited him. That smooth fabric worked its way from his forehead, down his cheeks and eventually found its way to his chin. It felt pleasant, slightly easing him. He saw that it was Cathy who had stretched her shawl over her hand and used the end to clean his forehead.

"My stay with you, from the moment you took me home from the hospital as an infant, until the day I had to leave, was more than any daughter could ask of a father, Mr. Turner. It was a rewarding seven years, but I am not your child. I never was. Your rightful child stands there," she explained, pointing to the frightened little girl standing next to Diane.

Since the day David had spotted Cathy at the ice cream truck, he has walked through one nightmarish incident to another, one jagged episode to the next, and when he tried to convince everyone that he was her father, no one would listen, short of throwing him into a mental institution. He now faced his most difficult test of all, one that was impossible to win: Cathy herself was telling him she was not his daughter. He had to recognize the spine-chilling truth that the girl standing next to Diane was the same child that she carried for eight and a half months and died along with her on that horrible morning. There was no rationalization or any natural explanation for what he saw or what was exposed to him in this room. It was what it was, his final chapter, and the end of his long and excruciating journey.

"I am forever indebted for the love you showed me all those years, Mr. Turner. Though I will miss what we once had, that same immense affection now belongs to your rightful daughter," Cathy told him.

David slowly looked back at his child as his real daughter for the first time. She was such a beautiful girl, adorably smiling at him much like Diane would when they couldn't see eye-to-eye on certain petty things, yet they both knew that her smile would win out in the end.

"From life's beginning, our Father bestows a soul, a heart, and the air to breathe. He reserves a place in heaven for all souls, including the innocent unborn," announced Mr. Steamer, proudly adding, "All unborn children are brought to heaven, David, as was yours on that day of the accident. Here in heaven they are nurtured and afforded the opportunity to flourish as every living soul has a right to under the sacred laws set forth by God."

David's child continued to smile at him, not certain if he would ever smile back, but when he eventually found the courage to grin at her, she let out a faint whimper and humbly squeezed Diane's hand. Seconds later David realized that his child was simply seeking the two basic things any daughter would in a father: love and acceptance.

There were only two words he could say to her, and he let them out slowly, "I'm sorry."

"It's all right, Daddy," replied his daughter, continuing with a gesture Cathy was known for; she winked at him, placing him more at ease. It took a few attempts, but he winked back, sparking the very first bond and a sudden craving for more. "I don't know your name."

"Iona Turner," she promptly replied.

Diane stepped forward. "I chose a fine Scottish name."

As was in life and now in life after death, Diane never ceased to amaze him.

"Yes. A fine Scottish name," he gently agreed.

"It is time to leave, David," Mr. Steamer said.

Those were the last words David wanted to hear, but they were expected. He focused on his child, soaking in her beauty, striving to absorb as strong a mental image of her as possible in the few seconds he had left with her, and though they had just met, he blurted out what came from his heart, "I love you, Iona," he said, feeling a welcoming closure for telling her that for the first time.

"And I love you, Daddy," Iona replied, looking at him in appeasement.

Diane and Iona had to leave. It was all coming to an end. Their time with him was over, and they were not granted anymore of it, not even for David to say a final goodbye. Both his wife and daughter disappeared, swallowed by the mist and leaving him staring at the bare platform. The stillness that followed was aching, the miracle given to him suddenly too brief. He missed them already and painfully understood only too well that he would not see them again until the day he died. By the principles governing his faith, he could only ever see them again if he died by accident or natural causes.

In spite of the abrupt ending, David felt that he was the luckiest man in the world. Even if he woke up to discover that this had all just been the dream of a lifetime, the incredible experience that went along with it was astounding. If this wasn't a dream, upon returning home he would share the experiences he had with the entire world.

Nick and Lee would be notified and told the truth about Tracie, and shortly afterwards he would seek out Father Mark and tell him that he was right all along—God did exist and that he was to continue preaching his values for the Almighty was as forgiving and virtuous as the Bible insisted he was. Father Mark and he could then arrange a meeting with the Pope himself, where he would tell him that miracles are indeed authentic.

Mr. Steamer read the enthusiasm on David's face, and it distressed him. He had been in this situation more times than he could count. He had seen stronger men than David emotionally wither away and live unhappy lives after leaving this holy setting.

"David, I must caution you that at this precise moment you have reached the uppermost pinnacle that any mortal man could ever reach. There is no mountain higher, no place on earth that exceeds the wonders you have experienced. When you step out that door, do not make the mistake of seeking an equal encounter or setting. Do not search for a heaven on earth, or your remaining days will be spent in anguish because no one will ever believe you," he warned.

David was mystified by his forewarning. "I don't understand why they would not."

"Perhaps it is best that you do not understand, David," he told him and then checked his watch. "We must leave now."

David glanced behind him and saw Detective Wood halfway out of the room, closely followed by Cathy; nevertheless he felt compelled to take one last look at the marble platform only to see it had vanished. His time was indeed over, and when he felt Mr. Steamer's hand on his shoulder, pulling him towards the exit, he did not resist.

"There will be other hurdles that face you when you get back, David," warned Mr. Steamer as they strolled towards the door. "Things will not be as they once were. People will insist that you have been missing for a long period of time. They will see that you have gone through a major transformation, not only of mind, but of a physical one as well. It will be impossible to explain and best not to question or to be frightened by your appearance."

"But I have only been here for one night.

"Time does not exist here, David, and no mortal can experience what you have and not expect to physically change," he reasoned.

"Thank you for your caution, Mr. Steamer, but I believe my work will begin the moment I get back. I want to tell the world of the things I have seen. I want to repay God and to shout to everyone of his kindness."

David spoke with the eagerness as all the others before him had when leaving heaven, but Mr. Steamer could warn him no more. They both had to move on; David to fulfill his remaining time in his world; Mr. Steamer had to continue to work for God as he would for eternity. He didn't know what would happen to David from this point forward, only God did, and though God shared many things with his superior messengers, he would not share the future with anyone.

"A bed waits for you so you can rest for a while before you leave."

"That is very thoughtful of you. I am very tired. A rest would do me good before I go. Even for a little while," he said, not asking how or when he would get home after his nap.

David stepped out into the corridor and found Detective Wood and Cathy waiting. Words were few and smiles where plentiful as the four of them walked to the end of the mirrored hallway until another room was reached. The detective opened the door. Inside was the butler, ready for them.

"Mr. Turner's room is ready," he said.

"Thank you," replied the detective, graciously moving to her side and giving the elderly spirit the space to walk out before she entered.

"You will find additional pillows and blankets in the closet should you require them, Mr. Turner," he told David when passing him.

Cathy stepped inside as well, followed by Mr. Steamer, but before David entered this new room, he took a final look back at heaven's door. The gap beneath the door was now dark. There were no more dazzling lights trying to escape from underneath as once before. It was as though someone had shut off all the lights from inside.

"Please come in, David," said Mr. Steamer.

This room was a simple one, no windows, and other than a standard queen-sized bed in the centre, there was very little else. The pillows appeared soft, and they were; the blankets were exceptionally clean, making the bed inviting. David did not have to be asked twice. He walked in, removed his shoes, and laid his weary body on top of the bed.

"I'm so tired," he was heard saying. "So, so tired." He then turned his head sideways to face Cathy. They had been through so much together and regardless of the fact that she didn't belong to him, he would miss her. "It's important to me that you know the years spent together, as father and daughter, will always be regarded as that—as father and daughter."

"Such kind words, Mr. Turner."

"Please tell Tracie that when I get back home, I will do my best to explain all of this to my brother Nick," he said.

"Should he not believe you, do not be upset, Mr. Turner," she replied back as best she could.

"Perhaps Mr. Steamer can have a chat with God and have you visit me from time to time," he said in jest, bringing a short giggle from everyone, more out of courtesy than of the intended humor.

He then turned to Detective Wood. From their first encounter, he always felt there was something exceptional about her, and he was right all along.

"It has been the utmost pleasure, Mr. Turner," she cut in before he had the opportunity to express his gratitude.

He smiled at her, and diverted his attention at Mr. Steamer. He didn't know how or where to begin. How could he possibly thank a kind spirit that he had mistaken for the devil? What could he tell that influential angel who risked his own reputation at his expense?

"I can't think of any words to thank you. I owe you so much. I hope that one day I will fully understand the extent of what has happened," he managed to tell him.

"It's because of people such as yourself that the struggle between good and evil will forever remain in our favor. You need not find words to thank me. Your actions are much more vigorous than any words can describe." Mr. Steamer grinned before carrying on. "From the day you drove Cathy home as an infant until the day we took her back, every second, every minute, and every hour was documented and now rests inside Father's library. Other spirits will read of your experience; they will study and learn from it. Not many can match a father's love for his daughter like you proved over and over. You truly are a remarkable family man, Mr. David Turner."

It was a lovely compliment coming from a superior messenger, and he felt honored. "And you are a remarkable"—he paused, longing for the right word and settling on—"a remarkable spirit."

Mr. Steamer laughed. "Go back in peace, Mr. Turner."

David slightly lifted his head, watching all three make their way out. Cathy was the last to leave. She took one closing glance at him, he at her. In the past this was the magical moment, the opening she needed to wink at him. He hoped she would, just one very last time, and when the gesture wasn't forthcoming, he took the initiative and winked at her in optimism. Cathy didn't wink back, perhaps not permitted to do so. She only grinned politely at him before shutting the door behind her.

The sound of the closing door dwindled to no sound at all. David knew that this chapter of his life had come to an end. He was now all alone, eyes heavy and pleading to be shut.

Eyes stinging to the point of being painful, he shut them and quickly fell into a deep sleep, a sleep like no other, a sleep that would thrust him into a new dimension.

CHAPTER FIFTEEN

David estimated that he had dozed off for fifteen to twenty minutes at the most, disappointed it wasn't longer, and was surprised that he would awaken so soon when only minutes earlier he was so worn out. He wiggled to his left, keeping his eyes shut in an unsuccessful attempt to fall back asleep but found he couldn't. His concern was that they would think of him as rude if he fell asleep in the limousine on his ride back home.

When he fidgeted to his right, he felt something very odd. That restful queen-sized bed he laid on now felt as hard as a piece of plywood, and gone also was that warm fresh feeling he had enjoyed earlier. He now felt as if he was outside and that his head was resting on a pile of newspapers. Most peculiar was the sound of buses, streetcars, and other automobiles, angrily honking at each other. Something was amiss. Something was very wrong.

"Mr. Turner," a voice called out.

He recalled that familiar voice, having heard it a handful of times before. Where and when, escaped him, but that raspy-toned voice was unmistakable. He opened his eyes wide enough to see a vague image of an older bald man sitting next to his feet.

"It's nice to see that you're finally awaking," the man said. "You have been asleep for a very long time. And, yes, you are lying on a bench just at the edge of the city in the most awful park anybody could wake up in."

David lifted his head, opened his eyes wider, and examined the surrounding area, recognizing this place. This man was right. He was lying on a park bench, not on a bed, in the most disgusting square, located just ten minutes north of the city considered a "humane" deposit for the homeless and the drug addicts. After what he went through, nothing was unexpected, not even waking up in a pigsty like this.

"What I am about to tell you can never be confirmed. You will never read or see any documentaries of it. It deals with the astronauts from the late sixties and mid-seventies," began the man.

The morning was cold and miserable; the clouds were thick, and a downpour inevitable. He slowly pulled himself up, placed his feet on the ground, and rubbed his shoulders in an attempt to shake the chill that penetrated his joints. The stranger removed his own jacket and had every intention of wrapping it around David's shoulders, but he grunted and quickly moved away, uninterested in the old man's generosity. The man wasn't offended, rather he made believe it didn't even happen and continued where he left off.

"Those brave spacemen were the first of many to walk on the moon," he said, placing his jacket back on.

Ignoring him, David sensed other differences. The back of his hands were dirty, his veins thick and dark purple, and the skin covering his arms appeared rougher and drier. His fingernails were filled with dirt, at least half an inch long if not longer, and when he breathed in, he smelled a sour odor about him, a stench accumulated over time due to his lack of bathing.

"Almost every one of those astronauts changed once they returned back from space. They were not the same men who left earth," continued the man.

David felt something tearing at his face, discovering he had grown a beard. It was messy, unkempt, and so long that he could see that most of it was grey. Remaining calm, he ran his hands along his head, finding that his hair reached his shoulders and was especially greasy. Grabbing a handful of locks, he turned sideways; a good portion of those strands were also grey. Without sound or reason, his appearance had drastically changed while "napping," just as Mr. Steamer had predicted.

The man leaned towards him as though about to disclose a vital secret. "I wouldn't worry too much about the grey hair. For some unexplained reason, no one can justify the aging process. All of my students have shared your experience, constantly debating that very subject, but it's never consistent. I have my own conclusion, contending it's God's fee for showing them his wonders and miracles."

It finally occurred to him that this man was Mr. Wright. The reason he didn't recognize him beforehand was due to his baldness and extreme weight loss. He had seen him just days ago, and now he was slimmer by at least a hundred pounds and missing were his bushy white hair and beard.

Mr. Wright read his mind, pointing to his slim belly and proudly proclaiming, "I finally overpowered my chocolate and ice cream addiction," he told him, not explaining his absence of hair.

David suddenly cramped up. He bent down in agony, holding on to his stomach, moaning from the tightening muscles whirling inside him.

"Do you need help?" he asked.

He shook his head, refusing any assistance, not wanting to be touched, not wanting to speak, and only wanting to be left alone so he could gather his senses.

"From what my students told me, those pains are common. I wouldn't worry too much about them either. We guessed they are reactions from a body that has not functioned properly for a very long time."

"For how long?" he mumbled, forcing an end to his silence by what Mr. Wright alluded to.

"It's varies from individual to individual."

"How long?" he firmly repeated.

Mr. Wright couldn't give him an exact number, only an estimate. "I don't know, Mr. Turner. The only thing I can tell you is that three years have gone by since I spoke to you last at a parking lot."

"You're crazy," he shot back, sweeping his long, greasy hair away from his eyes.

Mr. Wright understood his nervous reaction. It was the first phase of rejection with many more denials to come. He thought it best not to provoke him and to go back to where he left off. "As I was saying, once those astronauts were plucked out of the ocean, they were not the same people who blasted into space. When the congratulations, the ticker tape parades, and media interviews ended, they changed into secluded and unapproachable men, preferring to be left alone and giving up lucrative book and movie deals. No one could ever guess why they had changed so much in such a short time span, but I have a dear friend who works for the FBI that tells me the occasional dirty secret."

David held on to his stomach, unsure what would happen if he stood up. He decided to remain as still as possible.

"My friend told me that while these men were on the moon's surface, staring down at earth's breathtaking atmosphere, they were overwhelmed by a sudden and wonderful spiritual experience. Most of them claimed that God himself was standing beside them, explaining to them how he structured that wonderful blue layer surrounding the planet in order to protect us from ultraviolet solar radiation. One man even maintained that he answered God back, telling him of the marvelous job he did at creating earth." He threw his hands up in the air in bewilderment and added, "Who are we to dispute what these men claimed to see? We were not there."

David had a notion as to where this was leading.

"Standing shoulder to shoulder on the surface of the moon with God, whether true or not, is irrelevant, Mr. Turner. The point is that they were convinced it did happen and felt all the emotions that went along with such a spiritual occurrence. When back on earth, normal life for these astronauts, as they knew it, was impossible. They saw no reason to trim the grass anymore or to renew their golf membership. Everyday life became neither here nor there. Some fell into a deep depression, disheartened by the realization that they would never again come close to recapturing that sacred void they left back on the moon."

David became more uncomfortable, both from his aches that would not stop and from what Mr. Wright was telling him.

"My acquaintance also told me that a few of those brave men went insane, becoming an embarrassment to NASA and tragically even to their own families, but there was a deeper tragedy to all of this. Unlike you, they couldn't disclose why they had changed or what they saw. NASA wanted them to tell the world that Mars was next when all they wanted to do was talk about their conversations with God. It would make a mockery out of the space program if this ever got out, so NASA muzzled all of them. You have no one to place a muzzle on you, which makes it much more difficult. Be prepared to be looked upon as a hallucinatory, distorted drunk."

"They will believe me!" shouted David wanting to silence him.

"I hope you're correct, but imagining God standing next to you on the moon is one thing, trying to explain to others that you unknowingly raised an angel for seven years is another thing altogether. No one will believe you, and when the day comes when you can't even convince yourself is the day you will go insane, Mr. Turner."

"Father Mark will believe me!"

Mr. Wright hesitated momentarily. "I learned of the great relationship you had with Father Mark while researching your past," he replied, and then he lowered his tone to a whisper. "I'm sorry to inform you, Mr. Turner, but he passed away two years ago."

"Stop lying to me!" he shouted upon hearing that the only man in the world who would most likely have believed him was dead.

Mr. Wright stood up and gave him his card. "I gave you one of these before and asked you to keep it close to you, but I am sure it got misplaced."

David recalled his larger than life form of introduction, the two angels flying in midair and "Salt Lake University" printed below.

"I have maintained from the beginning that I represent a handful of unique individuals such as you; people who were chosen by God and taken on an incredible journey. As I stated the first time we met, I have eleven students in a class with one empty chair remaining. It is only fitting that you fill that last seat. You will be pleased to know that the rent and food are free." He smiled, getting ready to leave. "It may not seem fair, but a spiritual encounter is the most addictive drug conceivable. Once gone, it's replaced with an empty space that becomes intolerable."

"Why are you doing this? What's in it for you?" barked David, unconvinced by his authenticity or by his candid demeanor.

Mr. Wright didn't care for that question, but understood why it was asked. "I don't know. Perhaps I'm a wealthy old man who has too much time on his hands. Or perhaps I am bitter old man who is jealous that I will never experience the same wonders that you and all my students have had Mr. Turner. Honestly, I would like to believe that God simply chose me to look after all of you." He buttoned up his coat. "Challenging and confusing times await you, Mr. Turner. I pray that you call me, hopefully before any harm befalls you, and please keep in mind that Jesus Christ was eventually murdered in his attempt to be believed as the Son of God," he concluded before walking away.

David forced himself off the bench and took a few small steps towards the departing man with no serious intention of reaching him. It was more of a reaction because he didn't know what else to do. A piece of him wanted to angrily cry out, to make it clear that he was not interested in filling that twelfth empty chair, yet another part of him didn't want him to go.

"Bringing Christ into this wasn't necessary!" he shouted, disappointed when Mr. Wright didn't turn around; instead he kept on walking, crossed the street and jumped into the first waiting cab.

Left to stare at the disappearing taxi, he was unsure of what to do next or what to do about the stubborn pain in his gut that would not let up. He risked collapsing altogether and needed something solid to hold on to. Finding a lamppost nearby, he struggled to reach it, and when he did, he leaned his shoulder against it for support. It was then that he noticed a garbage bin chained around this same pole, and on top was a newspaper. He leaned over just enough to read the date. Mr. Wright was telling him the truth. His fifteen- to twenty-minute *nap* was, in reality, three long years.

Sitting in the backseat of the taxi, Mr. Wright placed his hand inside his pocket and removed a chocolate bar. He slowly peeled the wrapper away and took small bites. Within five minutes it was all consumed. He felt badly lying to David. His weight loss was not due to giving up sweets. He was dying from aggressive bowel cancer and had only four to six weeks to live. He mumbled a small prayer and asked God for a favour; to keep him alive long enough to see David sitting on that twelve chair.

Entering the city and in a confused state, David dragged his feet aimlessly for the next two hours, not grasping that people were distancing themselves from him and going to the trouble of crossing to the other side of the street in order to avoid him. When he entered into the city's core, he searched for the four-hundred-foot building, Mr. Steamer's publishing office, and eventually found it, but things were now different.

On the roof's edge, the six foot letters that once proudly proclaimed "STEAMER'S PUBLISHING INC." were now replaced with "S. DANAHER INSURANCE." The building had exchanged hands. He need not go any farther. Mr. Steamer was no longer there. He seriously didn't think it was going to be that uncomplicated, and it wasn't.

The smell of breakfast drifting out from a restaurant's air duct diverted his attention. The thought of a sizzling ham and egg sandwich and coffee resting beside the warm plate was appealing, but when he searched for his wallet, it wasn't there. Positive that it was inside his pocket before entering the white mansion, it was now gone. He didn't ask himself why it had vanished; rather he continued to walk and came to a stop before a glassed wall apartment building. Upon seeing his reflection, he barely recognized himself.

He expected the worst, but his appearance still astounded him. Disheartened, he turned around, slid down the wall and stretched his feet onto the busy sidewalk, ignorant to the fact that people were commuting to and from work. Some cursed at him while others simply walked around his legs, ignoring him as though he were just another "typical wino."

"You can't sit there!" he heard someone scream at him.

David recognized him immediately. It was the doorman whom he met when entering Lynda Stewart's apartment. He had somehow stumbled back to that same apartment.

"Did you hear me?"

He needed to share his spiritual experiences with this man, but before he could even open his mouth, the doorman again shouted angrily, "I'm calling the cops!" never dreaming that he was yelling at David Turner, the famed author whom had once handsomely tipped him.

"I'm David Turner!" he shouted to no one but himself since the doorman was already on his way back inside the apartment, waving his arms in disgust with every irate stride.

Whether the doorman was actually going to send for the police, he wasn't sure, and at this moment he didn't care. Something else had caught his interest. Approaching him, along with a wave of other people, was a woman. She had pitch-dark eyes, was clothed in a long traditional Uzbek-inspired embroidered Gosha dress and a hijab wrapped around her head. She appeared nervous, doing her best to go unnoticed, uncomfortably walking amongst other women who dressed more modern.

David quickly rose to his feet, waiting for her to get closer. Perhaps the doorman wouldn't take time to listen, but she would. He had amazing stories to share with this Muslim beauty, to tell her how he has seen representatives of all faiths come together as one, including her own.

She immediately noticed David and moved to the edge of the sidewalk in order to avoid him. When he moved in her direct path, she suddenly stopped, appalled by his chaotic appearance and was about to cross the street in order to avoid him.

"No, please. Don't go," he begged. The lady stopped, uneasily allowing him to take a step towards her. "I saw an angel of your faith," he told her. The lady didn't understand what was said and was intimidated. She swung her arm, not to strike him but rather to shoo him away from her, viewing David as just another deadbeat panhandler. He frantically searched for his wallet, forgetting that it had gone missing.

"I lost my wallet when I was in the white mansion," he tried to explain as sincerely as he could. "But if you can be as kind to buy me a cup of coffee we can sit down, and I can tell you all about the amalgamation of religions I have seen. I have been to heaven and back."

She shook her head, at the same time searching for anyone to intervene, but the morning crowd had no interest in getting involved, marching by them as though they didn't exist.

David put out his hand as a show of friendship. It came across as a demand for money. The lady panicked. She ran inside the apartment building where the doorman was already on the phone calling the police, leaving him no alternative but to leave before they arrived.

David stood so still he could have easily been mistaken for a statue. Only his beard and long hair moved, swaying back and forth to the wind's rhythm. He was gazing at charred remains of what was once his elegant home.

Most of the windows had been boarded up to keep the unwanted from entering or stealing whatever remaining sections of the home that might be still worth recycling. The garage seemed to have vanished; leaving only scorched, blistered half walls and split cement floors. The rear of the building was burned beyond recognition, so were most of the fruit trees that once grew graciously in the backyard. The swimming pool had never been cleaned, with ash and other unknown substances entrenched so deep inside that it turned to solid dirt and cracked the foundation beyond repair.

Other than a few stubborn outer walls, the only item still standing was the brick chimney. Even that was leaning, about to collapse, possibly from the next thunderstorm or the mildest of earthquakes. He could not even guess as to what might have happened to his beloved Jaguar. It was left at the cemetery when Detective Wood took him away and was nowhere to be seen.

The sight of his demolished house didn't bother him as much as it should have, with his only thoughts on his treasured photos of Diane and Cathy that once hung on the walls. They were now gone forever. He wasn't disturbed by the thought that his computer burnt along with the half a dozen unfinished manuscripts, including outlines for future stories. His writing career was over. His fingers would never pound on a keyboard again. Just as well that all his unfinished novels went up in smoke. Better they vanish along with his past than to be discovered later to make others rich after his death.

Some would have wailed while others would have been revengeful, keen to hunt down the culprits responsible, but he felt no sentiment for his home whatsoever. He felt that it represented a chapter of his life that was now over, and he had no interest in revisiting it. There was nothing left for him to see, no reason for him to hang about. He walked away, his destination in doubt, only that he would never return to this place again.

"Get away from there!" cried out Mrs. Robinson, his elderly neighbor, mistaking him for a homeless man.

He didn't even try to explain; soon making his way into some thick bushes before completely disappearing into a ravine, the same ravine he would often hide in when troubled.

Well into the evening, he hid deep inside the dark gorge for most of the night, hunger and fatigue getting the better of him. He felt lightheaded and worn out, and the threat of impending thunderstorms only depressed him further. He was disoriented, not thinking of ways to protect himself from the rain; rather he lay down to sleep, insulating his legs with dry leaves and loose weeds. Mixed with this shrub came ants, worms, beetles, and many other minuscule insects of the night. They didn't waste time, feasting on his flesh, biting the bottom of both legs as fast as he tried to brush them off. After a while he didn't mind the insects either, becoming immune to their sting, resting his head on a pile of damp soil and fell asleep.

All was calm at this lovely, large country home. Other than a half dozen low-energy garden lights mapping a path to the front door, it was clear that no one was home. An electrical sensor was installed above the garage door. This sensor sent out invisible beams across the driveway, which would activate a powerful lighting system, both inside and outside, if tripped.

A hungry coyote, searching for food, nervously scurried from one tree to another. When he came upon this house, he saw garbage can at the end of the driveway. The starving animal crossed a row of apple trees, made his way towards the driveway, hitting the invisible beam and activating the sensor.

The lights came on as they were meant to. With the home lit up, one could easily peek through the window and see family photos in every room hanging from the walls. A good portion of these pictures were of Tracie, either swimming or mini-putting with her cousin, Cathy.

The largest and most comical photograph hung to the left of the fireplace—one of Tracie and Cathy, both five years of age, identically dressed as Charlie Chaplin, smiling and ready to head out for Halloween. On the opposite side of the wall was a chain of enlarged and framed snapshots of Nick and Lee in certain stages of their relationship. The most recent one, laid face up on the kitchen table taken only a few days earlier and not yet framed. It was of Nick and a very pregnant Lee slicing a birthday cake together. Oddly, of all the photos, not one was of David. Other than a family print where his face had been unprofessionally brushed off and replaced with a very noticeable white gap, the impression given was that he was never a part of this family.

A car pulled up into the driveway and came to a slow stop. Realizing the lights were on, Lee would not get out of the car until Nick investigated first. Nick quickly got out and saw the coyote dash into a wooded area. Relieved, he opened Lee's door.

"The animals activated the system again," he told her. She stepped out, complained of dizziness, and held on to Nick's hand while he led her inside the house.

The first blow to the head was too sudden to hurt David. He was dazed by it, but it only served to awaken him from his deep sleep. He strived to make sense of what had just happened, not accustomed to the violence or the savagery of the unprovoked attack. It took a second blow behind the neck, sending a harsh sting up and down his spine for him to realize that he was being inhumanly assaulted and in very serious trouble.

He rolled his body numerous times in an attempt to escape a third blow, and when he stopped revolving, he caught a fuzzy glimpse of two enraged men running towards him carrying tree branches over their heads. When they reached him their incensed faces hit a patch of moonlight, disclosing their features.

One man's face was packed with deep scars, the other possessing a large reddish nose covered with blisters. He remembered them well. They were the two chilling drifters he had met before who stood on the opposite side of the river screaming that he had nice shoes.

He braced himself to be battered again, and though one of the men missed, the other didn't, thumping him on the ribs, cracking one. He screamed in pain, blindly crawling away on his hands and knees until his head collided with a tree stump. He turned around blindly and raised one arm to protect his face, the other wrapped around his broken rib, and yelled, "What do you want from me?"

"Where's your money?" snarled the scared one.

"I lost my wallet in heaven!"

The scared one raised his weapon in a threatening manner. "Damn lair!" he screamed back, striking him on the back of his leg, forcing him to tip over and land helplessly on his back.

David saw the other man positioning himself to strike again.

"I swear, God has my money!" he cried out, but it was too late.

The branch came crushing down, striking him on the side of his neck and sending him into a semi-conscious state. Convinced that they would not stop until he was dead, he shut his eyes, waiting for the final blow. One more hit to the head should have been enough. Although the pain was throbbing, he was not frightened of death.

He trusted that somehow Mr. Steamer would be there to welcome him just as he did with Diane; however, the finishing blow never came, instead he felt both legs being raised and his shoes brutally torn off his feet. One of the men then shoved his hand inside David's pocket, followed by his woeful cursing when no money was found.

"It's two bloody teeth," cried the other man when discovering Tracie's chain inside David's shirt pocket. More cursing followed before the scared one tore the two teeth off the chain, placed it inside his pocket and threw the loose teeth at David, which bounced off his forehead and got lost into the muddy dirt.

Just as quick as the senseless beating began, it ended. Everything was at a standstill. There were no more blows, no more cursing. The drifters left, breaking into a bitter squabble as to would be the rightful owner of the stolen shoes and chain, then laughing at David's remark about God stealing his money.

Strangely, David was disappointed that he was still breathing and ironically felt bitter towards the two vagabonds for all the wrong reasons. If only they weren't so selfish and had delivered that fatal blow, at this moment he could have been standing next to his loved ones, not in a ditch, bleeding, and in extruding pain.

The first of many cold raindrops splattered on his face followed by a thunderous bolt of lightning. He opened his eyes in time to see dark furious clouds swirling above him, all set to unleash that nasty downpour that had been threatening to let loose all day. When he tried to move, his battered ribs cried out in pain, forcing him to lie back down. He wondered if he should just remain still and simply allow himself to bleed to death, but he was fully aware that the word *suicide* was not found in the Bible for a reason; God would not hear of it and would deny anyone taking their own life a spot in heaven.

The skies cracked opened, letting loose an unforgiving deluge. He moaned and, with no one to hear him, turned his bruised body around and crawled like a snake until he hit a small bush. Ignoring the cold rain and his injuries, he pulled himself up to his knees and saw bright bolts of lightning threatening to strike at anything that dared move. He raised his head towards the angry clouds and between electrical bolts yelled at God.

"It would have made things so much easier if you allowed them to kill me!"

It was not his time to die, and neither David nor anyone else could tell the Almighty otherwise.

David threw himself down on the ground, landing in a puddle of water, and, with the little energy remaining, blindly ran both hands along the muddy sludge in search of Tracie's teeth.

Nick and Lee rested comfortably on the sofa, enjoying one of the two hundred specialty channels that came with the cable package. As was their practice for a Saturday night, the dial was set to the Silver Screen channel, which screened mostly black-and-white films from years gone by. They never tired of Clark Gable telling Vivien Leigh that he didn't give a damn or hearing for the umpteenth time that King Kong didn't die from the fall, but in reality, died from a broken heart.

A commercial break came on. Nick stood up, stretched, and excused himself, leaving the den and making his way to the washroom.

"I'll make more popcorn," Lee told him. Both left the den together, Lee making her way into the kitchen, Nick in the opposite direction towards the washroom.

Lee was in the middle of throwing a bag of popcorn into the microwave, when the doorbell rang. Startled, she looked over her shoulder, at the door.

"Someone is at the door!" she cried out, but Nick didn't hear her. When a lengthy pause ensued, she thought the door bell sound actually originated from the television. She waited an additional few seconds before setting the microwave timer for three minutes; when she heard the doorbell ring for the second time, her heart pounded. It was now one in the morning. Someone was standing outside in the pounding downpour this late at night, and it alarmed her.

"Nick, someone is at the door!" she cried out again. When the doorbell rang for the third time, she panicked.

Reminding herself that the locks were state of the art and that the door was not only fortified but had a view hole, she took it upon herself to see who it might be. She cautiously made her way to the door, rested her hands on the wall, discreetly placed one eye inside the view hole, and upon seeing a crazy-eyed, bloody-faced drifter staring back at her, she jumped back in horror.

"Nick!" she screamed, dashing back through the house, passing the kitchen, and meeting him as he stepped out from of the washroom.

"What's the matter? What is it?"

"Call the police!" she cried out. "There's someone standing outside covered in blood!"

"Stay here, and don't move," he ordered, moving her out of his way and quickly walking towards the entrance.

"Don't let him in!" she screamed at him.

The thumping on the door got louder. Nick placed an eye through the viewer. His jaw dropped, recognizing his little brother immediately. "Oh my God! Oh my God!"

"Who is it?"

He turned around, "Get Doctor Jones out of bed and over here right away!" he cried out.

"Why?" she yelled back.

"Just do what I tell you!"

"Who is it?" she repeated, demanding an answer.

"It's David."

A repulsive chill rushed throughout Lee's entire body from the mere mention of her brother-in-law's name. She rubbed her bare arms in an attempt to rid herself of the oversized shivers that suddenly plagued both arms.

Nick swung open the door. David stood there, drenched, his face covered in blood.

"God might have considered it suicide if I didn't fight for my life," he mumbled from the corner of his mouth before collapsing on the floor and into an unconscious state.

Nick quickly pulled his body inside, closing the door behind him, and when he looked back at Lee, she was in no state to make any call to any doctor. She thought David was dead, never to be dealt with again, and as far as she was concerned, Nick had just pulled in an incurable virus.

"What's the matter with you? It's David!" he shouted, expecting it would snap her out of whatever spell she was in and make the call.

Lee wouldn't place that emergency call. If Nick wanted that David nursed back to health he would have to do the calling. She didn't want any part of this and made it known by walking away and disappearing around the corridor.

The timer on the microwave rang, telling them that the popcorn was ready.

When David woke up the next morning he thought he might have fallen asleep with the television on, but as the arguing outside the room intensified, he realized that it was all authentic. Nick and Lee were quarrelling, and if he had to guess as to why, he would guess it was because of his sudden appearance.

He couldn't make out exactly what was being said, only that Lee cried out his name every so often. Ignoring the outside bickering for the time being, he focused his attention on the surroundings, remembering this spare room well. He kissed Cathy good night on this same bed whenever she slept overnight at *Uncle Nick's* house.

Resting on the dresser was a small gold-plated trophy with the engraving, "Congratulations on your Hole in One, Nick Turner." Then both members of a prestigious golf course, David recalled that morning when his brother pulled out his trusty seven iron, hitting the golf ball as perfectly as he could; the two of them tensing up as the ball trickled towards the hole and the jubilation immediately afterwards when it dropped in. That same night Diane and Lee scrambled to arrange a surprise party, complete with over thirty guests to celebrate Nick's athletic accomplishment. The buildup of dust on that trophy told him that it was not as special as it once was.

At the opposite side of the room was a small dresser, above it a mirror. Positioned too low to see his reflection, he struggled to sit up, eventually raising his head just enough to see himself. Clean white bandages were wrapped around his head, and all around his ribs. Whoever doctored his wounds had done so with professionalism, the best medical service that money could buy.

"What was I supposed to do? Slam the door in his face and let him bleed to death?" he heard Nick scream.

"You should have called an ambulance and let them worry about him!" Lee purposefully screamed back loud enough so David could hear. She wanted him to know exactly where she stood and held nothing back.

"He was bleeding, Lee. He was bleeding."

"Do I look like I care?" she brutally replied.

"You can't be serious. He's my brother."

David heard a pause followed by Lee's stomping feet and the slamming of doors. "I'm going to my mom's. You call me when he's out of this house. I can't stay under the same roof as him."

"That's not fair!" screamed Nick.

"Do you want me to tell you what's fair and what's not fair about your brother?"

"Don't go there. I don't want to hear it all over again," cried Nick.

"Not attending Tracie's funeral was not fair. Disappearing for three years was not fair. Do you want me to continue, because if I do, you know where it will lead? You know he's not right in the head. Do you want me to spell it out for you again?"

David heard the sound of a suitcase zipper and of bags being thrown about. Lee was leaving, and she made every effort to let him know that he was responsible.

"He's not a pervert, and you know it."

"No, I don't know it. I was the one who talked to him on the phone minutes before Tracie died. He knew before anybody that she was going to jump!"

That hideous line had been crossed again, a boundary that Nick couldn't bring himself to deal with—Lee's insistence that David might have had something to do with Tracie's death. Just short of accusing him of molesting Tracie, she had implied in the past that Tracie would not have died unless tormented by a horrendous occurrence, an unspeakable incident that had to involve David. Why not? He had been accused of chasing little girls in a conservation park. A sketch of his face was once front-page news.

"If you think that I'm bringing our new baby into this house with him still here, you're mistaken!" she said.

"Enough!" Nick screamed loud enough to shock her.

Lee had enough. She stormed out of the house, slammed the main door on his face, and left.

David grunted from the horrible pain but managed to raise his aching body in an upright position and then dragged the sheets off of him. He carefully lowered his left leg, followed by his right. Once both feet were firmly planted onto the floor, he sluggishly made his way to the side window in time to see Lee standing behind the opened trunk of the car.

Despite her advanced pregnancy, she somehow managed to launch the suitcase inside, immediately bending down afterwards to catch her breath. An eerie feeling overcame her. She felt that she was being stared at. She slowly raised her head, purposely avoiding the spare room window, but it seemed to be calling out her name, daring her to look over. She did and saw David stare back at her. Consumed with anger only seconds earlier, a look of terror now draped her face. She placed both hands on her belly as though David was about to transform himself into a monster, smash his way out of that room, and brutally tear at her baby.

David sensed her fear and hatred of him, but he was a forgiving man. He wanted to shout at her not to leave, to understand that he would pardon her repulsive accusations of him. Most important, he needed to disclose the incredible news that Tracie was an angel. He raised the window a few inches and lowered his head.

"Listen to me, Lee. Tracie is not dead," he said as loud as he was capable of and winced from a sharp pain when his whole rib section vibrated.

"Leave me alone!" she screamed. She then jumped into the car and backed up without looking behind, soon speeding away with the trunk still wide open.

With a blank expression, David followed the dust trail above the car, discovering that the tree house had been boarded up with a sign nailed to the door which read, "Opening Soon."

"Do you still like your eggs scrambled?"

David turned around. Nick was standing at the bedroom doorway, smiling as though nothing had happened.

"I'll leave," he said in a low pitch.

"You didn't answer my question; do you still like your eggs scrambled?"

Not knowing where to begin, he said, "I'm sorry."

"Dad told us that saying sorry between family members was a nice gesture but not an essential one."

"Yes, he did," he weakly agreed, enjoying the mere mention of his father.

Without a doubt, David was hungry, yet the past minute or so all he could do was single out loose crumbs off his toast with a fork. He didn't want to eat, not alone, preferring to wait until Nick finished frying his own eggs.

"Don't wait for me," Nick said, shaking the frying pan back and forth.

It was David's turn to quote his father, "We eat as a family."

"Or we starve as a family," laughed Nick, completing the citation.

"Dad was adamant about simple things like that. I think I'll wait for you."

"Fair enough," he replied, carefully flipping over the eggs over for the third time. He was very particular about his eggs. They needed to be fried a certain way so as the centre yolk was kept intact. Finally satisfied, he held out the plate with one hand, the scorching hot pan in the other, tilting his wrist as the carefully crafted eggs slid off the pan and onto the dish without unraveling.

"Look at that. Perfect!" He laughed and then sat down. He sprinkled his food with pepper, splattered ketchup at the corner of his plate, and—resembling a sculptor—carved the white part around the yolk with a knife.

"So what's new?" he asked sarcastically, betraying his dry sense of humor.

David laughed, an emotion he thought was lost forever, but chuckle he did, staring at Nick in admiration and at the same time feeling blessed to have him as a brother. It felt good to experience the love and respect that Nick was showering him with. Earlier, Lee stormed out on him, and here he was, cooking breakfast as though nothing happened.

"Congratulations on the new baby."

"Thank you," he replied between mouthfuls.

"You can call Lee back. I'll leave after breakfast."

Nick soaked his toast into the yolk, took a sizeable bite, and wiped his mouth. "You are not going anywhere until it's the right time to go."

"You need to be with her, not here with me."

"Lee is in good hands with her mother for now," he replied. "Now, go on, eat."

Breakfast smelt good and inviting. David picked up his fork, chewed thoroughly and swallowed, but he didn't enjoy it as he should have.

"It's very important to me that you know I'm not a pedophile. The sound of that word makes me sick."

"I don't cook breakfast for monsters." Nick smiled. "If for a moment I thought you were, you wouldn't be sitting here with me now. Besides, you aren't a wanted man anymore. It took a lot of doing and arm twisting, but in your absence my new lawyer lobbied on your behalf and found a judge that cleared your name."

David nodded his head in appreciation. He took another bite of the toast and perhaps might have shown more gratitude; but as far as he was concerned, he wasn't guilty to begin with.

"Why was Lee so frightened of me?" he asked. Nick didn't reply, nor did he offer any indication he would. Respecting his brother's decision not to answer, David moved on. "I passed by my house and saw the mess."

"It burnt down about two years ago. Before that it was used mainly as a motel for squatters. I hired a professional construction crew to have it sealed up, but they still found a way to get in. The fire marshal said that most likely drifters who live down at the ravine set it on fire because it was something for them to do. The insurance people are going to be disappointed when they see you. They were hoping you wouldn't appear for at least another four years. That would make you legally dead and easier for them to get a concession on any claim."

David took a drink of his coffee, ignoring news of any insurance entitlements.

A long pause elapsed before Nick asked, "Where have you been for the past three years?"

David pushed the cup away. "Mr. Steamer warned me I'd be asked that question."

Nick placed his fork on the side of the dish. Although brief, the time for eating was over. If he was going to be there for his brother, he would have to be more candid.

"When did he tell you this?"

"Two days ago."

"David"—he hesitated, clearing his throat—"Mr. Steamer died of a heart attack three years ago on the day you went missing. There was no possible way in the world that you could have been talking to him two days ago."

David's appetite disappeared as well, replaced with a different kind of hunger, a hunger to tell the truth and in turn to be believed. "It was two days ago, Nick. They placed me in a bed and somehow when I woke up I found myself sleeping on a park bench, three years later."

Nick forced a gulp of coffee down his throat.

David smirked at him, much like an adult would to a toddler and said factually, "Mr. Steamer is a very smart man. He is a genius. What better way to move to another location than to let everybody think he had died? As far as two days turning into three years, that doesn't surprise me. I learned that the spiritual world doesn't respect time as we know it."

Nick hid his frustration. Something menacing had happened to David that ill-fated day when he claimed he spotted Cathy at the park. He had gotten worse since then, and it tore his heart apart to see a once-successful writer transformed into a washed-up, unrecognizable, stray vagabond whose intelligence had withered down to that of a child.

"Mr. Steamer will appear again somewhere else. It depends on where and what location God thinks he is needed most."

Wiping his face with both hands, Nick sadly repeated, "Did you hear me? Mr. Steamer has been dead for over three years. As far as I know, Jesus Christ was the only man who rose from the dead, not Mr. Steamer."

"Funny you should mention Jesus Christ. Though Mr. Steamer never talked about him, I'm convinced the two of them crossed paths more than once," he replied without missing a beat.

Nick brushed his remarks aside, concentrating on the grotesque deep lines on David's face, dark facial marks that now covered his once unblemished handsome features. He saw grey hair on his brother's arms, head, chest, and even strands branching out from his ears. "You have aged in such a short time. Where could you have possibly been?"

David smiled. "Do you remember when we were kids and we used to watch the Ten Commandments every Easter?"

"Yes."

"Remember when Moses came down from the mountain all grey, and we couldn't figure out why," he continued as though putting Nick through a history lesson.

"Yes … I remember."

"It was because he spoke to God."

Nick hesitated before asking, "Are you trying to tell me you spoke to God as well?"

"No, I didn't, but he was looking down on me from heaven. But don't let the grey fool you. The ongoing joke is that this aging process is God's fee for the privilege of associating with him. To be honest with you, I have to guess that it is only meant to speed up our time on this earth and to get us to heaven earlier."

Listening to him as he did, it was obvious that David had finally gone mad. Possibly, he could find one word, one memory that just might snap him back to reality.

"David, the last time anyone had seen you or heard of you was at Cathy's graveyard fleeing from two officers and a detective trying to arrest you, but you fled and haven't been seen or heard of since."

"Not true, Nick. Those officers and that wonderful lady, Detective Wood, were actually angels. They took me to a white mansion where I saw things. I swear it's all true. I'm not crazy; I saw other things."

"Like what? What else did you see?" Nick forced himself to ask him.

David's face lit up. "Just things, things, things," he said over and over again as though Nick had granted him free rein to let loose. "I saw angels from all faiths, from around the globe, and if I told you who else was an angel, it would amaze you." At this point he was too excited to wait to be asked. "Your lawyer, Sam Balvati." He laughed, hurting his ribs in the process, thus far not letting the pain stop him. "And so was Jackie. That was the reason she disappeared after Cathy was supposed to have died the first time."

"The first time," replied Nick in utter disbelief at just how over the edge he had gone.

"God took her away from the Parkers the second time."

"Why would God take people's children away from them?" Nick bitterly asked in frustration.

"Because we all sinned. John Parker lost Cathy because he was about to cheat on his wife. I lost her for signing that book deal to write porn, and God took Tracie away from you because you signed that Woodbridge deal, but they really didn't die. They both returned to their rightful home in heaven."

If David thought his brother was fascinated by his spiritual revelations, he was wrong.

By this time Nick was weeping, recalling their childhood when their father filled the car with bags of food and took them downtown to feed the homeless. He remembered those desperate men constantly talking about God, not making any sense to anyone but themselves. He was now sitting across the table with one of those God-fearing, crazed, wretched men, and it happened to be his beloved little brother.

"Why are you crying, Nick? There is no reason to cry. You should be happy for me."

Nick got up from his chair, spread his arms around him and gave him a light hug. "I am so sorry for not being as strong as I should have been." He sobbed.

"But you are. You are a tower of strength and always have been."

Guilt ridden, Nick placed both hands around David's chin, kissed him on the forehead, and, when he let him go, he did his best to smile between sobs, but it was a difficult thing to do, for his brother's sad circumstance would forever symbolize his failure to protect him, a failed promise he made to his father.

"There is nothing wrong with me, Nick. Stop crying."

Hearing David insist that there was nothing wrong with him ignited a new set of emotions within Nick. He came clean and admitted that things could never be the same between the two. No more Sunday dinners as a family unit. No more spending Christmas together or celebrating New Year's together. What remained of the Turner family was pitiful: a fanatical brother who spoke of religious nonsense, a reclusive wife afraid of her shadow, and a memory of a daughter who died a suspicious death.

The past three years had not been kind to him; the only light at the end of his tunnel being that of his coming child, now complicated by David's return, and though he still believed that his brother was not a child molester, he could not bring himself to leave him alone with his new baby. Though he tried not to think of himself as selfish, he now hoped that David had remained in his bizarre world and not have returned. Things would have been so much better for everyone, including David. "I better go and see how Lee is doing."

"But I didn't finish, Nick. There is so much more to tell."

"Why don't you save it until I get back?" replied Nick, feeling the need to get away from him and walked towards the door.

"I saw Tracie," he quickly snapped, expecting the good news would astonish his brother into staying.

Nick stopped in his tracks, incensed that David would not let it go by bringing up Tracie's name for the second time. He stopped weeping long enough to cynically point at him. "I would appreciate it if you never mention Tracie's name again."

Suspecting his brother to be upset, David stood up. "If you must go, then go," he said, hinting at his own resentment. "I was also going to tell you that I talked to Diane, but that can wait until you get back."

The need to distance himself from David overpowered all else. Nick turned his back on him and walked out the door, crying louder with every step.

David followed him, stopping at the door, watching him heading to his car. "You were right all along. Cathy wasn't really my daughter!"

Sickened of it all, Nick got into his car, sat inside, and slammed the door shut, locking it as though it would also lock David from his life. He then furiously opened the window, "Well, then who was she if not your daughter?" he shouted at him.

"She was one of God's angels. My real child died with Diane and went to heaven where God saw to it that she grew into a lovely child. Diane named our daughter Iona. She's a real Scottish princess."

What Nick had just heard was repulsive, even if it came from the craziest of men. Short of cursing at David, he started the car and sped away.

With one hand resting on the doorframe for support, David watched the car disappear. In that silent moment, it finally occurred to him that Nick did not believe a single word he said, and when he thought of the things he ranted about, his brother was most likely going to make arrangements to have him locked up. There was only one last person that he had to try and convince. If that man couldn't be persuaded, then it was all over for him.

Nick stood waiting at the main entrance for his mother-in-law to bring Lee to him.

"I already called the police," he told Lee the moment she came to the door. "The way it works here, they will come with me to get him, and then he will be held for seventy-two hours."

"And then what?" she wanted to know.

"They assess him, and if they diagnose him to be mentally ill, they will keep him for another thirty days."

"And after that?"

"If they still feel he needs help, he could be held indefinitely."

"So that should be it then?"

He slowly looked away from her. "Yes. That should be it for him, but I have to give him time to heal. I can't have him taken away until he's physically better."

"Call me when he's out of my house, and then I'll come back," she told him.

David walked into the washroom and stood in front of the mirror, waiting for his reflection to appear, but after a while it became clear that his likeness would not show itself. It didn't want to hear his wild stories about talking to dead people and children turning into angels.

Holding on to his sanity by the thinnest of threads, he still had a fraction of intelligence remaining within to realize that if his own reflection didn't want to face or believe him, then he may have gone mad already and that Nick was now making arrangements to have him placed inside a psychiatric ward. It was at that moment that he realized he would never see his brother again.

CHAPTER SIXTEEN

It began with tiny pecking sounds coming from above a tree. They were sounds that only the mother could hear, but as the egg swayed slightly back and forth, a birth was about to occur. It began as a crack, followed by a section of the shell separating itself from the rest of the egg. Soon a blind newborn chick emerged and began to protest. It was completely helpless and hungry and wanted its mother to know of its entrance into the world.

A good half a mile away from the nest, two birds had their claws firmly clenched on top of a wooden sign which read "Welcome to Indian Pass Hills." When the mother of that newborn heard those cries, she spread her wings, sprang up in the air, and flew up the hill, towards that nest. She glided in circles around the tree, the same tree that the Kate the Scoutmaster had boasted about just before the incident with Tracie.

The bird flew downward and proficiently landed on the edge of the nest. By instinct she knew what to do next, lowering her head and calmly removing pieces of shell with her beak and tossing them down below. One single section swayed back and forth as it dropped, bouncing off a man's shoulder before getting lost among the leaves. That shoulder belonged to David Turner. He didn't feel a thing; his mind was focused on more important matters.

With one bag of groceries in each hand, Nick sluggishly walked into the house. He shouted David's name, needing a helpful hand with the groceries. When his third call went unanswered, he placed the bags on the floor.

"I bought you some fruit," he cried out, thinking it would be enough to entice him out from where he was hiding, but David neither answered nor appeared.

Nick shut the door behind him, slowly making his way along the corridor towards the spare room. He poked his head inside, surprised that the bed had been made up. At one time David used to be a quick learner, but one thing he had never mastered was to spread sheets as evenly as they were now.

Alarmed, he once again called out his name, and when he entered the kitchen, he came to an abrupt stop. On top of the table was an envelope shoved securely in an upright position sandwiched between the salt and peppershakers.

That envelope was not there when he left. He convinced himself that there was no need to be concerned; David had just left him a typical old-fashioned good-bye letter. With his brother possibly gone, he should have felt relieved. He should have been pleased that his brother left before he had the opportunity to have him committed and then spend a lifetime feeling guilty for doing so. Strangely the opposite was true. He was worried for him.

Every two hundred feet, installed deep into the soil, were courtesy benches along the side of the path. They were positioned that way for the general public to rest while making their hike up the wooded trails. It was while sitting on one of these benches that David knew he was where he wanted to be. Clean-shaven and his long hair tied into a ponytail, he took pleasure in absorbing the surrounding beauty. His break was short lived upon hearing aggressive chattering between a half dozen young university students climbing up the hill towards him. They ignored him except for a Scottish exchange student from Stirling University who stopped and stared.

"Aren't you David Turner?"

Ironically, David shunned the spotlight more often than not, forever denying who he was. It now seemed foolish. He was who he was.

"Yes, I'm David Turner," he replied.

"I told you he was," shouted the student to his colleagues who in return mocked him.

One other student shouted out, "Maybe in twenty years," while the rest blamed their Scottish friend's bad eyesight on last night's drinking binge.

The lad would not have any of it. He was positive that man sitting before him was indeed David Turner.

"Did you know you are a hero back home?" he told David.

"It's nice to know that I'm somebody's hero." He smiled.

Nick slowly tore the top off the envelope and pulled out a two-page letter. He began to read.

My Dearest Brother Nick,

I regret leaving this way. You don't deserve it, but I could not think of any other way. You have always been my idol and will forever remain my champion. Dad would have been so proud of you if he were alive today.

Please tell Lee that I had nothing to do with Tracie's death and that Tracie is fine where she is. I suspect that you both think I have been reduced to a hopeless lunatic. I will not attempt to change your view of me. Perhaps it's best that you continue to judge me insane. It will make things so much easier for us all.

I talked to a good entertainment lawyer and left his phone number on the back of this letter. He is expecting your call within the next few days. I have no use for money where I am going, and I have instructed him to set up a

trust fund for your new child. I still collect and will con-
tinue to collect royalties from future book sales and, with a
bit of luck, from any films based on my books. It hurts to
know that I will never see your baby, and my wish is for
her or him to remember Uncle David.

There is only one place for people like me to go, and that
is where I'm going. Sadly, you and Lee will never see me
again, nor will I see you. I will miss you both terribly, and
you will know just how much when we all meet in heaven.

Promise that you will not shed any more tears for me,
Nick. You have shed enough and I would hate to think of
you shedding any more.

Nick completed the first page, replacing it with the second and choking up.

"I will not cry," he whispered, giving way to David's wish.

David rose from the bench and headed towards the steep cliffs, the same overhang where Tracie once stood. He lifted his leg over the short protective fence and stood at the edge. If he thought of taking one more step, he would plunge to a certain death, thus far displaying no fear whatsoever.

He leaned over to get a better view of the thunderous rapids below, understanding how the river could mesmerize and seduce a weak-minded soul into jumping. The odds of survival were nonexistent. If one's body didn't mangle itself into an unrecognized state, then they would most surely drown.

A short distance away he found a bare spot, offering him a better view of the hazards below. For reasons known only to him, he smiled, shut his eyes, and spread out his arms as though he was about to jump. The wind that blew on his face felt good. It felt like freedom, and, most of all, it felt alive.

Nick began to read the second page.

I have no answer as to why God chose me to witness the immaculate miracles that I have witnessed. Dad always said there was a reason for everything. I know that I could never find happiness if I remain here, but I hope to find some answers in the place where I'm going. Then and only then can I be at peace with myself.

   Isn't it magnificent to know that there is a heaven, Nick? Isn't it grand to own a soul that lives forever?

   I have autographed every book of mine that I found in your house. You never know. They could be worth a fortune some day! (Wink)

   See you in heaven,
   Your little brother, David

Nick placed the letter on top of the table. He had promised David he wouldn't cry and would not. That letter would be the only part of his brother left, and he would cherish it. He would keep it forever, making a point of reading it to Lee. Perhaps then she might take away a layer of hatred she held for him.

Right then and there Nick decided that he would not go to search for him. David was right. Perhaps it was better this way. Most likely his brother would go back to his "kind" where he would be more at ease than if locked up.

It was difficult for him to come to terms with the fact that he had done all he could for David and could do no more. Now he was in a position to call Lee and tell her to come home. When he shoved the two-page letter back into the envelope, he unexpectedly noticed something else hidden inside that he missed the first time.

Confused, he turned the envelope upside down and shook it. Seemly in slow motion, Tracie's two teeth fell out, making a light sound as they hit the table. He stared at them, hypnotized, not able to move a single muscle, not blinking, barely even a heartbeat. Tracie was buried with those around her neck. He was there. He saw it for himself. There was only one place that they could have come from and that was from heaven, just as David had maintained all along.

As tears began to roll down Nick's checks, he sadly discovered that the truth was much more powerful than a promise not to cry.

The Scottish student lazily strolled back down the trail with one of his friends. He noticed a three foot monument entrenched deep into the ground. Made of expensive granite, it was light brown and the front was so polished and precise that it was difficult to read the inscription. The student got closer and lowered his head.

"What's it say?" asked his companions.

"Something about a little girl named Tracie who died here."

"That's too bad."

"She was only eight," replied the Scottish lad after subtracting the date of her death against the date of her birth. He then looked beyond the monument and noticed David standing dangerously at the edge of the cliff. He didn't give it much thought. After all, that was David Turner. He had so much to live for. He didn't need to jump to his death to become the "*tragic and misunderstood author*," yet something made the student call out David's name.

"Did you know a little girl died on this spot?" he yelled at him.

David lowered his arms, turned around, and said nothing.

"That's what's written on this monument."

"That's not David Turner, you jerk," said his mate, laughing and grabbing the Scottish student in a headlock and running down the hill with him.

David took half a dozen steps backwards, away from the dangerous edge, walked to the monument; when he read it, he smiled and softly whispered, "No one ever really dies Nick."

The university students trotted inside the bus station, fearing they might have missed their bus; relieved when they saw it idling. They ran up the steps, gave the driver their portion of the ticket, and moments later were seated at the back, adjusting their back packs into pillows and getting cozy for the long journey ahead.

David climbed on board, handing the driver his ticket.

"My son is trying to get me to do that," he told David, throwing his ticket stub inside a box.

"Do what?"

The driver pointed to David's ponytail. "To grow a tail like yours."

When David smiled, the driver asked, "How long did it take you to grow it that long?"

"A couple of days."

The driver laughed back at him. "That would take a miracle."

Chuckling, David looked down the aisle. The bus was relatively quiet and half empty with the university students making a minor fuss with each other. The other passengers were mostly Latino immigrants. Some were asleep, others either reading or staring blankly out the window.

He made his way along the aisle, noticing a mother with her tired son sleeping on her lap. On the floor he saw a Hell Boy toy, the anti-hero from the comic book and film notoriety. It had fallen from the boy's hand as he slept. David picked it up, studied it for a few brief seconds and laughed when it reminded him of Mr. Steamer. He carefully placed the toy back onto the boy's lap without waking him up and took a seat behind them.

"It's nice to see that you didn't jump to your death, Mr. Turner," the Scottish student yelled from the back in jest.

David turned around, chuckled, and said, "Life's too precious?"

When the bus drove out of the station and into the open highway, it occurred to him that it was a gorgeous day, and indeed, wonderful to be living and to have God on his side.

A gust of wind blew briskly through the window. Unbeknownst to the bus driver, a loose ticket stub flew out of the ticket box, landing between his feet. It was David's other half of his ticket. On it was printed his final destination. It read "Salt Lake City, Utah: Paid for by Mr. Jacob Wright."

David thought of the first two questions he would ask when sitting on that twelfth chair: why would God choose him over Nick, suspecting it might of have had something to do with Lee's character ruining it for his brother. The second question that had to be debated in class with his new companions was why God felt he needed to take his wallet away and the symbolism behind it.